MW00882627

Ghost in the Ring

Ghost Night #1

Jonathan Moeller

Copyright © 2017 by **Jonathan Moeller**

All rights reserved. No part of this publication may be reproduced, distributed or transmitted in any form or by any means, without prior written permission.

Jonathan Moeller
http://www.jonathanmoeller.com

Publisher's Note: This is a work of fiction. Names, characters, places, and incidents are a product of the author's imagination. Locales and public names are sometimes used for atmospheric purposes. Any resemblance to actual people, living or dead, or to businesses, companies, events, institutions, or locales is completely coincidental.

Book Layout © 2017 BookDesignTemplates.com

Ghost in the Ring / Jonathan Moeller. -- 1st ed.
ISBN 978-1547200252

To the readers of THE GHOSTS & GHOST EXILE series

OTHER BOOKS BY THE AUTHOR

CHAPTER ONE

THE DEAD CASTLE

On the night of her wedding to Kylon of House Kardamnos, Caina drew her husband after her into their bedchamber.

Prince Nasser had given them the use of a chamber high in the towers of the Palace of the Princes, the windows facing east towards the Alqaarin Sea. A large bed stood in the center of the chamber, and the air bore the faint scent of incense.

Caina barely noticed either of those things.

Nasser's wife Anzima had arranged for Caina to wear the traditional garments of an Iramisian bride, a white dress that left the arms bare and a cloak and mantle of white silk. Anzima's armies of maids had spent hours preparing Caina for the ceremony, applying makeup and arranging her hair and making certain that the dress hung just so.

Caina appreciated their work, but right now she was more concerned with getting the formal garments off.

Fortunately, Kylon was glad to help her.

She tugged at his own clothes as fast as she could manage. Anzima's troop of servants had also found suitable garb for Kylon, a formal tunic and cloak and boots in the Kyracian style. The cloak was pinned at his left shoulder with a jeweled brooch, which was easy enough to remove. Then the tunic went over his head, and he discarded the boots and then the trousers. By then Caina had gotten all the way out of her own elaborate dress.

She started to kiss him, but Kylon's left arm went over her shoulders and his right arm behind her knees. He lifted her from her feet in one smooth motion, and Caina let out a delighted laugh. Kylon laid her down on the bed, and Caina smiled and drew him to her.

The next several moments were intense. They shifted position, Caina straddling him, gazing into Kylon's face as the intensity within her built and built and…

Sudden confusion flooded across Kylon's face, followed by alarm.

What was wrong?

Caina felt the surge of sorcerous power against her back and shoulder blades, her skin prickling with it.

Ever since the disastrous day of her father's death and long before she had received the vision of the valikarion, she had been able to sense the presence of arcane forces. Now she felt sorcerous power behind her, a peculiar power that she had never sensed before.

But it felt like necromancy, with the same familiar tinge of corruption.

Caina turned her head in a sudden mixture of fear and rage. Fear that a wielder of sorcerous force would attack her in in the heart of Iramis. Rage that someone would interrupt them on their wedding night of all times.

The vortex exploded towards her.

It filled the room, a spinning maelstrom of shadow and ghostly green fire. With Caina's eyes of flesh, it looked like a miniature storm lit from within by green fire. With the vision of the valikarion, she saw the ancient necromancy that stirred within it, fueling the vortex with ribbons of eldritch fire.

Before Caina could move or even speak, the vortex engulfed her.

She felt herself ripped away from Kylon, and then she was tumbling through nothingness. She heard Kylon shout, and Caina lost his voice in the howl of the wind. The vortex stretched into an endless dark tunnel, green fire flickering and dancing in the gloom. Caina flailed, desperately trying to grab onto something, anything, as she fell. Had the spell knocked her from the tower window? Yet she didn't see the towers of Iramis anywhere, only writhing shadows lit from within by green fire.

Then she hit the ground with enough force to make her head ring and knock the breath from her lungs.

For a moment Caina lay motionless, stunned. Bit by bit her mind started to come back into focus, noting details. She was lying on her stomach on a flagstone floor, the stones icy cold against her skin. The howling roar of the strange vortex had vanished. Sorcerous power surged through the air, her skin crawling with pins and needles from it.

Caina got her hands beneath her, the floor flat and cold beneath her hands, pushed herself up, and sprang to her feet in one motion, ready to fight or to flee as necessary.

She was in…

Caina blinked in surprise.

She had no idea where she was.

A hall of stone yawned before her, the floor paved with smooth flagstones, thick pillars supporting the vaulted ceiling. The stones were rougher than Imperial or Istarish or Iramisian stonework, and the capitals of the pillars had been carved in a strange design that she did not recognize. A dais rose at the far end of the hall, supporting a bronze statue of a warrior in scale armor and a spiked helm, a greatsword in his hands. Caina did not recognize the statue, though she thought the style of the armor was common in the eastern Empire.

Despite that, the hall would have been unremarkable. It had a sort of barbaric splendor to it, and Caina could imagine an ancient Caerish or Szaldic chieftain reigning on the dais.

It would have been unremarkable…except for the veins in the stonework.

Caina had never seen anything like it.

Hundreds of black veins threaded their way through the stones of the walls and ceiling like blood vessels in flesh. Some were no larger than Caina's finger, and others were thicker than her leg. The veins pulsed and throbbed as if some massive heart pumped black slime through them. Portions of the walls and ceiling seemed…twisted, warped, as if the stone was growing tumors. To the vision of the valikarion, necromantic power flowed through the veins.

Caina didn't know where she was, but she was pretty sure it was not Iramis.

"Kylon?" she said, turning in a circle. "Kylon!"

There was no sign of her husband.

As far as Caina could tell, she was alone.

Where the hell was she? Some sort of spell had brought her to this place, that was clear. The cold air had a faint dusty smell as if no one had been in this room for a long, long time. Yet the very stone of the walls and floors and ceiling were charged with dark power. It was almost as if…

Was she back in the netherworld? In the netherworld, the air and ground blazed with sorcerous power. This room burned with sorcerous power, dark and necromantic, but it did not seem nearly as powerful.

Narrow windows lined the walls, and Caina walked to the nearest one. There was no glass or shutter, and a cold wind came through the window, so cold that her flesh stood out in goosebumps. Through the window, she saw…

It was so strange it took her a moment for her to process the sight.

One moment it seemed like she saw the bleak, lifeless plains of the netherworld, flat and desolate and dotted with menhirs of jagged obsidian. The next she gazed upon a snowy forest, silent and white. The sky kept shifting as well, blurring from the writhing storm clouds of the netherworld to a cold, crisp winter sky, the black expanse dotted with thousands of stars.

Caina looked left and right through the window, and saw a huge fortress rising around her.

It looked fantastical, a sprawling maze of towers and curtain walls and basilicas. It would have been a magnificent sight, but the black veins crawled everywhere over the walls, and tumorous growths bulged from the towers and the courtyards. The fortress should have been a thing of beauty, but it looked as if the stone of the citadel was being replaced by cancerous, tumorous flesh.

Caina stepped back from the window, shivering in the chill.

She suspected the fortress was caught halfway between the netherworld and the material world. That explained the powerful auras around her. And if the fortress was pulled all the way into the netherworld, Caina wanted to be long gone by the time that happened.

But how had she gotten here? Had it happened by accident?

Or had someone drawn Caina here deliberately?

No, she had to focus on the urgent problem, on escaping the fortress.

A shudder went through her limbs, and Caina realized that she had a more immediate difficulty.

She needed to find some clothing before she froze to death.

Save for her perfume, some smeared makeup, and a mixture of Kylon's sweat and her own, she was stark naked. If she didn't find some clothing or a source of heat, she was going to freeze to death, especially if she strayed too close to those windows.

Dread stabbed through her, not for herself, but for Kylon. What had happened to him? Had the vortex drawn him here? Or had something worse befallen him?

With considerable effort, Caina dismissed that fear. She could worry about Kylon once she made sure that she wasn't going to freeze to death. And in truth, Kylon could defend himself better than she could.

Caina turned, looking for a door, and a glint of light on her left wrist caught her eye.

She wasn't entirely naked.

Her pyrikon bracelet still rested on her left wrist, currently in the form of an intricate chain of ghostsilver links. In the heat of the moment with Kylon, she had forgotten to take it off, not that it had gotten into the way. The pyrikon had proven useful many times, and it might prove useful here.

And Caina wasn't unarmed.

She would never be completely unarmed for the rest of her life, thanks to the ordeals she had undergone in Istarinmul. The fingers of her right hand flexed a few times, and then she held out her hand and concentrated.

For a heartbeat, nothing happened, and then shards of silver light appeared out of nothingness and assembled themselves in her hand, forming into a short, curved sword forged of ghostsilver, the blade written with Iramisian characters. The valikon had been forged by the Iramisian loremasters, and it was proof against sorcery while the spells wrapped within its blade could destroy spirits. The sword shuddered Caina's hand, and the blade burned with white flames, reacting to the dark power in the air around her.

The valikon had bonded to her, and she could summon and dismiss it at will. Given her lifelong hatred of sorcery, Caina wasn't sure how she felt about that, but the sword was useful. And since she would have no weapons otherwise, she would not complain.

A pair of wooden doors stood at the opposite end of the hall from the dais, banded in dark iron. Save for the windows, they were the only way out of the hall, and Caina did not fancy climbing down the side of the fortress.

She crossed to the doors, listened at them for a moment, and heard nothing but the moan of the wind from the windows.

Caina nodded to herself and dismissed the valikon. It shattered into glowing shards and vanished. Its fire would be visible from some distance off. Better to remain unnoticed by whoever or whatever ruled this fortress.

A deep breath, and she eased open one of the doors, peering through the gap.

Beyond was a wide corridor. No, not a corridor – an arcade with pillars running alone one side. Through the pillars, she saw a wide courtyard overgrown with twisted, corrupted-looking vegetation. Towers and walls loomed over the other three sides of the garden, their surfaces covered with black veins and bulging, uneven growths. Caina looked up one side of the arcade and down the other, but it was deserted, and she saw nothing moving in the windows overlooking the garden.

Yet on one side of the arcade, she saw firelight leaking from a doorway.

She slipped through the doors and into the arcade, keeping close to the wall to remain out of sight of the windows. Her bare feet made no sound against the floor. A flicker of amusement went through her. She had never realized how easy it was to move in total silence while naked. Of course, a naked woman would draw attention, and gods, it was cold here. Caina was shivering, the muscles of her shoulders and arms jerking involuntarily, and if she didn't find some clothing or at least some warmth, she was going to be in a lot of trouble.

A flicker of motion caught her eye.

Had something moved in one of the windows? She froze, gazing at the mass of black-veined stone, her head jerking a little in the cold. As far as she could tell, nothing was moving behind the windows.

But Caina doubted she was alone in this place.

Something had brought her here. Better to get out of sight as soon as possible. Caina resumed walking and then broke into a jog.

Her bare footfalls made little enough sound. The doorway at the end of the arcade grew closer, the firelight brighter. Caina stopped and pressed herself against the wall next to the door, the chill from the stone soaking into her skin. She peered around the edge of the doorway, wondering if she was about to see a guardroom or a barracks...

Surprise flickered through her.

It was a library.

The room beyond was large, with high wooden shelves of books climbing the walls to the vaulted ceiling. More of those black veins and twisted growths covered the ceiling, but the shelves hid the stone walls. Four long wooden tables stood in a row, with four chairs at each table. The shelves sagged beneath the weight of hundreds of dusty books. On the right wall was an enormous fireplace, a fire blazing within it. No smoke came from the flames, but even from this distance Caina felt the heat, and it was a blessed relief.

She would have run to the fire at once, but the second half of her surprise held her back.

Because undead creatures wandered through the library.

There were six of the things, and Caina saw the currents of necromantic energy that animated them. Three of the undead wore armor and carried swords of archaic design. The other three wore dusty robes that had once been ornate and bright, hats of rotting fur perched atop their heads. All six creatures were skeletal and withered, leathery flesh cracking against brittle bone.

Caina stared at them for a moment, and then stepped through the doorway, making no effort to conceal herself.

And as she expected, none of the undead could see her.

She was a valikarion, and neither spirits nor sorcerous spells could detect her presence. The eyes and ears of the undead had rotted away long ago, and they relied upon their sorcerous senses to perceive living creatures. Since she could not be detected by any sorcery, they could not perceive her.

Caina crossed the library and stopped before the fireplace, spreading her hands before her and soaking in the warmth radiating from the fire. She could see the sorcery that sustained it, part of the power that surged through the stonework of the fortress, but she didn't care. Sorcerous or not, the fire gave off heat. She stepped to the side to let an undead soldier shuffle past her and then moved back into the warmth of the fire.

As her limbs warmed, she considered what to do next. Clothing? The undead wore robes, but the thought of putting the rotted, crumbling cloth against her skin made her stomach turn. Instead, her eyes turned instead to the dusty books on the shelves of the library. Perhaps they could tell her where she was.

Keeping one eye on the undead, Caina plucked the nearest book from the shelf and paged through it. The alphabet was unfamiliar to her, and she did not recognize the language. Wait, no, that wasn't right. The alphabet was the Kagari alphabet, which was used almost exclusively in the northeastern regions of the Empire. Long ago, the nomadic Kagari hordes had ruled most of what was now the eastern Empire, and the then-illiterate Kagari had forced one of their conquered peoples to devise an alphabet for them. The Emperor and the Legions had broken the power of the Kagari khans, but the alphabet lingered in the hinterlands of the eastern Empire.

Had the vortex brought her to the eastern half of the Empire? That seemed unlikely. And a book collector could certainly obtain a book in Kagari script easily enough. Caina shelved the volume and took another. This one was in High Nighmarian, her native tongue, and it was a history of the Empire. It was also an old history of the Empire. A very old history, come to think of it. The style of the High Nighmarian was ancient, and the book's account did not even reach the end of the Third Empire two thousand years ago.

She shelved the book and took another, glancing at the undead to check their positions. This book was a history of the Imperial Magisterium, the governing body of the Empire's sorcerers. At least it had been the governing body of the Empire's sorcerers until the Umbarian Order had come out of the shadows, but that was another story. Again, the book looked and felt ancient, and did not reach the end of the Third Empire. Caina took a third book in High Nighmarian. This one was about a man named Rasarion Yagar, the last King of Ulkaar, and his defeat of the Kagari Great Khan and his descent into madness after…

All the undead went motionless at once.

Caina looked at them, flexing her right hand as she prepared to call her valikon. Had the undead seen her? All six corpses were staring at the door on the other side of the library. It opened into a dim-lit corridor that vanished into darkness.

As Caina looked at the corridor, she noticed several things.

The first was a wet, rotting smell. The undead had been dead for so long that the creatures smelled of dust and dry bone. This odor put Caina in mind of a dead animal rotting in a swamp. The smell was coming from the dark corridor, and it seemed to be getting stronger.

The second was the sorcerous aura. The fortress all but glowed with sorcery, but the vision of the valikarion saw another aura approaching from the corridor. It was an aura of necromantic sorcery and some other kind of power she didn't recognize, appearing to her vision like a rippling haze of harsh green-purple light.

The final thing she noticed was the noise.

It was a faint squelching, slithering sound, like something wet crawling along a stone floor. The noise was getting louder.

Something was coming.

Caina shelved the book about the mad king and looked around. Should she retreat to the arcade? There was no place to hide there. Or would it be better to stand and fight? The valikon could destroy any creature of sorcery, but Caina didn't know what she faced.

But there was another option.

Caina turned away from the corridor and climbed up the bookshelves. She left handprints and footprints in the dust, but that was unavoidable. The top of the shelves was twelve feet off the floor, and there was a flat, empty space below the ceiling. Caina rolled onto it, the wood smooth and dusty against her skin, and watched the corridor, ready to summon her valikon.

About a minute later the source of the aura came into sight.

It was...

Caina had no idea what the creature was, but the sight of it was grotesque.

It looked vaguely like a man, and it wore a voluminous robe of the rough brown fabric favored by the ascetic priesthoods of the sterner gods. The robe was stained and greasy, and the cowl had been thrown back. The face of the creature was like something out of a nightmare. It had two human eyes, but the skin had turned a leprous gray, covered with a network of black veins, and a huge black eye bulged out of the center of its forehead. Strange antennae jutted from its head almost at random. Its right sleeve ended in a human hand, albeit one tipped with claws, but a tentacle came from its left sleeve, and Caina caught glimpses of more tentacles writhing beneath the hem of the robe.

She had no idea what the creature was, but she didn't want it to see her. And something about the pattern of the black veins and deformed growths on its face reminded her of the network of veins on the fortress walls. Was this creature the master of the fortress? If not, the creature had to be connected to it somehow.

The robed form glided into the library and paused.

Caina tensed and prepared to summon her valikon, fearing that the creature had sensed her, but the six undead fell in around the robed thing like an escort. The creature glided forward, and left the library and moved into the arcade, both it and the undead vanishing from sight. Caina watched their auras through the stone wall as they moved away. She thought both the robed thing and the undead were moving towards the hall where she had appeared. Were they coming to intercept her? The robed creature could not sense her presence, but it seemed to be a living thing with working eyes.

If it saw her, that would be bad.

Caina counted to a hundred, trying to keep her teeth from chattering in the chill, but the robed creature and the undead did not return. She lifted her head, looked around the library, and climbed down the shelves.

Caina had to press deeper into the fortress. As loathe as she was to leave the warmth, she dared not stay here. Sooner or later the robed creature would return, and if it saw her, she had no choice but to call her valikon and fight. She also needed to find clothing, and eventually, she would need water and food.

And most importantly, Caina needed to figure out where the hell she was and if Kylon had been brought here with her.

Again, a stab of terror went through her at the thought of Kylon. They had almost lost each other so many times. To be ripped apart on their wedding night, in the midst of their first time as husband and wife, seemed like a cruel joke.

She just hoped that he was safe, wherever he was.

And if someone had hurt or killed him…

Her right hand coiled into a fist, and she made it relax.

Caina would deal with that if it happened. And, she reminded herself, Kylon was probably safer than she was. He had his own valikon. He also had his abilities as a stormdancer and coupled with his skill with a sword, they made him into a formidably effective warrior. He could have destroyed all six of the undead and killed the robed creature in the space of about three heartbeats.

Right now, Caina had to stay alive long enough to find him again.

She took a deep breath, savoring the warmth of the fireplace for one last moment, and then headed into the gloomy, black-veined corridor, both her eyes of flesh and the vision of the valikarion watching for threats.

CHAPTER TWO

RESEMBLANCE

When the black vortex exploded into existence behind Caina's head, it happened so fast that even Kylon's reflexes had not responded in time.

That said, he had been somewhat distracted.

His whole attention was on Caina as she straddled him. Mortal men were water in the end, and Kylon's power with the sorcery of water let him sense the emotions of those around him. All except Caina, because as a valikarion, she was immune to his abilities to sense emotion with water sorcery.

Unless he happened to be touching her.

And when there was nothing between their skin, he felt her emotions like a blaze. Kylon had always thought her emotional sense felt like a fortress of ice around a molten heart, but when they lay together, the ice was gone, and there was nothing but the molten heat of her desire. She looked intoxicatingly beautiful, her black hair hanging sweaty around her head, her chest heaving with her rapid breathing, her face melting into a rapturous smile.

Then something dark and cold burned against Kylon's arcane senses.

The vortex of shadow erupted into existence behind their bed. Caina started to turn, and some colossal force seized her and ripped her off him. The same force gripped Kylon and pulled him after her. He just had time to shout her name, and then he was tumbling through an endless well of darkness, black shadows and green fire whirling around him. Kylon reached for Caina, but he lost sight of her pale form as she tumbled through the darkness, and he felt himself falling endlessly through the swirling void.

Then his fall came to a sudden stop.

A cold, wet stop.

The shock of falling naked into cold water was enough to make every muscle in his body contract at once, and Kylon sucked in a lungful of the icy water before he could stop himself. He started coughing, and the reflexes he had learned aboard the fleets of New Kyre asserted themselves. He began to swim upward, only to realize that the water came to his chest. Kylon spat out a mouthful of the stinking water and looked around.

A pool. Somehow, Kylon was in a large pool in an underground vault, probably a cistern. Windows high in the walls admitted a pale, flickering light, and at the far end of the cistern he saw a flight of stone stairs that climbed upward. Kylon hurried forward as fast as he could, gripped the edge of the stairs, and heaved himself out of the water.

That made him feel slightly less cold, but he was still drenched, and if he didn't do something he was going to freeze to death.

Fortunately, a stormdancer had options for dealing with water and cold that most men did not.

Kylon drew on the sorcery of water and worked a minor spell. The water started running off his limbs faster than it would have otherwise. He also felt quite a bit warmer. It was a spell he had learned long ago, early on in his training as a stormdancer. The fleets of New Kyre sailed to every civilized land and port, and some of those ports were in icy seas. Knowing how to keep warm in those places was the key between life and death.

Though there hadn't been much need for keeping warm in the arid lands of Istarinmul and Iramis.

Kylon looked around, details catching up with his stunned brain.

Just where the hell was he?

His first thought was that he had somehow fallen into a cistern below the Palace of the Prince. Yet it never got this cold in Iramis, not even underground. For that matter, the stonework did not look Iramisian. It was too rough-hewn, and this place looked as if it had been abandoned for a long time.

Kylon suspected he was no longer in Iramis.

Somehow that vortex had taken him far from the Palace of the Princes.

Caina. Where was Caina?

A surge of fear went through him, and Kylon drew on the sorcery of water, extending his senses.

He did not like what he sensed.

Sorcery radiated from the very stone around him. The power felt cold and malignant and necromantic. It did not seem like the sophisticated necromancy he had sensed from the Tomb of Kharnaces and the Great Necromancer Rhames and the Moroaica and her disciples, but somehow cruder and more elemental. Yet for all that, it was nonetheless powerful.

It made Kylon's hand itch to grasp the hilt of a sword.

He flexed his fingers, considering whether or not to call his valikon, but decided against it. The sword would come at his call quickly if he needed it, and the light from the sword's blade might draw unwelcome attention.

Because someone had brought him here, he was sure of it. Kylon had never heard of such a spell, but someone had brought him here deliberately, and possibly Caina as well. If these unknown summoners had done it with malicious intent, they would regret it.

Kylon climbed the stairs, the sorcery of water helping him to keep his balance on the wet stone. The stairs ascended to an archway near the top of the wall, and he reached the gate, walked through it, and stopped in surprise.

A hallway stretched beyond the end of the stairs, and there were…things growing on the stone wall.

A network of pulsing black veins covered the stonework, throbbing as if some distant, massive heart was driving dark blood through the vessels. Here and there things that looked like malignant growths sprouted from the wall, twisting the stone around them. Kylon stared at them, his disquiet growing. Necromantic power seemed to flow through the air around him like greasy smoke, and it seemed especially strong in the black veins and the strange growths.

He had killed more men in battle than he cared to remember, and the veins and the strange growths looked a great deal like the interior of a man's torso, albeit twisted and warped. It was almost as if the stone of the wall had merged with the blood and flesh of some monstrous living creature. He could not imagine the kind of sorcery that could do that…nor could he envision a creature large enough, because some of those veins were thicker than a grown man's leg.

Kylon kept walking, the stone cold beneath his bare feet. The strange dim light grew brighter, and soon the corridor ended in an archway. Kylon passed through the archway and entered a small courtyard.

Right away he noticed several strange things.

The first was the sky itself. One moment it looked like the cold, starry sky of a winter's night in the northern parts of the world, black and sharp with thousands of stars. The next it was filled with rippling black clouds moving with the speed of a hurricane wind, silent arcs of red lightning leaping from cloud to cloud. Kylon had never seen a sky like that, but Caina had described the sight to him once.

It was the sky of the netherworld.

If the sky kept changing...was this place, this fortress, whatever it was, caught halfway between the mortal world and the netherworld?

The second strange thing Kylon noticed was that more of the black veins and strange growths spread over the walls of the courtyard, reaching up to mantle the towers and basilicas that loomed over him. He could not shake the feeling that the fortress was some giant, twisted living thing.

The final strange thing was the statue.

It stood in the center of the courtyard, cast from greening bronze and over twelve feet tall. The statue displayed a proud-looking warrior wearing armor of a design that Kylon did not recognize. The warrior's face was lean and cruel-looking, with a hooked beak of a nose and a full mustache that hung down the sides of his thin mouth. He carried a sword, a dagger sheathed at his belt, and a strange amulet against his chest. A large signet ring was prominent on his right hand, a diadem resting upon his head.

A diadem? Was that a statue of a king? Kylon looked at the plinth. It bore an inscription in the Kagari alphabet. Some of the more barbarous nations of the eastern Empire used that alphabet, though Kylon supposed all those nations had fallen under the iron rule of the Umbarian Order. While he recognized the alphabet, he didn't recognize the language.

Did a statue with a plinth carved in the Kagari alphabet mean that Kylon was in the eastern Empire? The eastern Empire was a long way from Iramis, hundreds of miles as the bird flew. It seemed impossible that Kylon could have been transported there from Iramis in the blink of an eye.

Though he had seen stranger things.

Two archways led from the courtyard. One seemed opened into another, larger courtyard, while the second led to the base of one of the massive towers. Kylon hesitated, trying to decide which direction to take. The interior of the fortress might hold clothing and food and warmth, but the courtyard could lead him closer to an exit. But if Caina was here, she might be imprisoned inside the fortress, and...

A glint of metal caught his eye.

An armored boot lay in the next courtyard.

There was a spreading pool of fresh blood next to the boot.

Kylon lifted his right hand and called his valikon to his grasp.

The sword sprang into existence, a blade of ghostsilver with a delicately curved point, the flat of the weapon carved with Iramisian characters. Kylon was no valikarion, but after he had killed the Red Huntress, the valikon had bonded to him the way it might have bonded to a true valikarion, and he could summon it at will. The sword would penetrate any sorcerous ward and could destroy spirits of the underworld. The Iramisian characters upon the blade glowed, their forms blurred through the freezing white mist that encircled the sword.

Kylon strode into the next courtyard, sword raised, and saw the corpses.

Three men lay dead on the ground, their blood pooling beneath them. All three men had shaved heads, and all had a peculiar sigil carved into their foreheads, the symbol of a winged skull. Their armor was a strange carapace of close-fitting metal plates. In fact, the plates were so close-fitting that they had been grafted to their flesh like a second skin. His sorcery of water sensed the fading spells upon the armor, spells that would have given the dead men superhuman strength.

Kylon had fought and killed soldiers like these several times before.

The dead men were Adamant Guards, the elite soldiers of the Umbarian Order.

Was this fortress a stronghold of the Umbarian Order? Caina and Kylon had dealt a serious defeat to the Order when they had killed the Umbarian magus Lord Cassander Nilas and caused Istarinmul to ally with the Emperor against the Order. And it was well-known that Caina and Kylon had killed Cassander. Had the vortex that had brought them here been an Umbarian trap? The Umbarian Order had wanted to kill Caina even before she had been exiled to Istarinmul, and after Cassander's death, they would desire vengeance all the more.

Kylon's sword hand clenched, gripping the hilt of his valikon. If the Umbarians had hurt Caina, he would make sure they regretted it.

Then his brain caught up to his fears.

If this was an Umbarian stronghold, then who had killed the Adamant Guards?

That was a good question.

Kylon knew firsthand that the Guards were tenacious opponents and did not go down easily. He stepped closer, avoiding the puddles of blood, and looked at their wounds. All three men had been killed by sword blows to the neck, and one of the wounds was so deep that the Adamant Guard had nearly been beheaded. Caina couldn't have done that. She had a valikon of her own, but his wife simply didn't have the raw physical strength to drive a sword blade that far into a man's neck with a single blow, and all of these Guards had been killed with one powerful swing.

So who had killed them?

The presence of necromantic force brushed against his arcane senses.

Kylon looked up as dark shapes emerged from an archway on the far side of the courtyard.

They had the look of soldiers, but they had been dead for a long time, and their leathery, cracked flesh stretched over yellowing bone. The creatures wore rusted armor and carried ancient swords. Kylon had fought undead creatures multiple times, and he sensed the necromantic power that animated the walking corpses. His first thought was that the Umbarians had raised the creatures, but these things looked as if they had been dead for centuries, and the spells upon them were ancient.

Maybe this place wasn't an Umbarian fortress. Perhaps the Adamant Guards had been summoned here by the same spell that had brought Kylon. But he didn't think those undead had killed the Adamant Guards. The three Adamant Guards would have been enough to take down all seven of the undead without more than a few minor wounds.

The undead soldiers rushed towards Kylon, and he had no more time for thought.

In a way, it was a relief. Caina was the one suited for mysteries and puzzles and riddles. Kylon was a stormdancer, a soldier, a warrior. He preferred problems that he could solve while grasping the hilt of a sword.

This was one of them.

He drew on the sorcery of air to lend himself speed and hurtled forward, the valikon in both hands. The undead soldiers were fast, but he was faster, and he whipped the valikon in a sideways swing, the blade trailing white fire. The valikon crashed through the neck of an undead with the ease of an axe chopping a narrow branch, and the skull and rusted helm fell to the flagstones with a clang. The white fire from the sword flashed, dispelling the necromantic sorcery upon the undead and sending bones and ancient armor crashing to the ground. Two more undead came at Kylon, and the sorcery of water lent his arms extra strength. He hammered the valikon into the chest of the nearest undead with enough force to penetrate the rusted armor, and the ghostsilver blade undid the necromantic spells, bones scattering in all directions. The second one thrust a sword at his unprotected flesh, but Kylon raised the valikon in a parry. The undead soldier's ancient blade rebounded from the valikon, and Kylon ripped the valikon through the undead creature's skull, shattering the yellowed bone and sending fragments scattering in all directions.

The remaining four undead soldiers spread out around Kylon, trying to surround him, and he drew on the sorcery of water and air. He leaped backward, landing a half-dozen yards away, and recovered his balance. The four undead charged after him and Kylon focused on the one on the right and attacked, the sorcery of air boosting his speed. The valikon flashed in a swing as he ran past, and his timing was perfect. The blade shattered the creature's neck, the ghostsilver unraveling the necromantic spells.

The remaining three turned to face him, and Kylon fought them head on, the valikon flashing as he swung and thrust and hacked. Seven undead would have been dangerous, had they been able to surround him, but three proved little threat.

A few moments later the bones of the last undead rattled against the ground, and Kylon caught his breath.

Silence had fallen over the courtyard, save for the rapid draw of his breathing. Kylon reached for his arcane senses, sweeping them around the courtyard, but save for the pervasive necromantic aura, he detected no other threats nearby.

He looked at the archway behind the destroyed undead. It led into a broad, wide corridor, the walls distorted with more black veins and twisted growths. Kylon needed to find a way out of this strange fortress, but more importantly, he needed to find Caina. He didn't know what was going on, but it had something to do with the Umbarian Order, and they would kill Caina if they found her.

They would also try to kill Kylon if they found him...but they were welcome to the attempt. He had killed Cassander Nilas, but he had not forgotten the role the Order had played in his first wife Thalastre's murder.

And if they had forgotten, he would be pleased to remind them.

Kylon strode into the dark corridor, using the valikon's burning blade as a torch.

He spent the better part of an hour exploring the twisted fortress, trying to get a sense of its layout and size.

It was a surreal place. The fortress was far larger than any building Kylon had ever encountered, a tangled maze of towers and courtyards and keeps and turrets and walls, all of them covered in those black veins and tumorous growths. Kylon passed through grand halls with soaring roofs supported with towering pillars, the floor smooth and polished. Other times he walked through libraries filled with dusty books, or chapels of strange design, or vast courtyards that could have held entire villages. All the while the sky flickered, changing from the cold, starlit sky to the writhing black clouds of the netherworld.

He didn't know where he was going, but he had a trail to follow.

The Adamant Guards and the destroyed undead made sure of that.

Three times he encountered groups of destroyed undead similar to the seven that he had fought, and twice more he found dead pairs of Adamant Guards. Was there a battle raging through the fortress? As he looked at the dead Adamant Guards, he saw that they had all been killed in the same way, with powerful sword blows to the neck. Granted, with their heavy armor, that was one of the few reliable ways to kill an Adamant Guard. Yet Kylon suspected that the same swordsman had killed them.

A swordsman who had overcome so many Adamant Guards would be a dangerous opponent.

Kylon was standing in yet another courtyard, looking at a dead Adamant Guard, when he heard the distant sound of steel clashing against steel.

His head snapped up, seeking the source of the sound. It was coming from an archway on the far side of the courtyard. Was Caina fighting someone? Kylon jogged forward, valikon in hand. Stairs descended from the gate and then turned a corner. Kylon hurried down the stairs, turned the corner, and found himself overlooking a battle.

The stairs ended in a long pillared gallery with a high ceiling. Niches lined the walls, holding life-sized statues of warriors in archaic armor. Three Adamant Guards lay dead upon the floor, and six more still stood, attacking a man in black armor.

The man was a battle magus of the Imperial Magisterium.

He was moving too fast for Kylon to get a good look at him, but he wore the black plate armor of a battle magus, a black sword in his armored fist. Kylon sensed the psychokinetic sorcery the man employed to make himself faster and stronger…and he also sensed the man's growing exhaustion and desperation. He was holding his own, but so were the Adamant Guards, and they were wearing him down.

Was the battle magus an Umbarian? Both the Umbarians and the magi of the Imperial Magisterium wore that kind of battle armor. Then again, if the man was an Umbarian, why were the Adamant Guards trying to kill him?

The battle magus stumbled, his black sword flicking out, and he barely managed to deflect the thrust of a broadsword aimed at his head.

Kylon made up his mind. A battle magus would make a capable ally. With allies, Kylon had a better chance of escaping this twisted fortress and whatever dark power controlled it.

More importantly, he had a better chance of finding Caina.

He drew on the sorcery of water and air, lifted his valikon, and charged.

The Adamant Guards were focused upon the faltering battle magus and did not even realize Kylon was there until he attacked. He swung the valikon with all his strength and arcane power driving the blade, and he took off the head of the nearest Adamant Guard. No blood came from the stump of the man's neck, and the freezing mist wreathing his valikon turned the Guard's blood to ice before his corpse fell to the ground with a clang of armor.

The battle magus, to his credit, did not hesitate. He surged forward, and Kylon sensed the psychokinetic sorcery he used to drive himself with inhuman speed. The magus's black sword darted out and opened the throat of an Adamant Guard, blood spraying from the wound.

The other Guards whirled, moving to assess the new threat. Their heavy shields came up, presenting a solid wall of oak and steel. The black-armored magus stepped to the left, and Kylon moved to the right.

A flicker of incredulity went over the nearest Guard's face as he looked at Kylon. However strange this place, no doubt the Guard had never expected to be attacked by a naked man with a sword wreathed in fire and white mist.

Kylon attacked, thrusting the valikon at the shields. On the third thrust, he got past the shield, opening a shallow cut on the nearest Guard's sword arm. The wound was trivial, but the touch of a ghostsilver blade disrupted the spells that gave the Guard inhuman strength. That strength let the Guard bear the weight of his grafted armor, and the man stumbled, agony going over his expression as he tried to keep his feet.

The disruption lasted only a second, but that was more than enough time for Kylon to kill the struggling Guard.

Behind him, he sensed a surge of power, and the black-armored man cast a spell. A pulse of psychokinetic force rolled across the gallery and slammed into the three remaining Guards. The Guards stumbled, fighting to keep their balance. The spell hadn't been strong, but it had knocked them off balance, and that was all Kylon needed. The valikon blurred forward, and he slew another Adamant Guard.

The remaining two Guards split up, one coming at Kylon, the other attacking the battle magus. Kylon retreated as the Guard came in a rush, bashing with his shield and stabbing with his broadsword. The sorcery of air let Kylon stay ahead of the Guard's attack, but only just. Three times he had to raise the valikon to deflect thrusts that would otherwise have found his chest.

At last the Guard's momentum played out, and Kylon counterattacked. The Guard had seen the fate of his comrade, and he used his shield with skill, keeping Kylon's sword from finding his exposed skin. Kylon launched a series of blows towards the Guard's head, forcing the man to raise his shield higher and higher.

At last Kylon feinted high, sidestepped, and then swung the valikon low. The blade slashed across the Guard's left shin. It was a shallow wound, but the ghostsilver blade bit just deep enough to disrupt the spells upon the Guard's armor, and the man stumbled with a groan of pain.

Kylon killed him with a blow across the neck.

The Guard fell with a clatter of armor, his shield bouncing away, and Kylon turned to face the final Adamant Guard. But the battle magus had already killed the Guard, and blood dripped from the black sword as the magus ripped it free.

For a moment Kylon and the battle magus regarded each other. The magus had thick black hair and deep blue eyes, his jaw shaded with black stubble. Kylon was sure that he had never met the battle magus before, yet the man looked oddly familiar.

Disturbingly familiar, come to think of it, but Kylon could not quite place his features.

"I have to say," said the battle magus in High Nighmarian, "that of all the strange things that happened today, getting rescued by a naked Kyracian with a sword is still not the strangest one."

"Then you are not an Umbarian?" said Kylon. It took him a moment to recall the High Nighmarian words. He was grateful Andromache's tutors had forced him to learn the language as a child.

"Me?" said the battle magus. "No, no, no. They rather want me dead, I'm afraid. Who you are, I think, is a more interesting question." The magus blinked several times. Warding spells blocked off most of the battle magus's emotional sense, but Kylon felt the cold of concentration go over the man's aura. "You look Kyracian and speak High Nighmarian with a pronounced Kyracian accent. That, combined with the mist-wreathed sword in your right hand, suggests the obvious fact that you must be a Kyracian stormdancer. Factoring in your lack of clothing implies that an hour ago you were enjoying an activity that did not require clothes – sleeping, bathing, a woman, whatever – when you were suddenly snatched away from your activity by a peculiar vortex of shadows. Then you found yourself here. Am I correct?"

Kylon considered his answer. The man's deductions had been entirely correct. Caina often did the same thing. Yet Kylon didn't know if this battle magus would be an enemy. Still, Kylon would need allies to find Caina and escape this fortress.

"Yes," said Kylon. "I was a great distance from here, and the vortex appeared just as you said."

The magus frowned. "How much distance, if you don't mind my asking?"

"I don't know since I don't know where we are," said Kylon. "But I was a few days' ride east of Istarinmul." The battle magus might not believe that Kylon had been in Iramis since all the world knew that Iramis had burned a century and a half ago.

At least until Caina had brought it back.

"I see," said the magus. "I was with the Legions in their camps outside the walls of Artifel. We had just repulsed an Umbarian sortie, and I was walking back to the camp when the vortex took me."

"Artifel?" said Kylon. "There are a thousand miles of sea, mountain, forest, and plain between Istarinmul and Artifel."

"Aye," said the magus. "There are indeed. Which implies that whatever sorcery brought us here was a spell of exceeding power. I have never encountered nor heard of a spell that could do such a thing, and I've heard of many different spells."

"So have I," said Kylon. "Do you have any idea where we are?"

"No," said the magus. "Well…a suspicion. Wherever we are," he pointed at a window near the ceiling that showed the shifting sky, "it is quite clearly caught in the netherworld, at least partially. I suspect that we are in a portion of the netherworld that has been temporarily summoned and joined to the material world. That means…"

He fell silent, a frown going over his haggard face, and again Kylon was struck by a strange sense of familiarity.

"That sword," said the magus. "That's an Iramisian valikon. Where did you get it? Did you find it here?"

"No," said Kylon. "It came with me when the spell brought me here."

"Where did you find it, then?" said the magus. He didn't seem afraid, only fascinated. "Those weapons are legendary. There are only a few left in the world. All the rest were destroyed when the Alchemists burned Iramis."

"My wife gave it to me," said Kylon.

The magus snorted. "Clearly a woman of exquisite taste." He started to ask another question, and then stopped himself. "I suggest that we work together to escape. I have a thousand questions, and no doubt you do as well, but those can wait until we have secured our physical safety. If this place really is a part of the netherworld bound to the physical world, the spell will be unstable, and it might be pulled back into the netherworld at any moment."

"Very well," said Kylon. "I agree."

"Let us start with introductions, then," said the battle magus. "My name is Sebastian Scorneus, and I am a battle magus of the Imperial Magisterium. But that is something of a mouthful, and you did just save my life, so you can simply call me Seb."

"Sebastian?" said Kylon, startled.

Caina's father had been named Sebastian, though she rarely spoke of her parents. She had loved her father and hated her mother, though beyond that Kylon didn't think she had any other family. Still, Sebastian was a common enough name among those of Nighmarian birth.

But the last name. Scorneus? Caina had once disguised herself as a magus named Rania Scorneus. Her old mentor Halfdan had suggested the masquerade to her as if he had thought it would suit her...

"Yes," said Seb. "Have we met?"

"I don't think so," said Kylon. He considered giving the man a false name the way Caina would have done and decided against it. "My name is Kylon of House Kardamnos."

Seb's blue eyes widened. "Now that name I have heard before. Kylon Shipbreaker? The former Archon? They say you were banished from New Kyre and disappeared off the face of the earth."

"I ended up here, so evidently the rumors are true," said Kylon.

"I would be fascinated to hear the entire story," said Seb. "But we ought to move. The longer we stay here, the greater the danger that we will be drawn all the way into the netherworld."

He looked towards the window, and with a shock of recognition, Kylon realized why the man seemed so familiar.

Sebastian Scorneus looked like Caina.

He looked a lot like Caina.

His face in profile resembled hers. The line of his jaw and the shape of his ears were identical. His blue eyes were the exact same color as Caina's, and he had the same thick black hair. If Kylon didn't know better, he could have sworn that Seb and Caina were related.

In fact, he could have sworn they were siblings.

"Is there a problem?" said Seb.

Some of Kylon's confusion must have shown on his face. "Other than the obvious, no. You…just look a great deal like someone I know."

"Ah," said Seb. "Well, I'm afraid the House Scorneus is a large and powerful one, and we all look a great deal alike. Likely you met one of my cousins or my aunts at some point." He grimaced. "Depending on which aunt, my condolences. But I do think we should get moving."

"Yes," said Kylon. He could worry about the mystery later. "Do you know the way out?"

"No," said Seb, "but I can guess. We can solve a more immediate problem on the way. I passed through a barracks on my way here, and some of the items in there had been preserved. Including some clothing that ought to fit you."

"That," said Kylon, "would be welcome. Lead the way."

Seb nodded, and they started down the pillared gallery.

Kylon considered telling him about Caina but decided against it. As far as he could tell, Seb had been telling the truth. But the Umbarians were clever, and Seb was still a magus of the Magisterium. The Magisterium had wanted Caina dead in the past, and even with the civil war, they might not have forgotten their desire for vengeance.

And if Caina was here, and if Seb decided to attack her…well, Kylon would make sure the battle magus did not live long enough to regret his decision.

CHAPTER THREE

IRON RING

The corridor beyond the library was filled with darkness, and Caina had to make a decision.

It was too dark for her to see, and if she kept going, she could blunder into a trap or walk off a balcony. Worse, she suspected that the robed creature could see in the darkness, and if it had any companions, they could see her while she could not see them, though the vision of the valikon would give her some warning.

Which meant she either had to double back, or risk making some light.

She decided to risk the light.

Caina held out her left hand and concentrated on her pyrikon, asking it to change shape. The delicate ghostsilver bracelet unfolded and expanded. When it finished, Caina held a slender staff of ghostsilver links a few inches taller than she was, and its end gave off a pale silver light that threw back the gloom. In the light, the veins covering the walls looked stark and diseased, while the skin of her hands and arms seemed ghostly.

Well, that was appropriate. Caina was a Ghost. Or she had been. Now she was the adopted sister of the Padishah of Istarinmul, the Liberator of Iramis, a valikarion, and the wife of an exiled Kyracian nobleman. Could she be all those things and still be a Ghost of the Empire? Caina didn't know.

Of course, if she didn't get out of this place, she would become a corpse, and the question would be moot.

Caina moved down the corridor in silence, the staff glowing in her left hand, her eyes scanning the gloom and her ears listening for any sounds. She heard nothing but the soft draw of her breath, and nothing moved in the corridor save the shifting shadows of the veins and the growths on the walls. They made her feel like she was walking down the gullet of some malevolent beast.

Dread chewed through her, some for herself, but most of it for Kylon. She could not stop imagining what might have happened to him.

But the skills the Ghosts had taught her as a child were part of her very being, and Caina moved ahead in silence, watching for threats, the staff steady in her left hand.

There was a faint light ahead.

Caina sent a thought to her pyrikon, and it collapsed down to its bracelet form, the silvery light vanishing. She waited a moment for her eyes to adjust, and ahead she saw that the corridor ended in a tall arch. To judge from the color of the pale light coming from the archway, it opened into a courtyard of some kind.

She didn't see any necromantic auras ahead, save for the dark power saturating the entire fortress. The fingers of her right hand flexed, ready to call her valikon, and Caina walked to the end of the corridor.

She stepped into a small courtyard and looked around. Once, it must have been a beautiful place. There was a stone fountain in the center of the courtyard, a statue of an armored warrior with a gowned noblewoman upon his arm rising from a plinth, and a small garden surrounded the fountain. The walls of the courtyard rose for forty or fifty feet, fronted with balconies built of blue marble with golden veins, slender pillars supporting the railings and ceilings. Behind the balconies, narrow windows looked into small rooms.

It would have been a lovely place once, but now the black veins covered the pillars and the walls. The water in the fountain gave off a foul, reeking odor, and the vegetation in the garden looked poisonous and blighted. Despite that, the shape of the intricate railings had a somehow feminine look. Had this courtyard been the women's quarters of the fortress? Many of the emirs of Istarinmul maintained women's quarters in their palaces to house their wives and concubines. Maybe the builders of this fortress had the same custom.

Perhaps Caina could find some clothing here. The spells in the library had preserved the ancient books, so why not clothing? From what she had seen from the windows, the terrain outside the forest was a snow-choked forest. If Caina didn't find warm clothing before she escaped, she was going to die in a lot of pain. She had seen men that Kylon had killed using the sorcery of water to freeze the blood in their veins, and it did not look like a pleasant way to die.

Going naked into a frozen forest would be a death like that, albeit slower.

She crossed to the balconies and began investigating.

There were no doors on the first level, so she took the stairs to the second level and started opening doors. The first door opened into what looked like a dining room, with a polished table and a row of cushioned chairs. A faint layer of dust hung over everything, but despite that, the furnishings showed no sign of either age or recent use. The second door opened into a sitting room with tall wooden chairs.

The third door opened into a bedroom dominated by a huge bed piled high with pillows and blankets. The bedding should have rotted away long ago, but the sorcery of the fortress had preserved it. Caina thought that a good sign as she stepped into the bedroom. If nothing else, she could fashion a robe for herself out of the blankets. A massive wooden wardrobe stood against one wall, and Caina opened it.

For the first time since she had been brought to this strange place, she smiled.

The wardrobe was full of clothes.

Caina began sorting through them. Most of the garments were dresses of rich fabric – silk and velvet and damask, and some of them even had pearls or semiprecious stones worked into the collars and cuffs. The colors were bright, far more vivid than common among the nobles of the Empire, with bright reds and blues and yellows. One yellow dress caught her eye. She had always been partial to yellow, though with her work in the Ghosts she rarely got to wear such a conspicuous color, and Kylon liked her in yellow...

Caina smiled to herself. Odd that she could think of such things now.

Alas, the dress was beautiful, but it was an impractical garment. It would be difficult to run and fight and move with stealth in the elaborate dress, and if Caina saw more of those robed creatures, she might have to do all three in rapid succession.

Soon she found more practical clothes in the wardrobe. She donned a pair of black trousers that mostly fit and knee-high black boots that were comfortable. The leather should have been cracked and brittle with age, but it was still supple. After that came a white shirt and Caina found a red coat that hung to her knees, the collar stiff. It had ornate black trim on the cuffs and the lapels, and it looked like the sort of thing an archaic nobleman might have worn while hunting deer. Yet it was thick, and more importantly, it was warm. Caina shrugged into the heavy coat and found that it fit reasonably well. She took a few practice steps in the boots until she was sure that she could move in silence when necessary, and then left the bedroom.

No doubt she looked odd, but a frozen corpse would be far less attractive.

Caina left the bedroom and stepped onto the balcony, looking up at the sky. It kept blurring back and forth between the twisted, lightning-lashed sky of the netherworld and the star-scattered sky of the material world. She thought the sorcerous aura of the fortress pulsed in time to the changes in the sky.

And she thought the changes were coming faster, and that the sky spent more time as the twisted, writhing sky of the netherworld.

Did that mean the fortress was being drawn out of the material world?

Caina didn't like that thought at all. If the fortress was pulled back into the netherworld, she would have no way of getting back to the material world. Worse, if Kylon had been summoned to the fortress, he would be trapped here. Caina had hoped they would die alongside each other, but when they were old and full of years, not in some corrupted fortress that radiated necromantic energy.

It was time to move.

Caina went from door to door, checking until she found another corridor that led deeper into the fortress. She called her pyrikon back to its staff form, and in its pale silvery light, she saw more black veins and misshapen growths clinging to the walls. There was no sign of any undead or the robed creature she had seen earlier.

She started forward, a plan forming in her thoughts. Wandering this maze would be an inefficient method of escape. She decided to find a stairwell leading up. If she could get to the top of one of the towers, she would look at the layout of the fortress. Perhaps that would show her a way out.

Ahead Caina saw the dim light of yet another gate leading into yet another courtyard. This one seemed larger than the courtyard with the blue pillars, and...

Caina stopped.

The faint smell of blood came to her nostrils.

Human blood, and quite a lot of it. Someone had just been killed in the courtyard. Caina listened for a moment but heard nothing but her own breathing. Nevertheless, she sent her pyrikon back to its bracelet form and called her valikon to her right hand, the sword's weight reassuring in her hand.

By the Divine, she wished for a throwing knife or three.

Caina entered the courtyard.

It was like the ones she had seen earlier, an expanse of stern, cold stone, with pillared arcades running along all four walls. Three men lay dead on the ground, pools of fresh blood gathering beneath them. Broadswords and shields lay near their hands, and their armor was close-fitting...

Caina blinked, a cold suspicion settling over her.

No. Not close-fitting. It had been grafted to the flesh of the dead men.

The men were Adamant Guards. Which meant that the Umbarian Order was here, in the fortress. It was well known that she and Kylon had killed the Umbarian magus Cassander Nilas and stopped him from slaughtering everyone in Istarinmul. It seemed the Umbarians had decided that the hour had come for their revenge...and knowing the Umbarians, they had prepared thoroughly to take their revenge on Caina and Kylon.

Well, thorough preparations hadn't saved these three Adamant Guards, had they?

She examined the dead men.

All three of them had been killed with powerful sword blows to the neck. The sight heartened Caina. Kylon, with his strength enhanced by the sorcery of water, would leave wounds like that. His valikon would be a deadly weapon against the Guards since the ghostsilver blade would disrupt the spells of strength that allowed the Guards to bear their grafted armor.

Almost certainly Kylon had killed these Adamant Guards. Either Kylon or another skilled swordsman with the power of sorcery to drive his limbs.

If Kylon had killed the Adamant Guards, where would he have gone next?

Caina looked over the courtyard, but the flat flagstones preserved no marks of passage. Two other archways opened off the courtyard, but annoyingly both led to broad stairways going down, one on the left wall, and one on the right. Caina went to the right stairwell first, but it led into darkness, and she saw nothing. The stairwell on the left also went into the darkness...but in the distance, she saw flickers of light, and she also heard the clang of metal.

Like marching soldiers.

Or a battle?

Even as the thought came to her, she heard a hoarse shout, followed by a scream, and the vision of the valikarion saw the surge of a spell.

If Kylon was fighting, she would help him. He was one of the most effective fighters she had ever met, and with his valikon, he could deal with any number of Adamant Guards...but she also had a valikon, and two swords were better than one.

She hurried down the stairs in silence, collapsing her pyrikon down to its bracelet form once again. For a moment, she considered keeping her valikon ready but instead dismissed the sword. The valikon would give her a decisive advantage against the Adamant Guards, but it would still be a bad idea for her to fight a larger and stronger opponent face-to-face. Better to let the Guards underestimate her until it was too late.

As her mentor Halfdan had taught her so long ago, only fools fought fairly.

The stairs turned, and Caina slowed, peering around the corner.

A battlefield greeted her.

The steps ended in a small stone hall, and at the far end were a pair of massive iron-banded wooden doors that glowed with sorcerous power. Dead Adamant Guards and destroyed undead creatures lay scattered across the floor. Caina saw three of the robed creatures she had seen earlier, their features misshapen, their corpses leaking black slime.

Two Adamant Guards were still on their feet, broadswords in hand, though both men had taken wounds.

Am Umbarian magus stood with them.

The man could be nothing else. He was in his late thirties, with gray-shot black hair, hard brown eyes, and a thin, humorless mouth. He wore the black leather greatcoat favored by the Umbarian magi. To the sixth sense of Caina's valikarion sight, the coat shone with the sorcerous power of spells designed to make the material as strong as plate armor.

"We are almost there, sir," said one of the Adamant Guards. "It must be behind those doors. Else those creatures would not have put up such a fight."

The magus gave an irritated shake of his head. "But I can't get through the blasted wards on the doors. If the provost wants the damned thing so badly, she can come and get it herself."

Provost? Caina knew that the Umbarian Order was led by five provosts. Was one of them there?

"Magus Morett, we were commanded to take the ring," said the Guard.

The magus, evidently named Morett, scowled at him. "And you are welcome to do so. Go try to open those doors and see what happens."

Neither Guard leaped at the opportunity.

"We know the way to the chamber," said Morett. "We'll go back, get the provost, and she can break the seal on the doors."

"The fortress may not remain here that long," said the Guard.

"Then she can summon it back again with that precious amulet of hers," snapped Morett. "I thought this entire plan was folly. We have lost valuable resources dealing with those creatures." He kicked one of the robed things in sheer frustration. "Now, move."

The magus strode up the stairs, and the two Guards followed him.

Caina eased back around the corner, her mind racing. She had assumed the Umbarian Order was here to kill her and Kylon, but what if it was just a coincidence? Morett said the Order had come here to find something. Apparently, those robed creatures, whatever they were, didn't want the Order to have it.

So how had Caina gotten tangled up in all of this?

But she had a more immediate problem. In about three seconds, Morett and the two Guards would come around the corner, and she had no place to hide. Caina stepped to the center of the stairs, flexing her right hand as she prepared to call her valikon.

She would have to be quick.

Morett and the Guards came around the corner and froze in alarm as they saw her. To Caina's surprise, a flicker of recognition went over the Umbarian's face. Had she met him somewhere before? No, she had never seen the man, she was sure of it.

"Provost," said the Umbarian. "I didn't realize you would enter the fortress in person. We've located the relic, but I cannot breach the wards upon the doors to the vault. I…"

Morett fell silent, his eyes narrowing.

"No," he said. "No, you're not her." He drew himself up, the fear draining from his face. "Who are you?"

"I…I…" said Caina, making her eyes go wide.

"Identify yourself!" said Morett, raising his left hand. He didn't have one of the black gauntlets that let a Umbarian magus use pyromancy safely, but she saw the power as he drew together arcane energy for a spell of psychokinetic force.

"My name's Natalia," said Caina. "I don't know how I got here. I woke up in some dusty library, and…"

"Rubbish," spat Morett. "Look at you. You're obviously yet another one of the provost's damned relatives. Are there no end to them? Does she think to play games now of all times?" He scoffed. "She's gone too far." He released his spell of psychokinetic force and began another. Caina recognized it as a spell to break into the thoughts of another. "Let's compel the truth from you, shall we?"

"Please, sir," said Caina, stumbling as she backed away. "Please, I don't understand what is happening, I…"

"Kill her if she runs," said Morett.

Caina went motionless, making herself tremble with fear. It must have been a convincing performance, because the magus strode up without hesitation, put his right hand on her forehead, and cast his spell. She felt the surge of power as Morett's spell reached for her mind, and she saw it around his fingers as a flare of gray light.

It didn't do anything.

She was a valikarion. Mind-affecting spells could not touch her.

"What?" said Morett. "That doesn't make any sense. Why didn't that work? What…"

His eyes went wide, and he stepped back, beginning another spell.

"Kill her!" he shouted. "She must be one of those damned Temnoti! Kill her now!"

The Adamant Guards stepped forward, and Caina had no choice but to act.

She jumped after Morett, calling her valikon as she did. The blade coalesced in her hand, and Caina stabbed before the magus could dodge. The valikon sliced through the spell-armored coat and sank between his ribs, and Morett staggered back, collapsing to the stairs with a choked scream as his heart stopped.

The two Adamant Guards charged at Caina.

She ripped the valikon free and jumped back, and just kept ahead of their sweeping broadswords. The Adamant Guards came after her with slow, confident strides, spreading out on her left and her right, shields raised and broadswords drawn back to stab. Caina retreated, trying to keep her balance on the stairs, the valikon held out before her. The Guards probably didn't realize the danger the valikon posed to them, which meant she would have only one chance to do this right. The Guards had inhuman strength, but they had been trained like Legionaries, which meant they would fight like Legionaries...

One of the Guards stepped forward, shield dipping, sword stabbing over the shield's rim like a steel tongue. It was a terrifyingly fast blow, but the change in his footing had given the attack away, and Caina managed to dodge the stab by mere inches. She slashed with the valikon, and opened a glancing cut on the Guard's forearm, just above his bracer. It was a trivial wound and one that a seasoned Legionary might not even notice until the battle was over.

But when the ghostsilver blade broke his skin, it disrupted the spells wrapped around his flesh, and the Guard staggered beneath the weight of his armor. Before he could recover, Caina seized his sword arm and yanked him forward, his heavy armor driving him towards the ground. She raised her valikon and stabbed, hammering the blade down into the Guard's neck.

The wound didn't kill him, but he would bleed out before much longer.

Caina jumped back as the Adamant Guard fell, and the second one charged her. She dodged his sword, but his strike had been only a feint, and his shield slammed across her torso.

That hurt. A lot.

The impact threw Caina back, and she tumbled down the stairs, tucking her shoulder to roll with the fall. An instant later she reached the bottom of the stairs and slammed hard into the wall. That also hurt quite a bit, and the impact blasted the breath from her lungs.

The Adamant Guard leaped from the stairs, sword raised high to stab.

Fear gave Caina strength, and she kicked away from the wall and jumped to her feet, avoiding the Guard's landing by a few inches. He landed on his feet, his sword point bouncing off the ground. Caina scrambled backward, holding out her left hand and calling to her pyrikon, and the bracelet unfolded and took the shape of a slender staff.

The Guard looked at the staff and sneered. It was too thin to be a useful weapon, and Caina pointed the end at his face. The Guard advanced, and Caina held her ground.

A heartbeat later, the end of the staff burst into a brilliant glow at her mental command. The Guard was looking right at it, and he stumbled as the light dazzled his eyes. Caina darted forward, dodging around the Guard's furious thrust, and swung her valikon. The Guard almost avoided her strike, but the ghostsilver blade clipped his shaved head.

He staggered from the weight of his armor, and that made it easy to bring the valikon down against the back of his neck.

Caina stepped back, breathing hard, looking at the men she had just killed as her pyrikon collapsed back into its bracelet form around her wrist.

It was her wedding night. Her damned wedding night. Why did she have to fight for her life on her wedding night? Though she had to admit it wasn't inconsistent with the rest of her life. She could just imagine what Morgant might have said.

Caina shook her head, dismissed her valikon, and jogged back up the broad stairs to Morett's corpse. She took a moment to search it and found a small pouch carrying Imperial denarii, which she pocketed. Kylon was always a little appalled when she calmly went about looting the dead, but the dead had no further need of money, and if Caina escaped the fortress, she would need coin. She also took Morett's dagger, an unremarkable blade of normal steel, since she might need a dagger and could hardly cut her meat with the valikon.

Unfortunately, he had nothing else useful on him. For a moment Caina considered taking his medallion and his greatcoat and disguising herself as an Umbarian magus but discarded the idea. For one thing, any Umbarian magi in this fortress likely knew each other at sight. For another, the valikon had ripped a hole in the front of Morett's black coat, and that would be obvious at once.

He carried no clues indicating what the Umbarians were doing here.

But his conversation with the Guards had given something away, hadn't it? Wherever this twisted fortress was, the Umbarians had come here to claim a relic of some kind. Whatever the relic was, Caina had to assume that it was powerful and dangerous.

After the Staff and Seal of Iramis, the Conjurant Bloodcrystal, the Subjugant Bloodcrystal, the Throne of Corazain, and all the other dangerous weapons of sorcery she had encountered, Caina had hoped to never again find an ancient relic of arcane power.

Apparently, that hope was not going to be realized.

She looked at the massive doors at the end of the wide corridor. They were bound with thick bars of iron, and while they were not locked, that didn't matter. Potent spells bound them closed. Morett had only been a magus of average strength, and he wouldn't have been able to make a dent in those sorcerous defenses. It would either take a sorcerer of great power or a team of weaker magi to break through the doors.

Caina looked at the dead robed creatures. Black slime leaked from their wounds. Had they been the ones to create the ward on the doors? It seemed this fortress belonged to them, and the Umbarians had invaded the citadel to seize the relic.

The valikon could break through those wards with ease, but it didn't matter. Caina had no intention of digging out whatever blood-drenched old relic was behind those doors. She could find another way out of this place.

She turned, intending to go around the corner and back up the stairs.

Sorcerous auras flickered before her sight.

Caina froze, trying to make sense of the auras.

They were radiating from the top of the stairs, and they were coming closer.

As she looked, she realized that the auras were similar to the one she had seen around the first robed creature.

A dozen of the things were coming down the stairs.

Caina looked at the dead Adamant Guards before the doors. Some of them had been killed by the destroyed undead. Others looked as if their flesh had been twisted and withered by sorcery. Undoubtedly, they had been killed by the robed creatures.

Morett had thought Caina might be something called a Temnoti. Was that a nation or a tribe?

Or was that the name of the twisted creatures?

Caina didn't know. She did know, however, that she couldn't fight twelve of the robed things. Caina also doubted that the creatures would bother to distinguish between her and the Umbarians, which meant she had to get away from them.

And that left only one way out.

"Oh," muttered Caina, walking towards the doors. "I'm going to regret this, aren't I?"

She lifted the valikon and drove the blade into the crack between the doors. The hilt grew hot beneath her hands, almost too painful to hold, and Caina braced herself and forced the sword down. Wisps of smoke rose from the thick wood, and the ward began to snap and flicker, almost like a banner caught in the wind.

Then there was a flash of harsh green light, and the ward collapsed.

Caina wrenched her valikon free and stepped back, wisps of white smoke rising from the ghostsilver blade. To the vision of the valikarion, the threads of power that made up the ward jerked back and forth like cut ropes. Already the ward was rebuilding itself. Caina pushed on the right-hand door. It was heavy, but she strained, and it swung open a few feet.

She slipped through the gap, and the door boomed shut behind her, the ward relocking over the door.

Fearing she had trapped herself, she took a deep breath and looked around.

She found herself in another small courtyard, and two more doors opened on the left wall and the right wall, so at least she wasn't trapped. A stone plinth stood in the center of the courtyard, holding a twelve-foot-tall bronze statue of a proud warrior in armor. Before the statue stood a smaller pedestal, and atop it...

A powerful necromantic aura radiated from thing atop the pedestal.

Caina stepped forward, valikon raised, and looked at the object atop the short pillar of stone.

It was a ring.

It looked like a nobleman's signet ring, thick and heavy, but unlike most signet rings, it was made from gray iron rather than gold. It had a massive emerald set into the band, and someone with great skill had carved the emerald into the sigil of a dragon's roaring head. Necromantic sorcery radiated from the ring, fell and powerful.

A lot of necromantic sorcery...and as Caina examined the aura, she thought it was related to the aura hanging over the entire fortress. It seemed kin to the black veins pulsing through the walls, to the robed creatures that she had seen.

Similar, yet much stronger.

Her eyes moved from the ring to the statue of the warrior standing over it.

No, not a warrior. A king, she thought. The statue displayed a proud-looking man wearing armor of an archaic design common in the eastern Empire – Kagari, most likely. His face was lean and cruel, with a hooked beak of a nose and a full mustache that hung down the sides of his thin mouth. He carried a sword, a dagger sheathed at his belt and a strange amulet against his chest. A large signet ring was prominent on his right hand, a diadem resting upon his head.

Whoever had cast the statue had been a brilliant sculptor. There was a cold vitality to the image, a restless energy and cruelty. If the representation was accurate, that king had been a powerful and dangerous man in life.

Caina looked at the statue's ring, and then the ring upon the plinth. The statue's ring had the same dragon seal carved into the bronze.

Which meant that the ring upon the plinth had once belonged to the king whose bronze statue stood before her.

This ring had to be what the Umbarians had come here to claim.

Caina didn't know what the ring was or what it could do, but it was powerful. And if the Umbarians wanted it, they intended to use it work evil. Cassander Nilas had almost destroyed Istarinmul with the Throne of Corazain, and she shuddered to think of the destruction he could have wrought with the Staff and the Seal of Iramis.

She started to reach for it, and suddenly she felt that the ring was aware of her, that it knew she was a valikarion and it hated her for it. Caina stopped, staring at the ring. Its emerald dragon seal glowed with a harsh green light, identical to the green light she had seen before from necromantic spells.

Caina scooped it up, the metal icy against her palm. The necromantic aura pulsed and shrank into the cold metal of the ring, and she felt another wave of alien, furious rage from the relic.

"Yes," murmured Caina. "You don't like that, do you?"

The thing had a will of its own, she was sure of it. Her pyrikon had a will and a power of its own since it was a spirit of defense bound in material form. Had a malevolent spirit been bound within ring?

Whatever the source of its power, she didn't want the Umbarians to have the ring.

She glanced back, and beyond the warded doors she saw the auras of the robed creatures drawing near. Another few moments and they would find her, and she suspected they would take exception to her theft of the ring.

Best to be gone.

Caina looked at the bronze statue of the cruel-faced king one last time, turned, and picked the door on the left. It was a massive slab of wood and metal, bound with both iron bars and spells. In the center of the door was a massive lock fused to the door. The sorcerous flows centered upon an indentation in the center of the lock.

An indentation that looked exactly like the dragon seal upon the ring.

Caina pressed the ring into the lock.

The door shuddered, the spells flaring with power, and she heard bolts clang and gears turn. The door swung open, revealing a long corridor that led deeper into the fortress.

Caina hurried onward. The door swung shut behind her, and she continued down the corridor, the black veins in the walls throbbing.

CHAPTER FOUR

A LOST GIRL

Caina hesitated, looking around the windswept courtyard.

She wasn't sure, but she thought heard a voice.

The corridor had led her to another locked door, which the iron ring had opened for her. Caina still wasn't sure that taking the necromantic relic had been a good idea, but if it opened the fortress's locked doors, she might need it to escape. Beyond the locked door was another wide courtyard, this one filled with a dead garden, the plants and bushes nothing more than dry sticks clawing from the earth. Towers rose around the courtyard, covered in webs of black veins and tumorous growths. The sky overhead shifted back and forth between the cold winter's night and the writhing, cloud-choked sky of the netherworld.

Caina wasn't sure, but she thought the sky was looking more and more like the sky of the netherworld. Did that mean the fortress was shifting back all the way into the netherworld? If Caina did not find an exit soon, she might be trapped here.

If she did not find Kylon soon, they might both be trapped here.

She had crossed to the middle of the courtyard, looking for a way out, when the frightened voice reached her ears.

It was a girl's voice, and she shouted in a language that Caina did not recognize. Caina froze, looking around, but nothing moved in the dead courtyard, and nothing moved on the towers and ramparts overhead, save for the odd shadows cast by the sky's constant shifting.

The voice was coming from an archway behind a pillared arcade. The girl shouted again, her voice rising with fear. A second voice answered her, and that voice made Caina's skin crawl. There was a twisted, alien quality to the voice. If the black veins and tumorous growths clinging to the walls could have spoken, Caina thought, they would have a voice like that.

The girl shouted again. She was trying to sound threatening, but the fear overrode the anger.

Caina made up her mind and headed towards the archway. She ducked behind a pillar and peered through the archway, holding her valikon behind her back to conceal its light.

Behind the archway opened yet another large room that had the look of a ballroom, with a polished floor of gleaming marble and tall windows that looked over the twisted fortress and the flickering sky. Caina glimpsed ancient chandeliers hanging from the ceiling, heavy with dust and cobwebs. Four undead warriors like those she had seen earlier stood in the ballroom, ancient swords in skeletal hands. Behind them stood one of the robed creatures. Instead of a left hand, a thick tentacle covered in glistening suckers emerged from the voluminous sleeve. The creature's face was a misshapen horror of pincers and waving antenna, with three unblinking black eyes over its snapping pincers.

All three of the black eyes were fixed on a girl of about fifteen.

She was pretty with soft brown eyes, albeit with the lankiness of a girl who hadn't quite finished growing yet, with long black hair bound in an intricate braid. She was wearing trousers, heavy boots, a thick jacket, and a heavy cloak. In her left hand, she held a torch, and her right hand held a lump of white crystal that gave off a sputtering yellow light.

Raw terror filled the girl's expression, the dread of someone just inches from breaking down entirely.

And she was using sorcery.

Not with any degree of skill, and not powerfully. But to the vision of the valikarion, it was as plain as a flame in the darkness. The sorcerous aura looked like a far weaker version of Kylon's, and Caina realized the girl was trying to use the sorcery of water to keep the robed thing at bay. There was also a weak sorcerous aura coming from the rough crystal in her right hand.

Nevertheless, the sputtering yellow light was holding the undead warriors at bay. Every time they tried to reach for her, the crystal flared, and they reeled black. The robed creature did not seem to like the light as well, and its gray, glistening right hand came up to shield its black eyes. All the while, the creature kept speaking in that harsh language, and the girl screamed back at him in the same tongue. Caina did not recognize the language, but some words sounded Szaldic, and others Kagari. A language of the eastern Empire, perhaps?

The crystal flared and went dark, and the undead rushed at the girl. She waved her torch, but they knocked it aside and seized her arms, forcing the girl to her knees. Her courage at last broke, and she started screaming the lost, desperate scream of a frightened child. The robed creature loomed over her, a gloating note entering its rasping voice, and it reached down and caressed the side of the girl's head with a tentacle. That drove the girl into a horrified frenzy, and she tried to break free, but the undead held her fast.

Then she fell silent, staring at Caina in sudden incomprehension.

While the undead had overpowered the girl, Caina had glided up behind the robed creature in silence. The undead holding the girl were looking right at Caina, but they could not perceive a valikarion, and the robed thing's attention was on the kneeling girl. The robed creature stiffened, realized that something was wrong, and started to turn.

Before it did, Caina drove the valikon into its back. The robed creature loosed a hideous scream, black slime spraying from its mouth. She wrenched the valikon free and stepped back, the white fire on the blade burning away the creature's blood. It staggered to face her, starting a spell, and Caina ripped the valikon across its throat.

That proved fatal, and the creature collapsed, black slime pooling around it. The undead released the girl, and Caina went on the attack, cutting down the undead warriors. Since they couldn't see her, it was easy, and a few seconds later the last of the bones and ancient armor clattered away.

The girl got to her feet, staring at Caina with enormous eyes.

"Arvaltyr," she said, her voice awed.

"Hello," said Caina, speaking in Istarish out of habit.

The girl said another sentence in the harsh language.

"Do you speak High Nighmarian?" said Caina, switching to that tongue. The girl kept staring at her. "Or do you speak Kyracian?" She switched again. "Do you speak Anshani?" She changed languages once more. "Or maybe do you speak Caerish?"

The girl stirred with recognition at the final sentence and spoke in a halting voice.

"The...language of the traders, yes?" said the girl in Caerish. "The traders from the Empire speak that language when they come to Kostiv. Uncle Ivan said I had to learn it so I could be married someday."

"I see," said Caina. "Is that where we are? Kostiv?"

The girl let out a wild, terrified laugh. "What? No. You cannot be real. You must be a phantasm sent to torment me."

"Why is that?" said Caina.

"An Arvaltyr who speaks the traders' language and not the mother tongue of Ulkaar?" said the girl. "No. You must not be real. You must be a phantasm."

Ulkaar? Caina knew that name. Ulkaar was in the hinterlands of the northeastern Empire, nearly twelve hundred miles from Iramis. Her lost love Corvalis Aberon, slain defending her life and saving the world, had carried tattoos given to him by an Ulkaari witchfinder, tattoos that gave a measure of resistance to sorcery. Caina had never been to Ulkaar, and save for Corvalis, she had only spoken to a few men from Ulkaar. From what she had heard, either the Ulkaari provinces had remained neutral between the Emperor and the Umbarian Order, or they were contested in the war. Had the strange black vortex brought Caina to Ulkaar? If the girl was a native of Ulkaar, she might prove a valuable guide.

Caina considered the girl, her eyes noting details – the mud-splattered boots, the way her clothes were too large for her, the heavy pack over her shoulders, the marks of sweat around her collar, the dark circles under her eyes. The girl looked as if she had fled for her life in haste. And the flicker of water sorcery kept appearing around her...

Ah. That was it. She was trying to sense Caina's presence, and she could not. No doubt that was why she thought Caina was a phantasm. Likely the girl had been born with the ability to use water sorcery and had employed it on an intuitive level to sense the emotions of those around her without understanding what she was doing.

"I can prove to you that I'm not a phantasm," said Caina.

The girl frowned. "How?"

"Well, if I was a phantasm, I would be created from your own thoughts," said Caina. "Why I am speaking to you in the traders' language instead of Ulkaari?"

The girl opened her mouth, closed it again. "Because you are trying to deceive me with cunning stratagems?"

"If I was going to do that," said Caina, "would not it be easier to deceive you in your native tongue?"

"That...is a good argument," said the girl.

"But I know the real reason you think I'm a phantasm," said Caina. "You can't sense my emotions, can you?"

The girl's eyes went wide again.

"Almost all your life, I would wager," said Caina, "you've been able to sense the emotions of those around you. You can always sense the feelings of those around you. You could even sense that robed creature…"

"It was horrible," said the girl, her eyes darting to the misshapen corpse.

"But you can't sense me," said Caina.

"It is said," whispered the girl, "that no man can deceive an Arvaltyr."

"What is an Arvaltyr?" said Caina. "I do not know the word." Was that the Ulkaari word for valikarion? It seemed unlikely. The valikarion had been gone from the world for a century and a half until Caina had brought Iramis back to the waking world.

"The Arvaltyri are the great heroes of old," said the girl. "It is said they carried silver swords that burned with white fire, and they marched to war alongside the Warmaiden when she returned to fight the Iron King and his demons." She frowned. "But you might be lying to me. None of the Arvaltyri of old were women, and you have taken the form of a woman."

Caina pointed the burning valikon towards the floor and held out her left hand. "Take my hand."

The suspicion returned to the girl's face. "Why?"

"Because when you touch my skin, you will be able to sense that I am human," said Caina. "Then we can focus on finding a way to escape."

The girl hesitated.

"I won't hurt you," said Caina. "If I had wished you harm, I could have let the robed thing take you."

"The Temnoti?" The girl looked at the robed corpse and shuddered.

Caina waited, her left hand held out.

The girl looked at her, took a deep breath, and gave Caina's left hand a quick, hesitant touch. Caina saw the brief flare of water sorcery, and the girl's eyes went enormous. She took a hasty step back, gazing at Caina with a mixture of fear and confusion.

"You're real," said the girl. "You're human."

"All my life," said Caina.

"But I don't understand," said the girl. "Your sense is like...like...ice over fire." Kylon had said something similar once. "I...don't..."

"Have you ever sensed an Arvaltyr before?" said Caina.

The girl gave a quick shake of her head.

"Then maybe that is what the sense of Arvaltyr should be like," said Caina. "But you know I'm human. I'm not a phantasm or a trick of sorcery."

"Yes," said the girl.

"Listen to me," said Caina. "We need to escape from this place. I think we can escape if we work together. Can you tell me your name? I'll tell you my name if you tell me yours."

The girl hesitated, and then gathered her courage. "Sophia."

"My name is Caina, Sophia." Actually, her full name was Caina Amalas Tarshahzon Kardamnos, amirja of Istarinmul and Liberator of Iramis, but that was a mouthful. "Will you help me escape?"

Sophia nodded, something like relief coming over her face. Perhaps she had wanted an adult to take charge.

"Thank you," said Caina. "First, can you tell me where we are?"

Sophia blinked. "You...don't know?"

"No," said Caina. "I don't know how I came here. I was in my room, and a vortex of black shadow appeared. It pulled me here a few hours ago, and I've been avoiding those undead and robed things ever since."

"The Temnoti," said Sophia with a shudder, looking at the robed corpse once again. "The priests of the Great Master Temnuzash."

Caina hadn't heard the name before. "Where are we?"

"Oh, right," said Sophia. "We are in Sigilsoara, the castle of the Iron King."

"Castle?" said Caina, frowning at the strange word. Likely it came from the High Nighmarian word "castra," the fort an Imperial Legion constructed when it occupied a territory for any length of time. "Then we are in Ulkaar?"

"Yes," said Sophia. "Northern Ulkaar, near the town of Kostiv."

"How did you come to the castle, Sophia?" said Caina. Perhaps the black vortex had brought her here.

"I was in the woods, walking," said Sophia.

That was a lie.

Whatever else Sophia might have been, she was a terrible liar. The tells were almost painfully obvious. Her face flushed, and she looked down, unable to meet Caina's gaze.

When Sophia looked up, fear came over her face. "Then some wolves found me. I ran and ran until it became dark, and still the wolves followed me. I couldn't see, but then I came to the gate and ran inside. I didn't realize where I was at first, and then I saw the Temnoti and the skeletons. I ran some more, and they cornered me." She let out a shuddering breath. "Then you came."

Caina nodded. "Didn't you recognize where you were? If this Sigilsoara is so close to Kostiv..."

Sophia blinked. "Do you not know about Sigilsoara?"

"I do not," said Caina. "Before a few hours ago I have never been this far north. I've heard the title of the Iron King before, somewhere. Some king from the past of Ulkaar, yes?"

Sophia looked incredulous. "No, no, that's not it at all."

"Then what is Sigilsoara?" said Caina. "Please, tell me."

Sophia took no prompting to tell the story. Caina gathered that when Sophia was calmer, she liked to talk.

"It was in ancient days," said Sophia. "Long ago the Kagari horsemen ruled Ulkaar, and kept us as slaves. But the Iron King rose against them, and in twenty battles he smashed them utterly. All Ulkaar rejoiced, but the Iron King turned to evil and worshiped the Great Master Temnuzash. For a century, he kept the Ulkaari as his slaves, and then the Warmaiden and the Arvaltyri defeated him, though the Warmaiden was slain in the battle. To this day, the Ulkaari have no king, lest he turn to evil and madness as did the Iron King." She considered that. "Though we are loyal to the Emperor, of course, because the Emperor is above any king. But the Iron King's evil sorcery twisted his castle and pulled it into the shadow world. Sometimes it comes back to the world of the living, and foolish people blunder inside before Sigilsoara returns to the shadow world. I fear I am one of those foolish people."

"I see," said Caina. Perhaps the castle itself, this Sigilsoara, was some ancient relic of sorcery from Ulkaar's past. Caina wished she knew more about Ulkaar, but the province was in the hinterlands and she had never visited it. "One more question. Do you know about the Umbarian Order?"

Sophia flinched. "The sorcerers? You...you are not their friend, are you?"

"I am most certainly not their friend," said Caina. "I am their mortal enemy, I am afraid. There are people the Umbarians hate more than me, but there cannot be that many."

"Oh," said Sophia. "Uncle Ivan says they are bad men, that they have rebelled against the Emperor and brought war to the Empire. There are many of them in Ulkaar, and I heard a rumor that some of them had passed near Kostiv before I had to...before I went to walking in the woods."

Caina nodded. It seemed likely that the Umbarians had somehow summoned Sigilsoara and entered the castle in search of the iron ring Caina now carried. Likely it was a powerful relic of this Iron King, who must have been a mighty and terrible sorcerer-king of old. Caina thought about showing the ring to Sophia but decided against it. The girl was still on the edge of self-control, and seeing a relic of the dreaded Iron King might push her over the edge.

At least the path forward was now clear. Caina needed to escape from Sigilsoara, and once she did, she would find herself in Ulkaar, far from her friends. She would need to make her way across the Empire back to Iramis, and Sophia would make a useful local guide. At the very least, she could make sure that Sophia returned home safely.

"I have three more questions," said Caina. Sophia nodded. "Have you seen any Umbarians inside Sigilsoara?"

"No," said Sophia. "Just the undead and the Temnoti. And then you."

"Good," said Caina. "My next question. What is that glowing crystal in your hand?"

"This?" said Sophia, lifting the crystal. "Oh, it is a sunstar. The Warmaiden taught us how to make them long ago. The Temple grows the crystals, and they soak up sunlight like a sponge. Then if we go outside at night, we can release the light and keep the undead at bay." Sophia grimaced. "Unfortunately, I drained this one and need to recharge it."

"Interesting," said Caina. She had never heard of sunstars. "A final question." She took a deep breath. "Have you see a man wielding a valikon within Sigilsoara?"

"A valikon?" said Sophia. "I do not know the word."

"The sword of an Arvaltyr, you would call it," said Caina. She lifted her own valikon. "A sword like this. The man with the sword would have been Kyracian, over six feet tall, with brown hair and eyes."

"I have not," said Sophia. "Was he with you when the vortex took you here?"

Ah, she was clever.

"Yes," said Caina.

"Oh!" said Sophia. "He is...dear to you?" Caina nodded. "Then you will find him! The Divine must will it." The Divine? Caina had only heard the Iramisians use that phrase. Did that mean the Ulkaari followed the Iramisian religion?

"I hope so," said Caina. "Do you remember the path you took to come here? The way to the gate?"

"Yes."

"Good," said Caina. "Then tell me where to go, and follow me."

"I will do as you say, honored Arvaltyr," said Sophia.

"Just call me Caina."

"As you wish. We must go that way," said Sophia, pointing at an archway on the other side of the ballroom.

Caina led the way, valikon in hand, Sophia following close behind.

CHAPTER FIVE

SIGILSOARA

"Hold a moment," said Seb, raising an armored hand. "I believe there is fighting ahead."

"You're right," said Kylon, rolling his shoulders, the cloth of his tunic shifting. The tunic and jacket he had found in the barracks had been made for a man with smaller arms and a narrower chest, but the trousers and boots fit, and so did the heavy cloak. Given how cold it was inside the strange fortress, he was glad of any clothing.

"Of course," said Seb. "The senses of a stormdancer. I must say, Lord Kylon, that your abilities are of invaluable tactical utility."

"That's very kind," said Kylon.

"What do you sense?" said Seb.

Kylon concentrated, focusing his arcane senses.

He and Sebastian Scorneus stood in yet another long corridor of stone. To judge from the faint light coming from the end of the corridor, it opened into another courtyard. Kylon heard fighting coming from the courtyard ahead, steel clanging against steel. Through the sorcery of water, he sensed the presence of Adamant Guards, along with the cold, corrupt aura of necromancy.

"I'm not sure," said Kylon, "but I think there are some Adamant Guards fighting undead creatures."

"What manner of undead creatures?" said Seb.

"I'm not sure," said Kylon. "Not powerful ones, though. And I don't think they're Umbarian." He gestured at the black veins on the walls. "Likely they were raised by whoever controls this fortress. The spells on them feel ancient." He wondered if this place was a ruin of ancient Maat, like the Inferno and Pyramid Isle, but he doubted it. The architecture didn't look Maatish, and the spells he sensed on the undead did not feel Maatish.

"That is interesting," said Seb. "It suggests that the Umbarians are fighting the master of this citadel, whoever he is. Perhaps this master would make an ally against the Umbarians."

"Probably not," said Kylon. "The sorcerous aura around this place is malevolent. Whoever rules this citadel would probably exterminate us alongside the Umbarians."

"Most likely," said Seb. "Since your valikon is a potent weapon against the Adamant Guards, I suggest the following strategy. You will enter the courtyard first, and I shall follow. Wound the Guards with your blade. While their spells are disrupted, I will cut them down before they can recover."

"What about the undead?" said Kylon.

"If they are like the skeletal undead I fought earlier," said Seb, "I doubt they will prove a serious threat to either of us. Best to deal with the Adamant Guards first."

"Agreed," said Kylon. The plan would mean turning his back on Seb, but Kylon thought the battle magus would keep faith with him. Seb's story about how he had been brought here was implausible, but then so was Kylon's, and Seb had not yet given Kylon any reason to distrust him.

Kylon moved forward in silence, his valikon dismissed, lest the sword's glow give away his position. Seb, alas, did not move with nearly as much quiet, his armor rasping and creaking with every step. Whatever powers the battle magi of the Magisterium possessed, stealth was not one of them.

But the noise of battle drowned out any sound they made. Kylon heard the harsh breathing and grunts of the Adamant Guards. Unless he missed his guess, the courtyard held two or three times as many undead as Adamant Guards. Fortunately, the valikon could destroy most undead creatures with a single touch, the ghostsilver blade unraveling the necromantic spells upon the ancient bones.

Ahead Kylon saw another courtyard surrounded by pillared arcades, towers rising against the twisted sky. He caught a flash of the armored carapace of an Adamant Guard as the soldier struggled against an undead warrior in ancient armor.

Neither the Adamant Guards nor the undead warriors had noticed Kylon and Seb.

"Ready?" murmured Seb.

Kylon drew on the sorcery of water and air, filling himself with power. "Yes."

Seb inclined his head, his blue eyes glinting in the light from the courtyard. "After you, sir." Power crackled around him as he drew upon his own sorcery.

Kylon took a deep breath, called his valikon to his hand, and sprinted forward. The sorcery of water surged through him, augmenting his strength, and he leaped. The power of his jump carried him into the courtyard. His head came within a few inches of hitting the top of the archway, but Kylon had done this hundreds of times before, and he landed exactly where he wished to land.

Directly behind two Adamant Guards.

The valikon was a blur of silvery metal and white fire as Kylon lashed the blade across their legs. The sword opened shallow cuts on the back of their legs, not enough to cripple them and not even enough to hurt them much, but the ghostsilver blade disrupted their spells of strength. The Guards stumbled under the weight of their grafted armor for an instant, and in that instant, Seb attacked. The battle magus followed Kylon's leap with one of his own, landing behind the Guards, and his black sword stabbed out with the speed of a serpent's tongue, killing both Guards.

Kylon whirled, seeking more Guards to fight. He caught a brief glimpse of the courtyard, saw the Guards fighting the undead, saw a large bronze statue upon a pedestal, and then the Guards rushed at him. He fell back on the defensive, fighting alongside Seb. The courtyard turned into a three-way battle, with Kylon and Seb defending themselves from the Adamant Guards, the Guards trying to defend themselves from the undead, and the undead attacking anyone who drew too close.

An Adamant Guard came at Kylon, shield raised, broadsword drawn back to stab. Kylon beat aside the thrust with a sweep of his valikon, recovered his balance, and struck back, opening a shallow cut on the Guard's upper arm. The ghostsilver disrupted the Guard's spells, and Seb's black sword dealt a fatal wound before the Guard recovered his balance.

One by one Kylon and Seb cut down the remaining Guards, and they turned their attention to the undead. The undead looked ancient, clad in armor and carrying corroded swords. They were stronger than living men, but that made no difference. A single touch from the valikon broke the spells binding them, and with Seb covering him, Kylon cut his way through the undead with ease.

The final undead collapsed to the floor, bones and armor bouncing away, and Kylon sought more foes.

There were none.

Kylon turned to see Seb staring in fascination at the bronze statue.

"What is it?" said Kylon. The statue resembled the one he had seen earlier of the cruel-faced king with the sword and dagger and ring. Likely it was a statue of the same man.

"I think," said Seb, "that I know where we are."

"Then where are we?" said Kylon, looking at the bronze statue.

"Ulkaar."

Kylon blinked. "Ulkaar?"

It took him a moment to recall the name. Ulkaar was a province on the far northeastern edge of the Empire, beyond the Narrow Sea, the Disali Highlands, the city of Artifel, and then the Inner Sea. The southern portions of Ulkaar were accessible from the sea, but Kyracian traders rarely bothered to make the journey. Any ships had to pass the Imperial cities of Artifel and Arzaxia and their tolls, which rarely allowed traders to turn a profit on the cargoes of furs and timber and whiskey available in Ulkaar. For that matter, Ulkaar had a dark reputation as a haunt of demons and spirits and mad cultists.

Ulkaar was a long, long way from the bedchamber he had been sharing with Caina in Iramis when the vortex had taken them. Unless he missed his guess, the nearest part of Ulkaar was at least twelve hundred miles from Iramis. How the devil had the vortex taken them that far?

"Yes, Ulkaar," said Seb, his eyes distant as he gazed at the statue.

"How do you know?" said Kylon.

Seb looked at him. "Do you recognize this man?"

Kylon shrugged. "No. Should I?"

"Rasarion Yagar," said Seb.

"I don't know the name," said Kylon.

"He is simultaneously both the national hero and devil of Ulkaar," said Seb. "In the time of the Third Empire, the Kagari nomads came over Broken Shield Pass and conquered Ulkaar, reducing its people to slavery. Yagar was a nobleman who fought back, and he crushed the Kagari horde and killed their Great Khan with his own hands. He then declared himself the King of Ulkaar, and the people hailed him as their liberator."

"Then he went bad, I assume," said Kylon.

"Remarkably," said Seb. "He fell in with the cult of a god that called itself either the Great Master or Temnuzash, depending on the source, and the priests of Temnuzash were necromancers and conjurers. Yagar wound up living for a century and a half as some manner of undead creature, and he terrorized Ulkaar's neighbors. The Ulkaari called him the Iron King, for he ruled them with a rod of iron more terrible than that of the Great Khan."

"Then he was overthrown?" said Kylon. He had heard tales like this before. In ancient days, before the Magisterium had fully established itself, many of the nations of what became the Empire had been ruled by mad sorcerer-kings. Caina hated the Magisterium, but Kylon had to admit the Magisterium at least attempted to keep its more power-mad members in check.

At least, it had until the civil war started and its power-mad members joined the Umbarians.

"Even the Empire and the Magisterium working together could not stop him," said Seb. "Finally, an Iramisian loremaster who called herself the Warmaiden and a group of valikarion led the revolt against Yagar. The Warmaiden and the Iron King killed each other while he was casting some kind of great summoning spell. The spell failed and its power backlashed across Ulkaar, which is why the country is haunted by undead and spirits to this day. After Rasarion Yagar's death, the Ulkaari nobles petitioned to join the Empire, and they've been an Imperial province ever since."

"You look like a Nighmarian nobleman," said Kylon, "so it is surprising that you know so much about Ulkaar." What he wanted to say was that Seb looked like Caina, but he would not reveal that information yet. Not until he was more certain about Sebastian Scorneus.

Seb chuckled. "Technically, yes, but a minor one. My mother was something of a harlot, I'm afraid. And I spent a good deal of my childhood in Risiviri, the chief city of Ulkaar. House Scorneus has always had a strong presence in Ulkaar. Much to our detriment, I'm afraid." He shook his head. "But if I am correct about this citadel, then we had better hurry."

"Then what is this citadel?" said Kylon.

"Sigilsoara, the citadel of the Iron King himself," said Seb.

Kylon looked at the web of black veins on the walls. "I take it that his great summoning spell failed here."

"You see keenly," said Seb. "I don't know what happened. No one does but the Warmaiden and the Iron King, and they are both dead. Whatever happened, it caught Sigilsoara halfway between the netherworld and the material world. The citadel will sometimes appear randomly throughout Ulkaar for a few hours before it is drawn back into the netherworld." He pointed at the shifting sky. "If we are still inside the fortress when it is pulled back to the netherworld, I am afraid the experience will be quite fatal."

Based on what Caina had told Kylon about the netherworld, he feared that Seb's assessment was correct. But had Caina been summoned to Sigilsoara as well? Kylon decided he would follow Seb until they found the exit and the battle magus had gotten to safety. Then he would return to Sigilsoara and search for Caina until he found her.

Or they ran out of time.

With a flicker of dread, Kylon realized he might never know what had happened to Caina, might never know whether she was still in Iramis or if she had perished in this grim place. Gods, was the grim pattern of his life repeating once again? Kylon hadn't been able to save Andromache or Thalastre. He had gambled everything to save Caina, first at Rumarah and again in Istarinmul on the day of the mad Apotheosis. After all that, would she be killed on their wedding night?

It seemed impossibly cruel.

His fingers tightened against his valikon's hilt.

If the Umbarians had killed her, they would regret it bitterly.

"Lord Kylon?" said Seb.

Kylon realized that he had been glaring at the statue of Rasarion Yagar. "My mind wandered. We should find the exit from this place as soon as possible."

"Quite right," said Seb. "Fortunately, I have an idea." He pointed at the bronze statue of the Iron King. "The Iron King seemed the sort to appreciate his own grandeur and majesty, yes? I expect he would prefer any visitors to gaze upon his image as they entered his fortress, even after this place has been twisted by sorcery. Consequently, I expect all the statues are looking towards the exit."

Kylon shrugged. "Makes sense. Let's go."

Seb nodded, giving him one more curious look, and they left the courtyard, heading towards the archway facing the statue of the long-dead Iron King. As they walked, Kylon forced his emotions back under control. If Caina was still in Iramis, she would be safe, surrounded by the valikarion and the loremasters. If she had been brought to Sigilsoara with Kylon…well, she was still Caina. She was still the Balarigar, the woman who had slain the Moroaica, terrorized the Slavers' Brotherhood, burned the Inferno, and brought down Grand Master Callatas.

Perhaps she had already escaped and was awaiting him outside the gate of Sigilsoara.

Or so Kylon told himself as they hurried down the corridor.

"Wait a moment," murmured Caina.

Sophia nodded and came to a stop behind her.

They had entered what looked like another grand ballroom, the floor polished and gleaming, more of those dusty chandeliers hanging from the high ceiling overhead. This ballroom had another statue of the grim-faced man that Sophia had identified as the Iron King gazing towards the far doors.

Beyond the doors stretched a wide corridor, the floor a shallow staircase that descended downward at a gentle angle. Pillars and balconies lined the walls, the ornate ceiling adorned with glittering mosaic designs. Other doors opened off the central corridor, leading to gardens, courtyards, and more hallways.

Once the corridor would have been a magnificent place. Some of the various palaces and citadels Caina had visited during travels had boasted architectural features they had called Grand Corridors, and this place could have held its own with any of them.

At least, it could have. Now the black veins covering the pillars and the tumor-like growths jutting from the stone ruined the effect. Combined with the aura of necromantic sorcery that hung over the corridor, it reminded Caina of a rotting corpse clad in a beautiful dress.

But the battle held her attention.

Further down the grand corridor, perhaps thirty yards away, the vision of the valikarion saw the flash of spells and the flare of sorcerous power. She heard men shouting, the clang of steel against steel, and the harsh crackle and sizzle of unleashed sorcery. To judge from the auras, the Temnoti and their undead warriors were battling against the Adamant Guards.

"This is the way out, isn't it?" murmured Caina.

"It was the way I came in," said Sophia. "At least, it used to be. In the legends, the Iron King's castle can change itself. I came in to get away from the wolves, and then I realized where I was. Before I could leave, the undead started chasing me."

Caina nodded, watching the flickering auras of the battle. She glimpsed Adamant Guards struggling against undead, and in a flare of harsh green light, she saw a half-dozen robed Temnoti, the misshapen creatures leading their undead fighters against the Guards.

Could Caina and Sophia slip past the battle and escape? Caina didn't know, but they had no choice but to try. The aura of necromantic force surging through the black veins had begun to flicker, and she suspected that Sigilsoara was about to be pulled back into the netherworld.

If she and Sophia were still inside the castle when that happened, they were going to die.

If Kylon was inside the castle when that happened, he was going to die.

Caina gritted her teeth, forcing herself to calm. Kylon could defend himself. Certainly, any Adamant Guards or Temnoti who came for him would regret it. Likely Kylon could have carved a way through the battle raging further down the broad stairs.

Caina's skill lay in a different direction.

"We'll have to sneak our way past," said Caina. She spotted a narrow set of stairs that climbed their way up to the balcony running alongside the grand corridor. "No one ever looks up, and I think all the fighting is taking place on the stairs. We'll take the balcony and hope the Temnoti or the Guards don't notice us."

"But what if they do notice us?" said Sophia, the terror threatening to drown her expression once more.

Caina looked at the girl. "They might. But the only other option is to stay here." She decided to take a gamble. "You were brave enough to go into the forests, weren't you?"

"I'm not brave," said Sophia. "That's why I went into the forests. Because I'm not brave…"

"You were brave enough to talk to me when you thought I was a phantasm," said Caina. "I'd wager you're brave enough to follow me up some stairs. That's all. We're just going up some stairs."

Sophia took a few deep breaths and then nodded. "I…I can do that. Lead on, Arvaltyr."

Caina almost said she wasn't an Arvaltyr, but she stopped herself. She was a valikarion, and if that was the Ulkaari word for a valikarion, then she was an Arvaltyr. Besides, she had exploited the legend of the Balarigar again and again in Istarinmul. She could hardly quail from doing the same thing with the legend of the Arvaltyri to help a frightened girl escape from death.

Caina moved forward in silence. Sophia wasn't nearly as quiet, but that was all right, since the noise from the fighting below drowned out her footfalls. Caina took the stairwell on the right and climbed to the balcony, ready to call her valikon to her hand.

The long balcony was deserted. Once frescoes of forests and hunting scenes had covered the walls, but now the images were marred by the black veins. Every few yards a doorway opened into a narrow corridor. Caina wondered just how large Sigilsoara was. From what she had seen, it was larger than both the Imperial Citadel in Malarae and the Padishah's Golden Palace in Istarinmul, and it seemed unlikely that this Iron King had commanded engineers and builders equal to those found in the capitals of two of the world's most powerful nations. Perhaps Sigilsoara had...grown, somehow, expanded while in the netherworld.

She dismissed the thought. If they lingered too long here, Caina would have all the time she needed to explore Sigilsoara when the castle was pulled back into the netherworld.

At least until the Temnoti finally killed her.

"Come on," murmured Caina. "As quietly as you can. And when I tell you to run, run."

Sophia nodded, and they started down the balcony.

The corridor was deserted, but the sounds of fighting rang from the archway ahead. Beyond Kylon glimpsed something that looked like a promenade or perhaps a ceremonial grand corridor of some kind. Seb walked at his side, his sword and his sorcery held ready.

"Fighting?" said Seb.

"Yes," said Kylon. "I think…Adamant Guards and some undead. They're fighting…gods of storm and brine. I've never sensed an aura like that before." It reminded him a little of the malevolent aura of the nagataaru, but he could not sense any spirits nearby. The foes of the Adamant Guards were humans.

Or, at least, they had once been human. Now, he wasn't sure what they were. It felt as if their auras had been altered drastically, corrupted by a malefic sorcery he had never encountered before.

"It is possible you are sensing the Temnoti," said Seb.

"What the hell are the Temnoti?" said Kylon.

"Priests of the Iron King," said Seb. "Worshippers of Temnuzash. When the Warmaiden defeated the Iron King, and both were slain, Rasarion Yagar's sorcerous power collapsed rather dramatically. It mutated his priests, granting them immortality at the cost of their sanity and…well, most of their humanity."

"Then the Umbarians and the Temnoti deserve each other," said Kylon. "Let's try to slip past while they fight each other."

"An excellent plan," said Seb.

Kylon took a step forward and frowned. "Someone else is coming."

"Whom?" said Seb.

"I'm not sure." Kylon tried to focus the presence he felt through his water sorcery. "A woman? No, a girl. She's terrified. And…I think she has some sorcery of her own. Water sorcery, I think."

"Water?" said Seb. "Another Kyracian?"

"I don't know," said Kylon. "Perhaps the same vortex that brought us here also summoned her."

"Or her presence is a very clever trap," said Seb.

"Possibly," said Kylon. He took a deep breath. "Let's find out. I'll go first."

Seb nodded and lifted his black sword. Kylon strode forward and went around the corner, valikon raised and ready.

The first thing he saw was the girl.

She was about fourteen or fifteen and looked like she would become a woman of remarkable beauty in a few years. Her black hair had been pulled back in a thick braid, and her brown eyes widened in a mixture of surprise and fear as she saw Kylon. The girl wore heavy clothes suitable for winter, a jacket and trousers and boots and a thick cloak that were too large for her.

Next to her stood a woman Kylon had not sensed at all.

She was about five and a half feet tall, with sharp features, thick black hair that hung to her shoulders, and eyes like blue ice. She wore a strange costume, heavy boots and black trousers and an archaic-looking long red coat over a white shirt.

And Kylon could not sense her presence.

"Caina?" he said.

Caina looked at Kylon.

He was wearing peculiar clothes, a heavy tunic and trousers and boots beneath a jacket, and his valikon, longer than hers, burned with white fire in his right hand. Of course – he would have been naked when he had been drawn here, so like Caina, he must have scavenged clothing from somewhere in the castle. The vision of the valikarion saw the power in the ghostsilver blade, the aura of the water and air sorcery he held ready around him.

For a moment, she stared at him in surprise, and then relief, overwhelming relief, crashed through her.

It was really him. No illusion could deceive the vision of the valikarion. The strange vortex of shadows had pulled him here with her. They might have been yanked to a strange land, but they were still together.

"Kylon," said Caina.

Kylon hesitated, looking from her to Sophia.

"It's really me," said Caina. She dismissed her valikon and held out her hand. "I know you can't sense me."

He nodded and touched her hand, and Caina felt the presence of his water sorcery, a faint tingling sensation going over her skin.

Then his brown eyes widened, and he pulled her close and kissed her long and hard. Caina heard Sophia make a startled noise, but right now she did not care. Caina only felt relief that Kylon was with her, that he was safe. She offered up a silent prayer of thanks to the Divine that he was unharmed, that she would not be alone in a foreign land as she had been in Istarinmul two and a half years ago.

A dark thought crept into her joy.

They were as safe as he could be…given they were still in Sigilsoara.

Someone coughed behind Kylon.

"While this is indeed a touching reunion," said a man's voice in High Nighmarian, deep and a little dry, "perhaps such things ought to wait until we escape from the Iron King's fortress?"

Kylon broke away from her, and Caina nodded, collecting herself. She glanced back at Sophia and saw the girl grinning in surprise.

"Yes, you're right," said Kylon in High Nighmarian.

A black-armored man stepped from the corridor after Kylon, and Caina tensed. He wore the black armor of a battle magus of the Imperial Magisterium, and some of the Umbarian battle magi used the same armor. Yet if the man had been an Umbarian, Kylon would have killed him by now, and…

Then she saw the man's face, and a strange, strange sensation went through Caina.

She had never seen this man before, yet his face looked familiar.

He had blue eyes and thick black hair, black stubble shading his jaw. His features were sharp, his mouth hard and thin, and he looked a few years older than Caina, perhaps Kylon's age or so.

She saw her own confusion and recognition mirrored on the man's face.

"I thought," said the man, "that I knew everyone in the family."

"Oh, I see," said Sophia in Caerish, looking at Kylon and the battle magus. "This is your...husband and brother then, yes?"

Both Kylon and the battle magus gave Sophia a sharp look.

"He is my husband," said Caina in Caerish, "but I don't have any family."

The battle magus blinked several times. By the Divine, his eyes looked just like Caina's own.

Just like her mother's, now that she thought about it.

"It is possible, my lady," said the battle magus, taking a deep breath, "that you may have been misinformed."

Caina looked at Kylon. "Who is this? We should speak Caerish. I think it is the only language that the four of us have in common."

Kylon opened his mouth to speak, and then a furious shout from the stairs below caught Caina's attention.

One of the Temnoti looked up at them, its greasy brown robe rippling around its misshapen frame as the creature cast a spell. Its left hand had claws, and its right hand was only a barbed tentacle, but purple light blazed around both its tentacle and its hand as it gathered arcane force. To the vision of the valikarion, the creature shone with sorcerous power, and there was nothing Caina could do to stop it before it struck.

Kylon moved, drawing on the sorcery of air for speed.

The twisted robed creature, the creature that Seb had called a Temnoti, was casting a spell, gathering sorcery to unleash a necromantic strike. The Temnoti was taking its time, confident that it could kill them all before they could respond.

Evidently, the creature had never dealt with a Kyracian stormdancer before.

Kylon seized the stone railing and vaulted, the sorcery of water surging through him to strengthen his legs. The Temnoti gaped at him in sudden surprise, and before the creature could react, Kylon brought the valikon down.

His sword ripped from the creature's misshapen head to its belly, slicing open its innards, black slime spurting across the ragged brown robe. The Temnoti let out a screeching, rasping cry and collapsed to the floor, the black slime that served as its blood leaking over the broad stairs.

Kylon stepped back, looking down the stairs, and saw that the Temnoti and their undead guardians had prevailed against the Adamant Guards. A mob of undead rushed towards him, and behind them waited five of the Temnoti. He sensed the presence of their powerful spells, and while he could deal with any number of the undead, he could not fight that many sorcerers at once.

"Run!" he shouted to the others, looking at the balcony. He caught Caina's quick nod, and she, Seb, and the girl started running. Kylon sprinted towards the undead, valikon raised, and the Temnoti focused their powers towards him.

At the last minute, he changed direction and leaped, soaring back towards the balcony. The power of his jump carried him about two-thirds of the way up, but Kylon drew on the sorcery of water, sheathing his left hand in frost. He slapped it against one of the marble pillars, and the frost held him fast, almost as if he had dipped his hand in powerful glue. Kylon heaved himself up, vaulted back over the railing, and landed on the balcony.

Caina and Seb had slowed to watch him. The girl stared at him in astonishment, mouth hanging open. Evidently, like the Temnoti, she had never seen a Kyracian stormdancer before.

"Go!" said Kylon in Caerish.

Caina nodded, grabbed the girl's shoulder, and urged her forward. The girl spun and ran after Caina, and Kylon hastened after them. With the sorcery of air, he could have outdistanced them, but he stayed close to his wife, watching for any sign of attack from the Temnoti below.

The undead raced after them on the stairs, the robed Temnoti gliding after their undead servants.

The air grew colder against Caina's face. Ever since arriving in Sigilsoara, she had been breathing the stale, moldering air that filled the castle, but now the air smelled sharp and clear, like the wind on a cold winter's night.

Did that mean they were nearing the exit?

Caina hoped so, because the aura of the castle was pulsing around them. The black veins were throbbing as if the heartbeat within them had quickened. If Caina, Kylon, Sophia, and the black-armored magus were still inside the castle when it plunged back into the netherworld, they were going to die.

Unfortunately, the undead were keeping pace below them. They had outrun the robed Temnoti, but Caina could feel the creatures in pursuit. Perhaps the Temnoti planned to have their undead slow Caina and the others long enough to bring their sorcery to bear.

"There!" shouted Sophia, pointing. "There is the way out!"

At the end of the stairs was a wide gate, and beyond it, Caina saw a snowy forest, the trees bare, the night sky filled with a billion stars and the outline of mountains in the distance. Another set of narrow spiral stairs led from the balcony to the broad steps, but the undead had already reached the gate, dozens of them.

"We'll have to fight," said Kylon. "Seb, follow me over the railing." The man who bore a disturbing resemblance to Caina's mother nodded and raised the black sword of battle magus. "Caina, go down the stairs with the girl. Then all four of us will run for the gate."

Caina nodded and lifted her right hand, calling her valikon back. Seb blinked at her in surprise and then turned his attention back to Kylon.

"Go!" said Kylon.

Her husband seized the railing and vaulted over it, his valikon trailing white fire, and landed among the undead like a thunderbolt, his sword darting back and forth and destroying a half-dozen undead warriors in the blink of an eye. Seb was slower, but Caina saw the glow of his psychokinetic sorcery, and he landed with a clatter of armor, cutting down two of the undead.

"Come on!" said Caina, and she ran down the twisting stairs, Sophia following her. By the time they reached the bottom of the stairs, Kylon and Seb had cut down a score of undead between them.

The gate was thirty yards away, the image of the icy forest starting to waver. The currents of power flowing through the castle were growing stronger, pulling Sigilsoara back to the netherworld.

"Run!" said Caina.

Kylon and Seb slashed their way free from the undead and sprinted towards the gate. Caina and Sophia followed suit, boots slapping against the broad steps of the grand corridor. The undead pursued, and the image of the forest grew brighter before Caina's eyes.

Then, all at once, she plunged through the gate, snow crunching around her feet as the others followed her.

Caina whirled, valikon in hand, and looked back at Sigilsoara.

She blinked in astonishment and revulsion at the sight.

The castle was like something out of a nightmare, a twisted mixture of reality and demented fantasy. It was huge, so vast that it seemed to rise like a mountain, a fantastical pile of towers and keeps and battlements and turrets, its sides adorned with statues of countless winged monsters. It was larger than the Imperial Citadel, larger than the Golden Palace, larger than even the city of Malarae itself, and it was impossible, utterly impossible.

It was also alive.

Black veins throbbed through the outer walls and the towers were heavy with those strange growths. Sigilsoara looked like some towering, monstrous creature, like a horror risen out of the lightless depths of the sea to devour humanity. It radiated necromantic force, and through the gates, Caina saw the undead and the Temnoti rushing in pursuit.

"Here they come!" said Seb, pointing his black sword.

The necromantic aura surrounding Sigilsoara pulsed, and the towering fortress turned transparent. Caina saw the sorcerous power as Sigilsoara faded back into the netherworld. In a few heartbeats, the castle vanished entirely, with no hint that it had ever been there in the first place.

Caina stood in a cold forest, snow on the ground around her, mountains rising in the distance. The sun was just rising over those mountains, which meant they were to the east. She looked at the others, saw Sophia wilt with relief, saw Kylon and Seb looking around the forest with watchful eyes.

For a moment, they stood in silence.

"Well," said Seb. "Now what?"

CHAPTER SIX

MOTHER'S INDISRECTIONS

"I think," said Caina, "that some introductions are in order."

Seb returned his black sword to its scabbard, which eased Caina's tension somewhat. Against the horrors of Sigilsoara, they had all been allies, but now that they had escaped, she feared that Seb might prove hostile.

"I quite agree, madam," said Seb. His voice was deep and soft and a little hoarse. "Though I have a suspicion as to who you are."

"Oh?" said Caina, glancing at Kylon. "And who I am?"

Seb gestured to Kylon. "Lord Kylon saved my life when the Adamant Guards cornered me. Quite recently, rumors had come out of Istarinmul about the downfall of the Grand Wazir and the rise of a new Padishah. One of those rumors said that Lord Kylon, Kyracian exile, had wed the notorious Ghost spy Caina Amalas after the ascension of the new Padishah. Of course, all sorts of strange rumors have come out of Istarinmul in the last three months. But given your…enthusiastic greeting of Lord Kylon in the grand corridor, the logical deduction is that you are in fact the Ghost agent known variously as Caina Amalas or the Balarigar."

Caina sighed. So much for concealing her identity.

"My full name," she said, "would be Caina Amalas Tarshahzon Kardamnos. The new Padishah adopted me as his sister."

Seb raised his eyebrows. Sophia's eyes went wider.

"He did," said Kylon. "I was there."

"I see," said Seb. He offered a bow. "Then permit me to introduce myself, my lady. I am Sebastian Scorneus, a battle magus of the Imperial Magisterium. Until quite recently I was attached to the Legions fighting the Umbarians near Artifel…and then I happened to find myself here."

Scorneus? Caina knew that name. It was a noble family prominent in the eastern Empire, though she had never met any of them in person. A few years ago, before the Empire's war with New Kyre had ended, her old circlemaster Halfdan had instructed Caina to disguise herself as the magus Rania Scorneus, saying that Caina resembled the woman a great deal.

But as she looked at Sebastian, at his familiar features, Caina started to feel uneasy.

Just why had Caina resembled Rania Scorneus a great deal?

"How did you happen to find yourself in Sigilsoara, Master Sebastian?" said Caina.

Seb laughed a little. "Alas, I fear I am not a master magus, but a simple battle magus. But in answer to your question, I was returning from a raid on the Umbarian positions near Artifel. A black vortex of shadow fell over me, and when it cleared, I found myself in Sigilsoara."

"I see," said Caina.

"As I have said, I have heard of you before, I confess," said Seb.

"Nothing complimentary, I assume," said Caina.

Seb hesitated. "Not particularly, no. But I never dreamed you were part of the family."

"The family?" said Caina.

Seb gestured at his face, and then at Caina. "It is fairly obvious that we are related in some capacity."

"It could be a coincidence," said Caina.

"But a highly improbable one," said Seb. "What was your father's name, if I might inquire?"

Caina hesitated. Secrecy was an old, old habit with her. Secrets were like armor.

And yet…

"My father's name was Sebastian Amalas," said Caina. "A Nighmarian noble from the Bay of Empire."

Seb let out a quiet, tired laugh. "And I am willing to hazard a guess as to your mother's name."

"Go on," said Caina.

"Was your mother named Laeria Scorneus?"

Kylon gave her a sharp look.

Caina blinked, keeping the surprise from her face. "My mother was named Laeria, yes." She had known that her mother must have had family somewhere, but Caina had never bothered to find them. Caina had never bothered because she hated her mother as profoundly as she had ever hated anyone. Even after all the horrors and tyrants and mad sorcerers she had seen, Caina still hated her mother more than anyone else.

"Ah," said Sebastian. "Well, my mother was named Laeria Scorneus. At the age of sixteen, after she was expelled from the Imperial Magisterium for insufficient skill, she married a brother of the Magisterium. My twin sister and I were the result. However, their marriage was an unhappy one, and Laeria left him for a noble of the western Empire. Evidently, she believed that he would obtain sufficient standing to force the Magisterium to take her back. She disappeared into obscurity, and the family never found out what happened to her. My sister and I were raised by our Aunt Talmania," his mouth twisted a little at that name, "and by our Aunt Ariadne."

Caina stared at him, keeping the shock from her expression. She wanted to shout a denial at him, but the cold part of her mind, the part trained by the Ghosts and tempered by bitter experience, pointed out that his story rang true, that it matched what she knew of Laeria Amalas.

Or Laeria Scorneus Amalas, as it happened.

"Then, Lady Caina," said Sophia, looking back and forth in bewilderment, "does that mean he is your...your brother?"

"Half-brother, it would seem," said Seb. He smiled a little. "I confess you look a great deal like a Scorneus woman, my lady."

"And what are Scorneus women known for?" said Caina. Her voice sounded odd in her ears.

"Beauty," said Seb, "black hair, blue eyes, and both remarkable intellect and equally remarkable ruthlessness. My mother...our mother was the youngest of seven sisters, and she was the only one who did not become a powerful magus, whether of the Magisterium or the Umbarians."

Six sisters? Did that mean there were six more women like Laeria Amalas loose in the world?

Caina looked at Seb, and for a wild instant, she wanted to punch him.

She forced back the emotion, shocked by the intensity of her own reaction. Seb had done nothing to her, and he had helped Kylon in Sigilsoara. Yet the knowledge that her mother had a family, a large and powerful family, disturbed Caina. It was irrational, but the thought of other people with her mother's blood enraged her.

Though in hindsight, it was not at all surprising that Laeria Amalas had neglected to tell Caina's father.

Caina closed her eyes, trying to calm herself, annoyed that the news had affected her so profoundly.

She opened her eyes to see the others watching her. Kylon stepped closer and took her hand, and she squeezed his fingers.

"Is he telling the truth?" said Caina.

"Ah," said Seb. "One cannot lie to a Kyracian stormdancer."

"That's just a myth," said Kylon, "but...I think he's telling the truth, Caina. And the Umbarians were trying to kill him when I found him."

"I did not intend to upset you," said Seb. "I fear I am quite used to finding family in unexpected places. There are Scorneus cousins in half the cities of the eastern Empire." He paused. "I suspect your relationship with Laeria was not a pleasant one."

Caina laughed a little. "No. No, it wasn't."

"If it is a comfort," said Seb, "I grew up detesting the woman. She abandoned us and left us to the tender care of Talmania Scorneus, who raised us to be weapons." He hesitated. "Laeria is...not still alive, is she?"

"No," said Caina, remembering the poker from the fireplace, the sound that Laeria's head had made when it bounced off her father's desk. "She's been dead for fourteen years. Nearly fifteen, now"

"I see," said Seb. She wondered how much he had deduced about her. Like Caina herself, he seemed to have a gift for it.

"I suggest," said Kylon, "that we focus first on the matter of survival. We are alone in a strange country without supplies, and if we don't take action, we shall either starve or freeze to death."

"Yes," said Caina, grateful for the suggestion. "Yes, that is a good idea."

"Agreed, Lord Kylon," said Seb. "As to the matter of survival, I think we ought to first try to figure out how we got here and why. That black vortex brought all of us here..."

"It didn't, sir," said Sophia. "Not me. I was lost in the woods and seeking shelter," she gave the surrounding trees a wary glance, "and I ran into the gate of Sigilsoara to get away...to get away from some wolves." That was a lie. Caina was sure of it. "Once I realized where I was, I tried to flee, but it was too late. The Temnoti and their undead would have killed me if not for Lady Caina."

"Forgive me!" said Seb. He offered a polite bow to Sophia. "We have not been introduced, madam. I am Sebastian Scorneus of the Imperial Magisterium, and I am delighted and pleased to make your acquaintance."

Sophia blinked, and she smiled a little. "My name is Sophia Zomanek of Kostiv, and I am pleased to meet you, sir."

"So," said Seb, "of the four of us, three were brought to Sigilsoara by that vortex. Some sort of summoning spell, I would expect."

"Agreed," said Caina.

"But why the three of us?" said Seb. He gestured at Caina. "If you and I are indeed half-siblings, that would explain it. The common link of blood. Though why Lord Kylon might be included, I don't know."

Caina sighed. "I do. We were…close at the time."

Seb frowned. "Close?"

"It was our wedding night," said Caina.

"Ah," said Seb.

"Wedding night?" said Sophia, puzzled. "What has that got to do with…" Then her eyes went wide as she understood, and her face turned a bright shade of red.

And again, Caina saw that flicker of fear on Sophia's expression.

"I am less concerned about how we were brought here than why," said Caina.

Kylon frowned. "The sorcery of Sigilsoara? I have never seen anything like it. Or the Umbarians, maybe? I didn't see any Umbarian magi in the fortress, but with the Adamant Guards, there had to have been Umbarian magi nearby."

"I did talk to one Umbarian inside Sigilsoara," said Caina.

"Really?" said Seb, surprised. "Did you happen to catch his name?"

"Morett," said Caina.

Seb let out a long breath. "A necromancer of particular skill. And a close confidant of Aunt Talmania, I am afraid."

"Talmania is an Umbarian?" said Caina.

"Not only is she an Umbarian," said Seb, "she is one of the five Provosts who govern the Order." He hesitated. "And my oldest aunt, Rania Scorneus, is the High Provost of the Umbarians."

"Oh." That was just lovely. Not only did Caina have relatives from her mother's family, but they were also high-ranking Umbarian magi.

"Do you have any idea what Morett was doing in Sigilsoara?" said Seb.

"I think," said Caina, "he was looking for something. Some relic, some artifact of the Iron King."

Seb frowned. "I suppose he was trapped in Sigilsoara when it returned to the netherworld, the poor fool. I wonder if he found what he was looking for."

"I can say firsthand that he did not," said Caina, remembering the iron ring with the emerald seal in her pocket.

"Do you know what he wanted to find?" said Seb.

A calculation flashed through her mind. She didn't know if she could trust Seb or not, and she didn't know if she could trust Sophia. Neither one of them, she suspected, could sense the power of the ring while Caina carried it, its presence hidden by her nature as a valikarion. Seb's story made sense, but it could have been a carefully constructed lie…and even if it was true, the temptation of the ring's power might override his sense.

Caina's mother would have murdered anyone to possess a sorcerous relic of such power.

"He said he was looking for a ring," said Caina. "I know he didn't get the ring because I killed him."

Seb blinked in surprise. "Morett was a powerful magus. How did you kill him?"

"She is an Arvaltyr," said Sophia.

"Arvaltyr?" said Kylon.

"I think it is the Ulkaari word for a valikarion," said Caina.

"It is," said Seb, "but there are no valikarion. They all died out long ago. Lord Kylon might possess a valikon, but..."

"The girl is right," said Kylon. "She is a valikarion."

Seb stared at them for a long moment.

"Impossible," he said at last. "The valikarion were the knights of Iramis, and they perished with the city."

"They did," said Caina, "and you're not going to believe me, but Iramis has returned. Grand Master Callatas didn't destroy it. He banished it to the netherworld, and I brought it back. I brought the loremasters and the valikarion back to this world."

Seb laughed. "You are correct. I do not believe you."

"And I can prove that I'm a valikarion," said Caina. "You're holding your power ready, not for any specific reason, but to be ready for trouble. You have one spell on you now, one to make yourself faster, but it will likely wear off soon. You aren't carrying any enspelled objects." She smiled and held out her right hand. "Also, there's this."

Her valikon assembled itself out of shards of silver light and appeared in her hand.

Seb didn't say anything.

Caina watched him, wondering how he would react. Based on what Nasser and Annarah had told her, the magi of the Magisterium had always hated and feared the valikarion. No defensive spell could stop a valikon's blade, and no illusion spell could deceive the vision of a valikarion, and the magi had lived in fear that their misdeeds might draw the fatal attention of the valikarion.

But to her surprise, Seb smiled.

"Truly?" he said. "A living valikarion? I never thought to see one. Legends and myths walk among us."

"She is truly an Arvaltyr," said Sophia. "She called her silver sword and slew a Temnoti with it. Who else could do that but one of the Arvaltyri?"

"Gods of the Empire," said Seb, shaking his head. "I always loved the tales of the Arvaltyri when I was a child. If you ever have the misfortune to meet Aunt Talmania, you'll understand why the thought of a noble knight with a sword immune to sorcery is an appealing one." He laughed.

"What?" said Caina, baffled.

"It is a pleasing thought, madam," said Seb. "One of Laeria Scorneus's daughters became a valikarion? The thought of her displeasure is most entertaining."

Caina blinked, and then to her surprise, she burst out laughing. "She would have been furious."

"I suspect you two have a great deal to discuss," said Kylon, "but we should turn our attention back to survival."

"Yes, yes, of course," said Seb. "I suppose our first priority is to establish where we are. Northeastern Ulkaar, I think. Those are the Shield Mountains to the east, and…"

"Kostiv," said Sophia in a quiet voice, pulling her coat tighter around herself.

"Pardon?" said Seb.

"We're about a day northeast of the town of Kostiv," said Sophia.

"Where would that place us in Ulkaar?" said Caina. "I am afraid I know very little about Ulkaar." Not even the language, which could prove a problem.

"That would put us on the far northeastern edge of Ulkaar," said Seb, "and to be blunt, the somewhat less civilized region of Ulkaar."

Sophia started to bristle, and then the fear went over her face again, and she fell silent.

"Less civilized?" said Caina.

"Ulkaar is rather a harsh and dangerous land," said Seb. "The chief city of the southern half of Ulkaar is Risiviri, a port on the Inner Sea. Imperial influence is quite strong there, and the Ulkaari have cast off many of their more barbarous customs."

"What kind of customs?" said Kylon with bemusement. "The Empire of Nighmar tends to have a wide definition of barbarism."

Seb smiled. "I am afraid, my Kyracian friend, that in this our definitions of barbarism overlap." His smile faded. "In the northern hinterlands of Ulkaar, many of the old ways linger. The cult of Temnuzash," Sophia shivered at the name, "is outlawed, but it still flourishes in the shadows. And the Ulkaari themselves have a strong tradition of demon-worship, conjuration spells, and necromancy. Near Risiviri and the towns of the south, these practices have mostly been stamped out. Here in northern Ulkaar, though...the old ways are still strong, and the villagers sometimes come to shrines of Temnuzash in the dark of the night, and every village likely has a necromancer who knows how to speak to the dead, possibly two."

Caina frowned. "I'm surprised the Magisterium didn't stamp them out. If there's one thing the Magisterium was good at, it was destroying rival wielders of arcane force."

"The Magisterium was good at forcing them to go underground," said Seb. "But Ulkaar is something of a hinterland, and the Magisterium did not pay as much attention here as it should have. I also suspect the Umbarians made sure the magi looked the other way quite often. And now that the Order has declared itself openly and civil war rends the Empire...likely the Temnoti and the followers of the old ways are comfortable coming into the open."

"Yes," said Sophia in a quiet voice.

She did not elaborate further.

"I think," said Caina, looking at Kylon, "that my husband and I wish to return to Iramis. We have friends and obligations there. I suppose you will want to rejoin the Legions near Artifel?"

Seb nodded. "I have my duty." He sighed. "It is a long journey to Artifel from here, and an even longer journey to Iramis. If, as you say, Iramis has truly returned. But our first step must be to journey to Risiviri and hire a ship to take us to Artifel. I think it is about three hundred miles from Kostiv to Risiviri."

"We had best get started, then," said Caina.

"I think our best course of action is to visit the town of Kostiv first," said Seb. "We can obtain supplies there, and…"

"No!" said Sophia.

They all looked at her.

"What's wrong with Kostiv?" said Caina.

"I…I can't go back to Kostiv," said Sophia. "I just can't. Not ever."

"Why not?" said Caina.

Sophia seemed to shrink a little, and Caina wondered what had happened to her. Perhaps her sorcerous powers had manifested, and the townsmen had tried to kill her. Then again, if the Ulkaari were as familiar with necromancy as Seb claimed, it seemed unlikely the villagers would care. Or Sophia would have been recruited by the Umbarians or the Magisterium.

"The boyar will kill me if I return to Kostiv," said Sophia at last.

"Boyar?" said Caina, frowning at the strange word.

"Local nobleman," said Seb. "I believe the current boyar of Kostiv is a man named Vlad Nagrach. Thoroughly unpleasant fellow. He was brutal even by the standards of Ulkaari northerners."

"That is true," said Sophia, "but he died two years ago. His son Razdan is now the boyar of Kostiv." She shivered. "He is worse than his father ever was. Boyar Vlad was a hard man, but he only punished criminals. Boyar Razdan does what he wishes, and there is no one strong enough to stop him."

"So why does he want to kill you?" said Caina.

Sophia stared at her, stricken, and Caina could tell that the girl was at a loss for words. Then an idea seemed to come to Sophia, and she reached into her belt pouch and drew out the pale crystal of her sunstone.

"Because," she said, "I stole this from him."

"What is that?" said Kylon. "A gemstone?"

"No," said Caina. "It's her sunstone. Or the boyar's sunstone."

"What is a sunstone?" said Kylon.

"The Warmaiden taught the Ulkaari to make them in ancient days," said Seb. "A minor tool of sorcery and they are quite easy to grow. When exposed to sunlight, they soak it up like a sponge. The user then can release the sunlight at will. It is useful for keeping minor undead and some of the malevolent spirits of the forest at bay."

"Like…a waterskin for sunlight?" said Kylon.

Seb smiled. "Yes. The metaphor is precisely apt, Lord Kylon."

"So, you stole this sunstone," said Caina, "and the boyar will kill you for it?"

"Yes," said Sophia, shivering.

"That seems an overreaction," said Kylon, "if these sunstones are as common as Seb says."

"It is. If the boyar wants a new sunstone, the Temple can grow one for him in two or three weeks at minimal cost," said Seb. "But Vlad Nagrach was the kind of man to have a servant flogged to death for stealing a heel of bread. I imagine his son is no less brutal. Why on earth did you steal a sunstone, though? They are quite common, and the Temple gives them freely to anyone who asks."

Sophia blinked. "Because…because I wanted it. Because I knew I would need it when I went outside of the town's walls."

Caina shared a look with Kylon. Sophia had said she had stolen the sunstone because she knew she was leaving Kostiv. That meant that whatever had driven her from the town had happened before she had stolen the sunstone. And whatever had driven her from the town must have been dire. For the most part, pretty fifteen-year-old girls did not flee alone into the wilderness.

Not unless they had a very good reason.

"All right," said Caina. "We won't go to Kostiv." Sophia brightened. "We'll get supplies somewhere else."

"It is likely," said Seb, "that we have no choice in the matter. Kostiv is the northernmost frontier of Ulkaar. West and north are the demon-haunted forests of Iazn. East are the Shield Mountains. We must go southwest to Kostiv since there is no other place to find food. Additionally, we must also consider the weather. Blizzards are common in Ulkaar this time of year, and if we are caught in the woods by a blizzard, we will probably freeze to death or wander in circles until we starve."

"All right," said Caina, thinking it over. "We do need to go to Kostiv to get supplies, but there's no need for Sophia to return there. I'll wait outside with her. You and Kylon will go into the town and get food, and once we're ready, we'll head south."

"But I can't go anywhere near Kostiv," said Sophia.

Seb frowned. "Will the boyar be looking for you?"

Sophia hesitated. "He…might be. I don't know. He is a very vengeful man. He won't forgive that I…that I stole from him."

"Do you have any food in your pack?" said Caina.

"Just some loaves of bread and cheese," said Sophia. "Enough for three or four days. I had to flee in haste. I thought to head south to Vagraastrad, but I got lost and the…I had to take shelter. I ran towards some light, and I didn't realize where I was until it was too late."

The girl was a terrible liar.

"There is another problem," said Seb. "I suspect none of us have any money."

"No," said Kylon.

Caina shrugged. "I took some from Morett's corpse. If need be, I can steal some more from the boyar. It sounds like he's the sort of man who would deserve it."

Sophia's eyes went wide. "You wouldn't dare to steal from the boyar."

Caina smiled. She had robbed half the slave traders in Istarinmul and Grand Master Callatas himself. "I've had some experience in the matter."

Seb snorted. "No doubt, if half the stories about the Balarigar are true."

"Most of them aren't," said Caina. "Sophia, how long would it take to get to Kostiv?"

The girl hesitated. "About a day, maybe a little longer. But I can't go to Kostiv. I can't!" She looked on the verge of tears.

"I'm afraid our options are limited," said Caina. "We can stay out here and freeze or starve to death, or we can take our chances at Kostiv. If you don't want to come with us, I won't force you to do to anything...but what else will you do?"

Sophia stared at her, the fear playing over her face. "Are you...I need to ask something."

"Ask," said Caina.

Sophia took a deep breath. "Are you truly an Arvaltyr? Really and truly?"

"I am," said Caina. "I didn't want to be, but I am."

Sophia shivered. "All right. All right. I'll go with you to Kostiv. But it is a bad place. You shouldn't go there."

Caina inclined her head, wondering what had frightened Sophia Zomanek so badly.

"We ought to set off while we still have daylight," said Seb. "Which way to Kostiv?"

Sophia sighed and pointed with a finger.

"I'll take the lead," said Kylon. Seb nodded and fell in behind him, and Caina and Sophia brought up the back. She wondered at

Sophia's warning. The girl had said that Kostiv was a bad place. Was it because of the brutal Boyar Razdan Nagrach?

Or had something else driven her from the town?

Unfortunately, Caina thought she had no choice but to find out.

CHAPTER SEVEN

COLD FORESTS

The forests of Ulkaar put Kylon on edge.

The cold itself did not trouble him, though he didn't enjoy it. When he had sailed with the fleets of New Kyre, he had visited the colder northern ports, had helped clean the ice off the ship's oars and rigging. He had learned quickly that a mild effort of water sorcery could keep him warm, and he used that spell now. It was just as well that both he and Caina had found heavy clothing inside the twisted castle of Sigilsoara. Kylon's water sorcery could help keep him warm, but that would not have helped him and Caina if they had emerged naked into the forest.

The silence bothered him, but he conceded that it had its uses. Between the uneven ground of the forest and the layer of snow on the ground, it was almost impossible to move without making noise. If anyone approached, Kylon would hear them before he sensed their emotional auras.

He admitted the countryside was bleak. The combination of the looming Shield Mountains, the overcast sky, the frozen, leafless forest, and the chill created a sense of foreboding, but that was unimportant. Kylon had been in a lot of dangerous places, and the wild forest in Ulkaar was certainly better than the undead-haunted corridors of Sigilsoara. For that matter, it was better than Pyramid Isle, or the Inferno, or the ruins of Caer Magia.

Come to think of it, he and Caina had gone to a lot of dangerous places together.

No, what really bothered Kylon was the things he sensed in the forest around them.

The weaknesses he sensed.

Because the Surge had given him the ability to senses cracks in the walls between the world, ways that malevolent spirits could use to leave the netherworld and enter the material world to prey upon mortals.

"It's like," said Kylon when Caina asked what was wrong, "the forest is riddled with cracks."

Her face turned solemn.

"Cracks?" said Seb.

Sophia looked at the ground dubiously.

"No, not that kind of crack," said Kylon. "Caina, can you explain?"

They were walking along a deer trail in the forest. The barren trees rose over them, stark and bleak against the gray sky. Patches of snow lay scattered across the ground, and frozen leaves crackled beneath their boots as they walked.

"Kylon has the ability to sense weaknesses in the walls of the world," said Caina. "Places that spirits can use to enter the material world from the netherworld."

"Is that a useful ability?" said Seb.

"You might be surprised," said Caina.

Kylon shook his head. "The entire forest, as far as I can sense in all directions, is like a pane of glass with cracks in it."

"That makes a great deal of sense," said Seb.

"Does it?" said Kylon.

"I fear so," said Seb. "The properties of sorcery are altered in the boundaries of Ulkaar. Spells of necromancy and summoning are considerably more effective within this land."

"Necromancy?" said Caina. "Just as well the ancient Maatish never found out about this place."

"The Ulkaari tradition of necromancy is notably different than the Maatish one," said Seb. He kicked aside a branch, and it bounced away into the trees. "Rather cruder and less...refined, let's say. Among the magi who study such things, the necromancy of the Maatish is referred to as high necromancy, while the necromancy of the Ulkaari is called low necromancy."

Caina frowned. "You know a lot about necromancy."

Seb smiled and raised his black eyebrows, the blue eyes glinting in the gray winter light. By the Divine, he looked a lot like Caina's mother. Which, Caina supposed, meant that he looked a great deal like Caina. "Worried that I'm a necromancer, I presume? Do not fear. I chose my side, and it was not the Umbarian Order. And if you are a valikarion, you can see my sorcerous aura, which ought to be free of necromancy."

"It is," said Caina.

For a moment Caina and Seb stared each other, faces blank. Caina had a gift for keeping her emotions and thoughts off her expression, and it seemed Seb had the same ability. The battle magus's emotional sense was wary, but there was no alarm in it. Not yet.

"How did Ulkaar get this way?" said Kylon as the silence dragged on.

"It is the Iron King's curse, Lord Kylon," said Sophia. "I learned it from Brother Valexis in the Temple. The Iron King freed us from the Kagari khans, but he turned to necromancy and the worship of the Great Master Temnuzash. The Warmaiden came with the Arvaltyri to destroy him, but both the Iron King and the Warmaiden slew one another. In his dying throes, the Iron King laid his curse upon Ulkaar. Devils haunt the forest and the unsanctified dead rise to slay the living. But the Warmaiden taught us the lore of the Temple to defend ourselves, and of old the Arvaltyri hunted demons here. But then Iramis burned, and the Arvaltyri came to Ulkaar no more." Her eyes strayed to Caina. "Until today, perhaps."

"Admirably put, my dear," said Seb. "The Magisterium's histories say nearly the same thing. The Warmaiden was a loremaster of Iramis, and she led a force of valikarion against Rasarion Yagar and the priests of Temnuzash. She interrupted him in the middle of a great spell, and both were slain. The Iron King's castle of Sigilsoara was cast into the netherworld, and the Temnoti were mutated into the forms we saw in the fortress. And the backlash from the failed spell damaged the barriers between worlds in Ulkaar, which is why necromancy and summoning spells are easier here."

Caina blinked. "The Temple...they worship the Divine here? They follow Iramisian religion?"

"They do," said Seb. "If you have been to Iramis recently in truth, then no doubt you have seen a purer form of it. But the Temple keeps to Iramisian teachings and venerates the memory of the Warmaiden and the valikarion, and they even still have a vulgarized form of the Iramisian system of sorcery, the Words of...something, I forget what."

"Lore," said Caina in a quiet voice. "The Words of Lore."

Kylon watched her. Caina did not often talk about her religious leanings, but after her experiences in Istarinmul, she had grown more sympathetic to the Iramisian teachings of the Divine. Kylon supposed he was as religious as most men – best to appease the gods, lest misdeeds draw their wrath, though he hated oracles and seers and prophets. When he had been younger, he had believed that the gods punished wrongdoers, but as Kylon had grown older, he had seen enough prosperous wrongdoers to question that.

On the other hand, Caina had crossed the path of a lot of wrongdoers, and most of them were now dead. Maybe the Divine had sent her to deliver retribution to them, though she would scoff at that idea.

"Yes, that was it," said Seb. "The Words of Lore. Though I suppose if you brought Iramis back from the shadows, you're quite familiar with the Words of Lore."

Caina smiled. "You still don't believe that, do you?"

"Well, it is quite an unlikely story," said Seb. He shrugged. "Though no more unlikely that you should be transported to Sigilsoara on your wedding night, where you would meet your half-brother."

"It is unlikely," said Caina, "but it doesn't matter how unlikely it is because it happened. But I think we are wandering from the point at hand. If it is easier for spirits to enter the material world here...are the forests dangerous?"

"Yes," said Sophia in a small voice. "They are very dangerous."

"I'm afraid undead are quite common in Ulkaar," said Seb, "and corpses buried without proper rites from the Brothers and Sisters of the Temple often rise as undead. Malevolent spirits can slip into the material world and take control of animals, trees, corpses, and twist them into dangerous creatures." He shrugged. "Walking in the woods the way that we are is quite risky."

"Wolves, too," said Sophia.

A wave of dread rolled through her and pushed against Kylon's arcane senses. He looked at the girl, but she stared at the ground, her face blank. After a moment, the dread subsided.

But it did not leave her entirely.

"There are many ways to die in Ulkaar," said Seb, "but I think we should focus on a more immediate problem."

"Which one?" said Caina.

"The lack of food," said Seb.

Caina shrugged. "One way or another, we're getting food at Kostiv, even if I have to steal it. A little hunger for a day and a half won't kill us."

"Actually," said Kylon, "I might be able to help with that. Hold still for a moment."

The others went motionless. Kylon focused on the sorcery of water, extending his arcane senses. He sensed Seb's emotions, a mixture of wariness, amusement, and mild bemusement, but it was layered over a deep and abiding grief. Sophia seemed to be on the edge of terror, holding herself together only by a raw effort of will. Had their situation not been so dire, Kylon would have suggested to Caina that they bypass Kostiv entirely. Sophia dreaded the thought of returning to Kostiv, and while there was some guilt in her sense, there wasn't much of it. Kylon thought she had fled Kostiv out of sheer terror.

Perhaps Caina's plan was best. She would wait with Sophia while Kylon and Seb entered Kostiv.

From Caina, of course, Kylon sensed nothing at all.

But he did sense something else, a simple, instinctive mind, a mind concerned with food and cold and shelter and nothing else.

Kylon turned his head and saw the deer creeping through the trees. It hadn't scented them yet.

"Don't move," said Kylon.

"Is there danger?" said Seb, reaching for his sword hilt.

"No," said Kylon, drawing as much of the sorcery of water and air as he could.

The deer froze as it caught their scent.

Kylon sped forward, using the sorcery of air to lend himself speed. He hurtled towards the deer, his valikon's hilt grasped in both hands. The deer started to turn, but it was too late. Kylon brought the sword sweeping down, and he took off the animal's head in a single blow. There was no gore, since the freezing mist froze the blood, and the body collapsed to the ground while the head bounced away.

Sophia let out a shriek.

"I think," said Caina, "that will make an admirable breakfast."

Seb snorted. "Valikons are weapons of legend, but I confess I never thought to see one used to bring down a deer."

"It doesn't seem very sporting," said Sophia. "Uncle Ivan always said a proper hunter uses a bow or a boar spear."

"If your Uncle Ivan comes out here with us," said Kylon, "he's welcome to do better."

Sophia blinked, and then let out a startled laugh. "What? No. Uncle Ivan doesn't hunt any more, I'm afraid. His leg doesn't allow it."

"Well," said Caina, "if Uncle Ivan wouldn't approve, then you can watch the rest of us eat."

Sophia smiled, for the first time since Kylon had met her. "Uncle Ivan would tell me not to be stupid."

It did not take them long to skin and cook the deer. Sophia and Seb had daggers, and all four of them had experience preparing animals. Caina expected Sophia to flinch at the blood, but the girl handled the work with aplomb. If her Uncle Ivan had been a hunter in his youth, perhaps she had helped him clean his kills.

Caina tucked that observation away with the others she had noted about the girl

There was something wrong with Sophia.

Or, rather, there was something wrong in Kostiv, something frightening enough to drive Sophia into the dangers of Ulkaar's forests. Caina could think of a thousand things that might frighten a girl into fleeing into the wilderness, and most of them were not even unique to Ulkaar. And to be blunt, none of it was Caina's business. She wanted to return to Iramis.

And yet…

Perhaps she could find a way to help Sophia Zomanek. Certainly, the girl had been brave, and with her latent arcane talent, she would not stay in an isolated town like Kostiv forever. Either the Magisterium would find her and recruit her…or the Umbarians would.

Or some cult like the Temnoti or the various petty necromancers and conjurers that Seb had mentioned would corrupt her.

Thinking of Seb sent Caina's thoughts down a dark path.

It surprised her not at all that Laeria Amalas – in truth, Laeria Scorneus Amalas – had been willing to abandon her twin children to marry a young Count of the Empire. After all, Laeria had been willing to sell Caina to Maglarion in exchange for necromantic lore. Abandoning her children was easy by comparison.

It was all the more reason Caina wanted to return to Iramis. She wanted nothing to do with House Scorneus and her mother's family. She knew that not all the sons and daughters of House Scorneus would be like Laeria, that like any family, there would be good and bad men and women among them.

Caina still didn't want anything to do with them.

But to her surprise, she found that she liked her half-brother. Seb was a charming speaker, and like Caina, he had an eye for detail and a knack for making deductions from those details. Often, Caina found that she could guess what he was thinking, and Seb could do the same for her. That unsettled her a great deal, but for a battle magus of the Magisterium, he seemed a decent man. There was a sadness to him, and he did not seem inclined to indulge in the petty cruelties that some of the members of the Magisterium enjoyed.

Fortunately, the work of cooking the deer gave Caina something to occupy her thoughts. Kylon gathered firewood by the simple expedient of using the sorcery of water to augment his strength enough to rip branches off the trees, and Sophia started the fire with a piece of flint and the edge of her dagger.

"Can you not use sorcery to start the flames?" said Sophia.

"I could, dear girl," said Seb, "but pyromancy inevitably drives its wielders into homicidal madness, and then Lord Kylon's fair valikarion bride would cut off my head with her valikon, which would quite spoil our breakfast."

Caina laughed. "Is that an attempt at flattery?"

"Well," said Seb, "I have found that flattering a woman is frequently less harmful than refraining from flattering her."

"That seems sensible," said Sophia, perhaps hoping for a compliment. When none was forthcoming, she asked a question instead. "Does fire sorcery really drive its wielders insane?"

"I fear so," said Caina. "If you ever have the misfortune to meet an Umbarian magus, you will see that they often wear a black gauntlet on their right hands. That lets them use pyromancy without descending into madness."

"Lady Caina is quite correct," said Seb. "Therefore, descending into madness to cook our breakfast seems excessive, especially when you are doing an admirable job with the kindling." Even as he spoke, Sophia got the fire going. The winter seemed to have left the wood cold and dry, and it caught flame with gratifying speed. Caina held out her cold hands to the fire with relief. The long red coat she had taken from Sigilsoara was warm enough, but already she missed the searing, arid heat of Istarinmul and Iramis.

They finished butchering the deer and cooked the cuts of venison over the fire. Caina had not eaten anything since breakfast yesterday, and the meat was delicious. They ate their fill, and there was a good deal left over.

"There is no time to salt this properly," said Sophia, wrapping up some of the meat in her pack, "and we don't have salt anyway, but it is cold enough that it should last a few days. Maybe…maybe it will last long enough that we can travel past Kostiv without stopping there."

"Maybe," said Caina, watching the girl.

"It would be best to keep moving," said Seb, looking at the discarded pile of offal from the deer. "That will draw scavengers sooner rather than later."

"Agreed," said Kylon, and they walked southwest along the deer trail.

About two hours later they came to the road.

At least, it had once been a road. The wide track had been beaten through the forest, the brush cleared away, but the forest was reclaiming it. In another few years, Caina thought, there would be no sign that a road had ever been here. Still, it was smoother going than the deer trail, and their pace increased. Someone must have built this road, but it had been abandoned for a long time.

So Caina was not entirely surprised when she saw the ruined tower jutting out of the trees.

It looked old and crude, without the precision of Imperial stonework. The tower had been built of rough-mortared stone, and as they drew closer, Caina saw a crumbling wall encircling the tower's base. It occupied the top of a low hill, and despite the rough stonework, it nonetheless would have been a strong fortification. From the tower's crest, a man would have a view of the forest for miles in all directions.

Caina's first thought was that they ought to look around. The tower looked abandoned, and the previous occupants might have left useful supplies behind. Her next thought was that investigating the tower might be a bad idea. Such a place would almost certainly draw the eye of every bandit and renegade looking for a place to hide.

Then she saw the faint necromantic aura from within the tower.

"Caina," said Kylon, calling his valikon to his hand.

"Aye, I see it," said Caina. He must have sensed the aura at the same time that she had seen it.

"What is it?" said Seb, drawing his sword.

"That tower is a bad place," said Sophia. "We should not go there."

"Why not?" said Caina. "Are there bandits?"

Sophia shook her head. "It is cursed. It was the castle of a rebel szlacht."

"Szlacht?" said Caina. It must have been an Ulkaari word.

"Minor landed noble," said Seb. "Usually sworn to a stronger one, such as a local boyar. In exchange for a grant of land, the szlacht must equip himself with a horse, armor, and some men-at-arms, and then ride to the assistance of his boyar in times of war."

"Seems an inefficient way to raise an army," said Kylon.

"Compared to the professional armies of the Empire and New Kyre, yes," said Seb. "Which is likely why Malarae and New Kyre have never been conquered, but Ulkaar is a province of the Empire."

"That is not important," said Sophia. "The tower is cursed. Long ago there was a szlacht who refused the call to war from the boyar of Kostiv. When he died, he was cursed and rose again as an evil spirit. Anyone who enters the tower does not return."

"A local legend," said Seb, "but these things often have a kernel of truth to them, especially in Ulkaar."

"That kernel might have sprouted a strong crop," said Kylon. "There is a necromantic aura in the place."

"I can see it," said Caina, trying to make sense of the strange auras detected by the vision of the valikarion. "Undead creatures, I think, several of them. Inside the hill. A cellar below the tower, probably. But I think they're...dormant. If we enter the tower, they'll likely wake up. But if we stay away from the hill, I think they will leave us alone."

"Then for the love of the Divine," said Sophia, "let us stay away from the tower."

"Agreed," said Caina, and they pressed on.

The road was in better repair the further southwest they went, and they made good time. Caina kept the heavy red coat wrapped around herself, grateful that she had found the garment inside Sigilsoara.

After passing the ruined tower, they made about another five miles before the sun started to go down and the air grew colder. Kylon picked a small clearing off the road for the campsite, and Caina and Sophia gathered loose sticks for the fire while Seb and Kylon wrenched low-hanging branches from the trees with bursts of sorcery-enhanced strength. Soon they had a large fire going, and Caina settled close to it, enjoying the heat radiating from the flames.

Come to think of it, she also enjoyed the light. The forest grew dark around them and coupled with the soft moaning of the icy wind it made for an ominous scene. She looked at Kylon and was grateful that he was with her. Granted, she would have preferred to have been in bed with him, partly for warmth, and partly for other reasons. Their first night as husband and wife had been interrupted by that shadow vortex.

"I do not like this wind," said Seb, eating the rest of his venison.

"It isn't pleasant," said Caina.

"And it might get worse," said Seb.

"A blizzard, maybe," said Sophia, and she gazed at the darkness, the shadows from the fire dancing over her face. "The weather is right for it. If...if a blizzard hits, we'll have to shelter in Kostiv, won't we? If we're caught out in the forest, we'll freeze to death."

"Probably," said Seb. "But I thought you would be at risk if you returned to Kostiv."

"Yes," said Sophia, and she took a shuddering breath. "But compared to that or freezing to death from cold..." She lifted the sunstone and looked at it. "The boyar will kill me."

"Then we'll disguise you," said Caina.

"Disguise?" Sophia blinked.

"We'll think of something," said Caina. "I've pretended to be a man more times than I can remember."

Sophia laughed. "That's impossible. You don't look anything like a man."

Caina smiled. "I'm glad to hear that."

"I imagine Lord Kylon is as well," said Seb. Sophia laughed again and turned red.

"But I don't plan to march up to the gates of Kostiv and announce who I really am," said Caina. "Seb, you've never been to Kostiv?"

"No, never," said Seb.

"Then we'll say we're your attendants," said Caina. "Or your bodyguards. Or servants. If we do it right, no one will look at us twice, and we can leave Kostiv without anyone ever becoming the wiser. It's always best to hide in plain sight."

"Do you really think that can work?" said Sophia.

Caina shrugged. "I've done it before." She looked at Seb. "If Sebastian is willing to play along, I think we can manage it."

Seb snorted. "Well, since it seems we all must cooperate until we reach Artifel at the earliest, I am game if you are. Though I am curious how you shall conjure a disguise out of thin air since we have nothing but the clothes upon our backs. Is that one of the powers of the valikarion?"

"We'll think of something," said Caina. "Meanwhile, we should get some sleep. I will take the first watch. It will be harder for anything sorcerous to sneak up on me."

There was no disagreement. Sophia and Seb lay down on opposite sides of the fire and soon fell asleep. Caina walked a few yards from the flames, watching the shadows of the trees. Kylon joined her, and they stood side-by-side in silence for a while. Caina leaned close to him and rested her head on his shoulder. She wondered what he sensed from her. Her love for him? Her fear of the situation, and the unease of learning that Laeria Amalas had possessed a large and powerful family? Her discomfort at the cold and hunger? Her wish that she was still in bed with him in Iramis?

They stood like that for perhaps a quarter of an hour.

"They're asleep," said Kylon at last in a quiet voice. He spoke in Kyracian, which Sophia would not understand, and Caina didn't think Seb knew the language.

Caina straightened up and looked at him. "You are well?" She also spoke in Kyracian.

"As well as can be expected," said Kylon, "given that I was plucked out of my bed on the night of our wedding and flung twelve hundred miles in the blink of an eye."

Caina let out a breath. "I've lived through a lot of strange things, but I've never had that happen before. I didn't think such a thing was possible through sorcery."

"Neither did I," said Kylon. He hesitated. "Though I wonder…"

"What is it?" said Caina.

"Your…newly discovered family," said Kylon. Caina grimaced at that. "If you and Seb were both pulled to Sigilsoara, that suggests a blood link."

"You were summoned there as well," said Caina.

Kylon snorted. "I think that was only because you were on top of me at the time." Caina smiled. "But if you and Seb are half-siblings, and your mother's family is filled with sorcerers, I wondered if one of them summoned Sigilsoara."

"Summoned?" said Caina.

"Sophia and Seb said that Sigilsoara sometimes connects with the material world," said Kylon. "But the place was crawling with Adamant Guards, and you killed an Umbarian. That Morett necromancer was looking for a relic." He took a deep breath. "I wonder if one of your mother's relatives, one of the Umbarians, summoned Sigilsoara with a blood spell, and that spell happened to draw you and Seb along with it."

"I wondered that as well," said Caina. "It makes sense. One of my mother's Umbarian relatives wanted the relic from within

Sigilsoara, summoned it, and sent the Adamant Guards in to retrieve it."

"At least they didn't get the relic," said Kylon.

"Yes." Caina paused for a moment. "About that."

Kylon sighed. "You're about to surprise me unpleasantly, aren't you?"

"Well," said Caina. "Yes."

She glanced back to make sure that Seb and Sophia were sleeping, reached into her pocket, and drew out the iron ring.

Kylon stared at the ring for a moment, and then at her.

"That's what the Umbarians were after?" said Kylon.

Caina nodded. "I'm pretty sure."

Kylon let out a long breath. "Gods. Not even married a day and you still astonish me." Caina smiled again. "Was it a good idea to take it with us?"

"Not in the least," said Caina. "But leaving it behind would have been worse. I had to break down the wards on its vault to get away from a dozen Temnoti. If I had left the ring behind, one of the Adamant Guards could have picked it up."

"What is it?" said Kylon. "I can't sense any arcane force from it."

"I think that's because I'm holding it," said Caina. "Give it a tap. But don't pick it up."

Kylon nodded, tapped the ring with one finger, and jerked his hand back.

"Gods of storm and brine," he muttered. "That thing's powerful. And dangerous. I don't think you should let go of it. If you do, the aura will probably wake Seb and Sophia up, and draw the eye of every sorcerer for a dozen miles."

Caina nodded. "See why I didn't want to leave it behind for the Umbarians?"

"Aye." Kylon peered at the ring, frowning. "That dragon sigil in the emerald. Is that…"

"The same sigil we saw inside the castle?" said Caina. "It is. Did you see any statues of Rasarion Yagar in Sigilsoara?"

"The ugly fellow with the mustache?" said Kylon.

"That's him," said Caina. "In all his statues, he had this ring on his finger, with the same dragon sigil. I think this was his ring."

"What does it do?" said Kylon.

"I have no idea," said Caina. "Nothing good, I expect, if even half the stories about this Yagar are true...and the appearance of Sigilsoara suggests that quite a few of those stories were true."

Kylon sighed. "Then an Umbarian magus was looking for the ancient relic of some long-dead sorcerer-king?"

"It would seem so."

Kylon cursed softly. "Just like Cassander Nilas and the Throne of Corazain all over again."

"Yes," said Caina. "We did defeat him in the end."

But it had been a very close thing. Cassander had almost killed them both, and he had come within a hair's breadth of killing nearly a million people. Caina still remembered the pyromantic sorcery radiating from the Throne of Corazain, remembered Cassander's scarred face turning towards her as he cast a spell to strike her down.

"So, what do we do with the damned thing?" said Kylon. "I assume the valikons won't touch it?"

"I already tried. The ring just regenerates its spells. But the solution is simple," said Caina. "We take it back with us to Iramis and give it to the loremasters. They'll lock it up in the Towers of Lore, and it will never hurt anyone."

"That seems reasonable," said Kylon.

Caina hesitated. "I think we should take Sophia with us as well. Or at least give her the chance to accompany us to Iramis."

"Because of her arcane talent?" said Kylon.

Caina nodded. "It's still latent. I suspect she knows that she has sorcery, but she's only using it on an intuitive level. She doesn't really understand what she's doing or how she's doing it..."

"And if she keeps on like that," said Kylon, glancing at the sleeping girl, "she's going to hurt herself."

"Or the Magisterium will forcibly enroll her as an initiate," said Caina. "Or, worse, the Umbarians."

"Do you believe her story?" said Kylon.

"No," said Caina. "It's obvious that she's lying to us...but I think she's telling the truth that the boyar will kill her if she returns to Kostiv." She shrugged. "If I had to guess, I would say that the boyar or one of his men, one of his szlachts, decided that they wanted her. Based on what Seb said, a petty rural noble like Boyar Razdan Nagrach would be used to doing whatever he wanted..."

"And doing whatever he wished with his people," said Kylon

"So Sophia ran," said Caina.

"Brave of her."

"Brave and foolish," said Caina. "One of the Temnoti was about to capture her when I found her. I don't know what the Temnoti would have done with her, but it couldn't have been good."

They stood in silence for a moment.

"Do you believe Seb's story?" said Kylon.

Caina let out a long breath. "Yes. I'm afraid I do. If he is lying, he has put in his work."

"He looks like you," said Kylon.

"He looks like my mother," said Caina. She sighed. "And I look like my mother. He is my half-brother, Kylon, much as I might not wish to face that fact. And abandoning her first marriage and children was exactly the sort of thing that Laeria Amalas would have done. She probably told my father that she was an unmarried virgin when she met him." She sighed once more. "My father was a good man, but he was not the kind of man would have been able to tell if my mother was a virgin or not."

"I am sorry," said Kylon. "I regret that I never got the chance to meet him."

"I regret that, too," said Caina. She tried to smile. "I wonder what he would have thought of you. I doubt he thought his daughter would marry a Kyracian lord."

"Undoubtedly," said Kylon. "Do you trust Seb?"

Caina opened her mouth, closed it again. Sebastian Scorneus, by his simple presence, had brought a half-dozen competing emotions into her mind. His resemblance to Laeria Amalas had inspired an immediate dislike, and she liked the news of Laeria's family even less. And yet Seb himself had done nothing to warrant distrust. He had fought alongside Caina and Kylon as they escaped from Sigilsoara, and he had agreed to work with them until they reached Artifel.

"I...I don't know," said Caina at last. "We should not tell him about the ring."

"Of course not," said Kylon.

"But what do you think of him?" said Caina. She took Kylon's hand. "I cannot be rational about him, not yet. He reminds me of my mother, and I hated her more than anyone."

"I think," said Kylon, "that we can likely trust him."

Caina waited.

"He is not a coward," said Kylon. "He didn't flinch from fighting the undead and the Temnoti. And he did not suggest that we abandon you and Sophia at Sigilsoara. He could have – both he and I can run faster than you in a straight line."

"True," said Caina. "He also saw you kiss me. Perhaps he realized that you would make a valuable ally and that abandoning me would alienate you."

"Maybe," said Kylon. "If he could calculate like that in the heat of the moment, he would be a cold man indeed."

Caina stared into the forest. "I can calculate like that in the heat of the moment."

To her surprise, Kylon smiled. "True, but you forget. I can sense your emotions, at least when I am touching you, and I can sense his."

"So what do you sense?"

"As far as I can tell, he's telling the truth," said Kylon. "He's alarmed at our situation, but we all are. He's impressed by me, sympathetic for Sophia, and doesn't know what to make of you."

Caina laughed. "And I'm not sure what to make of him. We have that in common, at least."

"And he is…" Kylon thought for a moment. "Grieving, I think. I suspect he lost someone he loved recently."

Caina considered that. "Well, if we can all work together long enough to get out of Ulkaar, I suppose that is the most important thing."

"I think so," said Kylon. "And his hatred of your mother…his mother…was genuine. He also hates the Umbarians."

"That's a good quality in a man."

"I can take the watch if you need to rest," said Kylon.

"Thank you," said Caina, "but I'm too wound up to sleep. And I need to think for a while anyway."

"About Seb?" said Kylon.

"Mostly about what we're going to do when we get to Kostiv," said Caina. Though she supposed her thoughts would turn to Seb and her mother's family anyway. "Not that it matters. I won't be able to make a good plan until I see Kostiv firsthand."

"You'll think of something," said Kylon. He kissed her, wrapped himself in his cloak, lay down by the fire, and went to sleep.

For the next hour or so Caina kept watch, her eyes scanning the shadows of the forest. She was tired, but as she had told Kylon, she was too wound up to sleep. Her mind considered all the things she had seen – Sigilsoara, Sophia's terror and lies, Seb's tale, the history of Ulkaar. The Empire and the Umbarian Order were at war.

Istarinmul had been pulled into that fight and nearly destroyed, and perhaps the same thing was happening to Ulkaar.

She felt the weight of the iron ring in her pocket. The metal always seemed cold, no matter how long she held it. Yes, the sooner she got the thing to Iramis, the better...

A rustling noise caught her attention.

Caina turned her head to see Sophia standing and looking around.

"Is everything all right?" said Caina in a soft voice.

"Um." Sophia edged closer and bit her lip. "I have to...relieve myself, and I don't..." She looked at Kylon and Seb. "I don't want anyone to see."

"Go behind that tree," said Caina, pointing. "None of us will be able to see, and if there are any dangers, you can get back here quickly."

Relief went over Sophia's face, and she hastened to the tree. A few moments later she returned, tugging at her belt and adjusting her heavy coat and cloak.

"By the Divine, it is cold out," said Sophia. "I thought my legs would freeze off."

Caina nodded. "I've never wanted to be a man, but I imagine there are times when it is convenient."

Sophia blinked, looked confused, and then her brown eyes went wide, and her hand shot to her mouth to muffle a laugh.

"I never thought of it like that," said Sophia. She hesitated. "Can...can I ask you something?"

"Certainly," said Caina.

Sophia looked away. "It...is kind of an impertinent question."

"Then I'll just give you an impertinent answer."

Sophia almost smiled, but that mixture of hesitation and fear returned. "When...when you were brought to Sigilsoara, you and Lord Kylon...it was your wedding night?"

"That's right," said Caina, wondering why Sophia wanted to know.

"Then you were...you were..."

"In the midst of the consummation, to put it delicately," said Caina.

"Was that your first time?" said Sophia. "With Lord Kylon? I mean, Brother Valexis says that both the man and the woman should wait until they are married, but I know it doesn't always work that way. I'm not a child."

She looked very young as she asked it.

Young, and very, very frightened.

Caina considered her answer for a moment. "No. It wasn't the first time for either of us. Lord Kylon was married before, but his wife died. And I'm afraid I knew men before Lord Kylon. But I don't think that's what you really want to ask, is it?"

Sophia took a deep breath. "Does...does it hurt? The first time, I mean?"

Kylon's suspicion that Sophia had fled from the boyar and his szlachts flashed through Caina's mind.

"It can," said Caina. "It depends on the woman, and it depends on the man. My first time...well, it didn't hurt. It started out a little uncomfortable, yes, but I enjoyed it a great deal. Granted, it was a mistake to sleep with him, and I shouldn't have done it." She remembered poor Alastair Corus and his strange mixture of gallantry and resigned apathy. He hadn't deserved his death at the hands of Maglarion.

"Oh," said Sophia. "Weren't you worried about getting with child?"

"I wish I did," said Caina. "I was injured when I was a few years younger than you are. I can't have children."

Though "injured" was a delicate way to put it. But Caina would not burden Sophia with the true account of how she had lost her ability to bear children, how Maglarion had harvested her blood to build his great bloodcrystal.

"I'm sorry," said Sophia. "That must be both awful and a tremendous relief at the same time."

"It depends on the day," said Caina, though mostly the thought now brought her a resigned sadness. She had wanted children more than anything, but if she had not set upon the path of the Ghosts, then a lot of people would have died. "But I don't think that's what you really wanted to ask me, Sophia."

The girl frowned. "What do you mean?"

"I think you wanted to tell me something," said Caina. "I think you wanted to tell me the real reason you left Kostiv. It wasn't about the sunstone."

Sophia opened her mouth, closed it again, and finally started to speak. "It was said of old that no one could speak a lie to an Arvaltyr."

"I don't know about that," said Caina. "But I do know that sunstone isn't why you fled Kostiv. I know that you're frightened. I know that you've been very brave, maybe for a long time, but the fear is still there." Sophia swallowed, her eyes starting to glitter. "And I know that I might be able to help you."

For a long time, they stood in silence.

"No one can help me," whispered Sophia at last, trying to hold the tears back.

"Maybe," said Caina. "And maybe I really am a valikarion, an Arvaltyr."

"You haven't ever met anyone as horrible as the boyar," said Sophia.

"I very much doubt that," said Caina.

"He says that he's bringing back the old ways," said Sophia. "Brother Valexis and Uncle Ivan both told me to run, that there was no one I can trust in Kostiv. But I can't get away from Kostiv. I can't get away from the boyar and his hunt."

"His hunt?" said Caina, frowning. She had been expecting to hear the story of an arranged marriage, or that the boyar was the sort of man who snatched pretty girls from the street and imprisoned them for his own amusement.

But a hunt?

"He says that the war with the sorcerers is a sign," said Sophia. "The Warmaiden banned the hunt, and so does the Temple, but the boyar says the old ways are coming back." The words tumbled out of her faster and faster, her accent becoming thicker in the process, her Caerish harder to understand. "They told me to run, and I...and I..."

There was a flare of green light in the trees.

Caina went stiff, calling her valikon to her hand, and Sophia fell silent.

"What is it?" said Sophia.

"Go wake the others right now," said Caina. "The undead are coming."

CHAPTER EIGHT

THE WRAITH

Sebastian Scorneus was not entirely certain of what to make of Caina.

She looked like the rest of the women of House Scorneus. Caina had the same cold blue eyes, the same sharp features, the same thick black hair that would turn the color of hard iron as she aged. She looked like Aunt Talmania, who Seb hated, and Aunt Ariadne, who Seb loved, and Aunt Rania, who Seb feared. Caina also resembled Seb's twin sister Calvia, which made sense, since they were half-sisters.

It was nonetheless shocking that the Balarigar was not only a member of House Scorneus but Seb's half-sister.

He had heard the rumors about Caina Amalas, of course, the whispered tales about the Balarigar who had changed the course of the Empire. Some of the tales said she was a remorseless assassin, deadlier than the Kindred and a thousand times as cunning. Others claimed that she was a seductress, so beautiful that no man could resist her lures. Those rumors said she had seduced and murdered Aidan Maraeus, and Aidan's father Lord Corbould Maraeus still sought her death should Caina ever return to the Empire. The tales that had come out of Istarinmul had been even wilder – stories that she had destroyed the Slavers' Brotherhood, or deposed the Padishah and seduced his son, or convinced Istarinmul to turn against the Umbarian Order.

Of course, Caina herself claimed that Iramis had returned. That claim was just as incredible, but Seb thought she was telling the truth. Her valikon had come from somewhere, and he suspected that the ghostsilver bracelet on her left wrist was a loremaster's pyrikon.

And yet it seemed unlikely that she was at the center of so many rumors and legends. Caina looked like a lean young woman with black hair and cold eyes, pretty but otherwise unremarkable. But Seb was bemused to see how much Caina's patterns of thought matched his own, with the same penchant for observations and deductions.

And that valikon.

When he had been a child, Seb had wanted to be a valikarion instead of a magus, and when he had informed Aunt Talmania of that fact, she'd ordered her servants to beat sense into him.

He wondered what Katrina would have thought of Caina. That was a sad thought. She always had…

Seb put aside his musings and went to sleep, though not for long.

"Wake up!" screamed Sophia. "Wake up!"

Seb's eyes shot open, and he surged to his feet, the reflexes of two years of war sending his hand to his sword hilt and his mind to his arcane disciplines. He looked around as he called his power, slipping into a ready stance, his sword raised. The fire they had built still burned bright and hot, throwing tangled shadows across the clearing. The dark forests of northern Ulkaar loomed around them, bleak and barren, the sky masked with heavy clouds. Kylon had just gotten to his feet, his valikon assembling itself from shards of silver light in his hand. Seb wondered how he did that. Of the various contradictory legends and accounts he had read of the valikarion, they had claimed that only the most powerful valikarion could summon their swords, and Lord Kylon wasn't a valikarion.

A tale for another time.

Seb looked around, wondering what had caused the alarm, and then he saw the lights.

Flickers of ghostly green light danced in the trees, like tiny candle flames. Seb felt a chill, and not just from the icy weather. He had seen similar light on more occasions than he wished to remember.

Necromantic spells often produced such light

Seb cast a simple spell to sense the presence of arcane forces. At once he felt a powerful aura of elemental sorcery around Lord Kylon and a far weaker one around Sophia. Caina stood at the edge of the light from the fire, her valikon burning white in her right hand.

From her, of course, Seb sensed nothing at all.

He also felt the stirrings of necromantic power in the trees around him, spells old and ancient and rigid.

Undead creatures were approaching, he judged, and old ones at that.

"What's happening?" said Seb, stepping to join Caina and Kylon.

"I'm not sure," said Caina, staring into the darkness. "I can see them coming. Undead creatures, like the ones we saw in Sigilsoara. Sophia, stay between us and the fire."

Sophia hastened to obey, her eyes wide. "Did they follow us from the Iron King's castle?"

"Maybe," said Caina. "Or they came from that ruined tower. There were undead in there, I'm sure of it, but I thought they were dormant."

"Maybe something woke them up," said Kylon.

Husband and wife shared a concerned look. Seb wondered what that was about.

"It's possible," said Caina.

"It is the szlacht of the tower," said Sophia, her voice thin and frightened. "We trespassed upon his land and did not pay him homage, and now he is coming to take our souls."

"Perhaps," said Caina. She lifted the valikon, the white fire of the blade throwing harsh shadows against her face. "But I wager it has been a long time since these undead have seen anyone carrying a valikon."

"Then you think they will be overconfident?" said Seb.

"Yes," said Caina. "We'll have to use that against them."

"It could be just a wandering band of undead," said Kylon.

Caina nodded. "But they're heading right for us."

"Then we'll fight," said Kylon. "I'll take the lead. Seb, if you can knock them off balance, a single blow from my valikon ought to destroy them." Seb nodded and adjusted his grip on his black sword. The weapon, like his armor, had been made in the foundries of the Magisterium's motherhouse in Artifel and was lighter and stronger than conventional steel. It amused Seb how quickly he found himself following Kylon's instructions. Then again, Kylon had been one of the nine Archons of New Kyre. "Caina, if any of them get past us, strike them down."

Caina nodded again. "I wish had I some throwing knives."

Throwing knives? What would she do with throwing knives? An odd choice of weapon.

"What should I do?" said Sophia.

"Stay behind us and do whatever we tell you to do," said Caina.

Sophia hastened to obey.

"Here they come," said Kylon.

Seb cast another sequence of spells. He was only a mediocre magus at best, and he would never have the terrible power of someone like Ariadne or Talmania or Decius Aberon, the First Magus of the Magisterium. Nevertheless, he had been trained as a battle magus, and he was good with psychokinetic spells. The spells he cast would only last for a short time, but they would make him faster and allow him to hit far harder than he could otherwise. It was similar to how Kyracian stormdancers augmented their prowess, though Seb's spells did not rely on any elemental forces.

But with those spells driving his limbs, he could take a man's head off with a single swing, run faster than a horse, and absorb blows that would otherwise shatter his bones. Surviving two years of fighting with the soldiers of the Umbarian Order had increased his skill with those spells a great deal.

He watched the undead come into the edge of the light from the fire.

There were nearly twenty of them, withered creatures with leathery flesh clinging to yellowed bones. Ghostly green fires played in empty eye sockets, and wispy ribbons of green light served in place of their long-withered ligaments. The undead wore ancient armor of Ulkaari design, spiked helms and shirts of scale mail, and they held round shields with a spike set over the central boss. In their right hands, they carried curved sabers of Kagari design, a weapon that had become popular in Ulkaar since Rasarion Yagar had defeated the Kagari khans.

The undead stopped at the edge of the firelight and went motionless.

Seb heard Sophia's rapid, frightened breathing. Kylon stood grim and silent next to his wife, both hands grasping the hilt of his valikon, the sword burning with white fire as the Iramisian sigils on the blade glowed. This, Seb thought, this must have been what the valikarion of old must have looked like, grim warriors preparing for battle against monsters of sorcery.

But Kylon was not a valikarion.

Caina was, though she did not look anything like Seb would have thought a valikarion would look.

In the oversized red coat, she almost looked like a girl playing dress-up in her father's clothes. Yet she remained motionless next to Kylon, and while her valikon was shorter than her husband's, it burned no less brightly.

For a moment, the living and the undead stared at each other.

One of the undead warriors stepped forward and spoke in the Ulkaari language, its voice a rasping growl.

"You have entered the lands of our lord," said the warrior. "Your lives belong to our lord. You will surrender to us."

"What did he say?" said Caina in Caerish.

"He stated," said Seb, "that we have trespassed upon the lands of his lord, and that our lives are forfeit to him. He then presented a demand for surrender."

Caina smiled. She must have been forcing it. One could not survive as a Ghost nightfighter for very long without an excellent ability to lie. But she looked completely calm.

"Tell him," said Caina, "that they will leave us in peace, and we will leave them in peace."

Seb supposed he was going to serve as the translator, so he relayed Caina's message back to the undead.

The warrior stared at him, and it let out a croaking, wheezing laugh. The other undead joined in, and the harsh rasp of their laughter echoed over the clearing. Sophia let out a strangled, whimpering sound of fear.

"Does the woman speak for you?" said the undead warrior. "Tell her that she shall be the slave of our lord. Tell her that she shall attend to him in his silent halls for eternity. She is the one that our lord sent us to claim, and her torment shall continue long after she has perished."

"I gather," said Caina, "that it is saying unflattering things about me."

Seb snorted. "Something like that, yes. Also, he claims his lord has commanded him to take you personally."

"Me?" said Caina. Again, she shared a look with Kylon. "Ask him why his lord wants to capture me."

Sophia gaped at Caina. No doubt she found Caina's calm in the situation unnerving.

"Why this woman?" said Seb to the undead. "If your lord desires feminine companionship, surely it can be easier to obtain."

"The Syvashar commands it of our lord," said the undead warrior. "The hour is coming. The old ways return. The old lords awaken, and the shadows stir in their tombs."

"He says someone called the Syvashar commands it of his lord," said Seb.

"What's a Syvashar?" said Caina.

"The Syvashar?" said Sophia. "That is an old word. It is said in ancient days that the Syvashar was the High Priest of the Temnoti, and advised the Iron King from his right hand."

"So why are the Temnoti sending undead after us?" said Kylon.

"Perhaps they are offended that we killed several of them escaping from Sigilsoara," said Seb.

Yet Seb had the feeling that both Caina and Kylon knew exactly why the undead had come for them.

"Tell them," said Caina, pointing her burning valikon at the undead, "that if they want to take us, they are welcome to try. But if they do, they will see that the Arvaltyri of old have returned once more."

Seb doubted the undead understood Caerish, but they knew the name of the Arvaltyri.

When Caina spoke the word, the undead shifted. They had been standing motionless, but the warriors edged forward, raising their corroded weapons. The leader's face was too withered to show any expression, but Seb had the impression of overwhelming rage.

"Fools!" snarled the undead warrior. "The Arvaltyri passed from the world! Iramis perished in flame! The old ways shall rise again, and the Great Master shall ascend in glory! Kill them and bring their corpses to our lord!"

The undead surged forward in a tide of ghostly green fire and undead flesh, and Seb charged to meet them.

###

Kylon drew on the sorcery of water and air.

The undead warriors charged in a ragged line, no doubt expecting to overwhelm the four of them, but Kylon had a better idea. He jumped, and the power of his leap carried him over the heads of the undead. Kylon landed in their midst, and before his undead enemies reacted, he attacked.

The valikon snapped left and right in his hands as he swung. The undead wore heavy armor, strong enough to turn the edge of his sword, but Kylon did not bother to land powerful blows. The touch of the ghostsilver blade was enough to disrupt the necromantic spells binding the undead warriors. They either collapsed from the impact of the valikon, the spells broken, or staggered away from the sword's strike.

That gave Seb ample time to attack. While Kylon fought with speed and finesse, Seb relied on brute strength and psychokinetic force, but it served him just as well. He struck down the undead that Kylon stunned, his black sword smashing through necks and crushing skulls. Together they tore a path through the enemy, leaving dusty bones and dented armor scattered across the snowy ground.

They could not stop all the undead, and some rushed for Caina. She held her own, though her blade work was clumsy at best. She had always been better with daggers and knives instead of swords, though she had improved with a longer blade since becoming bonded to her valikon.

Fortunately, it didn't matter. The touch of the valikon destroyed the undead, and Caina's past training with the unarmed forms kept her ahead of their swords. It helped that the undead seemed unable to see her, likely due to her nature as a valikarion.

In a matter of moments, they had destroyed all the undead warriors, bones and armor and ancient swords lying across the forest floor.

"I daresay," said Seb, lowering his sword, "those valikons are useful weapons."

"They are," said Kylon, looking around. The undead had been destroyed, but he still sensed a great deal of necromantic power nearby. "But there are more coming."

He sensed the flicker of sorcerous force as Seb cast a spell. "I agree. Lady Caina?"

"It's coming from the northeast," said Caina, stepping over the prone form of an undead she had destroyed. "I don't know what…"

Green fire flared in the trees, harsh and bright, throwing black shadows from the barren branches.

A chill shot through Kylon. He hadn't been very cold, between the heat from their campfire and the exertions of battle, but suddenly he was shivering. Worse, it wasn't a chill he felt with his flesh. He seemed to feel it inside his mind and heart.

"Get back," said Caina. "Get back!"

To the vision of the valikarion, the necromantic aura rolled over the clearing like a hazy green mist.

Caina had encountered spells like this before, and the tingling sense of it against her skin was both familiar and unpleasant. It was a spell of necromantic science designed to drain away the life of its victims, feeding that energy to the caster. Maglarion and the Moroaica and Sicarion and Kharnaces had all used spells of that nature, and while this one was cruder, Caina feared it would be no less effective.

Kylon and Seb retreated to join her, swords raised, Sophia standing behind them.

A moment later the armored figure emerged from the trees.

Like the other undead, it was withered and ancient, leathery flesh clinging tight to yellowed bones. Unlike the others, it wore magnificent armor of polished steel, the plates worked with reliefs and adorned with gold and gems. A jeweled sword hung at its belt alongside a fine dagger.

And the creature's face...

Caina saw a ghostly image of green light superimposed over the undead creature's withered face. It showed the features of a nobleman, his hair and mustache cut in the same style as the statues of the Iron King. It was almost as if Caina looked at the translucent face of a living man to see long-dead flesh and bone beneath.

"That must be the szlacht of the tower," said Kylon.

Sophia let out a little sound of fear. "It is an ardivid."

"What is an ardivid?" said Caina.

"A powerful undead," said Seb. "Sometimes the worshippers of Temnuzash rise again as ardivids. Usually nobles. Very powerful. I suspect we now have the honor of meeting the lord of the tower we passed earlier."

The ardivid walked forward, the armor creaking, the necromantic aura creeping closer. The creature said something in the Ulkaari tongue, and both Seb and Sophia frowned.

"What did it just say?" said Caina.

"He says that we have slain his servants," said Seb, "so we shall be raised as undead to take their place. He says...that you bear the talisman of the Iron King, and for the glory of Temnuzash the Great Master, he will slay you and take the talisman for himself."

"I see," said Caina, frowning. The undead had come to kill her and claim the Iron King's ring. But how had they sensed it? Maybe they hadn't sensed it but had instead guessed the probable path she would take from Sigilsoara to Kostiv.

That, in turn, meant that the Temnoti knew that she had taken the ring from Sigilsoara, and had awakened the undead of the ruined tower and sent them after her.

Caina briefly wondered if it would be a good idea to give the ring back to the Temnoti. At once she dismissed the thought. The Temnoti had been fighting the Umbarians, but that did not mean the cult of Temnuzash was on Caina's side. For that matter, they hardly seemed any more benevolent than the Umbarians, and the ring was still a relic of great necromantic power.

No one should have it.

Again, the undead creature spoke, the ghostly face over the withered head sneering at Caina.

"He offers one last time to allow you to surrender," said Seb. "If you do, he shall kill us all and make us his vassals. If we resist, he will kill us all and make us his slaves, and he will torment us for centuries."

Caina said nothing, her eyes on the ardivid. The creature was powerful, she could see that with the senses of a valikarion. Yet powerful or not, it would still be vulnerable to the ghostsilver blade of a valikon. She glanced at the pyrikon on her left wrist. It had been able to shield her presence from spells of sensing and detection. Could it do the same to necromantic spells?

As if in response to her thought, the pyrikon moved.

The ghostsilver bracelet unfolded, seeming to crawl up the fingers of her left hand. When it had settled into its new configuration, a ghostsilver ring encircled each of her fingers and her thumb, the rings joined to the bracelet by a slender chain. It gave off a vibration, a faint buzzing noise coming from the rings.

"This is what I want to do," said Caina to Kylon in Kyracian. "I think the pyrikon can shield me from his aura. While I distract him, jump up and kill him. Our valikons have the best chance of destroying him."

Kylon let out a long breath. "All right."

Seb frowned at them. "What should I tell the ardivid?" he said in Caerish.

"Whatever you want," said Caina in the same language, and she started walking forward.

She walked into the creature's necromantic aura. It felt unpleasantly cold, and she started to shiver beneath her heavy coat but suffered no other ill effects. The pyrikon's vibration increased, growing so violent that it would make her left hand go numb before much longer.

The ghostly face shifted to her. Lesser undead, Caina knew, could not perceive her, since they did not have physical eyes and could not sense a valikarion. More powerful undead could perceive physical light, and the ardivid seemed able to see her as she walked towards it. Likely the undead szlacht assumed she was coming to surrender.

But the closer Caina drew, the more likely it was that the ardivid would realize something was wrong.

The creature focused on her, ghostly eyes narrowed, and said something in the Ulkaari tongue. Caina didn't know what the words meant, but she expected it wasn't even remotely complimentary. She kept walking at a steady, unhurried pace, the pyrikon buzzing on her left wrist, the valikon burning in her right hand.

Again, the undead szlacht said something. This time it sounded like a question. Caina only smiled and kept walking, her heartbeat like a drum in her ears. Fear pulsed through her in time to her heartbeat, but long practice kept her hands steady and the smile on her face.

Once more the ardivid barked its question. The translucent face shifted, the eyes narrowing as they looked at Caina, the valikon, and back at Caina.

Suddenly she saw the realization strike home.

The ghostly eyes widened, and the creature shouted and yanked the sword from its belt. Unlike its face, the sword was real, a curved Kagari-style saber with jewels glittering in the guard and pommel. Caina sprinted forward, covering the distance between them, and struck with the valikon. The ghostsilver blade scraped the ardivid's forearm, disrupting the spells, and the undead szlacht screamed in pain. Caina drove her valikon towards its neck, but the szlacht reacted with inhuman speed. The saber blurred towards her face, and Caina had no choice but to abandon her attack and raise the valikon in a parry, both hands clenching its hilt.

Her valikon turned the edge of its saber, but the impact drove Caina back with enough force that she lost her balance and fell in the snow. The ardivid stalked after her, raising its saber for the kill.

There was a blur and a flash of white fire, and Kylon landed in front of the ardivid, his valikon hammering down. His sword took of the undead szlacht's arms at the elbow, and both forearms and saber fell uselessly to the ground. The ardivid screamed, the ghostly face twisting in agony, and Kylon's valikon took the creature's head off.

The head rolled away across the snow, and the armored body collapsed with a clang to the ground.

The necromantic aura faded. Caina rolled to one knee, looking back and forth, but she saw no further necromantic auras, and no sorcerous auras save for those around Kylon and Seb.

Her pyrikon folded in on itself, returning to its bracelet form.

Kylon extended a hand, and Caina took it. He pulled her to her feet without the slightest hint of strain. By the Divine, he was strong, even without his water sorcery.

"Are you all right?" said Kylon.

"Yes," said Caina. She let out a long breath, the fear draining away. "A little bruised, but I've had worse."

A shadow moved through the trees, and a new aura blazed before Caina's vision.

She whirled, bringing up her valikon, and for a moment she saw a hooded shadow standing at the foot of a tree, hands tucked into its voluminous sleeves, its cowled head bowed. Caina caught a glimpse of tentacles writhing below the hem of the robe, and something in its crooked posture reminded her of the Temnoti she had seen in the corridors of Sigilsoara.

Then the shadow vanished without a trace, the arcane aura vanishing. It had never really been there, Caina realized. It had been a spell of illusion, a projection.

One of the Temnoti had been watching the fight.

Likely it had been the Syvashar that the undead szlacht had mentioned.

Seb jogged over, armor clanking, and Sophia trailed after him.

"You slew an ardivid," whispered Sophia.

"It was already dead," said Caina.

Sophia let out a strangled sound that was halfway between a laugh and a cough.

"A question," said Seb. "Why was that ardivid looking for you in particular?"

Caina sighed. "I didn't intend it, but I'm afraid I may have put our lives in danger."

CHAPTER NINE

BRONZE WITCH

In the two years since Boyar Vlad Nagrach had died, Sophia Zomanek had known fear.

Vlad Nagrach had been a brutal man, but he had been a predictable one. His taxes had been steep, but so long as they were paid, the boyar's szlachts and officers left the people of the town alone. Criminals had regularly been hanged from the gibbets in the town market, and the penalty for even minor crimes was death, but those who had stayed inside the law had nothing to fear. The boyar had also protected his people. Bandits and highwaymen met a swift and merciless end, and the boyar's szlachts and men-at-arms defended the town when the undead came wandering out of the wilderness. While Vlad Nagrach had not been a pious man, he had respected the Temple, and he had executed anyone caught following the old ways and the teachings of Temnuzash.

Then the old man had died, and his son Razdan became boyar.

With the Empire divided, and the Magisterium's attention turned elsewhere, Razdan had proclaimed his devotion to the old ways. It was said the new boyar and his young szlachts would go into the woods and visit the altars of the Temnoti, learning forbidden secrets. People caught outside at night were killed, sometimes torn apart. Rumors said that Razdan and his men wanted to follow the paths of the ancient Ulkaari nobles, to become the Hounds of the Iron King as their ancestors had been in the days of Rasarion Yagar.

Even if that were not true, Razdan was capricious where his father had been predictable, executing those who displeased him and taking whatever money and goods he wished. In the old days, the men of Kostiv could have appealed to the Imperial Lord Governor for succor, but the Lord Governor had been killed by the Umbarians, and no one had come to take his place. Razdan had the friendship of the Voivode of Vagraastrad, the most powerful pro-Umbarian noble in Ulkaar, and he could do whatever he wished.

All that was bad enough.

But as Sophia grew older, her ability to sense emotions became stronger, no matter how hard she tried to keep it secret. Brother Valexis knew, and he told her that in the old days the Magisterium would have taken her for training, but now they had to keep her abilities secret lest the Umbarians come for her.

And so she sensed the boyar's hungry lust whenever he looked at her.

Another girl would have been flattered. Razdan was handsome and rich and charming when he felt like it. But Sophia's ability meant she sensed the rage and hatred and hunger in his mind, a hunger that only sharpened when his eyes rested on her. More and more Sophia had feared that the boyar would kidnap her and take her to his castle as his unwilling concubine.

Then the boyar's szlachts had announced that Razdan would reinstitute the ancient custom of the Boyar's Hunt...and that Sophia had been one of the seven women chosen for the honor.

Compared to that, Sophia would have preferred to become the boyar's unwilling concubine.

So, Sophia had fled into the forest and stumbled into Sigilsoara, where she had learned a whole new kind of fear.

And then she had met Caina, and for the first time in two years, Sophia felt something other than fear.

Mostly bafflement.

Right now, Caina was kneeling next to the destroyed ardivid, using a scavenged dagger to lever the gemstones from its breastplate one by one.

"We need the money," said Caina as she began searching the destroyed undead. Some of the undead had been carrying ancient pouches of crumbled leather, and the pouches still held some silver and copper coins.

"Is this really the time to be looting corpses?" said Seb in a dry voice.

"Food isn't free," said Caina, taking more coins. "I can always steal what we need, but it's safe and easier to just buy it."

"More honest, too," said Sophia. Somehow, she never imagined the valikarion of ancient legend displaying Caina's streak of ruthless practicality.

"That, too," said Caina, looking at the ardivid's armored corpse. Sophia could barely make herself look at the thing. Ardivids were some of the most dangerous undead of the forests, second only to the vyrkolaki and a few others, and Sophia had never heard of anyone who had defeated one in a fight.

Perhaps Caina really was one of the Arvaltyri of old. Though Sophia had never imagined a valikarion who looked like an Imperial noblewoman.

"Isn't this grave robbing?" said Seb.

Caina grunted as she searched the ardivid's corpse. "I don't think it counts when the occupants of the graves try to kill you without provocation. I think…yes." She took the ardivid's sword belt, which had survived the passage of the centuries without decay, sheathed the saber, and passed the belt to her husband. "We'll get a good price for those if we're smart about it. I'll pry the jewels out of the armor. It's too heavy to take with us."

Kylon nodded and slung the sword belt over his shoulder.

Sophia was not quite sure what to make of Kylon and Caina. Brother Valexis had said a wife ought to obey her husband, but more often than not, Caina told Kylon what to do. On the other hand, on the infrequent occasions when Kylon told Caina to do something, she did it immediately. Perhaps he simply trusted her judgment as much as he trusted his own, and she trusted him in turn.

Sophia wondered if her own mother and father had been like that.

"Are not the jewels cursed?" said Sophia. "The szlacht was cursed to rise as an undead. Maybe the jewels will be cursed as well."

Caina shook her head. "No. There are no sorcerous auras on the gems."

"Trust me, she would know," said Kylon.

Caina flashed him a smile and resumed prying out gemstones. "But it's only fair that we split this four ways, I think. If you sell your share properly, Sophia, you'll have enough money to last at least a few years." She glanced at Sophia and then went back to her work. "Enough to get far away from Kostiv, if you want."

Sophia swallowed. Maybe the boyar would find her wherever she went. He had friends in the Umbarian Order. Maybe if the Umbarians defeated the Emperor, they would find Sophia and give her as a present to Razdan Nagrach.

"Once you have finished looting," said Seb, "perhaps you can explain just how you have placed our lives in danger." He gave the ardivid's head a kick, and it rolled away. "Other than the immediate dangers that threaten us, of course."

"Of course," said Caina, her voice just as dry as his. Sophia was struck by the resemblance between them. It was obvious that they were siblings, and strange that they had never met before Sigilsoara.

But perhaps Caina's mother had been someone like Razdan Nagrach.

A few moments they returned to the campfire.

"I didn't want to tell you this," said Caina, "since I suspect the knowledge is dangerous..."

"And you weren't sure," said Seb, "how I would react?"

Caina shrugged. "Can you blame me? My experiences with the Magisterium have not been pleasant in the past."

"Neither have mine," said Seb, "and I am a brother of the Magisterium. But to employ a metaphor that Lord Kylon would appreciate, we are all in this ship together, so it seems we must row together or sink together."

"Very well," said Caina. "While we were in Sigilsoara, I found out what the Umbarians wanted. I think it is a sorcerous relic of Rasarion Yagar."

Sophia shivered. All her life, the Iron King had been a legend of fear and dread. The Warmaiden had slain him long ago, but his creatures still haunted the forest...and Boyar Razdan wished to become one of his Hounds.

"Oh." Seb sighed. "And you took it with you."

"It was either that," said Caina, reaching into a pocket of the red coat, "or leave it behind for the Umbarians to find."

She drew out something. Sophia blinked in surprise, peering at the object. It was a man's heavy signet ring, but it was made from gray iron instead of gold or silver. It did have a stone, a massive emerald that glittered in the firelight, and the emerald had been carved into the shape of a roaring dragon...

Sophia's breath hissed through her teeth.

"That is his ring," she said. "That is the Ring of Rasarion Yagar."

"Dear gods," said Seb, as astonished as she had yet seen him.

"Why didn't you leave that evil thing in Sigilsoara?" said Sophia, horrified.

"Because," said Caina, still calm. "If I had, the Umbarians would have found it. And judging from your reaction, this is something the Umbarians should never have."

"No," said Seb. "And I know the Umbarians better than you do. You cannot imagine the kind of horror they could wreak."

"Do I not?" said Caina, those cold eyes glittering. "Because I have seen the kind of horrors the Umbarians have wreaked. Kylon and I killed Cassander Nilas, but before we did, he almost defeated us. An assassin he hired stabbed me in the back, and I barely survived. Cassander almost worked a spell that killed every man, woman, and child in Istarinmul. A million people, nearly burned to ashes, all so the Umbarian fleet could pass through the Starfall Straits and destroy the Empire."

"Perhaps I have not seen destruction on such a scale, my lady," said Seb. His eyes glittered in the same way as Caina's, like disks of blue ice. "But I spent years looking over my shoulder for an assassin's blade, lest the Umbarians kill me for refusing them. After they had declared themselves openly, I fought them openly. I have seen their Dead Legion, their cataphracti, their mutants and elemental spirits and all the other horrors they have called up. I have seen the slaughtered villages, the towns burned to ashes, the entire nations reduced to slavery. I fear I know the Umbarians just as well as you do."

For a moment, they stared at each other. It wasn't quite a glare, but it was close.

"So, you're just saying you both hate the Umbarian Order," said Sophia.

Kylon laughed. "Gods, the girl has the truth of it."

"If I had left the Ring behind," said Caina, "the Umbarians would have gotten it."

"You're right," said Seb. "The Umbarians cannot have this. Not for any reason."

"Then throw the evil thing away," said Sophia. Despite the heat from the fire, she shivered. "There are lakes and streams near Kostiv. Throw it into the waters and let it never see the sunlight again. Or wait until you get to the Inner Sea and throw it into the depths."

"We can't, I'm afraid," said Seb. "That ring will give off a powerful necromantic aura. I suspect the only reason that Lord Kylon and I are not overwhelmed by its presence is that it is in physical contact with a valikarion. If you dropped it on the ground or into the water, I expect every sorcerer for a dozen miles would sense it at once."

"Aye," said Caina. "I saw a shadow with that ardivid and its undead. I think it was a projection spell, that one of the Temnoti was watching the fight from a distance. If we leave it here, the Temnoti will take it, and I think that might be as bad as if the Umbarians claimed it."

"Then what do you suggest we do with the thing?" said Seb.

"We will take it to Iramis," said Caina. "In the Towers of Lore, the loremasters have secured many dangerous relics behind powerful wards. This Ring can be one more of them." She shrugged. "Of course, I doubt you'll want to travel all the way to Iramis. You'll probably need to return to duty with the Legions once we get past Artifel."

"I will," said Seb. He hesitated. "Though I will be obliged to report this to my superiors in the Magisterium and the Legion."

Caina shrugged. "Report anything you want. The Ring is going to Iramis where it can't hurt anyone."

Sophia looked back and forth between them. "What...what should I do? I can't go back to Kostiv. The boyar...Boyar Razdan will kill me for stealing his sunstone." Of course, that was a lie. The sunstone belonged to Sophia, had belonged to her since she had been a child. Razdan Nagrach would not give a damn if anyone stole a sunstone.

But Caina and Kylon were both nobles. Caina was even the adoptive sister of the Padishah of Istarinmul if she was telling the truth. Nobles looked out for each other. Granted, Sophia was technically a noble as well, which was why she simply couldn't join the Temple, since nobles could not take the Temple's vows. But if

Caina and Kylon knew the truth about why Sophia had fled, perhaps they would side with Razdan and insist that Sophia return for the Boyar's Hunt.

"You can do whatever you wish," said Caina. "I don't have any authority over you. But if you want, you can come with us to Iramis, to be trained by the loremasters of the Towers of Lore."

"Why would they want to train me?" said Sophia.

"Dear child," said Seb, "you might have been able to hide the truth from those in Kostiv, but I am afraid it will be much harder to conceal it from us. You have sorcerous talent, do you not? Some degree of water sorcery. Likely you can sense my emotions right now."

Sophia hesitated. "Brother Valexis in the Temple in Kostiv knows. So does my Uncle Ivan. No one else does. I've kept it a secret from everyone else."

"At some point," said Caina, "it will become obvious. You're...fifteen?" Sophia nodded. "As you get older, it will grow more powerful, and you will need training before you hurt yourself or someone else. If you stay in Ulkaar, sooner or later you'll get recruited into either the Magisterium or the Umbarians."

"I don't want anything to do with either one," said Sophia. She realized that might have been the wrong thing to say. "No offense, Lord Sebastian."

Seb snorted. "Sometimes I wish I never heard of the magi, and I am a brother of the Magisterium. But if you do not join the magi or the Umbarians, worse people might find you. There are many petty necromancers in Ulkaar who desire apprentices, and the various cults of the Temnoti might seek you out."

"No!" said Sophia. "I don't want anything to do with those people or the old ways. I am a daughter of the Temple, not Temnuzash." She looked at Caina. "But are the loremasters any better?"

"They are," said Caina. "I have often been...cynical about sorcerers, I will admit. And that cynicism is often justified." Seb snorted but did not protest. "But the loremasters are better than most. Their Words of Lore are devoted to healing, defense, and knowledge, and they cannot use their spells to hurt living mortals. If you went to Iramis, they could teach you to control your abilities, and you would be safe from the boyar of Kostiv there."

"Truly, my lady?" said Sophia. "You would take me with you?" It seemed too good to be true. Iramis had burned long ago, all men knew that. Yet if Caina really was friends with the Padishah of Istarinmul, and if Iramis had really returned...maybe Sophia could go somewhere where Razdan Nagrach could not reach her.

"Yes," said Caina. "I warn you, the training would not be easy, and it is a long journey from here to Iramis. But if you are willing, you can come with us."

Sophia shrugged. "Life is never easy. And this is Ulkaar. We are used to hardship here."

"Good," said Caina. She put the Ring back into her pocket. "That's settled, then. We'll get supplies at Kostiv, making sure no one there recognizes Sophia, and then continue to Risiviri and take ship to Artifel from there. Before we go back to sleep, though, I do have one question for both of you."

"Certainly," said Seb, and Sophia nodded.

"What is the Ring of Rasarion Yagar supposed to do?" said Caina.

Sophia blinked. "Do?"

"It must do something," said Caina. "It has powerful necromantic spells upon it. Yagar must have created it for a reason."

"In the old tales, it is said that the Ring of the Iron King gave him authority over all undead," said Sophia, "and that when demons from the netherworld beheld its power, they bowed down before him and carried out his will."

"In the histories," said Seb, "Rasarion Yagar created several enspelled objects of great power with the aid of his Temnoti. I believe there were five – his sword, his dagger, his diadem, his amulet, and his ring, presumably the ring you found in Sigilsoara. There are constant rumors that one or another has been found. I think the last time I was in Risiviri, you could equip an entire Imperial Legion all the genuine Swords of the Iron King sold by enterprising street peddlers."

"Whatever the Ring does," said Caina, "it won't be able to do it once it is secure within the Towers of Lore. We ought to get some more sleep before dawn."

"I'll take the watch this time," said Kylon.

"I'll get some more wood for the fire," said Caina.

Sophia followed her. "I'll help."

Together they gathered more branches and carried them to the fire, feeding the flames. Sophia looked at Caina, her emotions twisting inside her chest. Could Caina keep that promise? Could Sophia really come with her to Iramis?

Perhaps she would become a loremaster of Iramis, just as the Warmaiden herself had been in ancient days.

For the first time in two years, Sophia Zomanek started to feel a flicker of hope.

But only a flicker. They were still close to Kostiv and within the power of Razdan Nagrach.

If Razdan and his szlachts truly thought to become the Boyar's Hunt…they would not let her go without a fight.

The next morning, they ate a breakfast of cold venison, covered the ashes of their campfire, and continued southwest. As they walked, the road was in better repair, and Caina saw signs of regular passage. Likely the townsfolk of Kostiv came this far north to hunt and trap and harvest lumber. Caina kept watch, seeking for both movement in the trees and signs of sorcerous auras. If the Temnoti and the Syvashar were hunting for the Ring, Caina doubted they would give up after a single failure.

But she saw no sign of anyone else.

Sophia said they would reach Kostiv in the afternoon, and Caina pondered how best to approach the town and obtain the supplies they needed. As they walked, she questioned Sophia at length about Kostiv, and Sophia answered with bemusement. About three and a half thousand people lived in Kostiv. The town had a stone wall twelve feet high to keep out bandits and undead. The wall had gates in the north and the south, and the gates were always guarded. Brother Valexis maintained the town's Temple to the Divine with the help of a few part-time acolytes. A man named Magur was the burgomaster of the town (Seb explained the office was a bit like an urban prefect in the Empire), and while Magur hated the boyar, he would obey Razdan Nagrach for fear of his life. The burgomaster had some full-time sergeants in his employ to keep the peace, but all the men of fighting age of the town could be roused to form a militia in an emergency. The boyar's castle was several miles west of the town, on a hill overlooking the forests and the cleared fields outside of Kostiv's walls.

Caina would want to look for herself, but as she considered Sophia's answers, she decided that the original plan was likely best. She would wait with Sophia in the forest while Kylon and Seb went into Kostiv to purchase supplies. Given that the boyar was friendly with the Umbarian Order, Seb could masquerade as an Umbarian battle magus and Kylon as his bodyguard. Once Seb and Kylon returned with food and supplies, they could depart, and by the time the boyar realized that an "Umbarian" had visited his town, Caina and the others would be long gone.

Sophia was still unwilling to talk about what had driven her from the town, but Caina suspected that Boyar Razdan had wanted her for something. Either it was for the usual reason a nobleman wanted to abduct a pretty girl, or perhaps the boyar had realized she had arcane talent and wanted to make a present of her to the Umbarians.

Either way, Caina hoped to help Sophia escape the fate the boyar had planned for her.

"After we pass Kostiv," said Kylon, "what will be our best path?"

"Through the city of Vagraastrad and then to Risiviri," said Seb. "The Voivode of Vagraastrad is quite friendly to the Umbarians, alas, so we shall have to keep a low profile. The Boyar of Risiviri is openly pro-Imperial, and from there it should be easy to hire a ship to take us to Artifel."

Kylon frowned. "Won't the Umbarians have ships on the Inner Sea?"

"And on the Narrow Sea, and the entirety of the Alqaarin Sea," said Seb. "I'm afraid the Empire doesn't yet have enough ships to contest them. As I recall, you destroyed most the Empire's western fleet a few years ago." Sophia gave Kylon a startled look. "So, the Umbarians have a far stronger naval force in the seas of the eastern Empire. That said, it is hard for them to get ships past the defenses of Artifel. I doubt we will encounter many Umbarians on the Inner Sea. From Artifel, you can make your way through the Disali Highlands to Malarae with ease."

"I've never been to the Disali Highlands," said Kylon.

"I have." Caina frowned with the memory. "It was just about six years ago. There was a chieftain and his mistress, and she found this enspelled dagger the Ashbringers of old had left..."

In the distance, in the trees, she saw the sudden glow of an arcane aura.

"Wait a minute," said Caina, coming to a stop. The others halted around her. "I see something ahead."

"I don't see anything," said Seb, hand grasping his sword hilt.

"Kylon?" said Caina. "Do you sense anything?"

The steady glow of the arcane aura was coming nearer.

Kylon concentrated, and Caina saw the pale blue-silver glow as he used a spell of water sorcery. "I'm not...yes. There is something approaching. I think it's someone wrapped in a warding spell. I can't sense their emotions."

"Just one?" said Caina.

"I think so," said Kylon. "A single sorcerer, probably."

"Maybe an ambitious Temnoti," said Caina. "Or an Umbarian."

"Or another brother or sister of the Magisterium," said Seb.

"That could be just as bad," said Caina.

Seb grimaced but conceded the point with a nod.

"I think he's coming right up the road," said Kylon.

"Then let's wait here to greet him," said Caina, looking to the southwest. Ahead the road twisted slightly, moving around a stand of barren trees and a pile of tumbled boulders, perhaps the wreckage of a long-fallen watch tower. Through the pile of stones and the trunk of the trees, Caina saw the approaching glow of a warding spell. Caina braced herself but did not call her valikon to her hand. If the approaching sorcerer proved to be hostile, she wanted to be ready to fight, but she would prefer it if the sorcerer underestimated her.

It was useful to be underestimated.

She heard the faint rasp of boots against the frozen road and the tap of a cane or staff.

A moment later the figure came into sight, and Caina blinked in surprise.

Whatever she had been expecting, this had not been it.

A towering figure walked towards her, standing nearly seven feet tall. The shape looked vaguely female and wore a heavy brown dress of rough material beneath a long, tattered gray cloak, the massive cowl concealing the woman's face. The left hand and arm were hidden beneath the heavy cloak. The woman's right hand was gnarled and thick and age-spotted and clutched a twisted wooden staff with a peculiar sheen to it.

No, the staff wasn't wooden – it was made of bronze, corroded and green with age, though shiny spots still showed here and there. To Caina's eyes, it gave off a faint glow of sorcerous power, a glow that wrapped around the woman and sheathed her in a warding spell.

Caina heard Sophia's startled inhalation of breath.

"No," said Seb, amazed. "It cannot be."

The woman hobbled towards them, the cracked leather of her boots rasping against the ground.

"Do you know her?" said Caina.

"The Bronze Witch," breathed Sophia.

"Who is that?" said Caina.

Seb's eyes were fixed on the approaching figure. "A legend."

"It is said that the Bronze Witch roams the forests of Ulkaar," said Sophia in a small, frightened voice. "If travelers are kind to her, she gives them blessings and gifts. If travelers are cruel to her, the Witch unveils her power and gives them riddles. If they answer the riddles, she lets them live. If they fail…she eats them alive."

"I have already seen Sigilsoara and the Ring of Rasarion Yagar," said Seb. "What is one more legend out of the deeps of the past?"

The woman stopped and let out a cracking, croaking sound, her head still bowed. It took Caina a moment to realize that she was laughing.

"Tut, tut, tut, children," said the old woman in Caerish with a thick, near-impenetrable Ulkaari accent. "Talking about your elders in front of them." She lifted her face and gazed at them. "It is most impolite."

Caina blinked in surprise. The shadows remained gathered in the old woman's cowl, concealing most of her face. Yet enough light penetrated the hood that Caina could see shape of the lined, ancient face, could see the old woman's teeth.

They, liked her staff, were made of corroded bronze.

"Greetings," said Caina. "We were unaware that you spoke Caerish."

"Well, I do, dear girl, I do," said the old woman. She hobbled closer a few steps and stopped as if the effort had exhausted her. "Young people are so overconfident these days."

"Are…are you the Bronze Witch, ma'am?" said Sophia, her eyes still wide.

"Oh, they call me that," said the Witch, her shadowed face turning towards Sophia. "But that is one of the nicer things they call me, come to think of it. I suppose you can call me that too, if you like. But people collect names as they get older." The cowl turned towards Caina. "Your friend, for instance, is called the Balarigar in some places."

"You've heard of me, then?" said Caina.

"Oh, yes. I hear people speaking the tales of the Balarigar in the taverns of Risiviri."

"Then you've heard bad things, then," said Caina.

The Witch cackled again. "Well. It's so hard to tell the truth and so easy to repeat a lie, isn't it? Rumors spread like weeds and choke out the truth. I heard one rumor that a valikarion had returned to Ulkaar, that she had taken the Ring of Rasarion Yagar from Sigilsoara, and the Temnoti were interested in finding her."

"One cannot believe everything that one hears," said Caina.

"One cannot," said the Witch. "Why, the tales I have heard of the Balarigar are almost as unbelievable as the things they say about me, and those are only mostly true."

Caina stared at the old woman. The Bronze Witch might have been a fearsome legend among the Ulkaari, but Caina had her doubts. The aura of power around the Witch was nowhere near as strong as those around the Temnoti she had seen in Sigilsoara. The woman in the cloak had some sorcerous power, but Caina suspected not very much. And it was possible to achieve the rough voice through practice and the ragged appearance with makeup and changes in stance.

Caina ought to know. She had done it herself many times.

Someone was putting on a performance for them. But why?

"I don't know if you'll believe this," said Caina, "but we don't want any trouble, and we shall be happy to leave you in peace if you return the favor."

Again the old woman cackled. "And I never want any trouble either, but trouble finds me nonetheless."

"Well," said Caina, "you'll get not trouble from us."

"And if I desire to give you trouble?" said the Witch.

"If you do," said Caina, glancing at Kylon. "You see the sword he has. If you really are the Bronze Witch," the old woman chuckled, while Sophia blinked, "then you'll know that no sorcerer has a defense against a sword like that. I think it is in everyone's best interest, especially yours, if no one starts a fight."

"You mean his valikon will tear through my wards and strike me down, the wicked old sinner that I am?" said the Witch. "Well, it would. I never thought to see a valikon in the hands of a Kyracian stormdancer, but stranger things have happened. But I do not wish to start a fight with you, Balarigar and Arvaltyr. Merely to share news."

"Oh," said Caina. "And what news is that, if I might ask?"

"You may not seek trouble," said the Witch, "but while you carry the Ring of Rasarion Yagar, trouble will seek you. Many people desire that evil thing, and you would do well to keep it from them."

"That is what I intend," said Caina.

"And you," said the Witch, "have brought trouble on their heads, haven't you?"

Caina frowned, wondering what that meant, and then realized that the Bronze Witch had been speaking to Sophia.

Sophia shrank away from the old woman's shadowed gaze. "I don't...I don't understand."

"You understand perfectly well, child," said the Witch. "You know the real reason you fled Kostiv. Have you told your new friends? Or were you planning on waiting until the trouble caught up to you all?"

"I just want to get away from Kostiv," said Sophia. "I don't want to hurt anyone. I just want to get far away from the town."

"No, dear child," said the Witch. "You wanted to get away from the boyar and his szlachts. You wanted to get away from what they had become."

"Sophia?" said Caina.

Sophia said nothing, her face tight with fear. She suddenly reminded Caina of a deer caught motionless by the approach of a wolf.

"Balarigar," said the Witch, and there was a sudden urgency in that rough voice. "Listen to me. You are about to be in great danger."

"More than I already am?" said Caina.

"More immediate, let us say," said the Witch. "I will give you this piece of advice." She leveled her bronze staff, pointing it east. "Directly east of here, about a mile away, is a place called a Sanctuary Stone."

"What?" said Seb, astonished. "One of the Warmaiden's Sanctuaries is here?"

"Yes," said the Witch. "Nadezhda scattered them far and wide across Ulkaar for the protection of her people from the Iron King's servants. Many of them are still in use, but some have been forgotten. Save by me, of course. One such Stone is a mile east of this road."

"What is a Sanctuary Stone?" said Caina.

"A relic of the Warmaiden," said Seb. "But a beneficial one. When she returned from Iramis to overthrow the Iron King, she planted them across Ulkaar, dozens of them. The stones give off a warding spell, and no undead can enter within the radius of the ward.

They are still widely used today, and rural inns and villages have been built around them."

"Yes," said the Witch. "And you shall need that protection shortly. The boyar's szlachts are coming to claim Sophia...and the worse things within the szlachts. They will kill you and take the girl if they can. Perhaps the Stone will help protect you. Perhaps you truly are a valikarion, and you will fight them off. Or maybe they will kill you." The shoulders shrugged beneath the massive cloak. "We shall find out soon, will we not? If you are victorious, Balarigar, we shall speak again."

There was a surge of arcane power from the staff, and the Bronze Witch vanished from sight. Caina blinked. The Bronze Witch hadn't turned invisible or used an illusion spell to vanish. If she had, the vision of the valikarion would have let Caina see through the spell. Instead, the Witch had somehow used sorcery to transport herself away.

"That was...unsettling, to say the least," said Seb.

Kylon shook his head. "Was that truly the Bronze Witch, do you think? Or someone playing the part?"

"Someone playing the part," said Caina.

On the other hand, there really had been a Moroaica, and there really had been a Red Huntress.

"It was her," whispered Sophia. "It was her. She knew the truth."

"What do you mean?" said Caina.

She met Caina's gaze, tears starting in her eyes. "I'm so sorry."

Caina started to ask a question, and then the sounds of howls rang over the frozen forest.

CHAPTER TEN

MAVROKHI

Kylon did not like or trust oracles.

That said, the Surge, the oracle of the Kyracian people, had given him a useful ability.

She had given him the power to sense the presence of spirits from the netherworld. At first, he had thought the ability had been limited to the nagataaru. Later, Kylon had realized he could sense the presence of any spirit of the netherworld that made its way to the material world, and there were countless different kinds of spirits. They organized themselves into kingdoms and orders and empires as mortals did, and most of the spirits of the netherworld were indifferent to humans and the material world.

Some were not. Some preyed upon mortals. The nagataaru did. The ifriti spirits that Cassander Nilas had summoned also preyed upon mortals.

Kylon had never before sensed the spirits that now approached them, but they were just as malevolent as the nagataaru and just as furious as the ifriti. Yet there was something...bestial about them, something that made him think of rabid animals. The nagataaru had been cold and sadistic, creatures that gorged themselves on pain. The ifriti were all hunger, burning with the desire to consume the world in their flames.

These spirits were also hungry, and they desired to rend and tear and kill, to feast on their victims...

"Kylon?"

Caina grabbed his arm.

Her emotions suddenly flooded through his arcane sense. He felt the layer of ice in her mind, the cold calculation that her training and experiences as a Ghost had imparted to her. Kylon also sensed her fear. She was mostly frightened for him, and the howls that rang around them were inspiring that fear.

Those howls almost sounded like wolves.

"Those aren't wolves," said Seb.

"Are they?" said Caina. "I don't think I've ever heard wolves howl before."

"I have." Seb's emotional sense grew grim and hard as he drew his sword. "Wolves don't sound like this. The howls are too deep. Whatever they are, they aren't wolves."

"No," said Kylon. "They're spirits."

"Spirits?" said Caina.

"I've never sensed them before," said Kylon. "They're like...animals, rabid animals..."

"Mavrokhi," said Sophia.

The girl's voice was calm, glassy calm, but her sense was pure, unbroken terror.

"Mavrokhi?" said Caina.

"Impossible," said Seb. "They were all exterminated by the Magisterium years ago..."

"What the hell is a mavrokh?" said Caina.

"The Hounds of the Iron King," said Sophia, still in that brittle voice. "His wolves and his hunters. They're coming for me. I'm sorry. I brought them to you. I should have told you the truth. I should have let the Temnoti kill me. I..."

"Sophia, stop talking," said Caina. "Kylon, how far away are they?"

"Not far," said Kylon. The malevolent spirits were just at the edge of his senses. "A third of a mile, maybe half a mile away. They're not moving fast, and they're spread out."

"A hunting pack," said Seb. "They'll start circling and try to surround us."

"That Sanctuary Stone the Bronze Witch mentioned," said Kylon.

Seb frowned. "Do you think she was lying? She might have been working with the mavrokhi. This Sanctuary Stone might be a trap."

"It might be," said Caina, "but if those spirits catch us, they'll find they caught more than they wanted." She gestured, and her valikon sprang into existence in her right hand. "These can destroy spirits. That might make the mavrokhi change their minds. We'll run east."

"Leave me behind," said Sophia. "It's me they want. It's…"

"No." Caina grabbed Sophia's shoulder and spun her to the east, and some of the girl's fear eased. "Run! Move!"

They ran from the road and into the trees to the east, the deep howls ringing behind them.

Caina darted through the trees as fast as she could, looking back to make sure the others were keeping pace. She also wanted to make sure that Sophia did not fall behind. The girl had the blank, empty expression of someone facing certain and irrevocable doom. Perhaps the boyar's creatures had been coming for Sophia, but Caina refused to leave the girl for them.

They ran through the trees, the snow crunching beneath their boots. Caina wished they could have concealed their tracks, but the snow made that impossible. And if these Hounds of the Iron King were anything like real hounds, they might have the same keen sense of smell.

The howls rang again, deep and cold and malevolent. Just listening to them made all the hair on the back of Caina's neck stand on end, made a wave of fear roll through her gut. She had never suffered any particular fear of animals, but listening to those awful howls made her understand why some people were terrified of dogs and wolves.

Because those creatures were hunting for her, and she heard the hungry rage in those howls.

"It sounds like they're getting closer," said Seb, jumping over a tangled root, his armor clattering as he did. He wasn't even breathing hard yet. Evidently, the training of a battle magus had left him in good physical condition.

"They are," said Kylon, his voice hard with concentration and strain. The valikon in his right hand swirled with freezing mist. "But not by much. They're just following us."

"Can you tell how many?" said Seb.

"Five to seven, I think," said Kylon.

"Likely they are driving us," said Caina. But to where, though? An ambush? Caina wanted to ask Sophia more, but the girl was breathing hard, her whole attention turned towards running.

"It depends if this Bronze Witch was helping us or leading us into a trap," said Kylon.

Caina didn't know, but she suspected the Witch had been at least attempting to help them. If she had wanted to betray them, she could have simply kept talking until the mavrokhi arrived. Or she could have said nothing at all and remained hidden, watching from concealment as the mavrokhi attacked.

"She told us about the Sanctuary Stone," said Caina.

"She could have been lying," said Seb. "Or she could have been pretending to be the Bronze Witch. Children in Ulkaar are told tales of the Bronze Witch to frighten them into behaving…"

"It was her!" said Sophia, wheezing as she ran. "She knew the truth. She knew my heart. I'm sorry, I..."

"Keep going!" said Caina. She dodged around another root and kept running.

Kylon cursed. "There are two more of those spirits ahead."

"Then they are herding us," said Seb.

Caina opened her mouth to suggest they change direction, and then she saw the glow.

It was invisible to her eyes of flesh, but it was clear as daylight to the vision of the valikarion. It was the glow of an Iramisian warding spell, an old and strong one, and it was right ahead of them.

"I can see the Sanctuary Stone!" said Caina. "Straight ahead! Keep running!"

A chorus of those deep, unnatural howls rang out, sending a chill down her spine. The fear also gave her strength, and she forced her legs to further speed.

Then the forest opened into a clearing, and Caina saw the Sanctuary Stone.

Caina had not known what to expect. Based on Seb's description of the Warmaiden, she expected perhaps a crumbling Iramisian tower. Maybe it would look like a smaller version of Silent Ash Temple in the Kaltari Highlands.

Instead, she ran into a half-overgrown garden.

Caina stopped, looking around in surprise, the others halting around her. A frozen pond dominated the clearing. A small island stood in the center of the pond, and from it rose an obelisk of white stone about twenty feet tall. Iramisian characters had been carved on all four sides, and Caina recognized the symbols of warding and protection. The symbols glowed, giving off a pale white light. Barren bushes stood around the pond, separated by paths of flat flagstones. Time had taken its toll on the garden, and the flagstones were cracked and worn. Yet this had clearly been a garden, planted by someone with skill and an eye for beauty.

A powerful warding spell had been placed on the obelisk, and it radiated out to cover most of the clearing and the garden.

"I'll be damned," said Seb. "A Sanctuary Stone of the Warmaiden, here in the wilds of northern Ulkaar. I wonder why it was forgotten."

"Maybe it doesn't work properly," said Kylon. He looked at Caina. "Do you think the spell will keep these mavrokh things at bay?"

"I don't know," said Caina, looking at the light radiating from the obelisk. "It's a warding spell of the Words of Lore. I saw Annarah use something similar. I don't think it will stop a malevolent spirit, but the spell will hinder them." She turned to Seb, who stood with his sword ready, his eyes scanning the trees around the clearing. "Just what is a mavrokh?"

"A human possessed by a mavrokh spirit," said Seb.

Caina shared a look with Kylon. They had encountered humans possessed by malevolent spirits before.

The Red Huntress had almost killed them both.

"Is a mavrokh like a nagataaru?" said Caina.

"A what?" said Seb. "I've never heard the word nagataaru, I fear."

"Fine," said Caina. Another chorus of howls rang out from the trees. Sophia shivered and stepped back, her eyes darting back and forth. "Then what can you tell me about the mavrokhi?"

"The Hounds of the Iron King," said Sophia.

"They were one of Rasarion Yagar's creations," said Seb. "He summoned bestial spirits from the netherworld and bound them into his szlachts. The szlachts gained the ability to shapeshift and become wolf-like creatures, though far larger and faster than any natural wolf. The Ulkaari called these spirits the mavrokhi, and the name also came to apply to the Hounds themselves." He shook his head. "But the mavrokhi are extinct. The witch hunters of the Temple wiped them out long ago. Sometimes the petty necromancers or the followers of the

Temnoti figure out how to transform themselves into mavrokhi, and the Magisterium kills them."

"But the Magisterium is occupied with the civil war," said Caina, looking at Sophia, "and Boyar Razdan and his friends are interested in the old ways, aren't they?

Sophia said nothing but gave a miserable nod.

"Here they come," said Kylon. "Get behind me."

Caina stepped behind Kylon, her valikon in hand, Sophia shivering next to her. Seb came to Kylon's side, sword in hand, and she saw the auras as both men prepared spells for battle. Caina held her valikon ready, the blade burning white, the Iramisian sigils glowing. She didn't see any sorcerous auras in the trees as the mavrokhi approached. That didn't mean anything, though. The Red Huntress hadn't been able to use sorcery, but the nagataaru-possessed assassin had been one of the most dangerous enemies Caina had ever encountered.

Another chorus of those blood-freezing howls rang out, and she heard something heavy crashing through the trees. She saw dark shapes blurring between the trunks, and glimpsed something massive and covered in black fur.

Then the noises and the howls stopped.

"They've seen us," said Kylon. "I think they're trying to decide what to do."

Caina nodded, her mind racing. That proved the mavrokhi, whatever they were, were not mindless beasts. She supposed wolves would have either come right at them or circled around the clearing to surround them. Caina waited. Once again, she wished she had throwing knives, though she didn't know if the weapons would have been of any use against the mavrokhi.

The trees started rustling again, and a group of seven men entered the clearing, stopping at the edge of the light from the Sanctuary Stone.

They looked like young noblemen, and they wore dark clothing, heavy jackets lined with fur and long cloaks edged with wolf fur, their boots spattered with mud. All seven noblemen carried swords and daggers at their belts. They look like a group of young nobles out for a hunt. But hunters would have been mounted, and none of the men carried bows or arrows.

"They're possessed," said Kylon in Caerish. "All seven of them. I can sense the spirits. They're...not pleasant."

One of the men stepped forward. He was somewhere in his thirties, with slicked-back black hair and a drooping mustache styled like the statues of the Iron King that Caina had seen in Sigilsoara. The man walked into the area of the warding spell, grimacing a little, but shook off the effect.

He looked at Sophia and grinned, and she flinched.

"Sophia Zomanek," said the nobleman, and he said something in Ulkaari that made Sophia go white.

"What did he say?" said Caina.

Seb frowned. "He said that he looks forward to experiencing her with both the senses of touch and taste."

"Your friends speak the trader's language, it seems," said the nobleman in Caerish, looking at Kylon, Seb, and Caina with undisguised disdain. "Then perhaps they ought to learn that tradesmen ought not to interfere with their betters."

"Who are you?" said Caina in Caerish.

The nobleman laughed at her. "Will the woman speak for the men?" He smirked at Sophia. "How pathetic you are. You run from the honor offered you, and hide behind a foreign woman."

"If we are to have the honor of addressing our betters," said Caina, "then perhaps we should know who they are."

The nobleman stared at her. Despite his bluster and sneer, his eyes were cold and hard, the eyes of a man accustomed to killing. And she could tell the burning valikons that she and Kylon carried made him uneasy. Likely he had planned to simply rush Sophia with his friends, but caution had stayed his hand. Even if he did not recognize the valikons, it was possible the malevolent spirit in his head would, and the mavrokh would be whispering counsels of caution.

"After all," said Caina, "this is very strange, isn't it?"

The nobleman scoffed. "What do you mean?"

"You came out here to capture the girl, didn't you?" said Caina. "You thought she would be alone, and that you could run her down with ease. Instead, you found her standing at a Sanctuary Stone of the Warmaiden, in the company of a battle magus," she nodded at Seb, "and a Kyracian stormdancer." She nodded toward her husband.

"And you, Nighmarian," said the nobleman. His voice and face sneered, but his eyes were as cold as the frozen forest around him. "Whoever you are."

"Whoever I am," said Caina with a smile. She took a few steps forward, the valikon held low in her right hand. Kylon and Seb shifted, and so did the Ulkaari noblemen, but their leader remained motionless. "So. Who are you to threaten us?"

"My name," said the nobleman, "is Rudjak, and I am a szlacht sworn to Razdan Nagrach, the boyar of Kostiv."

"This is foolishness, Rudjak," snarled another nobleman. "Kill them and take the girl. The boyar is not patient…"

"Silence, Varlov," snapped Rudjak. "The boyar gave me this task, not you. And only a fool rushes forward without surveying the ground." His eyes turned back to Caina. "Now. Who are you?"

"We are simply messengers," said Caina. "By accident, our path took us to this region of Ulkaar, and we are returning home. While finding our way back to the road, we came across the girl, and she asked to travel with us. We accepted."

Rudjak grunted. "You sound Imperial."

"So I'm told," said Caina. "I could use another accent if you like."

"Then do you support the Umbarians?" said Rudjak. "Or are you loyalists of the Empire?"

"To be blunt," said Caina, "I have been exiled from the Empire, and the Umbarians want me dead. I'm not terribly welcome anywhere."

Rudjak barked a harsh laugh. "A clever answer. The common fate of bearers of bad news, I suppose. Then what is your business in Ulkaar?"

"I have no business in Ulkaar," said Caina. "Our errand is elsewhere. We want to leave as quickly as possible. We don't wish any trouble with you or your boyar. Let us pass through your lands, and you'll never hear from us again."

Rudjak considered this. "We live in troubled times. The Emperor and the Umbarians battle against each other, and those who are unprepared will find themselves destroyed. Perhaps it would be for the best to allow you and your...bodyguards to pass unharmed through the boyar's lands."

"Rudjak!" said Varlov.

"The boyar has no need of further enemies," said Rudjak with irritation. "And the Voivode will be furious if we provoke hostilities with another power, especially while he contests with that idiot in Risiviri."

Caina kept the surprise from her face. It seemed that Rudjak had concluded that she and Kylon and Seb were emissaries from either the Empire or the Umbarians, and had no wish to draw the attention of either power. Perhaps Caina could bluff her way out of this yet.

"The boyar will soon be strong enough to destroy his enemies!" said Varlov. "No one can stop us. The old ways are coming back. The old powers are awakening. Soon both the Emperor and the Umbarians will bow to the true ruler of Ulkaar, and we shall stand at his right hand!" He glared at Caina. "I say we kill the two men and take the girl and the woman both back with us. We can listen to her scream when she joins the Boyar's Hunt." He looked at Caina and licked his lips. "I would enjoy that."

Caina looked at Sophia, but the girl had gone rigid with fear. Kylon's face was a cold mask. If it came to a fight, he was probably going to kill Varlov first.

Just what was the Boyar's Hunt?

"Shut up, Varlov," said Rudjak. The two men glared at each other for a moment, and then Varlov looked away, muttering under his breath.

"We seem to have provoked a disagreement," said Caina.

"Disagreement is irrelevant," said Rudjak, his glare turning back towards her. "The boyar gave me this task, and my men will obey my orders. But that is not your concern, just as Ulkaar is not your concern. The boyar has enough enemies, and he will not thank us for earning him new ones. I am prepared to let you and your companions go unharmed, provided you leave at once and do not return."

Caina nodded. "And what price will you ask for this?"

"No price," said Rudjak. "Simply go at once and do not return…but you will leave Sophia Zomanek with us."

"No," whispered Sophia. "No, please, please don't."

One of the szlachts behind Rudjak and Varlov laughed. "Beg all you want, you little bitch. It won't save you. You'll beg and beg and…"

"Bashkir!" snapped Rudjak. "I said to shut up!" Bashkir fell silent, though he still grinned at Sophia.

"Tell me," said Caina. "What is the Boyar's Hunt?"

"It is not the concern of foreigners," said Rudjak, controlling his irritation with an effort. "Razdan Nagrach is the ruler of Kostiv. Its people are his to do with as he pleases. The girl is his to do with as he pleases. Go about your business, and leave the girl. It is not your concern."

"There is one more thing I wish to know, szlacht," said Caina. "What is a mavrokh?"

Rudjak said nothing. Some of the other men chuckled. Varlov and Bashkir smirked at Caina.

"You don't know, then?" said Rudjak.

"Not entirely," said Caina. "I do know you like to call yourselves of the Hounds of the Iron King." The smirks faded. "I do know that each one of you is possessed by a malevolent spirit you call a mavrokh. That likely means that you are a follower of the old ways, a worshipper of Temnuzash, and so is your boyar Razdan. You're taking advantage of the civil war to return to the old ways of the Iron King since the Temple is too weak and the Empire too distracted to stop you."

No one said anything for a moment.

"She knows too much, Rudjak," said Bashkir. "If she goes back to the Empire and tells the Magisterium…"

"It doesn't matter," said Rudjak. "The Umbarians support the old ways, and the Emperor is busy with them." He looked at Caina. The sneer had vanished, and now his face was cold and hard, the expression of a dangerous man evaluating a potential foe. "But for a foreigner, you are very well informed."

Caina shrugged. "I keep my eyes open."

"This is your last chance," said Rudjak. "Leave. Now. We'll permit you to depart if you leave the girl."

"You're mistaken," said Caina.

"Am I?" said Rudjak. "About what?"

"Enough!" roared Varlov, taking a step forward. He seemed on the verge of flying into a rage, and his dark eyes were taking on a yellowish shade. "I will not permit…"

"He'll attack first," said Caina to Kylon in Kyracian, and he gave a sharp nod. "Be ready."

Rudjak raised a hand, and Varlov fell silent.

"About what," said Rudjak, "am I mistaken?"

"This isn't my last chance," said Caina. "It's yours."

"And why is that?" said Rudjak.

"Because this sword," Caina lifted her weapon, her free hand pointing at Kylon, "and that one are both valikons."

"Impossible," said Rudjak.

Caina smiled. "Do you often see swords that burn with white fire?"

"A trick," snarled Bashkir. "An illusion wrought by the battle magus."

"No, they're not," said Caina. "They're real. And I am a valikarion."

The szlachts roared with laughter. Only Rudjak did not laugh.

But the strange yellow gleam had appeared in his eyes as well.

"Impossible," said Rudjak. "In ancient days, the Warmaiden and her valikarion warriors overthrew the Iron King. But Iramis burned, and all the loremasters and valikarion were hunted down and slain."

"Care to wager your life on that, my lord Rudjak?" Caina pointed her valikon at them. "Because that's what you're doing right now. Either I'm bluffing, and these are not valikons...or I'm telling the truth, and you're about to die. Those mavrokhi spirits might make you faster and stronger than normal men, but a valikon can destroy even a spirit and..."

She had been talking to Rudjak, but her words had been aimed at Varlov, and the gamble paid off.

"Enough!" roared Varlov, stalking forward. "If you lack the spine, Rudjak, then I shall act! I will kill them all, and take the girl back to the boyar!"

He walked forward, and then his body changed.

The transformation was swift and horrifying. On the first step, his eyes turned a venomous shade of yellow, the color of a seeping, infected wound. On the second step, black claws sprouted from his fingers, and black fur covered his face and hands.

On the third step, his transformation was complete, and Varlov had become a creature that looked like a wolf the size of a horse. Varlov still stood on his hind legs, and his head looked too blunt to truly be that of a wolf, and malicious intelligence gleamed in his yellow eyes. Somehow his twisted face and muzzle conveyed both lust and hunger and contempt. Slime dripped from his fangs, and he lifted his hands, his claws like daggers.

The stench was hideous. Even from twenty feet away, Caina smelled the reek of rotting meat and musk rolling off the wolf-like creature.

If this was a Hound of the Iron King, no wonder the Ulkaari held them in such dread.

Varlov threw back his head and loosed that chilling howl, and then surged forward like a crossbow bolt, his black-furred body a blur. Sophia started screaming the keening, high-pitched scream of a girl terrified beyond all reason.

Except Kylon was already moving, the valikon trailing white fire in his fists.

He leaped, and his sorcery-enhanced jump carried him right into Varlov's path. He swept his sword around in a sideways swing, and the blade ripped deep into Varlov's side, black slime spraying from the wound.

The creature staggered with a howl of agony and fell to his knees, and Kylon stepped back, valikon raised in guard. Caina moved to join him, and Seb followed suit, but it was unnecessary. Varlov's form shivered and twisted, and he shrank back into human shape. His coat and cloak had been torn, wet with blood pumping from the hideous wound Kylon had carved into his side.

The arrogance and rage had vanished from his face, replaced by terror.

He suddenly looked no different than the other frightened young men that Caina had seen die.

"No," croaked Varlov, clutching at his side. "You...you killed it. You killed my mavrokh. You..."

He pitched forward into the snow, his blood sinking into the overgrown garden. If he wasn't dead yet, blood loss would take him soon.

The other szlachts stared at the dying man, their shock and chagrin plain. Caina suspected the wolf-form of the mavrokhi was resistant to weapons of normal steel or could heal so quickly that it didn't matter. They must have expected that Varlov would tear them all apart, and then they would change form and join the attack.

They had not expected Kylon to cut down Varlov with a single blow.

For a moment, they would not be thinking clearly.

"Behold!" roared Caina at the top of her lungs, using one of the theatrical voices that Theodosia had taught her all those years ago. "The Arvaltyri have returned! Once more the bearers of the valikons walk the lands of Ulkaar, hunting for those who follow the old ways of blood and necromancy!" She pointed her valikon at Rudjak. "Come! Which of you is next? Which of you will dare to face the wrath of the valikarion?"

Rudjak took a step back, and as one, all six remaining szlachts shifted form, becoming those monstrous, misshapen wolf-things.

A bolt of pure terror went down Caina's spine. The mavrokhi in their wolf-forms were things out of a nightmare. Each one towered over her by a good two or three feet, and they had to be four or five times her weight, and most of their weight was muscle and claw and fang. Even one mavrokh could take her apart with ease, and standing before six of the things was an unnerving experience.

Yet she kept the fear from her expression…and the mavrokhi flinched from the burning valikon in her hand.

She might have been frightened of them, but they were just as frightened of her.

Perhaps they were even more terrified. Caina was very familiar with the idea of her own mortality, but no doubt Rudjak and his men thought that their mavrokhi had made them invincible.

Several of Grand Master Callatas's disciples had been the same way, their thinking so twisted by the nagataaru inhabiting their flesh that they had believed themselves invincible.

The mavrokhi dropped to all fours. Caina was sure they would attack her, but instead, they whirled and fled into the frozen trees. They vanished from sight in short order, and silence fell over the clearing and the overgrown garden of the Sanctuary Stone once more.

"They're gone," said Kylon. "They've moved far enough away that I can't sense them any longer." He lowered his valikon, and Caina felt a flash of guilt. He had watched her stride toward the mavrokhi, and had likely been ready to throw himself at the beasts to save her life.

Well, her bluff had worked. But if it hadn't...

Seb was laughing.

"What the hell is so funny?" said Caina.

"You just bullied the Hounds of the Iron King into fleeing," said Seb.

"I didn't bully them." Caina looked at the corpse of Varlov. "We persuaded them."

Seb's laughter faded. "And they'll run right to Boyar Razdan to tell him what happened."

"Yes," said Caina, looking to the trees.

The mavrokhi had fled, but she knew they would be back.

"Are...are we safe?" said Sophia. She was still shaking, tears in her eyes.

"For now," said Caina. "But I'm afraid that we're about to be in a tremendous amount of danger."

CHAPTER ELEVEN

FIGHT OR FLIGHT

Kylon looked at the corpse of the szlacht Varlov.

Killing the man did not trouble him in the slightest. Kylon had killed many men in battle. If they had been faster or stronger or simply luckier, they would have killed him, but they hadn't, so he was still alive, and they were not. For that matter, Varlov had been possessed by a mavrokh spirit, and Kylon had sensed the bestial hunger and fury within the spirit. Varlov had apparently taken that wicked spirit into himself of his own free will, and evidently, his character had matched that of the mavrokh.

Plus, he had threatened Caina.

No, Varlov's death did not trouble Kylon.

What troubled him was Varlov's friends.

If Caina had not frightened off those other six mavrokhi, the creatures might have killed them all. The Hounds were strong and fast, and if Kylon had been a half-second slower, Varlov would have killed Caina. If Varlov had kept his wits about him, he might have been able to hold Kylon at bay long enough for Rudjak and Bashkir and the others to transform and join the fray.

Kylon knew he could have defeated Varlov in a straight fight. He could have taken two or three of the mavrokhi at once, thanks to his valikon and his abilities as a stormdancer. But seven of them would have been fatal. Even with Seb's help, the mavrokhi would have won the fight.

"How did you know?" said Kylon.

"Know what?" said Caina. She stooped next to Varlov's corpse, searching it with brisk efficiency. Kylon was still not comfortable looting the dead, though he supposed Caina was right and they would need the money.

"That you could scare them off."

"I didn't." Caina took a dagger from Varlov's belt, tested the edge, nodded in satisfaction, and claimed the weapon, along with Varlov's money pouch. "But I guessed the boyar's pet mavrokhi were men like the disciples of Grand Master Callatas, proud and arrogant and hungry for power. Rudjak and Varlov and their friends likely thought their mavrokhi made them invincible. And the valikarion were all slain long ago, everyone in Ulkaar seems to know that. So, when they encountered an actual valikarion, when they saw Varlov slain and his mavrokh spirit destroyed…"

"They panicked," said Seb in a quiet voice.

"So it would seem," said Caina, straightening up and brushing the snow from her knees.

"That was a hell of a gamble," said Seb.

"It was," said Caina. "But I didn't have any choice. If we hadn't frightened off the mavrokhi, they would have killed us. And then probably eaten us."

She looked at Sophia, and the girl gave an unsteady nod.

Sophia's emotional aura was chaotic against Kylon's senses. Utter fear had paralyzed her as Rudjak and his szlachts arrived, the cold and terrible fear of a long-awaited doom arriving at last. Shock had replaced the fear as Kylon cut down Varlov and Caina had bullied the mavrokhi into fleeing, and now the predominant emotion in her aura was bewilderment.

But the fear was still strong.

"Because they would have eaten us, wouldn't they?" said Caina.

"Yes," said Sophia, her voice an unsteady whisper. "They would have. After they had kept you and me alive for some other torments first."

"Rudjak and his men seemed the type," said Caina. "Sophia. I think it's time that we were honest with each other, don't you?"

Sophia sighed, and guilt entered her sense. "It is my fault. Rudjak will tell the boyar about you, and he will kill you. It is my fault."

"I very much doubt that," said Caina. She turned to Seb. "Tell me about the mavrokhi, these Hounds of the Iron King."

"They are possessed by malevolent spirits of the netherworld," said Seb, "turning them into hybrids of mortal man and bestial spirit." Caina's mouth twisted. "You have encountered such creatures before?"

Kylon remembered Kalgri's mad, giggling laughter as she killed.

"Oh, yes," said Caina. "Please continue."

"You have heard the account of Rasarion Yagar the Iron King by now," said Seb. "To drive the Kagari horsemen from Ulkaar, Yagar turned to necromancy and the worship of Temnuzash, and he created many different creatures to serve him. The Hounds of the Iron King, the mavrokhi, were one of them. The mavrokhi are bestial spirits, and they hunt and devour other spirits in the netherworld, though mortals are their preferred food. Yagar summoned them and bound them into the flesh of his most loyal szlachts. Those men gained the ability to take the form of giant, twisted wolves, which you just observed firsthand. In wolf form, they are deadly fighters. Some of the old tales claim they are immune to iron and vulnerable only to weapons of silver, but that's not true. They heal incredibly fast, and the only way to kill one in wolf form is to cut off its head and cut out its heart. The mavrokhi can regenerate almost anything else."

"Sounds familiar," said Kylon, scowling as he remembered the nagataaru.

"And, of course," said Seb, "they are profoundly vulnerable to the blade of a valikon."

"Just as well that we have two," said Caina. She stared at the trees for a moment, her expression distant with thought, and then she looked back at Seb. "I thought you said the mavrokhi were extinct."

Sophia let out a bitter little laugh.

"Allegedly," said Seb, "though we have seen firsthand that information is incorrect. After the Warmaiden slew Rasarion Yagar and interrupted his great spell, most of the nobility of Ulkaar were Yagar's hybrids – mavrokhi and vyrkolaki and undead creatures and the like. The Temple devoted themselves to hunting down the mavrokhi and the Iron King's other creatures, and once the Empire conquered Ulkaar, the Magisterium did the same." He shrugged. "Almost certainly they didn't kill all of the mavrokhi. Most likely the smarter ones went underground and kept their abilities concealed, like the Temnoti. Though for the boyar to flaunt his mavrokhi so openly…just a few years ago that would have invited destruction from both the witchfinders of the Temple and the battle magi of the Magisterium."

"But the Empire is fighting for its life against the Umbarian Order," said Caina, "and there is no one to stop the mavrokhi."

"You heard what Varlov said," said Seb, looking at the corpse. "The old ways will rise again. Though, alas, it seems that the lord Varlov shall not be alive to see them."

"Such a pity," said Caina. She turned to Sophia. "I would like you to tell me everything about the boyar now."

"Why bother?" said Sophia. That stupor-like bewilderment still filled her emotional sense.

"The more I know about him, the better chance we have against him if it comes to a fight," said Caina.

"You can't...you can't fight the boyar," said Sophia. She took a shuddering breath. "He'll kill us. He'll kill us all. He'll kill you for helping me. I'm sorry, I'm so sorry, but he's going to kill us all."

"He can try," said Caina.

"It is foreordained," said Sophia. "It was always my destiny." She started to cry. "And now it's yours, too. It's yours, and you're going to die, and it's all my fault..."

Caina stepped forward, caught Sophia's chin in her right hand, and forced the weeping girl to look at her.

"Listen to me," said Caina, her voice gentle. "Listen to me, Sophia Zomanek. Varlov knew his destiny. It was to be a Hound of the Iron King in service to his boyar. He was going to bring you back to Razdan Nagrach." She gestured at the corpse. "How did that work out for him?"

Uncertainty entered the girl's bewilderment. "Lord Kylon killed him. But...but Varlov was just a szlacht. You can't fight the boyar. He's too strong."

"Listen to me," said Caina again, her voice almost a whisper. Sophia stared at Caina, transfixed by those cold eyes. "I've heard that before. I've heard that so many times. And do you know what happened? I fought two Great Necromancers of Maat, lords of power who would make the boyar and his szlachts look like puppies, and I defeated them both. I went into the netherworld four times, and I came out alive again four times. I burned the Widow's Tower and the Craven's Tower, I robbed the Maze of Grand Master Callatas himself, and I escaped. I went into the Inferno and commanded the ancient dead to follow me. I fought the Moroaica herself, the sorceress of legend called the Bloodmaiden and the Herald of Ruin, and I killed her with my own hands."

"Dear gods," muttered Seb. "She's telling the truth, isn't she?"

Kylon gave a sharp nod, watching Caina. Granted, it had been a bit more complicated than that, but every word was true.

"And my husband," said Caina, gesturing at Kylon. He blinked in surprise. "Do you know what he has done? He killed the Lieutenant of the Inferno, the Iron Hell where the Immortals were trained. He defeated the Master Alchemist Rhataban when an entire army ran from him. He killed the Lord Cassander Nilas and broke the Throne of Corazain and saved a million men, women, and children from being burned alive in Istarinmul. He broke the western fleet of the Empire, and they still call him Kylon Shipbreaker for it. And he killed the Red Huntress with that valikon. An assassin a century and a half old, who had killed and killed and never been defeated, and he cut her down and avenged the oceans of innocent blood she had spilled. And you just saw him slay Varlov with that same valikon. A mavrokh invincible and powerful, and he died in a second and a half."

Caina made it sound so much more impressive than it really had been.

Sophia gaped at Caina. That uncertainty filled her emotional sense, but now there was something else.

A flicker of hope. Tentative and dim, but it was there.

"The boyar will kill us all," said Sophia. "You should be afraid of him."

"Perhaps I should be," said Caina. "Only a fool doesn't fear her enemies." She leaned a little closer. "But do you know something?"

Sophia tried to shake her head, but Caina's fingers held her fast.

"Maybe the boyar," said Caina, "should be afraid of us."

She let go of Sophia and stepped back.

For a moment, no one said anything.

Kylon sensed the furious churn in Sophia's emotions. He had seen Caina do this kind of thing before. She had convinced the undead of the Inferno to fight for her, persuaded Cronmer's Circus Of Marvels And Wonders to help them against Cassander, had convinced the men of the Imperial Guard and New Kyre to fight alongside each other on the day of the golden dead. When she set her mind to it, she was an astonishing orator and could persuade people to push themselves far harder than they would have otherwise. No wonder the Ghosts of Istarinmul had been devoted to her. Old Agabyzus and his sister Damla had loved her the way loyal soldiers loved a victorious commander.

Little wonder the legend of the Balarigar had grown around her like a pearl.

"Maybe," said Sophia, and she swallowed, "maybe the Arvaltyri of old talked the way you do."

"Maybe," said Caina, and suddenly she grinned. "I met a few of them in Iramis, but they didn't like to talk very much."

Sophia laughed and then blinked in surprise. "All right. Maybe you really are an Arvaltyr of old, and I shall put myself into your hands." She shrugged. "What do you want to know?"

"Why does the boyar want you back so badly?" said Caina.

"The Boyar's Hunt," said Sophia.

"Ah," said Seb, his expression grim.

"What is the Boyar's Hunt?" said Caina.

"How I shall die," said Sophia. She grimaced and waved at Seb. "Let Lord Sebastian describe it. His Caerish is better. If he is wrong, I shall say so."

"Thank you, madam," said Seb with a slight bow. He turned back to Caina. "Do you recall when Lord Kylon and I discussed what the Empire would consider barbarous?" Caina nodded. "The Boyar's Hunt is one such custom. Rasarion Yagar instituted it during his reign, a privilege accorded to his boyars and szlachts who had become mavrokhi. For the Boyar's Hunt, a boyar could select seven young women from the lands under his control." Kylon suspected he knew where this was going. "On the day of the Hunt, the women would be deprived of their clothing and driven into the forest, and the boyar and his szlachts would assume their wolf-forms. They would then hunt the women chosen for the Hunt, and a mavrokh who caught one of the women could claim her for his own, to use her to slake whatever appetites he wished." He shrugged. "Almost always the women were eaten alive after various…indignities."

"I see," said Caina. Kylon knew that look on her face. That had often been her expression when she had spoken of the Slavers' Brotherhood of Istarinmul. "I take it Razdan Nagrach has brought back this custom, and you were chosen for it?"

"Yes," said Sophia. "Last week. I live with my uncle Ivan in Kostiv. Rudjak came from the boyar's castle. He said that I was one of the girls chosen for the Hunt. I…I didn't know what to do. No one can fight the boyar. Uncle Ivan would, but he is old and sick, and Brother Valexis would, but his powers are not strong enough. If I stayed, they would be killed, and I would be taken for the Hunt anyway."

"The boyar," said Caina. "How many szlachts does he have?"

"Sixteen," said Sophia.

"Fifteen, now," said Seb, looking at Varlov.

"They all have men-at-arms," said Sophia, "but only the boyar's szlachts have become mavrokhi."

"When did it start?" said Caina. "Two years ago, I assume? Soon after the civil war began?"

"Aye," said Sophia. "The rumors said that the Temnoti visited the boyar's castle. Soon after the boyar proclaimed that he was now a follower of Temnuzash and that he was a Hound of the Iron King. His father Boyar Vlad hanged criminals. Boyar Razdan would take wolf-shape and devour them alive. Before the war started, my uncle and the burgomaster would have written to the Imperial Lord Governor or the Magisterium for help." She shrugged. "But they are fighting the Umbarians, and we are on our own."

"And there is no one," said Caina, "to stop the boyar from doing as he wishes."

"Aye," said Sophia again. "We tried sending messengers to the Voivode of Vagraastrad for help, but the Voivode had the messengers flogged and sent back with instructions not to question our lawful lords."

"I see," said Caina again.

"We should run," said Sophia. "We should run right now, and go to Vagraastrad or Risiviri. There are many people in both cities. Maybe the boyar's men will miss us there, and we can escape from Ulkaar."

"I'm afraid," said Caina, "that it is too late to run."

Caina considered what Sophia and Seb had told her.

She had seen how fast and strong Varlov had been in his wolf-form, and she had to assume that the other mavrokhi that Razdan Nagrach commanded would have the same abilities. A single Hound would be dangerous. Sixteen of them at once would be lethal.

"Why can't we run?" said Sophia.

"Because," said Kylon before Caina could answer, "Rudjak and Bashkir and the others will run right to the boyar to tell him what happened."

Caina nodded. "And the boyar will have no choice but to strike back at once. He can't let a challenge to his authority like this pass unanswered."

"Yes," said Seb. "I fear we have dropped a gauntlet at his feet. It might mean a battle to the death."

"Perhaps," said Caina. She supposed that deepened on whether or not Razdan Nagrach was a fool. That he was cruel and brutal was beyond all debate. The question was if his lust for Sophia would override his thinking, whether he could set aside his pride and listen to reason. It was obvious that the valikons were a deadly danger to the boyar and his Hounds.

The question was how Razdan Nagrach would respond to that danger. Would the boyar attack in a blind fury, seeking to destroy the threat? Would he take a more cautious approach, hoping to lure Caina and Kylon into a situation where they could not escape? Or would he feign friendship, hoping to stab Caina in the back at the soonest opportunity?

Caina didn't know. And until she knew more about the boyar, she would not guess how he might respond to the threat.

But she did know two things.

They could not stay here, and they had to get out of the forest and find more defensible ground as soon as possible. The power of the Sanctuary Stone had slowed the mavrokhi, but it had not stopped them. The frozen forests of northern Ulkaar gave all the advantages to the mavrokhi. More, Caina needed to keep the initiative. Better to have the boyar reacting to her actions than the other way around. Right now, she had the initiative. Rudjak and his men would return to the boyar's castle, and then Razdan Nagrach would act.

Caina needed to be ready by then. More importantly, they needed to be out of the forest before the boyar came hunting for them.

"So," said Seb. "I suppose the most important question of all is what we shall do next."

"Agreed," said Caina. "We can't run. Those mavrokhi will catch us if we try. That means we have no choice but to fight or to bluff, and if we try to fight the Hounds in the forest, we'll lose."

"They have all the advantages in the forest," said Kylon.

"They do," said Caina. She looked to Sophia. "How far is it to the boyar's castle from here?"

"About a day," said Sophia.

"And to the gates of Kostiv?"

Sophia considered. "Less than half a day. We might get there before dark if we hurry."

Caina nodded. "Then it seems we have no choice but to go to Kostiv, all of us."

Seb frowned. "And what will we do at Kostiv?"

Caina thought about her answer. Once again, it seemed, she had to play a dangerous game with high stakes. Their own lives were in the balance, of course. Yet the presence of the Ring of Rasarion Yagar in her pocket ensured that the stakes were far higher. If they were killed, the Ring would fall into the hands of Razdan Nagrach. If that happened, almost certainly the boyar would hand the Ring over to the Umbarians to curry favor, or the Umbarians would simply take the Ring from him.

Caina didn't know what powers the Ring possessed, and she didn't want to find out. She especially did not want to find out when the Umbarians used the Ring to destroy the Empire.

Of course, if they did that, she would already be dead.

Caina had thought that she would settle in Iramis and serve as an advisor to Prince Nasser. She might have been finished with dangerous games...but it seemed that deadly games were not done with her.

But maybe that was all right. Caina was good at dangerous games.

"We are going to bluff," said Caina.

CHAPTER TWELVE

THE COUNTESS

They took the road to the southwest as fast as they could.

Kylon kept his arcane senses extended, watching the trees for any sign of danger. The only other people he sensed nearby were Sophia and Seb. Sophia's aura veered between stark terror and wild hope, while Seb simply had the grim sense of a warrior preparing himself for battle. Nothing moved in the trees, and Kylon sensed no one else nearby.

Nevertheless, Kylon kept his senses extended and his valikon ready in his hand. Rudjak and his men might recover their nerve and come back. For that matter, once Razdan Nagrach learned of the news, he would respond with force.

Kylon had once been one of the nine Archons of New Kyre, the chief magistrates of the city. And if someone had blatantly challenged the authority of the Archons the way that he and Caina had just challenged the authority of Razdan Nagrach, the Archons would have had no choice but to respond with deadly force.

He doubted the boyar would feel differently.

Of course, while New Kyre was reliant upon slavery, the Kyracians had nothing so brutal as the Boyar's Hunt. Kylon could not recall hearing of a Kyracian nobleman who hunted people for sport. And save for those few who had been possessed by a nagataaru after the day of the golden dead, Kylon could not recall a Kyracian nobleman who had voluntarily chosen to become possessed by a malevolent spirit. Necromancy and summoning malevolent spirits from the netherworld were forbidden in New Kyre, likely because it resulted in creatures like the Red Huntress and cruelties like the Boyar's Hunt.

Seb kept watching the trees. He, too, knew that Rudjak might return. Sophia walked in silence, staring at the road, looking neither right or left. Kylon found himself admiring the girl's bravery. He sensed the terror that the thought of returning to Kostiv summoned in her, yet she kept going.

Of course, if she stayed in the forest, she was going to die. Or the mavrokhi would find her, and then she would die. Kylon supposed she might have killed herself in terror, but she kept pushing on.

Kylon and Seb spent the time watching for enemies. Sophia brooded.

Caina fussed with her hair.

"I wish," she said, her hands weaving her hair into a braid, "that I had a mirror. Or some horses."

"Horses?" said Seb, bemused.

Caina's hair had been hanging loose around her shoulders, but she had arranged it into the elaborate crown favored by the noblewomen of Malarae, a braid encircling her head and a few loose locks hanging against her neck. Kylon was impressed that she could do that without a mirror while walking in a forest. She had also been rearranging her clothes, buttoning the red coat to her neck and turning up the collar. The net effect almost made the coat look like the elaborate dress of a self-important noblewoman.

"Yes, horses," said Caina. "We could make a more impressive entrance that way. Also, some jewelry. None of us cut very impressive figures, I'm afraid. Well, Seb does, but a battle magus of the Magisterium is a different kind of impressive."

"If a lone noblewoman walked up to the gates of Kostiv covered in jewels," said Sophia, baffled, "the boyar's men would probably rob her."

"I have a stormdancer and a battle magus to keep that from happening," said Caina. "And, also, all the jewels I took from the ardivid are safely concealed in my pockets." She looked at her wrist. "I suppose this will have to do."

Her pyrikon bracelet unfolded itself in a flicker of white light and jumped to her forehead. Kylon watched as the pyrikon reshaped itself into a slender diadem that encircled her forehead and black hair, glinting in the cold winter light as it did.

"A crown?" said Sophia, baffled.

"A diadem." Seb gave Caina an amused glance. "I imagine the difference is significant."

"Quite." Caina grinned at him. "The difference is between good taste and too much. And some Imperial women wear diadems. It depends on their lineage and the offices that their husbands hold. But that doesn't matter right now. What matters is impressing the men of the town enough that they don't kill us or turn us away."

"And what do we want them to do?" said Seb.

"Not kill us," said Caina. "And to send a message to the boyar."

"You want to send a message to the boyar?" said Sophia, incredulous. "What will it say? 'Here we are, come eat us?'"

"I will phrase it differently than that," said Caina.

Kylon watched his wife as she returned to arranging her hair. He knew her well enough to guess her thoughts. "You have a plan."

"I think so," said Caina, "but that depends on how the boyar reacts to what we do next."

"How he reacts?" said Sophia. "What are we going to do?"

Seb snorted. "I think I can guess at that, madam. We are going to show confidence. We are going to stride into Kostiv as if we own the town. Caina Amalas Tarshahzon Kardamnos will be at her most lordly. Or ladylike, I suppose, and Lord Kylon and I will punch anyone who offers her the slightest disrespect."

"Why?" said Sophia, blinking at Caina.

Caina looked at Seb. "Can you guess why?"

"Because the boyar is a predator," said Seb, "and there is one thing you must never, ever do when confronted by a predator."

Caina nodded. "Show weakness."

They walked in silence for a while.

"I hope you are right," said Sophia.

Kylon shrugged. "We're about to find out." The trees were thinning, cut down to provide firewood, and Kylon saw the signs of cultivation ahead.

"Truly, Lady Caina and Lord Sebastian must be half-siblings," said Sophia. "They both have the same...the same sideways method of thinking."

Caina and Seb shared a look. Kylon could tell they were not entirely pleased by the comparison because they were both hated Laeria Scorneus Amalas. Though Sophia was right. Caina and Sebastian Scorneus did tend to think along parallel paths.

Then the trees thinned out, and Kylon saw Kostiv.

The dirt road led into a broad, shallow valley, a wide river flowing through its center. The town stood alongside the wide river, huddled within a thick wall of stone. The wall was twelve feet high, and many of the houses rose far higher than the wall, some of them four or five stories tall. Smoke drifted from the chimneys of the houses, and the empty fields outside the town were deserted. On the far side of the town, near the river, Kylon glimpsed the water wheel of a mill, and he saw the distant figures of men guarding the town's gate.

"Kylon," said Caina, gazing at Kostiv. "I think you should dismiss your valikon." She held out the sword belt holding the jeweled saber they had taken from the ardivid. "Wear this instead. It would look odd if you approached the gate unarmed."

"Why?" He took the sword belt and wound it around his waist, the weight of the jeweled weapon tugging at his left hip. "If there are mavrokhi in the town, we'll need the valikon."

"We will," said Caina, "but I would wager all the mavrokhi went right to Boyar Razdan's castle to tell him what happened. I don't think there will be any inside Kostiv, at least not yet. Besides, we might need to persuade some of the townspeople to our side, and it will be hard to do that if we're holding burning swords of ghostsilver." She paused. "Unless we need to persuade them by holding burning swords of ghostsilver."

Kylon nodded and dismissed his valikon, the sword collapsing into shards of silver light and vanishing from sight. He did not understand the process by which the sword had bonded to him and allowed him to summon it, but it was certainly useful. He drew the ancient saber and tested its balance. It was a good weapon, the steel sharp, and despite the gaudy jeweled hilt and guard, it would be a useful weapon in a fight.

Caina lifted her own valikon before her face, frowning. Kylon wondered what was wrong, and then realized she was using the weapon as a mirror to check her reflection.

"Ah, well," she said. "As good as it is going to get, I suppose." She dismissed the weapon, and it collapsed into shards of light. "When we get to the gate, let me do the talking and follow my lead. Seb, I might need you to translate."

"Very well." Seb smiled a little. "I confess I am looking forward to watching this."

"Then I'll try not to disappoint," said Caina.

###

Caina led the way toward Kostiv, donning her disguise as she did so.

At least, the disguise she would wear inside her thoughts.

A disguise, Theodosia and Halfdan had taught her long ago, was almost as much about attitude and accent and expression as it was about a costume and makeup. Caina's costume was inadequate, and she didn't have any makeup, so she would need to rely on her posture and accent and poise.

Maybe that would be enough. Or maybe it wouldn't.

Caina changed her posture and expression as they walked. Usually, she tried to move without making any sound at all, a habit reinforced by training and years of experience. Now she walked with a confident stride, her boots striking the road. She kept her chin up, her expression a mask of calm arrogance. Everything about her posture and expression radiated confidence and calm, a noblewoman who expected to be obeyed immediately and without question.

The town drew closer, and Caina took a good look at the men who guarded the open gate. Both were middle-aged, with graying black hair and beards. Not Legion veterans, she thought, but they weren't plump enough to be merchants. Likely farmers who had taken refuge in the town for the winter. Both men recognized Sophia, that was plain, and both seemed uneasy at the sight of Seb.

A battle magus's black armor often had that effect.

Caina stopped and gazed at them for a moment.

"Do either of you speak the Emperor's tongue?" said Caina in High Nighmarian, keeping her voice cool and remote. "I would prefer to make my wishes known directly, rather than having to rely upon the services of a translator."

The two militiamen exchanged a look.

"I speak some High Nighmarian, my lady," said the man on the left. He had dark eyes and an old scar beneath his graying beard, his hands heavy with calluses, his trousers and boots marked with dust

"Capital," said Caina. "What is your name, townsman?"

The farmer hesitated, looking at Sophia. "That girl…my lady, you might have some trouble…"

"That does not answer my question," said Caina, letting her voice cool. "What is your name?"

She saw a lifetime of trying to avoid trouble with nobles kick in. "Vasily, my lady." He gestured at the other man, who was alarmed and trying to avoid showing it. "This is Costin, but he doesn't speak the Emperor's tongue. We both farm the valley."

"Splendid," said Caina. She glanced at Sophia. "The girl I have taken into my service tells me that this is the town of Kostiv, and these lands are ruled by the Boyar Razdan Nagrach. Is that correct?"

"Your service?" said Vasily, gaping at Sophia. "But..."

"Answer her ladyship's question," said Kylon in High Nighmarian. Vasily flinched. Caina kept the smile from her face. Kylon could look downright intimidating when he wanted, and right now his face looked as if it had been carved from stone.

"Ah...yes, of course," said Vasily. "Yes, this is the town of Kostiv, my lady, and the lord Razdan Nagrach is our boyar."

"Excellent," said Caina. "I am pleased to see that we are not lost. Now. Does this town support the Umbarians or the Emperor?"

Vasily managed to look even more alarmed. "Ah...the lord Razdan follows the wishes of the Voivode of Vagraastrad, my lady. But we of Kostiv wish to keep our heads down. We pay our taxes and do our duty to our lord, and otherwise, we keep to ourselves and out of the troubles of others."

"A sensible attitude, master Vasily," said Caina. "A pity more men do not share it. Well, I have a long journey behind me and a longer journey ahead of me, and some rest shall be welcome. I presume your town has an inn for travelers?"

"It...it does," said Vasily, "but perhaps it would be better for you to travel on." He looked at Sophia. "Perhaps it would be better for you to leave the girl and travel onward. The city of Vagraastrad is only a week away, and there are many fine inns there worthy of your ladyship."

"Certainly not," said Caina. "Do not presume to tell me my own mind." Vasily started to stammer an apology, but Caina talked right over him. "I require rest and fresh supplies, and I understand Ulkaar often suffers from simply dreadful blizzards at this time of year. I have no wish to be caught in the forest when such a storm strikes. No, I shall take my rest here at your inn, and then continue on my way..."

"The boyar might...take exception, my lady," said Vasily, looking at Sophia again.

"Why should he, my good man?" said Caina. "I always enjoy meeting the local nobles of the provinces. They are always so quaintly...rustic, yes, that is the word." Vasily blinked in alarm. Caina suspected Razdan Nagrach was not the sort of man to tolerate condescension from anyone. "I suppose I shall have to invite the boyar to dinner. I doubt he has the manners to know that he ought to invite the guest to dinner, but one cannot expect refined etiquette in this distant corner of the Empire."

"You have taken Sophia Zomanek into your service, my lady?" said Vasily.

"Certainly," said Caina. "The journey has been difficult, and one must always be on the lookout for talent in the provinces. Sophia comes from a good local family. Minor nobility, to be sure, but nobility nonetheless. Perhaps she shall accompany me to the Imperial capital of Malarae and make something of herself." Caina made an airy, dismissive gesture. "But I shall not worry about the distant future today. The name of the local inn, townsman Vasily?"

"Ah...the White Boar, my lady," said Vasily. That matched what Sophia had told Caina. "In the town square, facing the Temple and the burgomaster's house. It...it is not anything fancy, but it's clean, and the food doesn't have maggots."

"Splendid," said Caina. She produced a silver coin and handed it to Kylon, who caught the hint and handed it to Vasily. "Please conduct me there at once."

Vasily blinked. "I shouldn't leave the gate while I am on duty, my lady. The burgomaster wouldn't like it."

"Nonsense," said Caina. "I say it is all right, and I am sure that your comrade can keep watch in your absence. Now then, please conduct me to the White Boar. Surely you do not mean to leave me standing outside the gate all night?" She let disapproval creep into her tone. "The wilderness of Ulkaar is quite dangerous after dark."

Vasily turned to Costin and had a hurried conversation with him in Ulkaari. Caina still did not understand the language, but the tone of the conversation was clear enough. They were trying to decide what to do about her. At last Costin shrugged, Vasily made a disgusted noise and then turned back to Caina.

"Please come this way, my lady," said Vasily, his voice far calmer. "I will be happy to conduct you to the White Boar inn. But then I must return to my post at once."

"Of course," said Caina. "Please lead the way."

Vasily took a deep breath and walked through the gate. Caina shot a quick look at Kylon, but he only shook his head. He didn't sense any mavrokhi nearby. For her own part, Caina only saw one faint, weak arcane aura within the town, coming from the direction of the river. It was the sort of aura created by the spells of the Words of Lore. If the ancient loremasters had indeed taught some of the Words of Lore to the Temple of Ulkaar, and if the priesthood continued the practice to this day, Caina supposed she was looking at the town's Temple.

They walked down the main street, cobblestones beneath their boots. The houses had their first floors built from stone, the second of whitewashed wood, and the third and above of dark wood. The roofs were steep, likely to dislodge accumulations of snow during the winters, and every house, no matter how small, had a covered porch. Caina supposed the families gathered on the porches in the heat of the summer, or that the town's wives would gossip there.

Right now, she supposed they were about to generate some gossip.

Every house had a sunstone over the door, and most had sunstones over at least some of the windows. Caina supposed the glow would light the town at night. It would help keep the undead at bay, but it would do nothing against the mavrokhi.

There were people on the streets, men and women both. The women wore long dresses of blue or green with close-fitting black sleeves, while the men preferred black trousers, white shirts, and long black vests. Both men and women wore heavy cloaks and coats to keep the cold at bay, along with cylindrical fur hats. Given how cold it had been in the forest, Caina found herself envying those hats. Maybe if they lived through the next few days, she could buy herself one.

The townspeople stared at her as she passed. Muttered whispers in Ulkaari accompanied her passage. Sophia seemed to wilt under their attention at first, but then her expression turned angry. Caina could guess her thoughts well enough. The townspeople of Kostiv had not been willing to lift a finger to save Sophia from the boyar and his Hunt.

Of course, the townspeople of Kostiv could do nothing to protect themselves from the mavrokhi. Had they objected to the Boyar's Hunt, no doubt the boyar and his szlachts would have made a few bloody examples to inspire obedience.

Caina took note of the details as she walked through the town, keeping her icy mask in place. She saw the narrow windows, the high, peaked roofs, the narrow alleyways between the houses. Towards the end of the main street, the houses began to have workshops on the lower levels – a forge, a carpentry shop, a cooper, a shoemaker, a chandler, and so on.

Kostiv was not large, and it did not take them long to reach the main square. Caina examined it with interest. On her left was a tall, boxy building that had the familiar look of a large inn. On the right side of the square was an octagonal building of stone with a domed roof that looked vaguely Iramisian. The arcane aura came from the building, so Caina supposed that it was the Temple. Next to the Temple stood a house like the others in the town, but larger and of better construction. Likely it was the burgomaster's house.

On the other side of the square, overlooking the river, rose the mill. It was a big building, the biggest building in Kostiv, with thick stone walls and narrow iron-barred windows. It had double doors wide enough for a wagon and a team of oxen, though they had been locked and chained shut until the harvest came.

"I wonder why those walls are so thick," said Kylon in Caerish, pointing at the mill. "That place could practically be a fortress in its own right."

Seb snorted. "You don't know very much about farming, do you, Lord Kylon?"

Kylon offered an indifferent shrug. "The wealth of New Kyre comes from the sea, not from the land."

"Mills, silos, and barns all suffer from a specific danger," said Seb. "A large quantity of grain dust gets into the air, and grain dust is flammable. So is flour, and flour burns even more quickly than grain dust. If there is enough flour and grain dust in the air when a spark is struck, the entire building can explode. Likely the mill was constructed of stone to keep the fire from burning down the entire town in the event of an explosion."

Kylon glanced at Caina.

"Don't look at me like that. I am not stupid enough to set a fire in a mill," said Caina. "I might have set fire to one or two buildings in an emergency, but I am not mad enough to set fire to a mill."

Seb blinked. "Do you often burn down buildings?"

Caina sighed. "Once or twice."

"On the day we met," said Kylon, "she tried to burn down a warehouse with me inside it."

Sophia frowned at them, her fear momentarily forgotten. "Truly?"

"It was a long story," said Caina.

"Oh." Sophia considered that. "What a peculiar way to meet a husband."

"I must take my leave of you now," said Vasily in High Nighmarian, who had been watching the conversation with unease, since he did not speak Caerish. "The White Boar is there." He pointed, and Caina saw a sign with a painted white boar hanging over the door. "The innkeeper Rachov is an honest man, and he will see to you."

"Thank you, townsman," said Caina. "Your service has been most appreciated."

Vasily bowed and left the square as fast as he could without actually running.

"We may have frightened him," said Seb in Caerish.

"Likely he fears the retribution of the boyar falling upon his head for speaking to us," said Caina. "But we may be able to forestall that."

She walked to the inn. Kylon opened the door and went first, followed by Seb, and then Caina and Sophia went inside. The common room of the White Boar looked like the common rooms of a hundred other inns that Caina had visited. A dozen sturdy wooden tables stood around the room, their surfaces scarred and worn, a half-dozen chairs sitting around each table. A massive fieldstone hearth stood on one side of the common room, radiating heat from its fire, and opposite the hearth stood a long counter.

The master of the inn stood next to the counter, staring at them with wide black eyes. He was an elderly man with a paunch, his hair and beard white. The innkeeper wore an immaculate white apron over his white shirt and black trousers, and a tremor went through his hands at the sight of Sophia. Behind the innkeeper stood a stocky boy of about twelve who was either the man's son or grandson.

"Sophia Zomanek," said the innkeeper. He let out a barrage of questions in Ulkaari. Sophia answered back, and the innkeeper frowned.

"The traders' language?" he said in Caerish. "But why?"

"Because it is the common tongue of the Empire of Nighmar, master innkeeper," said Caina in Caerish with a strong Nighmarian accent, "and that, therefore, is the best way to make my wishes known to you."

He blinked as Caina stepped towards him. "My…my lady?"

"What is your name?" said Caina.

"Rachov, my lady," said the innkeeper. "This is the White Boar. The inn has been in my family for nine generations."

"Splendid," said Caina. "My name is Caina Amalas Tarshahzon Kardamnos, Countess of the Empire of Nighmar and amirja of the realm of Istarinmul." Rachov gaped at her. "I shall require three rooms." One for her and Kylon, one for Seb, and one for Sophia. "I trust that your rates are reasonable, master innkeeper?"

Rachov recovered his power of speech. "They…they are, my lady." He named a price that was indeed reasonable, and Caina handed over some of the coins she had taken from the undead warriors of the ardivid. Rachov looked at the coins, blinked at the ancient inscriptions…but money was money, and he took the coins. "Do…you know how long you will be staying, my lady?"

"I do not know," said Caina. If she underestimated the boyar, Caina supposed she would end her life in Kostiv. "A few days, most likely. I would like to reach Vagraastrad before the worst of the winter sets in, so I will no doubt depart soon."

"I see," said Rachov. He stepped back to the door behind the counter and opened it, and Caina saw a group of women standing there. Rachov's wife and daughters, by the look of them, listening fearfully. Rachov gave instructions in Ulkaari, and the women vanished. "My wife and daughters will make your rooms ready, my lady. I fear the White Boar inn is a humble place and is unworthy of a Countess of the Empire…"

"And an amirja of Istarinmul," said Seb, who seemed amused at the poor innkeeper's discomfort.

"Er. Yes." Rachov blinked a few times. "But my rooms are clean and free of lice and rats, I would give my oath upon that."

"Capital," said Caina. "I assure you, master innkeeper, after the wilds of Ulkaar in the winter the White Boar seems a finer residence than all the palaces of Istarinmul. Might we prevail upon you for some food?"

"Of course, my lady," said Rachov.

Caina gave him a reassuring smile. "I don't suppose you have any coffee?"

The innkeeper blinked. "Coffee? I've never heard of it."

Well, that had been a long shot. Caina never had drunk coffee until Kylon had introduced her and Corvalis to the drink in Catekharon.

"Tea will be fine," said Caina. "The stronger, the better."

Rachov bowed, turned, and issued a string of instructions to the boy in Ulkaari, and Caina caught Sophia's name in the torrent of words. The boy nodded and took off across the common room, vanishing into the town square. Caina sat at one of the round tables, and Kylon and Seb followed suit, the wooden chair creaking beneath Seb's armored weight. Caina hoped his armor did not carve any grooves into the chair. Sophia hovered nervously behind them until Caina beckoned for her to sit down.

"Let me guess," said Caina to Seb. "Master Rachov sent the boy to fetch someone in authority?"

"The burgomaster." Seb's eyes flicked over the common room. "Specifically, told the boy…"

"His grandson," said Sophia. "Tormin."

Seb inclined his head. "He told young Tormin to speak with the burgomaster at once, and to tell him that Sophia Zomanek has returned in the company of a foreign noblewoman, an Imperial or Umbarian magus, and a Kyracian." He grunted. "A foreign noblewoman, a magus, and a Kyracian walk into a common room. It sounds like the beginning of a joke of remarkably poor taste."

"It seems," said Kylon, adjusting the saber at his belt, "that we have set the storm among the fishermen."

Seb blinked. "Eh?"

"Kyracian metaphor." Caina watched the door, wondering how the burgomaster would react. "The closest equivalent in the Empire is to say that we have set the fox among the henhouse, or kicked the hornet's nest."

Sophia frowned. "Who would kick a hornet's nest? That seems like a very foolish thing to do."

"It means," said Caina, "that we're about to cause a lot of trouble. Everyone in the town knows about the Boyar's Hunt, I assume. They know you disappeared. Likely they think you either ran for your life, or the boyar just killed you himself. But after missing for a few days, you return in the company of powerful strangers. How do you think they will react?"

Sophia blinked. "It will be the chief gossip for many days."

"Exactly," said Caina. "I wonder whether Rachov will bring out our meal before Tormin returns with an invitation for us."

As it turned out, Tormin won the race. The door burst open, and Tormin came inside, breathing hard. He looked around and trotted over to his grandfather, and Rachov and the boy spoke in low voices for a few moments. Then Rachov grunted, straightened up, and approached the table with an apologetic air.

"My lady," said Rachov, "I am sorry to trouble you, but our burgomaster has issued an invitation for you to speak with him at once. Forgive me, but...but I think it would be best if you talked with him right away. Things are not well in Kostiv," his eyes flicked to Sophia, "and we would not want for you to become caught in our troubles."

Caina smiled at him. "Oh, it's much too late for that."

The poor innkeeper gaped at her.

"Could you hold our meal for us?" said Caina, rising to her feet. "I think we will be hungry after we speak with the burgomaster."

CHAPTER THIRTEEN

KNIGHTS OF LEGEND

Sophia followed Caina, Kylon, and Seb as they left the White Boar and walked into the town's square.

Sophia had never liked the town square. True, on market days the square was full of farmers selling crops and pigs and cows, and on the festival days the square filled with dancing and laughter and music.

But on days when old Boyar Vlad had visited the town to dispense his justice, his men had built gallows in the center of the square and hanged those who had earned the boyar's justice. The boyar himself had watched the executions, grim and unsmiling. Vlad Nagrach had been an iron-hearted, unyielding man, and he never had so much as blinked as criminals begged for his nonexistent mercy. Sophia had been terrified of the boyar as a little girl.

How strange that she now found his son far more frightening. Boyar Vlad had only hung thieves and murderers and petty criminals. He had never demanded that the town surrender seven girls and women for the Boyar's Hunt.

Caina strode across the square, the cold wind tugging at the skirts of her long coat, a few strands of black hair dancing alongside her head. Sophia had to admit that she had no idea what a proper Nighmarian noblewoman was supposed to look like, but she thought Caina looked...important. Like someone in authority. Certainly, if someone looking like that had given Sophia a command, she would have jumped to obey it.

The transformation was astonishing. When Sophia had met Caina, the woman had seemed calm and collected and soft-spoken. Now she spoke in tones of ringing command, her Caerish overlaid with a heavy Imperial accent. Even her stride and posture had changed. It was like she had transformed herself into another woman. Seb seemed amused by it. Lord Kylon took it calmly. Perhaps he was used to it.

"Sophia," murmured Caina, her queenly expression still in place. "The burgomaster's name. Magur?"

Sophia nodded.

"What is his wife's name?"

"Olya," said Sophia. "They have seven children." She hesitated. "Their daughters are twins about two years older than me. The boyar also chose them for the Hunt."

Caina's eyes flashed. "Did he? Interesting. Thank you, Sophia."

They walked to the burgomaster's house. Sophia liked both the burgomaster's house and the Temple far better than the square. Old Magur was a kindly man and sometimes gave sweets to children on festival days. And Sophia had spent many contented hours in the Temple, listening to Brother Valexis and his acolytes lead prayers to the Divine or sitting in the old man's lessons as he taught the children of the town to read and write and do sums. A few of the town's women had whispered about Sophia learning to read and write, but Uncle Ivan had laughed at them.

"I'm an old man, and the girl's got to look after her own damn self when I'm gone," Ivan had said. "If she knows how to do sums so no one can cheat her."

A burst of fear went through Sophia. She hoped that the boyar had left Uncle Ivan alone. She hoped that Ivan would not suffer for her decision to flee.

They strode up to the door to the burgomaster's house, and Kylon knocked three times. The door swung open. Magur's youngest son Yuri stood there, a shaggy-headed boy of about nine, and he gaped at them with fear. Sophia could sense the mixture of confusion and excitement and fear coming from him.

Then Yuri bowed.

"Please, my noblest lady, come inside," he said in Caerish, pronouncing the words carefully. "The burgomaster welcomes you to his...his...horny home."

"Humble," Sophia corrected him.

Yuri flashed her a grateful look. "His humble home."

"I am honored to accept the burgomaster's invitation," said Caina in a grave voice. "Please, young sir, lead the way."

Flustered, Yuri bowed again and led the way inside. They walked through the small entry hall and into the dining hall. A long, polished wooden table ran the length of the hall, lined by sturdy chairs. A fire crackled in the large hearth, and the paneled walls were covered by tapestries showing the Warmaiden's victory over the Iron King and the Iron King's victory over the Kagari khans.

Three old men stood near the fire, waiting for them.

The first was Magur, burgomaster of Kostiv. He was bald as an egg, with barely a fringe of gray hair left on the back of his head. His clothes were little different than the other men of Kostiv, save that he wore his golden chain of office around his neck.

The second man was Brother Valexis, the keeper of Kostiv's Temple. He was even older than Magur, so old that he looked withered, and his brown robe nearly swallowed him. The seven-pointed star of the Divine hung from a chain around his neck, and she saw the fear in both his expression and in his emotional sense.

It was fear for her.

Ivan Zomanek was the final man. Despite his crippled right leg, her uncle was still a big man, with arms like tree trunks, and he wielded his blacksmith's hammer with vigor. He leaned on a cane of iron that he had forged himself, his face like old leather, his hair and beard the color of the iron he worked.

Sophia barely remembered the fire that had killed her parents and crippled her uncle. All she remembered was the smoke and the flames and the screaming, remembered coughing as she called for her mother. A fallen beam had crushed Ivan's leg, but he had clawed his way free from the burning house, taking Sophia with him.

That had been eight years ago.

For a moment Ivan, Valexis, and Magur stared at her in silence.

"Oh, child," said Magur in Ulkaari at last, his voice heavy with sorrow. "Shall we bring our disasters upon these strangers as well?"

Sophia swallowed and gathered her courage. "We should speak the traders' language, your honor. All of our guests speak it, but only the Lord Sebastian speaks Ulkaari."

"Very well," said Magur in Caerish. He bowed in Caina's direction. "I am Magur Kostakov, the burgomaster of Kostiv, as my father was before me. This is Ivan Zomanek, the best blacksmith in the village, and Brother Valexis of the Temple."

"A pleasure," said Caina. "I am Caina Amalas Tarshahzon Kardamnos, a Countess of the Empire of Nighmar and an amirja of Istarinmul. This is Kylon of House Kardamnos, my husband, and Sebastian Scorneus, a battle magus of the Imperial Magisterium."

She didn't mention that Sebastian was her half-brother, despite their obvious resemblance. Perhaps Caina still wasn't happy with that fact.

Ivan scoffed and looked at Kylon. "You let your wife do your talking, son?"

Kylon gave an indifferent shrug. "She's better at talking to strangers. I'm better at killing them."

Magur and Valexis both flinched, but Ivan barked his harsh laugh. "Ha! A good answer. My Malia was the same way." Aunt Malia had died before Sophia had been born, and Ivan had never remarried. "She could always talk me down when I wanted to thrash some damn idiot or another." He sighed. "Pity she's not here now. Though maybe it's just as well she has not lived to see such dark days."

"My lady, forgive us," said Magur. "I fear you have walked into something of a...local problem. Nothing to trouble you with, I think." He hesitated. "Might I ask your business in Kostiv?"

Sophia wondered how Caina could answer that. The truth was wildly implausible.

"You may," said Caina. "I am simply passing through. We are departing Ulkaar, and Kostiv happened to be in our path. We met young Sophia upon the road, and she has been a most useful local guide."

Magur frowned. "Then you intend to take her with you when you depart Ulkaar?"

Caina shrugged. "If it does not cause strife with her family, but I understand her parents are dead. Sophia is a talented young lady, and she will go far in the courts of the cities. And if her parents are dead, perhaps there is nothing to tie her to Kostiv."

"Yes," said Ivan at once, and Valexis nodded his agreement. "Yes, my lady, if you are willing, you should take Sophia from Kostiv at once."

Magur turned an anguished look at the other two men. "And what of the rest of us? What of those of us who have daughters and cannot flee?"

"Then we should write to the Boyar of Risiviri," said Ivan at once. "He is a bitter enemy of the Voivode of Vagraastrad. He will aid us."

"Or to the High Temple in Risiviri," said Valexis. "If they can dispatch witchfinders to Kostiv, they might be able to aid us. Or perhaps they can even send magi." He glanced at Seb. "One has already come. Perhaps more shall arrive as well."

"One magus could do nothing against the boyar's men," said Magur, his pain and fear visible both on his face and in his emotional sense. He shifted to Ulkaari, not wanting the outlanders to hear and forgetting that Sophia had said that Seb spoke Ulkaari. "The boyar would kill them all. A lone battle magus could not stand against the mavrokhi, no matter how skillful and powerful. As for this foreign Countess? The boyar would take her and make her run in his Hunt as well. You know Razdan Nagrach as well as I do, and humbling a proud foreign noblewoman would please him to no end."

"Perhaps she can help us," said Ivan in the same language.

Valexis shook his head. "I doubt it. A Countess of the Empire and an amirja of Istarinmul? A ridiculous story! Likely she is a scoundrel who assumes we are rural simpletons and seeks to fleece us for our money. Even in Kostiv, we have heard of the woman Caina Amalas. What would this so-called Balarigar be doing in northern Ulkaar? No, this is a trick."

"Men of Kostiv," said Caina in Caerish, raising her hands. "A moment."

Magur, Ivan, and Valexis all looked at her.

"I should remind you," said Caina, "that Lord Sebastian speaks fluent Ulkaari, and will tell me everything you just said."

Magur made a strangled sound. Valexis looked dismayed, and Uncle Ivan only seemed amused. Of course, he would find it funny. He had always had the most inappropriate sense of humor.

"Well," said Seb, "they think you are a scoundrel, and that you are impersonating an Imperial noblewoman to steal money from them."

Caina laughed.

"Why is that funny?" said Sophia.

"I've been accused of a lot of things," said Caina, "but I don't think I've ever been accused of impersonating myself." She shook her head and turned her attention back to Magur. "Let me see if I understand correctly, burgomaster. If I take Sophia from Kostiv, you fear the boyar's wrath will fall upon you."

"I wish to speak bluntly, my lady," said Magur.

"I would prefer it."

"Good." The burgomaster took a deep breath. "You should leave at one, my lady. Leave Kostiv and never return. The boyar will punish us for letting Sophia run. We all knew she would run. To look the other way as she fled into the haunted forests was like looking the other way while she tied a noose around her neck, but at least in the forest she had a chance of escape. But now you have brought her back into the boyar's reach. He will kill her...and he will kill you, my lady."

Caina raised an eyebrow. "He would dare to kill an Imperial noblewoman?"

Magur's face was harsh. "Yes. It is time for more blunt speech. You are a long way from the Imperial capital, and you are traveling without guards, save for your husband and this battle magus. They will not be enough to protect you from Boyar Razdan. If he decides he wishes you dead, he will kill all three of you, and no one in the Empire will ever know your fate."

"He may also keep you alive, Countess," said Valexis, "and that would make death preferable, I fear."

Caina looked at the Brother for a moment and said something in a strange, fluid-sounding language that Sophia did not know. She recognized it, though. It was the language of the solemn liturgies of the Temple, the language of the Warmaiden as she had led her Arvaltyri against the Iron King and his demons.

Whatever Caina had said, Valexis reacted as if she had slapped him. What little color was in his face drained away, and he stared at her in shock. Both Magur and Ivan gave the old Brother a surprised look, and then Magur shrugged and turned back to Caina.

"Brother Valexis did not exaggerate the danger." The burgomaster tugged at his chain of office. "For your own sake, my lady, please. Leave at once. If the boyar turns his wrath towards you, then nothing will save you."

"It is possible," said Caina, "that you are wrong about that. And it is already too late."

Magur frowned. "What do you mean?"

"Does the boyar have many szlachts in his service?" said Caina.

"Not many," said Magur. "Only sixteen, but they are all…ah, they are all dangerous warriors." Sophia had seen him start to say the word "mavrokhi" but change his mind at the last moment.

"Is one of them named Varlov?" said Caina.

"Yes." Magur's frown deepened. "He is a cruel man, and takes what he wishes from the town's merchants without paying."

"He's also dead," said Caina.

Stunned silence greeted her announcement.

"Impossible," said Valexis at last.

"I saw it with my own eyes," said Sophia. "Lord Kylon killed Varlov."

"He was with another szlacht named Rudjak," said Caina. "It seems the boyar told Rudjak and his szlachts to hunt down Sophia after she fled from Kostiv." Ivan's expression tightened. "They caught up to us about half a day northeast of here. Rudjak demanded that we hand Sophia over to him. I refused."

"You are lying," said Magur, his anger pushing against Sophia's senses. "You are all lying. If you challenged Rudjak and the szlachts, they would have killed you all and carried off Sophia to the castle to await the Hunt."

"Why?" said Caina. "Because they are mavrokhi?"

Silence answered her.

"Varlov transformed in front of us," said Caina. "His eyes turned the yellow of an infected wound, fur covered his skin, fangs filled his mouth, and claws like daggers grew from his fingers and toes. I would say he looked like a giant wolf, but no wolf ever looked so ugly or smelled so foul. He charged us, and Lord Kylon cut him open and killed him."

"Impossible," breathed Magur. "The mavrokhi...Varlov would have just healed from even a grievous wound, and Rudjak and the others would have killed you all."

"They were frightened," said Caina, "and they fled. I expect they ran right back to the boyar to tell him what happened. Meanwhile, Sophia led us here, and we are now speaking with you."

"That is impossible," said Ivan, wariness in his sense. "The mavrokhi are very hard to kill. One of them is a match for a score of stout men, and you are two men, a woman, and a girl. Varlov alone could have killed you all. You couldn't have defeated Rudjak and his men."

"We didn't," said Caina. "They were dismayed after Varlov's death."

Ivan frowned and looked at Seb. "What, then? Are you a magus of mighty spells? One of the high magi, maybe?"

"I fear not, sir," said Seb. "I am quite good with a sword, but with my spells, I am only middling, much to the lasting despair of my teachers."

"Then how," said Ivan, "did you..."

Magur's temper snapped.

"Enough!" bellowed the burgomaster, his face turning red.

They all looked at him, save for Valexis. The Brother of the Temple was still staring at Caina, shaken. Sophia wondered what Caina had said to him.

"This is intolerable," said Magur, his hands and voice shaking with rage. "Bad enough that we must live under Razdan Nagrach's tyranny. Bad enough that we must surrender our daughters to slake his lusts, and there is no one to defend us or help us. But now you come here and give us false hope!" He leveled a thick finger at Caina. "I know what you are."

Caina remained calm. "What am I?"

Her voice was quiet now, the imperious accent gone, just as her voice had been when Sophia had met her in Sigilsoara.

"You are a trickster," said Magur.

"I cannot disagree."

Magur gave a shake of his head. "No. No. You've spun a web of lies around us. You've convinced Sophia that you can save her, but nothing can save her. Nothing can save us. If we don't hand over those seven girls to the boyar, he'll kill more of us." He shook his head, despair and rage filling his sense, the grief of a father watching two of his daughters go to a horrible fate. "Maybe if we hand you over to the boyar, he will show us mercy."

Caina only raised an eyebrow. "Do you really believe that, burgomaster?"

Magur's expression crumpled. The strain of the last two years had aged him. "No."

"Perhaps we can help you," said Caina.

Magur scoffed. "No one can help us."

"Then there is nothing I can say that will convince you?" said Caina.

"No."

Caina smiled. "What about something I can do?"

Caina watched the three leading men of Kostiv.

They were, for the most part, beaten men. Ivan had some defiance left in him, and she guessed that he wanted to go out fighting. But he was not a fool, and he knew that would be a useless gesture that would get people killed. Magur seemed utterly beaten, crushed by fear of what would befall his daughters in the Boyar's Hunt.

Valexis was shocked.

But, then, telling him in flawless Iramisian that both Iramis and the valikarion of old had returned would have that effect on a man who knew the history of Iramis.

"Do?" said Magur, his bitterness plain. "What can you do?"

Caina took a deep breath. What she did next might save all their lives…or lead to the deaths of many innocent people beneath the claws of the mavrokhi.

Once again, she was playing a deadly game, and these men before her, their families and neighbors and children, they were the stakes in this game.

"This," said Caina.

She raised her right hand with a flourish, turning her palm and pulling up her sleeve to show them that her hand was empty and that she had nothing up her sleeve.

Magur glared at her, his hands balling as if he wanted to strike her. "What nonsense is this…"

Caina called her valikon.

The shards of silver light leaped out of nowhere and assembled themselves into the valikon in a heartbeat, the curved blade of ghostsilver erupting into white flames. Caina saw the flicker of light as Kylon called his own valikon, and she sent a request to her pyrikon. The diadem unfolded itself into her left hand and expanded into the form of its slender staff, the end giving off a white glow. She supposed that was a bit excessive for the point she wanted to make.

But it worked.

Magur rocked back with a croaking noise, his eyes bulging. Ivan said several words that Caina supposed he did not use in front of Sophia all that often. Brother Valexis let out a little cry of wonder, his watery eyes wide, his lined face transformed with amazement.

"What?" managed Magur at last. "What is this?"

"You know what it is! It is a valikon!" said Valexis, gazing at the sword. His voice shook with powerful emotion, and Caina was surprised to recognize it as joy. "It is one of the holy valikons carried by the Arvaltyri in ancient days when they marched alongside the Warmaiden, when they kept Ulkaar free of necromancy and the demons of the netherworld."

"That is impossible," said Magur. "All the Arvaltyri were slain long ago."

"They were," said Caina, pointing her valikon at him. Magur flinched. "But my name is Caina Amalas Tarshahzon Kardamnos. I went into the netherworld and came out again, and I am a valikarion. I found this sword in the tomb of a Great Necromancer, and I have borne it ever since. I saw Iramis return from the netherworld and rise again, and the valikarion of old returned to the world of the living. How do you think my husband slew Varlov? Why do you think Rudjak fled? The touch of the valikon slew the mavrokh spirit, and Varlov died in his wickedness. Lest they share his fate, Rudjak and the others fled."

For a moment, no one spoke. Magur kept trembling.

"Can it be true?" said Magur at last. "Can the valikarion really have returned?"

"They have," said Sophia. Caina glanced at the girl. "Burgomaster, it is true. When I fled into the forest, in my terror I ran heedlessly into Sigilsoara itself."

"Speak not that evil name!" said Magur.

"But it is true," said Sophia. "I saw it with my own eyes. Lady Caina slew one of the Temnoti and its undead soldiers. Together she and Lord Kylon escaped from Sigilsoara. And Lord Kylon killed Vaclav, even after he took his wolf-form! I swear by the Divine it is all true!"

Valexis began to whisper under his breath. Caina recognized it as a prayer of thanksgiving to the Divine. Tears of joy trickled down his face as he recited the prayer.

A strange sensation of unreality went through Caina. How had this happened? She had been trained as a spy and a Ghost nightfighter, and spies were supposed to remain invisible, unnoticed.

And now she stood before the leading men of a town while holding a burning sword. If there was a better way to draw attention, Caina could not think of it.

She had been a spy, but that path had taken her in a different direction. Now she was the adopted sister of the Padishah of Istarinmul, the Liberator of Iramis, and a valikarion. Caina the Ghost nightfighter would not have been able to help the people of Kostiv.

But perhaps Caina the valikarion could.

Or, a dark voice whispered in her head, maybe Caina the valikarion would get them all killed.

No. Now was not the time to show doubt or weakness.

"I know what the Boyar's Hunt is," said Caina in a quiet voice. "I know what Razdan Nagrach wants to do to your town and your daughters. If you wish it, I will depart and never return. But I can help you. We might be the only people for a thousand miles who can help you."

Magur hesitated and looked at the others.

"Yes," said Valexis. "It is the will of the Divine. The valikarion have returned at last. Perhaps the shadows shall start to lift from Ulkaar."

"By the Divine, let's fight!" said Ivan. "It's past time we stood up for ourselves! Perhaps we shall fight alongside the valikarion like the men of Ulkaar did in ancient days. Maybe we'll all die, aye. But better to die fighting like men than to die quaking in our own sweat and waiting to see who the Hounds of the Iron King will claim next."

Magur closed his eyes and took a deep breath, and then another.

"So be it," he said at last. "So be it. If we are to embark upon this folly, then embark upon it we shall. Maybe you will get us all killed. Or maybe you really are an Arvaltyr. What would you have of us?"

"Just one thing," said Caina, lowering her hand and dismissing her valikon. Her pyrikon settled back into its bracelet form upon her wrist. "I need you to send a message to the boyar's castle right now."

"A message?" said Magur with a frown.

"Yes." Caina smiled. "I'd like to invite the boyar to dine with me."

CHAPTER FOURTEEN

NO INTERRUPTIONS

They had indeed, Kylon reflected, set the storm among the fleet. Or the fox among the chickens.

But regardless of the metaphor, they had stirred up the town of Kostiv.

Kylon had visited countless small fishing villages near New Kyre and its colonies on the islands of the western sea, and he knew how small towns worked. Likely most of the families of Kostiv were all related to one another to some degree, and that meant gossip traveled faster than the wind itself.

Caina had claimed most of the upper floor of the White Boar for her plan. From the common room, a flight of stairs led up to a wooden balcony overlooking the lower level, and Kylon stationed himself at the top of the stairs to keep watch as Caina and Sophia prepared with the help of Rachov's family. The emotions of the people of the town had been roused enough that Kylon sensed them without even trying. Before, an aura of sullen fear had hung over the town. Caina's arrival and her little demonstration had ignited the emotions of Kostiv like a torch thrown into a vat of oil. Kylon sensed wild hope and terror from the townspeople, mixed with a bit of awe.

Their reactions had been almost religious.

Come to think of it, their reactions had been religious. The Warmaiden might have introduced Ulkaar to the Iramisian faith of the

Divine, but the valikarion had been wrapped up in her legend. Sophia had not been the only child in Ulkaar raised on tales of the mighty Arvaltyri of old. The thought that one of the Arvaltyri might have returned to deliver them from the cruel boyar had set off a wild elation in the people of Kostiv.

But a great deal of fear tempered that elation. And Kylon knew that a terrified townsman might try to stave off Razdan Nagrach's fury by killing the so-called valikarion and presenting her head to the boyar.

So, just in case, Kylon stood guard at the top of the stairs and watched the common room, his hand resting on the saber's jeweled hilt. For now, he kept his valikon dismissed. Caina had said they should only summon the weapons at need, given the effect their appearance had on the Ulkaari, and Kylon agreed with that assessment.

A crowd filled the common room of the White Boar, ostensibly to drink, but Kylon heard the low murmur of conversation. He couldn't understand their language, but he knew they were speculating about Caina, about whether or not she was really a valikarion. None of them climbed the stairs to see for themselves. Kylon was amused that he was intimidating enough to keep them at bay even without the valikon in hand.

The door to the market opened, and Sebastian Scorneus stepped inside, a gust of cold wind following him. At once silence fell, and the townsmen stared at him. The valikarion might have passed into legend, but the black-armored battle magi were very real and often very dangerous. Seb paid no heed to the stares, strode to the counter, and purchased two cups of beer from Rachov.

Then he climbed up the stairs, stood next to Kylon, and passed him one of the cups.

"I have spent half my life on guard duty," said Seb, "and by all the gods, it is thirsty work."

"Not as thirsty as some tasks," said Kylon. He took a drink of the beer. "Thank you." The Ulkaari beer was so thick it was almost like drinking a loaf of fermented bread.

"The messenger is off to the boyar's castle," said Seb. He took a drink of his own beer. "Magur and Ivan think that the boyar should arrive at the town tomorrow by noon."

"He'll ride at once," said Kylon, watching the townsmen. "He won't have any choice. It's too much of a challenge to his authority. First, we killed one of his men, and then he received an invitation from another noble in his own town? Caina thinks Razdan has too much pride in being a noble to refuse the invitation, so he'll come."

"And then?" said Seb.

Kylon shrugged. "And then we'll see what happens." He was reasonably sure this confrontation was going to end in a fight. If so, the town of Kostiv would be a far better battlefield than the forest. The mavrokhi were fast and strong, but the narrow streets and alleys would limit their speed.

Of course, Razdan Nagrach had to know that as well.

"Lady Caina seems quite confident in her assessment of a man she has never met," said Seb.

"She's usually right about that kind of thing," said Kylon. "She spent all that time talking to Magur and Valexis and Ivan about him, and they probably know the boyar better than anyone in Kostiv." He looked at the battle magus. "And you don't disagree with her. You think in the same sideways manner that she does, and you agree with her opinion of Nagrach."

Seb blinked in confusion and then laughed. "Is it that obvious? Yes, I think she is correct. Obviously, Razdan Nagrach is a young man newly come to a great deal of power, both as the new boyar and as a new mavrokh. He's insecure in that power and wishes to prove it, both to himself and to his subjects." His cold blue eyes took on the same distant cast that Caina's did when she was thinking. "Else why reinstitute the Boyar's Hunt? It is a wasteful and violent exercise of power that will only alienate the townsfolk from him and make the task of government more difficult. A young man's folly."

"Or that of a man who enjoys cruelty," said Kylon, thinking of the Red Huntress. Perhaps the mavrokhi fed upon pain in the same way that the nagataaru did.

"Alas, both men who love cruelty and foolish young men are all too common," said Seb. He looked away, and a flicker of old pain went through his emotional sense. "Men and women both." His gaze turned back to Kylon. "I wish to ask you a question."

Kylon snorted. "Can't you simply deduce the answer?"

"I suppose I could, but your reaction will be informative. Since we shall likely be fighting alongside each other tomorrow or the day after tomorrow, it would be useful to know."

Kylon inclined his head.

"Does taking orders from your wife annoy you?" said Seb.

Kylon burst out laughing. Some of the townsmen turned surprised looks in his direction. Kylon supposed the laughter would detract from his image as a grim warrior.

"She doesn't tell me what to do," said Kylon.

Seb hesitated and then smiled. "Then you have done a very good job of fooling me."

Kylon shrugged. "She's right, most of the time. If I think she's right, I'll do what she wants, and if I think she's wrong, I'll change her mind. I trust her completely." He thought back. "I suppose I trusted her even before I loved her."

"Then you married for love?" said Seb. There was an odd note in his voice.

"I'm an exiled Kyracian noble, and she is, or was, a Ghost nightfighter and circlemaster," said Kylon. "People like us don't marry except for love." An insight occurred to him. "What about you? You married for love, didn't you?"

Seb blinked in surprise.

"Ah," said Kylon. "That's another way you two are similar. Caina never likes it when people figure things out about her, and neither do you."

"How did you guess?" said Seb.

"Caina's smarter than I am," said Kylon, "and you probably are too, but I'm not an idiot."

They stood in silence for a moment.

"I was," said Seb. "Married for love, I mean."

Kylon nodded. "She died?"

"Yes," said Seb. "You will understand if I do not wish to discuss the matter further."

"I do," said Kylon. "Better than you think, probably. I was married before Caina. My first wife was assassinated."

They lapsed into silence. Kylon took another drink of his beer. He would have preferred Kyracian wine, but the White Boar's beer was good, at least as beer went.

"Might I confess something to you, Lord Kylon?" said Seb.

"I really wish you wouldn't."

Seb smiled. "Ha! A true answer. The Ulkaari have a proverb that an honest answer is like a kiss on the lips."

"The Iramisians have the same proverb," said Kylon, "but if you try to kiss me, I'm not going to react well."

Seb laughed at that. "Another honest answer! But I wish only to confess this." He waved a hand at the room. "When I was a child, I wanted to be a valikarion."

Kylon blinked. "I think you mentioned that in the forest."

"Yes, but not the extent of it," said Seb. "My sister Calvia and I were raised by Talmania Scorneus and Ariadne Scorneus after our mother abandoned us. Well, at least by Talmania's servants, anyway. Talmania herself had little interest in us. She wanted to raise us to be her…vassals, essentially, her supporters in the Magisterium when we became full magi."

Kylon nodded. "Like Decius Aberon the First Magus does with his bastard children."

"Precisely," said Seb. "I fear the arrangement is quite common for more powerful magi. Anyway, thankfully I spent more time with my tutors than with Aunt Talmania herself. The lessons in swordplay and history were my favorites...and I confess I loved the stories of the valikarion, the Arvaltyri of ancient days. I wanted to be a valikarion. I wanted to be a heroic knight who rode into the village and slew the wicked monsters that terrorized the people."

"I thought something similar," said Kylon. "I wanted to be a strong and just Kyracian lord, a defender of the Kyracian people." He supposed he had become something like that, at least for a time of his life. And now he was...what, exactly? A landless exile wed to the Liberator of Iramis?

Of course, at the moment they were both landless exiles in Ulkaar.

The idea did not trouble him. The Surge had given him a chance to return to New Kyre, and he had turned it down to stay with Caina. A flicker of old irritation went through him at the thought. What had the oracle been thinking, asking him to return to New Kyre without Caina? Surely, she had known he would refuse.

Damned oracles.

"But I grew up," said Seb, "and I found that there were no valikarion. And, truth be told, no heroes. I thought being a battle magus would be the closest I could come to a valikarion, but I rarely spent any time hunting down creatures of sorcery. Instead, I fought in the Empire's wars, first against the Kyracians and the Istarish and then against the Umbarians."

"I lost many illusions in war as well," said Kylon. When he had gone to Marsis with Andromache, he had been certain of his place in the world and confident in his sister.

Then everything had changed.

"To see all this," said Seb, "is unsettling."

"What do you mean?" said Kylon, though he thought he knew.

"Your wife claims to be a valikarion," started Seb.

"She is a valikarion," said Kylon. "I was there. It happened by accident, but she is a valikarion. You know that as well as I do. She can see spells, and you can't sense her with any spells."

"She is a valikarion," conceded Seb, "but is she ready to be one?"

"What do you mean?" said Kylon.

"Look at these people," said Seb, lowering his voice. "They want to believe. They want to believe that a valikarion has shown up to save them from the mavrokhi, that they won't have to hand their daughters over to the boyar. Some of them think that if they just placate Razdan Nagrach, he'll leave them alone, but the wiser ones know better. Maybe next year the boyar will call another Hunt. Or maybe once this year's harvest is complete, even. But maybe a valikarion can save them from all of that."

"Or," said Kylon, "we'll fail, we'll all be killed, and the boyar will take his revenge on Kostiv."

"The thought had occurred to me," said Seb. "The thought has occurred to them as well. And it is not as if Lady Caina could fight hand-to-hand with a mavrokh and survive. You and I could, but she could not."

"No," said Kylon. "But she doesn't need to. She should have been killed a long time ago."

Seb frowned. "What do you mean?"

"I first met her during the battle for Marsis," said Kylon. "She should have died there, but she didn't." It sometimes unsettled him to think of how close he had come to killing his future wife with his own hand.

How different would his life have been then.

For one thing, his life would have been much shorter, since Scorikhon would have possessed Andromache and then killed Kylon.

Seb shrugged. "Luck ever rules the battlefield."

"It does," said Kylon, "but she was both lucky and clever. And I've seen it happen again and again." Catekharon and Caer Magia and the Craven's Tower and the Inferno flashed through his memory. "You heard that speech she gave to Sophia. It wasn't an exaggeration. I killed Cassander, but she was the one who outwitted him, twice. And if Razdan Nagrach won't see reason, she'll find a way to outwit him, too."

"And then you'll kill him," said Seb.

Kylon shrugged again. "If I must."

"She does the clever things, and you kill her enemies when they try to stop her from doing clever things," said Seb. "I suppose there are worse foundations for a marriage."

Kylon laughed. "I am pleased we have your approval."

Seb snorted. "My approval is of no consequence to anyone." His amusement faded. "Many of us in House Scorneus are clever, too. But I don't think any of them would lift a finger to help someone like Sophia Zomanek. Most of them would not approve of the Boyar's Hunt, true, but they would not help."

"Caina would," said Kylon, looking at the people in the common room. "She's more ruthless than I am, but she has a stronger conscience."

"I believe that is a contradiction, Lord Kylon," said Seb.

"It's not." Kylon finished his beer and set the cup on the railing. "Once Caina learned why Sophia fled Kostiv, the conflict was inevitable. She wouldn't have turned back. If I were alone, I could have walked away from Kostiv. The Boyar's Hunt is an evil thing, but there are evil things everywhere, and a man cannot save the world from itself. But Caina..." He paused, arranging his thoughts. "If there is a way to stop the boyar, she will find it."

"Your confidence cheers me," said Seb. "To be blunt, I wish I shared it."

Kylon smiled. "That will make Caina happy."

Seb looked confused. "Why?"

"Because she prefers to be underestimated."

"That ought to do," said Caina, looking over the dining room.

The top floor of the White Boar had a private dining room, a large, rectangular chamber with a long wooden table and its own hearth. With the help of Rachov's wife and daughters, Caina had prepared the table, covering it with white linen and setting out plates and silverware. One of Rachov's daughters had also located a dress for Caina to wear, which she had paid for using coins taken from the ardivid's soldiers. By the standards of Malarae, the blue dress would have been a common garment. By the standards of Kostiv and northern Ulkaar, it was one of the finest garments in the village.

The dress would serve its purpose. Caina doubted that Razdan Nagrach had ever been out of Ulkaar, and if he had, he likely would not have traveled far. The Nighmarian nobles of the capital often considered provincial nobility to be little more than haughty peasants. That attitude had come back to haunt them, given how many of those "haughty peasants" had sided with the Umbarians, but Razdan Nagrach struck Caina as someone who would have taken that condescension to heart.

She hoped to use that insecurity to her advantage.

But the dining room was ready, and Caina was ready.

She hoped that it would be enough.

If it wasn't…well, she had already started working out a backup plan. Kostiv's narrow streets offered advantages against creatures like the mavrokhi, as did the high roofs. Hunting was common in Kostiv, and Ivan Zomanek had told her about the many different kinds of traps he made at his forge. Wolves hunted through scent, and if the mavrokhi did the same, Kostiv had a carpenter's shop…

"Is there anything else we need to do?" said Sophia, hovering at Caina's elbow.

Caina looked at the girl. "No. Not yet. Now, all we need to do is wait."

Sophia shivered. "Do you really think the boyar will come?"

"Oh, yes," said Caina. "I'm certain of it." If she guessed right, Boyar Razdan would be unable to stop himself from coming to meet her. "And when he does…I want you to stay out of sight. Go into one of the inn's upper rooms, close the door, and don't come out again until I come for you. If the boyar sees you, he might lose his temper, and then we'll have a fight right then."

It would be a fair fight, and Caina did not like fair fights. She had advantages in such a fight – the valikons that she and Kylon carried, Kylon's and Seb's skill at sorcery and swordplay, and the relatively cramped confines of the inn. But the mavrokhi would have speed and strength, and the boyar might bring every single one of his Hounds with him.

No. For now, best to avoid a fight. Perhaps Caina would even be able to persuade Razdan to let them go.

She doubted it.

"I will, my lady," said Sophia. She shivered. "I don't want to see the boyar ever again."

"Good," said Caina. "Go get some dinner, and then you should probably go to sleep." She glanced out the shutters at the darkened town below. "Tomorrow is going to probably be a long day."

Sophia turned to go, and then hesitated. "My lady…thank you for all this. You didn't have to help me."

"I haven't helped anyone yet," said Caina. "Good night, Sophia."

"Good night, my lady," said Sophia. She left the dining room.

Caina watched her go, and then opened a side door and stepped into the room she had rented for Kylon and herself. The furnishings were simple but clean, with a large bed, a wooden table, a small fireplace, and a pair of chairs. Given how cold Caina had been since they had arrived in Ulkaar, she looked forward to lighting a fire and sleeping beneath a pile of blankets.

She would likely need to rest for tomorrow.

The door to the balcony in the common room opened, and Kylon stepped inside, closing and latching the door behind him.

"Sophia's gone to sleep," he said. "Seb's keeping first watch. He'll wake me at midnight to take his place."

Caina nodded. "That is wise." It was possible she had misjudged Razdan Nagrach, and he would send an assassin to kill her in her sleep. Or the townsmen might panic and try to kill them to placate the boyar. The lives of their children were at stake, and nothing made people more irrational and more dangerous than threats against their children.

That was something, Caina thought, she would never know. It left her with a twinge of sadness. Then again, she had seen the anguish written upon Magur's face as he thought of his daughters' fate in the Hunt.

That was something else Caina would never have to know.

"I think," said Caina, "that we..."

Before she could finish the question, Kylon crossed the room, grabbed her hips, pulled her close, and kissed her hard. For a moment, sheer surprise froze Caina, and then the surprise melted into something else, something far more pleasant.

While she had been with Corvalis, Caina had learned something about herself that surprised her. A brush with death often put a fire in her blood, and as soon as she and Corvalis had been alone, she had all but jumped into his arms. The same thing was true with Kylon. There were many things about Kylon that she loved – his decency, his courage, his refusal to indulge in cruelty, the way his brown eyes were more amber-colored when she was close to him.

But if she was honest with herself, it was his strength that aroused her. It was a side of herself that she only felt comfortable sharing with him.

"We didn't get to finish," whispered Caina when they broke apart. Her heartbeat had quickened, and she felt a spreading warmth in her chest. "On our wedding night. The spell brought us here first."

"No," said Kylon. His eyes glittered in the firelight from the hearth. "No interruptions here, I hope."

"What are you going to do about that?" said Caina.

He showed her. It involved pulling off all her clothes and carrying her to the bed. In short order, he had removed his own garments and joined her, and Caina wrapped her arms around him, and then her legs, pulling him as close to her as she could manage. She pressed her face into his shoulder to muffle her cry as she finished. Perhaps the townspeople would overhear them, but for the moment she did not care.

After they were done, Caina curled beneath the blanket and dozed, her head resting against Kylon's chest, her mind and heart clearer than they had been since she had arrived in Ulkaar.

Later she awoke and found that Kylon was not there. Caina blinked in surprise. Was it midnight already? He must have gone to relieve Seb at watch. She turned her head and instead saw Kylon on one knee by the fireplace, arranging some fresh logs with the iron poker. He hadn't gotten dressed, and his skin seemed to glow in the light from the fire, the flickering light tracing the muscles of his arms and chest and legs.

It was a compelling sight. Kylon must have felt the weight of Caina's gaze, because he looked up from the fire.

Caina smiled and tossed aside the blankets, propping herself up on her elbow.

"I'm cold," she said.

"The fire should warm up shortly," said Kylon.

"I don't care about the fire."

He put aside the poker, got to his feet, and joined her.

After they finished Caina and Kylon lay on their backs, the fire throwing dancing shadows across the rafters of the ceiling. Caina caught her breath, her heart racing within her chest, and wiped the sweat from her face and eyes. It was just as well that Master Rachov's inn had a good bath. She would need it before she was presentable again.

Kylon rose, and Caina watched as he crossed to the table. There was a carafe and two cups there, and he poured them both some water and returned. She took the cup gratefully and drained the entire thing in two gulps.

"It's so cold outside," she said at last, her voice a little shaky. "Strange that we were sweating so much."

"Not really," said Kylon, and he gave her quick kiss as she lowered her cup. "We were busy."

"Yes, I suppose we were," said Caina. "Most busy indeed. We are properly married now."

"Hmm?" said Kylon. "As if the ceremony before half of Iramis wasn't enough?"

"We hadn't consummated it yet," said Caina. She always tended to babble after the act was done, but she was lightheaded enough that she didn't care. "That damned spell interrupted us. We spent the first night of our marriage wandering through some old sorcerer-king's damned maze of castle, the second going through a frozen forest. Now we've consummated it."

Kylon smiled. "It wasn't as if this was the first time for us."

"No, no," said Caina. She kissed him again, a little harder this time. "And I wasn't lying here trembling in fear of your touch." She grinned at him. "If I was trembling, it was because the valikon isn't the only sword you wield most skillfully."

Kylon laughed, and Caina let herself fall back on the bed with a contented sigh.

For a while, they lay in silence. Caina luxuriated in the softness of the bed, the heat of the room, and the warmth of Kylon's skin against hers. He could sense what she was feeling, she knew, so long as they were in physical contact. Caina supposed that gave him an advantage that most husbands did not have with their wives, but since she benefited from it, she would not complain when life was unfair in her favor.

But what did she feel right now? Her emotions were a confused tangle. She felt a pleasant lassitude, a deep affection for Kylon mixed with fear for his safety, fear for what might happen to Kostiv...and the cold calculation in the Ghost-trained parts of her mind that always preceded a fight.

"I am glad," Caina heard herself say, "that you are here with me. But I wish you were safe in Iramis."

"I don't," said Kylon. "If you had been drawn here and I had been left behind, that would have been intolerable. I would rather that you were safe in Iramis and I was here...but I suppose that you would have followed me through twelve hundred miles of ocean, mountains, and war. To know that you would have put yourself in such danger would have been...difficult."

"And for me to know the same of you," said Caina. She closed her eyes and laughed a little. "Just as well we were both brought here. Otherwise, we would have tried to find each other and likely passed each other in the night."

"Aye," said Kylon. He was quiet for a moment. "I wish I knew why we were here. Or even how."

Caina shrugged, her bare shoulders shifting against the bed. "We'll know once we return to Iramis. Annarah will know. Or one of the high loremasters. Then they can lock up this damned Ring of Rasarion Yagar, train Sophia as a loremaster, and that will be that."

"Do you think the boyar will listen to you?" said Kylon.

Caina stared at the shadows on the ceiling for a while.

"No," she said at last. "At least, I don't think he will. Kalgri and Malik Rolukhan wouldn't have listened to reason either. Their nagataaru twisted their thinking. No doubt the mavrokhi do the same to their hosts. But maybe I'm wrong. Maybe he'll listen. And if not...then I'll understand him better."

"And to defeat a man," said Kylon in a quiet voice, "you have to understand him."

"Yes," said Caina. She shuddered a little as a dark memory cut through the pleasant warmth filling her body. "It reminds me of when Claudia and Martin and Nasser and I were waiting for Kalgri at Silent Ash Temple. We had set a trap for her, and we thought it would be enough. But we didn't really understand her, not back then. We won the fight, but she recovered and returned at Rumarah."

Kylon's arm slid around her shoulders and tightened against her, and Caina rested her head against his chest. Silent Ash Temple was a dark memory. Rumarah was a far worse one. She had almost died there...but she had not, and the ordeal had given her the abilities of a valikarion.

Those abilities and the valikon she had taken from Silent Ash Temple might be what they needed to defeat Razdan Nagrach.

The next morning Caina finished getting dressed and stepped onto the balcony overlooking the common room.

Just as she did, a middle-aged man in leather armor ran up the stairs, breathing hard, his spear in hand.

"Master Vasily," said Caina, recognizing the townsman who had greeted them at Kostiv's gate.

Vasily blinked at her, no doubt surprised to see her wearing a proper dress. "Ah...my lady Arvaltyr," he said in halting High Nighmarian as he caught his breath. "You should know. We have seen horsemen on the road from the castle, about seven of them. The boyar is coming to Kostiv."

Caina looked back as Kylon followed her onto the balcony.

"The boyar?" he said.

Caina took a deep breath and nodded. "It's time."

CHAPTER FIFTEEN

RUIN

Razdan Nagrach, the boyar of Kostiv and lord of Castle Nagrach, led six of his pack brothers to the gates of his town.

It was cold winter day, the sky gray and overcast, the fields barren and frosted with snow, the river frozen beneath a sheet of ice. Yet even this icy day was alive to Razdan's senses in a way it would not have been a few short years past. He could smell the musk and sweat of his horse, could hear its heartbeat, could hear the rustling of its tail and the hairs stirring in its mane.

Around him, he smelled Rudjak and Bashkir and the other brothers of his pack of Hounds, heard the rasp of their breath and the faint thrum of their heartbeats. More than that, he was aware of their location in a way that did not involve his physical senses. He could sense the mavrokhi spirits bound within each of them, could feel the powerful spirits lying primed and ready, like a deadly wolf ready to spring upon its prey.

His enhanced senses were just one of the gifts of the mavrokh spirit stirring beneath Razdan's thoughts.

And all that the mavrokh asked in return for such powers was to be fed.

It was a request that Razdan was more than happy to oblige.

He slowed his horse to walk as they approached the gates of Kostiv. Two militiamen stood guard, and even from a distance,

Razdan smelled their fear, smelled the sweat starting to roll down their backs as their lord and master approached. The reaction pleased him. What was more, the mavrokh could sense the presence of the men. The spirit did not perceive the physical world as he did, but it sensed the life forces of the men waiting by the gate.

And it hungered to feed upon them.

"I urge caution, my lord," said Rudjak in a low voice. "Both the woman and her husband carry valikons, and the man is a Kyracian stormdancer. She would not have issued such a bold invitation unless she was certain of her safety."

"Bah!" said another of Razdan's sworn szlachts and his pack brothers. Balmin was a big, ferocious man with shaggy black hair and a bushy black beard, and his horse all but sagged beneath his bulk. Very little of his weight was fat, and he was almost as dangerous in human form as he was when his mavrokh manifested in its power. "Are we not the Hounds of the Iron King? If this outlander bitch thinks to threaten us, let us teach her the meaning of her folly. She will not be so haughty once we have each taken our turn with her. Perhaps we can even make her run in our lord's Hunt."

Rudjak glared at Balmin, his mavrokh stirring in wrath, a yellow cast coming into his eyes. "You were not there, Balmin. You did not see that sword the Kyracian carried. It was a valikon of old, I am certain of it." Balmin started to sneer, but Rudjak cut him off. "I sensed Varlov's mavrokh perish! No, it was no trick."

A shiver of fury went through Razdan. Some of it came from his mavrokh. The spirit demanded that he hunt down the threat and destroy it. Some of the rage belonged to Razdan himself. This foreign woman had dared to strike down one of his szlachts? She and her companions would suffer for this…

He forced back the rage, forced the mavrokh to subside.

Control. Control was vital. He was a mavrokh, a Hound of the Iron King, a predator moving among the herds of sheep that were the common men…but he still needed to exercise caution. An incautious predator was a dead predator.

Even prey still had teeth.

And something had killed Varlov and destroyed his mavrokh.

Balmin sneered at Rudjak. "Are you so unmanned by the stories of the old Arvaltyri? Perhaps I should put you to bed with a glass of warm milk, so you don't have nightmares."

Rudjak started to snarl back.

"Silence, both of you," said Razdan.

At once his szlachts fell silent, flinching from the anger in his gaze.

Razdan rode towards the gate to his town.

He could not help but wonder if his transformation into a mavrokh had drawn a reprisal at last. Had he become a mavrokh and reinstituted the Boyar's Hunt while his father had still been alive, it would not have lasted long. Someone would have sent word to the Imperial Lord Governor of Ulkaar. The Magisterium would have fallen on him like a storm, or the witchfinders of the Temple. The Umbarian Order had offered friendship in secret to many lords of Ulkaar for years, but they would not have lifted a finger to protect a lord who brought such attention to himself.

But the world had changed. The Empire would fall to the Umbarian Order. The old ways would come into the light, and Ulkaar would rise again in glory and power. The Syvashar had showed Razdan the truth. They would be victorious over both the Empire and the Umbarian Order.

Yet Razdan was not foolish enough to believe that victory was inevitable. And even if victory was inevitable, he still knew that carelessness might mean he would not live to see that victory.

After all, no doubt Varlov had thought he would live to see victory, and now Varlov was dead.

"We shall play this out," he informed his pack brothers. The szlachts nodded. "A parley before a battle is customary, after all. Remain vigilant, and I shall decide how to deal with this threat."

They rode in silence the rest of the way to the town, and Razdan reined up before the gate, glaring at the guards. The men went to one knee before their lord and bowed their heads.

"Costin, isn't it?" said Razdan, recognizing the man on the right.

"Yes, lord boyar," said Costin.

"What news from the town?" said Razdan.

"Foreigners have come to Kostiv, my lord, and are in the White Boar inn." He swallowed. "They…they claim to be Arvaltyri, my lord, like the knights of ancient legend."

"I see," said Razdan. "Have you seen their valikons?"

"No, my lord."

"Who has?"

Costin swallowed. He was doing a good job of keeping a calm face, but the fear filled Razdan's nostrils, and the mavrokh stirred with hunger inside his mind. "The burgomaster, my lord. Also, Brother Valexis of the Temple and Ivan Zomanek."

"Have they, then?" This time Razdan did not bother to keep the contempt from his face. All three men had been irritations that he had been unable to remove. He would have liked to have killed the sanctimonious old priest, but if he did, that might be the final act that turned the pious townsmen against him, that sent them to seek help against their demon-worshipping lord. Kostiv needed a burgomaster, though Razdan thought that fat old Magur ought to have been appreciative that not one but two of his daughters had been chosen for the honor of the Boyar's Hunt. As for Ivan, the Zomanek family had noble blood, so he couldn't simply kill Ivan out of hand. Worse, Ivan had the respect of the townsmen, and his death might also drive the town to desperate acts.

Still. If they had been conspiring with this foreigner, this woman who claimed to be Caina Amalas the Balarigar, perhaps Razdan had the excuse he needed to rid himself of all three.

"Yes, my lord," said Costin. He had interpreted Razdan's musing as a question. "At the burgomaster's house. Then the Arval...the Countess asked us to send a message to you, so we did." He swallowed again. "The burgomaster has been notified of your arrival, and awaits you in the market."

"Very well," said Razdan. He beckoned to his pack brothers. "Come."

They rode into Kostiv, leaving the guards behind without a second glance. Razdan looked over the houses lining the main street as the horses' shoes rang against the cobblestones. All the houses had been locked and shuttered shut, the townsfolk hiding in fear as their lord passed. His mavrokh sensed them hiding within their feeble little houses, and their dread pleased him. The lesser ought to cower in fear before the greater. The Empire had never really understood that, even under its more tyrannical Emperors, but the Umbarian Order did.

And no one had understood that better than the Iron King himself.

Razdan and his pack brothers came to the market square, the White Boar on his left, the Temple and the burgomaster's house on the right, and the town's mill rising before him. The burgomaster and Brother Valexis awaited him in the center of the market. Magur's face was composed, though Razdan smelled his terror. Valexis was calm, and he smelled of nothing but age and sickness. The ancient fool was old enough that death no longer held any terror for him.

But Razdan could still make him scream.

The two old men went to their knees as Razdan brought his horse to a halt.

"My lord boyar," said Magur. "We welcome you to Kostiv."

Razdan stared at them for a moment. Neither man could meet his gaze.

"It seems," he said at last, "that you have sent me a message."

"Yes, my lord," said Magur. "The Countess Caina Amalas Tarshahzon Kardamnos is residing at the White Boar, and requests the honor of a meeting with you at your convenience."

Balmin let out a sneering laugh. "The Countess Caina…such a load of foreign nonsense! Does this outlander woman think she can summon the Boyar of Kostiv at her whim? She should be whipped for such impudence!"

"There is no harm," said Razdan, "in one noble extending an invitation to another." He stared at Magur for a moment, enjoying the man's fear and helpless rage. "I have heard some interesting rumors about this woman and her companions."

"My lord?" said Magur.

"They killed the szlacht Varlov," said Razdan, letting a growl come into his voice. Magur flinched. "And the woman claims to be an Arvaltyr, a…valikarion." He disliked the feel of the ancient Iramisian word upon his tongue.

"She does, my lord," said Magur.

"And she is as she claims to be, my lord." It was the first time Valexis had spoken, and the old Brother lifted his eyes to look at Razdan. "Both she and her husband carry holy valikons, as the Arvaltyri did in the days of the Iron King."

"You dare to speak defiance to the boyar?" thundered Balmin.

"I speak no defiance, honored szlacht," said Valexis. His calm annoyed Razdan. "I simply state the truth, as a Brother of the Temple of the Divine is sworn to do."

Yet there was a threat in his simple words. The Warmaiden and her valikarion had overthrown Rasarion Yagar, and they had destroyed the Hounds of the Iron King. The old priest didn't need to make any threats. He only had to state facts.

"You are certain they both had valikons?" said Razdan.

"I swear it on the name of the Divine," said Valexis.

Razdan's lips pressed into a thin line, his mavrokh screaming in fury. He had hoped that Rudjak had been wrong, that Varlov had gotten himself killed in a fit of bad luck. Varlov always had more enthusiasm than brains. Yet Razdan could not deny Rudjak's testimony, the warning of his mavrokh, and the confidence of Brother Valexis. The old man was not strong with the Words of Lore, the secrets of the Temple, but he was strong enough to sense the presence of a valikon. That meant the foreigners did indeed have valikons.

And that made them a deadly threat to Razdan.

"Very well," said Razdan, swinging down from his saddle. "Come!" He passed his reins to Magur. "Watch our horses."

It was an insult to a man of Magur's rank to ask him to watch the horses, but the burgomaster only nodded.

Razdan crossed the square, his szlachts following him, and strode into the common room of the White Boar.

It was a wretched peasant hovel, but decent enough for the commoners, and it was also warm, and the roof didn't leak. In his younger days, before he had become the boyar and a Hound of the Iron King, Razdan had bedded a few peasant women here, and the inn had been a reasonable enough place for wenching. Old Rachov stood near the counter, trying to keep the fear from his face. Razdan sensed the presence of the innkeeper's family in the kitchen, hiding away from him. He barely paid them any mind.

The two men standing at the foot of the stairs to the upper floor held his attention.

Razdan stepped towards them, the szlachts fanning out around him.

The man on the left was a battle magus of the Magisterium, clad in black armor, a sword at his belt. He had thick black hair and cold blue eyes and watched Razdan with faint interest. Next to him stood a Kyracian man in his early thirties, with brown eyes and close-cropped brown hair. He looked dangerous. The battle magus would be dangerous, of course, but the Kyracian had the balance that Razdan associated with a master swordsman.

And both men had arcane auras. That likely meant the Kyracian was a stormdancer, one of the warrior-sorcerers of the Kyracian Assembly. The thought of a valikon in the hands of such a man was an unsettling one.

Both men smelled like warriors. Razdan did not detect fear on them, not quite. Rather, they smelled like experienced fighters readying themselves for a battle.

For a moment, they stared at each other.

"You," said Razdan in Caerish at last, pointing at the battle magus, "are a Scorneus. I would recognize the look anywhere."

The magus inclined his head. "You are correct, sir. I am Sebastian Scorneus, a battle magus of the Imperial Magisterium of the Empire of Nighmar."

"And the Kyracian?" said Razdan.

The hard brown eyes turned to him as if assessing how best to strike. "I am Kylon of House Kardamnos."

"The Shipbreaker," said Razdan. Ulkaar was a long way from the western sea and even farther from New Kyre, but even in Kostiv, they had heard the account of the destruction of the Emperor's western fleet.

"So some call me," said Kylon. He did not seem a man inclined to excessive speech.

Sebastian Scorneus, on the other hand, did. "Might I presume that we have the honor of speaking with Razdan Nagrach, the boyar of Kostiv?"

"You do," said Razdan. "I am here by the invitation of the Countess Caina Kardamnos." He did not bother with the full ridiculous name. The pompous Imperial nobles had always been so concerned with their titles and ancient House names. Let them see how such empty words protected them when the Iron King's tide swept across the world.

"She did extend such an invitation," said Sebastian. He gestured to the balcony. "The Countess awaits you in the upper dining room. She would speak with you alone."

"Why alone?" said Razdan. That seemed bold of her. If she was alone with him, he could do whatever he wanted to her. He could kill her, and neither her husband or her pet battle magus could arrive in time to save her from him. Razdan wouldn't even need to change shape to do it.

Unless...

"Because," said Sebastian with a smile. "She is the only one among us who is a valikarion. She will be quite perfectly safe from you."

"Is that a threat?" said Razdan. Behind him, Balmin and a few others bristled. Rudjak kept his eyes on Kylon. If Kylon was the one who had killed Varlov, then he was the biggest danger.

"Certainly not," said Sebastian. "This is a cordial meeting, nothing more. So long as there is no need for us to defend ourselves, there is no need for you to defend yourself."

"Indeed," said Razdan. His mavrokh screamed for him to attack and to kill these intruders, and he felt the similar fury from his pack brothers. Yet his rational mind counseled caution. Razdan had heard tales of the skill of the Kyracian stormdancers, of how fast they could move, and he was standing close to Kylon. The man might be able to attack before Razdan could react.

Though Razdan neither saw nor sensed a valikon on him. Kylon's only weapon seemed to be a curious jeweled saber of ancient design.

"The Countess awaits you upstairs," said Sebastian. "I imagine she is quite eager to begin your discussion."

Razdan looked towards the door to the private dining room. He knew the room. In fact, he had once pulled a woman into the room and taken her there...had it been five years ago? Six? It wasn't important.

What was important was the fact that he couldn't sense anyone inside the room. Razdan could sense his pack brothers, Sebastian and Kylon, and Rachov. Come to think of it, he could also sense Sophia Zomanek and her damned uncle. They were in one of the private rooms, no doubt listening to the conversation.

A thrill of lust went through Razdan at the thought of Sophia. She was a beautiful young woman, and she belonged to the boyar of Kostiv. Her uncle would have married her off to a minor merchant or nobleman of Risiviri, or the Magisterium would have found Sophia once her sorcerous abilities became obvious.

Instead, Razdan would put her to better use. First, to slake his lust. And then, once he tired of her, he would take his wolf-form and devour her, letting her screams feed his mavrokh.

"Do not go alone, my boyar," said Balmin at once. "It could be a trap."

"For once I agree with Balmin," said Rudjak. "She is dangerous."

Rudjak and Balmin never agreed on anything. If they both thought this might be a trap...

"There is no reason to fear," said Sebastian. "There will be no fighting unless you or one of your men start it, my lord boyar."

"But if you do," said Kylon, "then we will have violence."

"Do you think I fear one lone woman?" said Razdan to Balmin. He looked at Sebastian. "Very well. I will speak with this Countess of yours." He turned back to Rudjak. "At the first sign of treachery, kill them both." Razdan glanced at Rachov. "And everyone in the White Boar inn, for failing to warn their lawful lord of treachery."

He had the distinct satisfaction of seeing the desperate terror go over Rachov's face. The satisfaction curdled. An old innkeeper was far easier to bully than a battle magus and a Kyracian stormdancer.

And, perhaps, a valikarion.

Without another word Razdan turned and walked towards the stairs. Sebastian stepped aside to let him pass, though Kylon did not move. He felt Kylon's and Sebastian's stares on him as he climbed the stairs, walked down the balcony, and opened the door to the dining room.

Caina waited at the head of the table, clad in her borrowed dress, her pyrikon in its diadem form and resting atop her black hair. She had redone her hair in the crown-like style of Nighmarian noblewomen, though this time she had done it properly since there had been more time and Sophia had helped her. The girl had proven quite adept at braiding hair.

Deep voices rose from the common room, and a moment later she heard the creak of footsteps upon the stairs.

The door swung open, and Razdan Nagrach stepped into the dining room.

Caina had not been sure what to expect. Based on what the others had said, she had expected a fat lordling, a man who relied on his mavrokh for strength. Instead, the boyar was sharply handsome and quite fit. He was in his early twenties, and his black hair and mustache had been styled in the same fashion as the statues of the Iron King in Sigilsoara. Like Rudjak and the others, Caina had seen at the Sanctuary Stone, Razdan wore dark clothing, his jacket and cloak trimmed with fur, a sword and a dagger at his belt.

They stared at each other. Caina's mind raced, sorting details about him. His eyes were brown. His clothes were clean, despite the ride from his castle, which indicated a fastidious nature, and likely pride in his station as boyar. He was in good physical condition, which meant he possessed at least some self-control, and there was no sign of excessive alcohol consumption. His sword and dagger were fine weapons, but the leather wrappings around the hilts showed the signs of much use. His face was a cold mask as he stared at her, his brown eyes hard as stone, though she saw hints of lust and hunger there.

Overall, he struck her as a dangerous man.

Caina rose, slowly, not taking her eyes from his, and began speaking in High Nighmarian. "Thank you for coming, my lord boyar. As you have no doubt guessed, I am Countess Caina Amalas Tarshahzon Kardamnos." She stepped around the table and offered him a bow, and then extended her left hand towards him.

His lips twitched in something that might have been amusement, or perhaps contempt, and he bowed over her hand and pressed a brief kiss onto her knuckles.

"And I am Razdan Nagrach, boyar of Kostiv," he said, his High Nighmarian thick with an Ulkaari accent, his voice a deep rumble.

"Shall we be seated?" said Caina.

She sat at one end of the table, and the boyar at the other, the chair creaking a little beneath his weight.

Razdan was not quite sure what to make of Caina.

He had heard the rumors about Caina Amalas, of course, the stories about the Balarigar and the Umbarians and Istarinmul, but he knew such stories were always exaggerated in the telling.

He had not been sure what to expect when he met the woman in the flesh.

Perhaps she would be a broad-shouldered ox of a woman, the sort of woman who would be mistaken for a man at the first or even third glance. Certainly, that fit some of the tales about the terrible Balarigar. Or maybe she would be a woman of stunning beauty, capable of beguiling the men around her into doing whatever she wished. That would explain why a man like Kylon Shipbreaker followed her.

To his mild surprise, she was neither.

Caina Amalas Tarshahzon Kardamnos was a young woman of average height and lean build. Her black hair, blue eyes, and noble birth marked her as yet another scion of House Scorneus, but the damned troublemakers seemed to be everywhere. She was pretty, certainly, and he would have no objection to bedding her with or without her approval, but her mouth was too thin and her features too sharp for her to be exceptionally beautiful. Frankly, he could not decide if she looked like a Szaldic peasant girl or a Nighmarian noblewoman, but certainly she had the eyes of a noblewoman. They were large and blue and very, very cold, and did not blink as they met his gaze.

That was the first indication that there might be something odd about her.

Few people could meet his gaze any longer. Most of his own men could no longer do it, and only a few of his fellow Hounds.

The second indication was that he could not sense her at all.

It surprised Razdan how much that alarmed him. He had only been a mavrokh for two and a half years, had only possessed the enhanced senses and the spirit's abilities for that long. Yet he had grown accustomed to sensing the presence of others around him. He could see Caina, and he could smell her, but his mavrokh could not sense her presence at all.

The silence stretched on and on.

"How old were you," said Caina in High Nighmarian at last, "when you killed your father?"

He blinked in surprise, a little flicker of alarm going through him.

Perhaps some of those rumors about the Balarigar were true.

"What makes you think I killed my father?" said Razdan.

Caina raised one black eyebrow. "Isn't it obvious?"

It was aggravating that he could not sense her at all. He could smell her easily enough. She had washed and bathed recently, though he still smelled Kylon's scent on her. Likely she had lain with him earlier. She was a little afraid of Razdan, but not as much as she should have been.

But none of it, no hint of her emotions, showed on her face.

She looked perfectly calm. Perhaps she was too stupid or too overconfident to realize just how frightened she should have been.

"Obvious?" said Razdan. He needed to find out more about her before he acted. He leaned back in his chair, watching her. "Enlighten me. Why is it obvious?"

"The townsmen say you took your father's place about two and a half years ago," said Caina. "That would be just after the day of the golden dead. Vlad Nagrach died unexpectedly. Everyone thought he had at least another ten or fifteen years left in him. But he died, and you took his place, and you displayed yourself openly as a Hound of the Iron King." She smiled a little. "Was he your first kill as a mavrokh? Or one of the first?"

"The second," said Razdan, irritated that she had guessed the truth. There had been an initiation ceremony, and the Temnoti and the Syvashar had brought his first victim, some peasant woman or another he had killed and then devoured to seal his transformation into a mavrokh. After that, Vlad Nagrach had been his second kill. By the name of Temnuzash, it had been satisfying to watch the horror on the old tyrant's face, to listen to his shrieks as Razdan had devoured him alive.

He was beginning to suspect he would enjoy doing the same to the woman in front of him.

He was also beginning to suspect that killing her might not be nearly as easy as killing his father had been.

"I suppose there have been many others since then," murmured Caina. "It is easy to kill when they cannot fight back, is it not?"

"That is of no consequence right now," said Razdan, "and of no consequence to you." He tapped his fingers against the arm of the chair, watching that calm face. "So you are a valikarion, hmm? You need only look at me, and all my secrets are revealed to you, is that it?"

"Not at all," said Caina. "I'm merely observant, and I can make deductions from the things I observe. Being a valikarion has nothing to do with it."

"If you are a valikarion," said Razdan, "then where is your valikon? The Arvaltyri of old always carried valikons for their glorious battles against the Iron King."

"Elsewhere," said Caina with a faint smile.

"Show me," said Razdan, leaning forward. "Perhaps you really are a valikarion with a valikon. Or perhaps you are a skillful deceiver, and this is all nonsense."

The faint smile didn't waver. "I am an excellently skilled deceiver, my lord boyar. And, no, I'm not going to show you my valikon."

"Why not?"

"For the same reason," said Caina, "that you aren't going to transform into your wolf-form in front of me."

Razdan smiled at her, showing his teeth, and his mavrokh snarled in his thoughts. "And why won't I do that? We are alone. I could transform and rip out your throat before your husband and your pet battle magus could rescue you."

"You could," said Caina, "but that would be like drawing a sword at a parley. If you transform, you'll find out just where I have hidden my valikon...and my husband and Lord Sebastian are very fast. Maybe faster than you are. They might kill you before your szlachts can transform and join the fight." She reached for the table, and Razdan tensed. But instead of a weapon, she held up a corroded old silver coin. "Do you like to gamble?"

"What are you talking about?" said Razdan.

"Because if you transform and I summon my valikon, that's what you're doing, my lord," said Caina. "Gambling." She tossed the coin to herself and slapped it against her palm. "A fifty-fifty chance, most likely. Either we kill you, or you kill me."

Razdan almost did it. The fact that this foreign woman would dare to challenge him to his face was infuriating, and it certainly enraged his mavrokh. He wanted to transform, leap across the table, and rip out her throat with his jaws while his claws tore open her chest. He started to call his mavrokh, let its power transform him into the pure fury of the beast...

No. Control. His rational mind needed to govern this confrontation. This woman looked harmless, fit either only as a concubine for his amusement or a meal for his mavrokh, but he suspected she might be the most dangerous foe he had faced since becoming the Boyar of Kostiv.

And even if she was not a valikarion, Sebastian Scorneus was still a battle magus and Kylon was still a stormdancer.

He had the irritating feeling that she guessed just what was going through his head.

"Very well," said Razdan once he had mastered himself. "But you have not summoned your valikon. I assume that you then have a reason for speaking with me?"

"Yes," said Caina.

"Well?" said Razdan. "What is it?"

Another irritating thought occurred to him.

He couldn't decide what color her eyes were.

They were blue, obviously, but what shade of blue? The water of the river? The ice of the river when it froze? Or the ice upon the mountains? The steel forged in the southlands? It was an absurd thought, and one utterly unlike Razdan. He had no use for poetry. Yet he realized his mind had gone in such a strange direction because he could not sense her presence.

But they were cold eyes, were they not? The eyes of someone accustomed to killing.

"Simply to talk," said Caina.

"Talk?" said Razdan. "I am a mavrokh, a Hound of the Iron King. You are a valikarion, or you claim to be. We are natural enemies as the hawk and the mouse are, as the…"

"As the wolf and the sheepdog?" said Caina.

He inclined his head in acknowledgment of the metaphor. It would be a mistake to see her as a mouse.

"As you say," said Razdan. "Then what do you wish to discuss?"

"The Boyar's Hunt," said Caina.

He smiled at her, leered really, and let his eyes flick up and down over her body, imagining what her unclad form would look like while running for her life in the Hunt. It failed to draw a response from her.

"I see," said Razdan, "you have spoken with Sophia Zomanek."

"I have," said Caina. "And the burgomaster, and Ivan Zomanek, and the families of the other girls and women you selected for the Hunt."

"Did you, now?" said Razdan. He sneered. "Come to judge the customs of Ulkaar, Nighmarian?"

"It seems quite a few of the people of Ulkaar judge the custom of the Boyar's Hunt as well," said Caina. "I spoke to all the families of those chosen for the Hunt, but I failed to learn what I wished."

"And what did you wish to learn?" said Razdan.

"Why?" said Caina.

"Why what?"

"Why did you bring back the Boyar's Hunt?" said Caina.

Razdan smirked. "Have you a theory, valikarion? Have you looked at me and deduced the truth?"

Caina shrugged. "The most logical explanation is that you are a cruel and stupid man, that you are tormenting your subjects for no better reason than to slake your own lust and to feed the wretched spirit that you stuffed inside your skull." The rage pulsed through him again, and the chair's arms creaked in his fingers. "But I wondered if you had a better reason."

"I have the best of reasons," said Razdan, his voice hard.

"Oh? Do enlighten me."

"I am a Hound of the Iron King," said Razdan, "a true vassal of Rasarion Yagar."

"It is a challenge to serve a dead man."

He ignored her disrespect. He would make her show fear before the end of this meeting, one way or another. "It was Rasarion Yagar who freed us from the yoke of the Kagari khans, Rasarion Yagar who raised Ulkaar to greatness. He showed us the path to power. The great god Temnuzash gave him the power to free us, and Temnuzash shall give the lords of Ulkaar the power to rule the world."

"Nadezhda the Warmaiden disagreed," Caina said, her voice mild.

"She is dead," said Razdan. "Have you yet failed to realize the truth, valikarion? The Iron King shall return. The lords of Ulkaar will rise in power. We shall sweep aside both the Empire and the Umbarian Order, and the world will kneel to the Iron King."

"Indeed?" said Caina, raising her eyebrows again. "The Iron King will return? Most curious. I had not heard that rumor before."

Razdan blinked, and then rebuked himself. He was giving her information. The rumors about the Balarigar had claimed that the woman was a spy for the Emperor. The Empire was preoccupied with the Umbarian Order, but the Syvashar would still be furious if Razdan spilled the secrets of the Temnoti to an agent of the Emperor.

"Let us not speak of rumors," said Razdan. "You asked why I had reinstituted the ancient ritual of the Boyar's Hunt? I did so because it is my right. I am a Hound of the Iron King. The people of Kostiv are mine to do with as I please...and I do not suffer outlanders to interfere with what is mine."

"Do you not?" said Caina. "I've already interfered."

Razdan smiled again, showing his teeth. "Your husband killed Varlov."

"Varlov would have killed us."

"Well." Razdan tapped the arms of his chair again. "Perhaps Varlov was rash. Rudjak says that Varlov attacked you alone while the others hung back."

"They were wiser than Varlov," said Caina.

"So it would seem." Razdan looked at the table and saw that she had set out cups and a carafe of wine, or at least the swill that passed for wine at the White Boar. He took the carafe, poured himself a cup, poured a second for her, and slid it down the table to her reach.

"That's very trusting of you," said Caina as Razdan lifted the cup to his lips. "I could have poisoned the wine."

"Yes," said Razdan, taking a drink. By Temnuzash, it was vile, but Risiviri was the only place in all Ulkaar to get proper wine. "But if you poison me, Rudjak and the others will simply kill you all."

"And the mavrokh will, no doubt, heal you from any poisons at once," said Caina, taking a sip of her own wine.

Razdan cursed again. Likely the wine had been another test, a way of probing the limits of his abilities. Still, all this talking made him thirsty.

"Why are you here?" said Razdan at last. "Let us accept for the moment that you really are a valikarion. No doubt you are on some righteous crusade to rid the world of evil sorcerers. But there are far greater foes loose in the world. The Umbarians, for one. Kostiv is a distant corner of the Empire. Why come here?"

"If you must know, it was an accident," said Caina. "I don't understand how it happened. Some freak of sorcery drew us here and deposited us in the forests to the north. The same thing happened to Sebastian." She shrugged. "It is an unbelievable story, I know, but if I was going to lie to you, I would do a better job of it."

"I see," said Razdan. Perhaps that was a way out of this dilemma. He decided to share some information. "In truth, I find your story believable."

"Why is that?"

"Because a few days ago, a large party of Umbarian magi and Adamant Guards passed near Kostiv, heading to the northeast," said Razdan.

Caina blinked. "No one in the town spoke of this."

"Likely no one in the town knew," said Razdan. "They remain huddled in their walls until winter passes, save for those few brave enough to dare the dangers of the haunted forest and venture forth to hunt." He smiled at her again. "But my pack brothers were hunting the forest, and we watched them from afar."

"And you did not slay them for daring to trespass upon your lands?" said Caina.

"You know better than that." Razdan took another drink of the bitter wine. "The Umbarians do not care if we follow the old ways of Temnuzash. For that matter, I am sworn to the Voivode of Vagraastrad, and he supports the Umbarians. Finally, the Umbarians are not the sort to allow others to meddle in their affairs." He offered her a thin smile. "As you already know, if the rumors of Caina Amalas and the Umbarians in Istarinmul are true."

She did not respond to the taunt. "Do you know what they were doing in the forest?"

Razdan shrugged. "Some work of sorcery. We left them alone, and they left us alone. They departed to the south before your encounter with Rudjak at the Sanctuary Stone. Therefore, I am perfectly willing to believe that the Umbarians summoned you here by accident, and that offers a solution to our disagreement."

"And what is that?" said Caina.

"You wish to return home, yes?" said Razdan. He set aside the wine cup. "To Istarinmul or Malarae or wherever the legendary Balarigar makes her dwelling. I can accept that. Take your husband

and your sibling or cousin or whatever Sebastian Scorneus is and go. You did kill Varlov, but perhaps Varlov acted rashly. Leave Kostiv and never return, and I shall be satisfied."

Caina said nothing for a moment.

"That would be acceptable." She set down her wine cup, and those cold eyes met his. "I also wish to take Sophia Zomanek with me."

A snarl of anger went through Razdan, the mavrokh growling inside his head.

"No," he said. "The girl remains. You, Lord Kylon, and Lord Sebastian may depart my lands in peace, so long as you never return. But Sophia stays in Kostiv."

"Sophia has done me great service," said Caina. "Ever since I found her, she has acted as a guide and a translator. I would reward such service. She will come with me when I depart."

"If you want to reward her, fine," said Razdan. "Give her a purse of gold or a pat on the head, whatever you wish. But she will remain in Kostiv."

The blue eyes got colder. Now they reminded Razdan of ice more than anything else. "So she can run in your Boyar's Hunt."

"Yes," said Razdan.

"The Boyar's Hunt," said Caina. "Such a fine and noble-sounding name. Though given that you plan to force yourself upon her and then kill and eat her, I suppose that calling the Boyar's Hunt by its true name of murderous cannibalism might upset you."

"She should be honored," said Razdan. "Of all the women and girls of Kostiv, she was one of the seven most beautiful, and only the most beautiful women are chosen for the Hunt."

"She appreciated the honor," said Caina. "She appreciated it so much that she fled into the woods and risked death rather than face it."

"Foolish child," said Razdan. "A quick death at my hands is better than what she would suffer if she fell into the hands of an ardivid or a wraith. And who knows? If she pleases me, perhaps I will spare her life and allow one of my szlachts to keep her as a concubine."

"A barbarous custom," said Caina with a faint hint of contempt.

That contempt made Razdan angrier than anything else she had said. "Barbarous? You dare to call us barbarous? Do not presume to judge your betters. You are a long way from Malarae, Nighmarian. Yes, you are so cold and so proud, but if you flee naked through the woods with the Hounds of Iron King hunting you, let us see how long that pride lasts. You will scream and weep and beg on your knees before the end, just like all the others."

"And what gives you the right?" said Caina. "What makes you better?"

"Strength," said Razdan. "I am a Hound of the Iron King, and I may do what pleases me."

Caina scoffed. "Does it? Many a bandit thought the same before meeting his end at your father's gallows, I'll wager." She leaned back in her chair, her face still calm, but he was starting to smell some fear from her, which pleased him. But there was something else in her scent.

Rage. She was furious at him. And still nothing of it showed on her face.

Razdan smiled. "And my father thought the same until I killed him."

"All right," said Caina, her voice soft. "This, then, is my offer. You will let us depart. I will take Sophia with me, and the six other women you have chosen for the Hunt. In exchange, I will never return."

"No," said Razdan. "The people are Kostiv are mine to do with as I please. I will not suffer anyone to interfere with what is mine. And certainly I will not tolerate interference from a haughty Nighmarian whore and her Kyracian lover."

"It seems I was wrong, then," said Caina.

"About what?" said Razdan.

"You," said Caina. "There isn't a better reason for the Hunt. You really are just a stupid and cruel man."

The rage thundered through Razdan this time, and he shoved to his feet and kicked away his chair. He stalked around the table, and to his surprise, Caina rose as well and walked towards him. Razdan realized that he was losing control, that he could feel his teeth changing to fangs and claws sprouting from his fingers. No doubt his eyes were changing color as well.

But Caina did not flinch from him, the fingers of her right hand flexing.

They stood two yards apart, staring at each other.

"Is this it?" whispered Caina. She grinned at him. By Temnuzash, the woman had to be insane. "Are we going to flip that coin, Razdan Nagrach? Right here, right now, are we going to flip the coin and see which one of us lives and which one of us dies?"

He almost did it. He almost lifted his hand to rip out her damned throat, but his rational mind stopped him. She was right, at least about this. He could kill her...but if he did, he might not leave the White Boar alive.

He would give her one last chance.

"This is not your country. These are not your people. You have no business here." Razdan leaned closer, forcing back the fury of his mavrokh. "Go home with your lives while I still permit it, and never return."

Caina stared at him without blinking. Maybe those damned eyes were the color of steel. Well, if she defied him, he looked forward to seeing those eyes fill with terror.

"You're right," Caina said. "This is not my country, and these are not my people. But I promise you one thing. I give you one warning. If you come for Sophia Zomanek, I shall give to you what I do best."

Razdan sneered. "And what is that?"

Caina smiled. "Ruin."

The word hung in the air between them like a sword.

"Then you shall have your will, Caina Amalas Tarshahzon Kardamnos," said Razdan, spitting each of her names like a curse. "Your cup will overflow with ruin before I am finished, and you will think back on this moment and curse your folly."

He did not wait for her answer, but turned and strode from the dining room without looking back. Razdan descended the stairs, shoved past Kylon and Sebastian, and gestured to Rudjak. The szlachts followed him into the square, and Razdan strode to where Magur and Valexis waited with the horses.

"My lord," said Magur. "I…"

Razdan shoved him aside, and the burgomaster fell to the ground. "Get out of my way, you old fool."

He swung into the saddle and rode from the square, his szlachts following him.

"My lord?" said Rudjak. "What are your wishes?"

"We are returning to the castle," said Razdan. "We will gather all of us, all our pack brothers, all of us who have become Hounds of the Iron King. Then we shall return, and we will teach this foreign whore what it means to challenge the Hounds."

Balmin laughed in delight, and a few of the other szlachts cheered. Razdan did not. He was too angry.

Yes, he would return with his pack brothers, and he would tear a path of blood and slaughter through Kostiv. He would show his power to the imbecilic peasants of Kostiv, and he would kill Kylon of House Kardamnos and Sebastian Scorneus with his own claws.

He would show Caina what fear was really like. The rumors said the Balarigar had bested all manner of foes, but he would show her what it meant to face a Hound of the Iron King.

Perhaps he could decide what color her eyes really were once she was dead.

Caina let out a long breath as she stepped onto the balcony, her heart racing.

She had been certain, absolutely certain, that she had pushed the boyar too far, that he would transform all the way and kill her. The process had begun. Fangs had grown in his mouth, and claws sprouted from his fingers, his eyes turning a poisonous shade of yellow.

She had been ready to call her valikon and plunge it into his chest. Perhaps she would be able to kill him before he killed her.

But at the last minute, Razdan had stopped himself. Caution overrode his fury, and he had left with his szlachts.

But he would be back.

She knew he would be back…and more of his men would be with him.

Caina looked down at Kylon and Seb.

"I take it," said Seb, "that the meeting did not go well?"

"We had better get Magur and Valexis and Ivan," said Caina. She took one more deep breath. "I think we're going to have to plan a battle."

Razdan Nagrach rode into the forest, following the road to his castle, the rage boiling within him. He pushed it aside and focused on planning. Sixteen Hounds of the Iron King could destroy a small army. They would prove more than enough to deal with Caina and her few allies. Kylon and Sebastian would be dangerous, but they would be alone. The townsmen would be too frightened and fearful of the boyar's vengeance to help her. Razdan would lose a few of his szlachts, but they could be replaced at…

Something cold and dark washed against the senses of his mavrokh.

The others felt it as well and reined up as Razdan did.

He looked to the forest ahead and saw a brown-robed figure step from the trees, hands tucked into voluminous sleeves, head bowed beneath a heavy cowl. The robe looked greasy as if it covered something damp and slimy, and the stench of decay and mutated flesh filled Razdan's nostrils.

He knew that figure.

"Wait here," said Razdan.

The szlachts were only too happy to comply.

Razdan took a deep breath, swung from the saddle, and walked towards the robed figure.

"Honored Syvashar," said Razdan with a bow.

The Syvashar, the High Priest of the Temnoti, lifted his head and looked at Razdan.

Razdan was proud that he did not flinch. The Temnoti had been promised immortality, and they had received it after a fashion. The Syvashar's face was distorted, a third eye bugling in his gray, pallid forehead, his mouth twisted by jagged pincers. Razdan also knew that the Syvashar's left arm had been replaced by a slime-coated tentacle, and he could glimpse the ends of tentacles occasionally darting beneath the hem of the brown robe.

The smell was hideous.

The enhanced senses granted by his mavrokh had occasional drawbacks.

"Boyar Razdan," said the Syvashar, his voice thick and wet and deep. The ancient sorcerer shuddered, all three of his eyes staring at Razdan. "You face an outlander enemy."

"I will destroy her utterly," said Razdan. "I am a Hound of the Iron King, a follower of the Great Master Temnuzash, and a true son of Ulkaar. I will show the bitch the price she must pay for meddling in our affairs."

"Mmm." The Syvashar was silent for a moment. "Be wary. She is a valikarion, an Arvaltyr. In other lands, they name her Balarigar and Liberator."

"Legends," sneered Razdan.

"No," said the Syvashar. "Not this time. She is dangerous. It is foretold that the Iron King shall rise again, and inaugurate the era of Temnuzash."

"It shall be a glorious day," said Syvashar.

"But a foreseeing is a two-edged sword, Hound of the Iron King," rasped the Syvashar. "Not all destinies are foreordained. For while the Iron King shall return, the Warmaiden may yet return as well to oppose us...and if she does, the valikarion woman shall be the one to bring her to the waking world."

"What?" said Razdan, alarmed. "That is not possible."

"The priests of the Great Master have performed their divinations," said the Syvashar. "Such are the potentialities of the future. This is your great test, Razdan Nagrach. Slay the Balarigar, and you shall be the greatest of the Hounds, and you will stand at the Iron King's right hand as he conquers the world. Fail, and you shall perish."

"I shall not fail," said Razdan. "I will be victorious."

"Perhaps," said the Syvashar. "When you triumph, upon the body of the valikarion woman you shall find an iron ring adorned with the seal of Rasarion Yagar. Kill her and bring this ring to me. Bring me the iron ring, and you shall have a province of your own to rule when the Iron King breaks the Empire."

"It shall be done, honored Syvashar," said Razdan.

The Syvashar had vanished before Razdan finished speaking, disappearing from both sight and the senses of Razdan's mavrokh. The High Priest of the Temnoti came and went as he pleased, and he had disappeared just as quickly after he had inducted Razdan and his szlachts into the way of the Hounds.

Razdan smiled and walked back to his horse.

"My lord?" said Rudjak. "What did the honored Syvashar want?"

"I acted wisely, Rudjak," said Razdan, swinging back into his saddle. "Killing the woman at the White Boar would have been too risky. She has made herself an enemy of the priests of Temnuzash, and the Temnoti will reward us well once we bring her head to them." He grinned at his pack brothers. "Once we've had our fun with her, of course."

Balmin cheered, and this time the others followed suit.

Razdan rode for his castle, planning the death of Caina.

CHAPTER SIXTEEN

WIN OR DIE

"Come along, girl," said Ivan Zomanek, peering through the door at the common room. "Looks like the boyar has left in a huff." The old blacksmith grimaced. "Guess there's going to be trouble."

Sophia nodded, fighting back the dread. She had been certain, utterly certain, that the boyar would see her and take her back with him to the dungeons of Castle Nagrach. When that hadn't happened, she had been certain that the boyar would kill Caina, that the szlachts would transform and kill Kylon and Seb as well.

Instead, the boyar had departed in a rage, and Caina had emerged from the dining room.

Sophia still felt dread, but now there was more bewilderment. Why hadn't the boyar killed them? The only possible reason was that he had gone back to the castle for more men. But why go back to the castle? Surely seven mavrokhi could destroy any foe.

Perhaps he had gone back to the castle because he was frightened of Caina.

Sophia still felt fear and bewilderment, but mixed with them was a growing flicker of hope.

The boyar was afraid of Caina and Kylon and Seb.

Sophia hadn't thought that Razdan Nagrach feared anything in the world. She had thought him and the mavrokhi invincible. Then Kylon had cut down Varlov at the Sanctuary Stone…and Sophia had started to feel the first stirrings of hope. Maybe the boyar wasn't invincible. Maybe Caina could save Sophia and the rest of Kostiv from this nightmare.

Or maybe they were all about to die in agony.

Sophia followed her uncle onto the balcony. Caina had descended to the common room and stood talking with Kylon. Seb walked through the door and into the market, no doubt to summon Magur and Brother Valexis. Sophia sensed nothing of Caina's emotions, but she felt some of Kylon's, and she sensed his growing grim determination.

It seemed that Lord Kylon agreed with her uncle. A battle was coming.

"How did your parley with the boyar go?" said Ivan, limping down the stairs.

Caina sighed. "We're not dead yet. I'll give you the full story when the others arrive." She looked at Sophia. "How are you?"

"I'm...I'm fine," said Sophia, which she supposed was still true. "Confronting the boyar like that, my lady...I don't think anyone has ever done that. That was very brave."

"Or foolish," said Caina. "I suppose we'll find out soon enough."

The door swung open with a blast of cold air, and Seb returned with the burgomaster and Brother Valexis.

"Did he leave?" said Kylon to the burgomaster.

Magur swallowed and nodded. "He...he did, Lord Kylon. The boyar left without another word."

"He rode off in the direction of the castle," said Valexis. "Lady Caina, I fear he has gone to retrieve the rest of his szlachts, and he will return to kill you."

"Most likely," said Caina, frowning as she looked off into the distance. "Probably he will gather every single mavrokh among his men and come back to Kostiv. About sixteen total, I think."

"Sixteen," said Sophia, shuddering at the thought. One Hound of the Iron King was dangerous. But sixteen of them at once? Sixteen would be a nightmare beyond imagining.

No one could fight sixteen mavrokhi at once and live.

Sophia looked around the common room and swallowed. She knew everyone here, had grown up around them. Sophia had met Caina and Kylon and Seb only a few days ago, but they had saved her life at Sigilsoara, and again when the ardivid found them and once more when Rudjak hunted her down.

Now they were very likely all going to die.

And it was Sophia's fault. Perhaps if she hadn't run, if she had just accepted her fate and gone to her death, then none of this would have happened.

"We're doomed, aren't we?" said Magur, sagging. "When the boyar comes in wrath with his mavrokhi, after they kill Lady Caina they'll run amok through the town. Dozens of people will die. Maybe hundreds."

Ivan scowled. "Don't be so lily-livered, Magur. We ought to fight. We should have fought a long time ago!"

"Easy for you to say!" snapped Magur. "It is not your daughters who are going to the Boyar's Hunt."

"It is my niece," said Ivan. "I promised my brother I would look after her if anything happened to him. How shall I face his shade knowing that I surrendered her to the wolves without fighting?"

"It doesn't matter if you fight or not, we shall still lose my daughters and your niece," said Magur. "All we can do is hope to save whatever we can save from the boyar."

"And the next year?" growled Ivan, his face darkening. Sophia hoped he kept himself under control. His heart was bad, and Brother Valexis's healing prayers could only go so far. "And the year after that? And that? Will we have to sacrifice seven women to that monster every year?"

"And what else can we do?" said Magur, stepping forward and pointing at Ivan. The old burgomaster was shaking with rage and sorrow. "If we..."

"Enough!"

Kylon's voice cut through the shouting, and everyone fell silent and stared at him. For a man who did not talk all that much, he could be loud when he wanted.

"What happened with the boyar?" he said to Caina.

"He made me an offer," said Caina, speaking to Kylon, but her gaze swept over the others. "The boyar offered to let me, Lord Kylon, and Lord Sebastian depart from his lands without any interference, on the condition that we never returned."

"Why would he do that?" said Valexis, his voice quavering a little. "The boyar is not a man inclined to mercy."

"Is it not obvious, Brother?" said Seb, stepping forward. "Razdan Nagrach is afraid of the valikons. He knows that Lady Caina is a valikarion. He doesn't want to face those valikons because he knows that in the right hands those swords could kill him. All the savagery and fury of his mavrokh spirit would avail him nothing. The valikon would destroy his mavrokh and end his life."

"I made Nagrach a counteroffer," said Caina. "I said we would leave Kostiv, but only if we could take Sophia and the other six women with us." Sophia blinked, grateful. "The boyar refused. We then exchanged a few insults, and he left in a rage to summon the rest of his Hounds." Her mouth twisted. "Or his 'pack brothers', as he called them. As if they were real wolves and not simply evil men."

"Then he will return?" said Magur.

"Oh, yes," said Caina. "He'll kill me and Kylon and Sebastian, and anyone who gets in his way or annoys him. He'll also take Sophia and the others, and he'll probably kill some townsmen just to make the point that he can do whatever he wants."

Magur sighed. "Then we are all dead."

Ivan scowled and pointed at the burgomaster. "And you would have us submit to this...this tyranny? The boyar's father was a hard man and had no mercy in him, but he knew the law and respected its boundaries. Razdan Nagrach cares nothing for law and custom, and does whatever pleases him."

"And our deaths will please him," said Magur, "and that..."

Ivan, Valexis, Magur, and Seb all started trying to talk at once.

"It is my fault!" shouted Sophia.

They all stared at her, astonished.

"It is my fault," she whispered. "I shouldn't have run. I should have just waited for the Hunt and...and accepted it. If I hadn't run, I wouldn't have met Lady Caina. If I hadn't met her, Lord Kylon wouldn't have killed Varlov, and the boyar wouldn't be coming to kill us all."

"Child," said Magur, his voice weary, "this is not your fault."

"No," growled Ivan. "It's the damned boyar's fault, for his pride and cruelty."

"I'll run," said Sophia, trying to pull herself together. "I'll run into the forest like I did before. The boyar and his men will hunt for me, and...and..." She tried not to think about what would happen then. "And while I do that, Lady Caina and the others can leave Kostiv and go to Vagraastrad. The boyar won't chase them if they leave, not if he's scared of them, and once he has me, maybe the boyar will show mercy to Kostiv."

No one said anything for a while.

"A noble gesture," said Ivan. "A very noble sacrifice." He tried to smile. "But it wouldn't matter. The boyar would still take his revenge upon Kostiv, and the Boyar's Hunt would continue. And if the Countess and her companions fled into the wilderness, they would be at the mercy of the mavrokhi or maybe the other horrors that haunt the forests of Ulkaar."

"Then it seems we are doomed to die no matter what we do," said Brother Valexis. "Perhaps there is nothing left for us to do but to make our peace with the Divine."

"There is another way," said Caina.

The leaders of Kostiv looked at her.

"We kill Razdan Nagrach," said Caina.

"That is far easier said than done," said Valexis.

"Yes," said Caina, "but it can be done."

"You seem so confident," said Magur, his face slack with fear and exhaustion.

"Because I am," said Caina. "Varlov is dead, and he didn't fall and crack his head, did he? Kylon killed him. Varlov died on the edge of a valikon, and so can Razdan Nagrach and the rest of his thugs."

"But you took them off-guard," said Valexis. "They won't make the same mistake twice."

"Of course they won't," said Caina. "Which means we'll have to be cleverer this time."

"My lady," said Magur, hesitant. "I don't doubt that you are truly a valikarion. To the end of my days, I will never forget the sight of that valikon burning in your hand. But...you must think me an appalling coward. I wish had the vigor of old Ivan, and he is half a cripple. But we cannot fight the boyar. If we do, he will kill us all."

"Burgomaster," said Caina in a soft voice. "I'm afraid you don't have any choice but to fight. Even if we had never come to Kostiv, even if Sophia had been killed by the undead in the forest, you still would have had no choice but to fight. The boyar will not stop. The mavrokh spirit within him will not stop. I have encountered such spirits before, along with men and women evil enough to invite those creatures into their flesh. Their lust for death will override the judgment of their hosts. Razdan Nagrach likely will not stop until he has killed most of Kostiv. Eventually, he would have pushed you too far, and you would have fought back, and then he would have killed you all."

Magur stared at Caina, and Sophia did not need to use her abilities to sense the despair radiating from the old burgomaster. Valexis had the weary sorrow of an old man approaching death. Even Ivan seemed grimmer than usual.

"Then what are we to do?" said Magur.

"You have no choice but to fight," said Caina, "but this is the best moment you will ever have. The boyar has shown his true self to you. And you have two valikons wielded by a valikarion and a Kyracian stormdancer, along with an Imperial battle magus."

"Three against sixteen?" said Magur.

"We will fight," said Ivan. "Those of us who are sick of the boyar's tyranny will fight alongside you, Arvaltyr. But I fear we can do little against the mavrokhi."

"I'll give you a choice, burgomaster," said Caina. "If you tell us to go, we'll go. We'll take our chances in the forests." She rolled her hand, and the valikon appeared in her fingers, assembling itself from shards of silver light. "But if you let us stay, we will fight...and maybe we'll be able to kill Razdan Nagrach for you."

Her voice was compelling. It reminded Sophia of the speech she had made at the Sanctuary Stone when she had talked about the Great Necromancers and Cassander Nilas and all the other terrible enemies that she and Lord Kylon had survived.

And it was working. Sophia sensed the flickers of faint, disbelieving hope coming from the others. It was the same faint, disbelieving hope she had felt at the Sanctuary Stone. Somehow Caina was making them believe.

Sophia would have thought that Caina was a sorceress, save that she sensed no arcane power around the woman.

"All right," said Magur. The burgomaster drew himself up. "All right, then. For my daughters. If the boyar will torment us until we have no choice but to fight…then by the Divine, he shall have a fight."

"I have been waiting two years to hear you say that, Magur," said Ivan.

Magur sighed. "I suppose there are worse ways to die than fighting side-by-side with the Arvaltyri of legend."

"What?" said Caina. "No. I don't want any of you to die. And I don't want to fight the boyar. I want to kill him."

Valexis blinked. "What…what do you mean?"

Caina smiled. "I have a plan."

CHAPTER SEVENTEEN

GAMBLING

The militia of Kostiv came alive under Caina's commands.

It did amuse Kylon a little. He had seen Caina do this kind of thing before, after all, with Cronmer's circus and the undead of the Inferno.

And Caina was doing the same thing once again.

The men of Kostiv had no reason, no reason at all to listen to Caina, but listen they did. Part of it was their own history. The valikarion were so thoroughly embedded into the legend of Ulkaar that when an actual valikarion showed up holding an actual valikon, they wanted to obey. Kylon supposed it was as if the First Emperor Nicokator had turned up at Malarae to issue commands to the Legions, or if the ancient Archons of Old Kyrace had come to the Assembly to guide the Kyracian people.

And some of it was simple desperation.

Everyone knew what the boyar intended to do with the girls and women he took for his Hunt. Razdan Nagrach would choose another seven women next year. The people of Kostiv were not even remotely warlike, but desperation drove them to heed the warnings of the strange valikarion who had appeared among them.

Part of Kylon was amused by it, but part of him was chilled. He loved Caina with all his heart, but he knew that she was extraordinarily ruthless when she felt it justified. Kylon had told Seb that Caina had a stronger conscience and a greater tendency towards ruthlessness than he did, and once again he saw that the proof. Kylon could have left Kostiv without much self-recrimination. Razdan Nagrach was a monster and the Boyar's Hunt an atrocity, but the world was full of monsters, and Kylon could not fight them all.

But Caina's conscience would not let her turn aside. And since her conscience would not let her turn back from the fight, she would use every weapon at hand to defeat Razdan Nagrach.

Including the people of Kostiv.

Nevertheless, there were three thousand people in Kostiv. Some of them might not view Caina's plans with enthusiasm. Others might try to kill her to gain favor with the boyar. So Kylon accompanied Caina as she turned her plans into reality, watching for any sign of treachery.

Sophia Zomanek accompanied them at Kylon's insistence. It had occurred to him that the girl might make an easier target for any of the boyar's loyalists, that kidnapping her and spiriting her away to Castle Nagrach was a possibility. Caina had agreed, and Sophia put up no argument. Perhaps she was relieved to stay close to Caina and Kylon. The girl's emotional sense churned with a mixture of fear and guilt and hope and rage.

First, they went to Ivan Zomanek's blacksmith shop.

Ivan might have suffered a crippled leg, but it had done nothing to impair the strength of his arms. He was a versatile smith, and horseshoes, pots, pans, shields, and axes hung on the walls of his shop. Ivan had four journeymen and ten apprentices, and they toiled at the forges, keeping the fires lit and the work continuing. Kylon supposed not even the threat of the boyar's wrath slowed the demands of commerce. Likely the boyar and his household were one of Ivan's biggest customers.

"I don't suppose," said Caina, looking at the array of items on the walls, "that you could make throwing knives?"

"Throwing knives?" grunted Ivan. "What a peculiar thought. Why would you throw a knife at someone? You'd be as likely to hit your enemy with the handle as the blade."

"Never mind," said Caina. She stopped before a row of nasty-looking devices. The machines were rings of iron about two feet across, their circumference lined with sharpened teeth, a hinge on either side and a pressure plate in the center. "At the moment, I'm much more interested in these."

"Those?" Ivan limped closer. "Bear traps. You two!" Ivan pointed his cane at two of the apprentices, who obediently trotted over. "Demonstrate the trap for the Countess!"

The apprentices took one of the traps from the wall and set it on the sooty floor. One apprentice wrestled the jaws of the trap all the way open until they locked into place with a click. The second apprentice drew out a stick of firewood from the pile and pressed the end of the stick against the pressure plate.

Again, Kylon heard the click, and the jaws snapped shut with a clang. They closed with enough force to snap the stick in two. The apprentice dropped the stub, and both pieces of the stick clattered against the floor.

"Are bears a problem in Ulkaar?" said Caina.

Sophia answered first. "Constantly. They infest the woods, and make off with our sheep and pigs." She shuddered. "And sometimes malevolent spirits enter the bears and make them into monsters."

Kylon grunted. "Just as well we didn't run into any of those things."

Sophia gave him a tremulous smile. "The undead and the Temnoti and the mavrokhi were bad enough, my lord."

"How many do you have?" said Caina, looking at the traps.

"Right now?" said Ivan. "Twenty. Suppose we could make another ten by the end of the day if we push."

Caina nodded. "Are there any others in the town?"

"Lots of the damned things," said Ivan. "Everyone in town who farms outside the walls has at least two or three. I suppose we could gather a bunch more. How many do you want?"

"Why, all of them."

After that, they went to the town's carpentry shop. It was owned by one of Magur's sons, a gaunt-faced man named Kiril with a receding hairline and a limp. The shop was about the size of a barn, and like Ivan, Kiril had a team of journeymen and apprentices laboring on various half-finished chairs and benches and tables.

"Do you have any turpentine?" said Caina.

Kylon had never heard of turpentine, but then the only kind of carpentry he understood was the kind involved in the construction of Kyracian warships.

"It is a solvent, Lord Kylon," said Sophia in a quiet voice as Kiril turned and limped to the wall. "Made from pine sap. The carpenters use it to strip paint from wooden walls."

Kiril wrestled over a wooden cask with a metal stopper and opened the top, taking a step back.

At once the vile smell flooded Kylon's nostrils. He grimaced and took a prudent step away, as did Caina and Sophia. The odor was vaguely like pine trees, but far, far fouler. A pine tree rotting in a swamp for a year might smell like that.

"Yes," said Caina. "Yes, that's exactly what we need. How many casks of that do you have?"

"Six, my lady," said Kiril, the Ulkaari accent on his Caerish so thick that Kylon could barely understand him.

"Splendid," said Caina. "How much for all six?" Kiril named a price, and Caina paid him with coins taken from the ardivid's undead warriors. "Oh, by the way, any sawdust sweepings that you have? I'll want those, too."

Once Caina had purchased her collection of sawdust sweepings and turpentine casks, she went to the Temple.

Kylon had expected the interior of the Temple to be solemn and austere, similar to the temples of the gods of the Empire. Instead, he found himself confronted with a riot of color, the walls painted with frescoes in bright golds and blues and reds. Each of the eight walls had been painted with a scene from the life of the Warmaiden. One displayed her escaping from slavery in the Iron King's court. Another showed her learning the Words of Lore in Iramis. A third displayed the army she had gathered. A fourth showed the Warmaiden leading that host against the twisted towers of a castle Kylon recognized as Sigilsoara.

Within the Temple, Brother Valexis oversaw the collection of sunstones from the town.

"The townspeople were not happy to volunteer their sunstones," said Valexis, looking at the rows of sunstones set before the altar. The altar was a massive block of stone carved with Iramisian symbols, and Iramisian seemed to serve as the language of the Temple of Ulkaar. It was yet another language which Kylon didn't know, so it was just as well that Caina spoke the tongue. Behind the altar, a door opened into the Temple's "garden," though the garden was a row of shallow stone troughs in which sunstones were grown from specially prepared salts.

"It is for the best," said Caina. "How many can you spare from the Temple's treasury?"

"Twenty-seven in all," said Valexis.

Caina nodded. "Between that and what the townsmen have volunteered, that should be enough. Make sure these get in the sunlight for at least a few hours before we put them into position."

"I must warn you," said Valexis. "The light of a sunstone will keep the undead at bay. It will do nothing against the mavrokhi."

"Oh, I know." She flashed a smile at the old priest. "I'm counting on it, actually."

Once Caina finished at the Temple, they went to the main street that led from the northern gate to the town's market. Halfway from the market to the gate, Magur supervised workmen as they constructed a wall. Well, it was more of a barricade, built out of overturned wagons, broken barrels, old tables, and whatever other debris could be found.

"The work goes well, burgomaster," said Caina.

"Aye," said Magur, wiping sweat from his forehead. The burgomaster of Kostiv was not too proud to get his hands dirty, which Kylon thought spoke well of him. "We'll have this wall finished by sundown, don't you fear."

"I know," said Caina. "One way or another, we'll see the end of this by the dawn."

She sounded optimistic, but Kylon knew her well enough to hear the grim warning in her words.

"That barricade won't slow them down," said Kylon in a low voice once they were out of earshot. Sophia gave him an alarmed look. "If the mavrokhi are as strong as Varlov, they'll jump right over it."

Caina nodded. "I hope they will. I want them to go in a specific direction. Hopefully, the barricade will encourage them. Let's visit the river warehouse next. Magur mentioned they would have stored some coal from the mines there. After that, I want to look at that mill."

A few hours later, Caina walked through a narrow alley leading to the main street. In the distance, she heard the steady click as the townsmen labored to set the bear traps on the main street, heard the thud of hammers against wood. She cast a wary glance at the sky. They had enjoyed nearly a full afternoon of sunlight to fill up the soulstones, but the sun was dipping to the west...and the southern sky was a solid mass of gray clouds.

A storm was coming, and it looked like a strong one. Sophia, Ivan, Magur, and all the other people of Kostiv were united in their opinion that a blizzard was coming and that it was probably a strong one. Brother Valexis thought that there might be a foot of snow on the ground by this time tomorrow, maybe more.

And that meant Razdan Nagrach's attack would come tonight.

They were almost ready to meet the boyar's attack. Or, at least, as ready as they ever could be. Caina wished she had a score of valikarion and a half-dozen Iramisian loremasters with her. Then they could have stormed Castle Nagrach and killed the boyar without risking the people of the town. Instead, Caina had Kylon, Sebastian Scorneus, a bag of tricks, and her own wits.

She hoped that would be enough.

They would find out soon.

"Yes, torches and archers on the rooftops overlooking this alley," said Caina, pointing. Kylon, Magur, and Sophia followed her, and Magur squinted at the rooftops. "When the boyar and his wolves come, I want them to meet a rain of arrows."

Magur looked dubious. "That will not slow them down much. It is said that the mavrokhi can shrug off wounds the way a normal man might shrug off a splinter."

"They can," said Caina, "but enough splinters will still kill a man. And they will slow down the mavrokhi long enough for us to kill them."

Of course, if things went the way she wanted to them to go, they wouldn't have to fight the mavrokhi hand-to-hand, or at least not many of them. But she had been in enough fights to know that battles rarely went according to plan. The day she had met Kylon, his sister Andromache and the Istarish emir Rezir Shahan had planned to conquer Marsis.

They had all sorts of plans…and a few days later, they were dead, and Marsis was still in the hands of the Empire.

"As you say, then," said Magur. "I will round up every militiaman who has a bow and send them to the roof."

"I suggest that we only use those who have experience hunting in the wilderness," said Caina.

"There are no poachers in Kostiv," said Magur. "The woods belong to the boyar."

Caina stared at him.

Magur sighed again. "Well…maybe a few. I will go speak to them, and make sure they have torches and enough arrows."

The burgomaster walked away, leaving Caina and Kylon and Sophia alone in the alley.

"It won't work," said Kylon in a quiet voice.

"Oh?" said Caina. "Which part?" Truth be told, none of it might work. She thought she understood the boyar, and she thought she grasped what drove Razdan Nagrach.

But she had been wrong before.

"This alley," said Kylon. "It will be too obvious. A torchlit alley lined by archers? The boyar might be rash, but I don't think he is a stupid man. Between that and the barricade, he'll see that you're trying to lure him in this direction. A dozen mavrokhi would go right through that barricade."

"Probably," said Caina. "At least, I hope that's what will happen."

Kylon blinked and then snorted. "You want them to go in that direction."

"Yes," said Caina. "I do."

"The turpentine," said Sophia, understanding going over her face. "That's why you took all of Kiril's turpentine. It's because they're wolves."

"Aye," said Caina, pleased that she had figured it out. "The mavrokhi spirits can sense the presence of others around them…but I don't think they'll sense a barrel or two of turpentine. And the Hounds hunt with their noses, I think. The boyar kept sniffing in my direction during our talk. At a guess, I think he was trying to smell me to determine my mood since he couldn't sense me. Spill some turpentine over the ground, and they won't be able to smell anything else for a while." She looked at the sky, gauging the time. They had maybe two hours left before sundown, and Caina knew that the boyar and the mavrokhi would prefer to attack in the darkness. "Let's head back to the market and check on Seb."

"This way," said Sophia, and she led them through the narrow back alleyways of Kostiv, avoiding the work on the main street until they walked past the White Boar's yard and into the square. Seb was there, talking with Brother Valexis, and at last the old priest nodded and shuffled off towards the main street.

"Lady Caina, Lord Kylon," said Seb. "All the sunstones are in position."

Caina nodded. "And the volunteers?"

"In place," said Seb. He turned a wary eye toward the mill, and then looked back at her. "Mostly acolytes from the Temple, and those with family chosen for the Hunt. I think they were the only ones brave enough to stand behind the windows."

Caina looked north along the main street and saw the glint of metal. "I think that will have to be enough."

Seb nodded. "The boyar will almost certainly attack tonight."

"Yes," said Caina.

"You present too much of a challenge to his authority," said Seb. "In a normal man with the character of Razdan Nagrach, that would be a danger. But if you're right and his mavrokh has twisted his mind, if he is thinking like a predator, then he would find the risk intolerable. The strongest male of a wolf pack responds to a challenger in only one way."

Caina nodded and drew a finger across her throat. "He will speak in the only language that someone like him truly understands."

"But it is a tongue in which he is most fluent," said Sophia in a small voice.

"Sophia," said Caina. "Go to the White Boar's common room and have dinner. I'll join you shortly." She looked at the sky again. "It might be the last chance we have to eat for a while."

Sophia nodded and trotted off to the inn.

"You are gambling with her life, you know," said Seb.

"Yes," said Caina. "But her life was already lost. The boyar would have killed her and the six others in that wretched Hunt of his. Maybe this way we can win those lives back."

"And you're gambling with our lives and the lives of everyone in Kostiv," said Seb.

Caina frowned. "If you want to leave, this is an excellent time to head south. I don't have any right to command you. Whatever happens tonight, Razdan Nagrach will be too busy to care what happens to you."

"No," said Seb. "I will not leave until this is finished. Besides, you have a much better chance of success with my help." He shrugged. "And in a way, I am still doing my duty to the Magisterium and the Empire. The Boyar of Kostiv supports the Voivode of Vagraastrad, who in turn supports the Umbarian Order. So, anything I do to harm the boyar harms the Umbarian Order."

"Perfectly logical," said Caina. "I'm glad you see it that way."

Seb grinned, and then his mirth faded. "But this is indeed a colossal roll of the dice, and the coins upon the table are the lives of the town."

"Yes." Caina stared at the town, at the people she had set to their tasks. "I know that. If we fail, we'll be killed. And then Razdan Nagrach will take revenge on the town for helping us. He'll probably kill Valexis and Ivan and Magur's family. I expect he would have the Boyar's Hunt right away, maybe with twice as many women."

Seb nodded. "At least you understand the stakes."

"I wouldn't have expected a magus of the Magisterium to care so much about innocent life," said Caina, growing irritated with his questions.

"That is fair." Seb shrugged. "But neither would I have expected a Ghost nightfighter to care so much. The Ghosts are known to be ruthless to those who get in their way. And I should point out that I never actually wanted to be a magus."

"Yes, that's right," said Caina. "You wanted to be a valikarion."

"Did you?"

Caina blinked. "I'm sorry?"

"Did you want to be a valikarion when you were a child?"

Caina sighed. "If you must know, when I was a child what I wanted most was to be a mother. I wanted as many children as I could have." She shrugged. "But we don't always get what we want, do we?"

"No," said Seb. "How long have you been a valikarion?"

It took a moment for Caina to sort through the time in her head. The last two and a half years of her life had been both eventful and chaotic. "About six months."

"Really?" said Seb. "Only six months?"

"Is that a surprise?"

Seb rolled his shoulders, his black armor creaking. "Is it."

"Why?"

"Because." He thought for a moment, the blue eyes distant. "Because you are acting the way the valikarion did in the old tales. A lost girl who needs your help, a town terrorized by a cruel demon-possessed boyar...by the gods of the Empire. You even won the townsmen to your side with a rousing speech."

The comparison annoyed Caina. "But this isn't a tale, and this isn't a gamble with lives or a game or any other clever comparison you can think up. This is life and death. We either win, or we die."

Seb nodded. "I just wanted to make sure that you understood that."

To her surprise, Kylon laughed.

"What?" said Caina.

"I know what troubles him," said Kylon. "He's worried that you became a valikarion recently and that your head is filled with legends of glory and renown." His eyes shifted to Seb. "If it makes you feel better, Caina has done this kind of thing for as long as I have known her."

"What do you mean?" said Seb.

"When we met," said Kylon, "she went out of her way to free the slaves Rezir Shahan took in Marsis. Later she defeated a Great Necromancer of ancient Maat and the Moroaica herself. And that was long before she became a valikarion. She has always done this kind of thing. Now she just does it as a valikarion."

"So she was acting like a valikarion before she even became a valikarion?" said Seb.

"More or less," said Kylon.

Caina shook her head. She was to have been a Ghost nightfighter and then a Ghost circlemaster, one of the eyes and ears of the Emperor of Nighmar. Spies were supposed to be discreet. But after New Kyre and Istarinmul and Iramis, she had started to become famous, much to her annoyance.

Seb snorted. "After facing the Moroaica and the Great Necromancers of legend, a pack of mavrokhi must seem like a minor threat."

"Do you think so?" Caina looked again at the sky. "The Moroaica and the Great Necromancers never threatened to eat me alive." She looked back at Seb. "I'm going to go change. Have Vasily and Kiril keep watch over the northern gate. If the boyar arrives, they're not to fight him or challenge him or to speak with him. They are to run."

"I'll tell them," said Seb. He hesitated. "And one way or another, I will see this through with you to the end. I just hope we know what we are doing."

"As do I," said Caina. "It seems we are about to find out."

Seb nodded and headed towards the northern gate.

"I think I will keep watch as well," said Kylon. "If the boyar and his Hounds try to approach with stealth, I'll be able to sense them."

Caina nodded. "If they do show up, withdraw from the wall at once with Seb."

"Fighting them on the wall would be suicide, anyway," said Kylon. "I suspect they'll be able to jump over the walls anyway. Best to shape the battlefield to our advantage."

"Which is the whole point of this, anyway." Caina sighed. "Kylon, I'm a spy. Or, at least, I was supposed to be. How do I keep finding myself in all these damned battles?"

"Bad luck, I suppose." He smiled and kissed her. "Or you were acting as a valikarion even before you heard the word, and valikarion find themselves in battles."

"Maybe," said Caina. "Maybe. Do you want some food? I can have Rachov set out something for you."

"No," said Kylon. "It's better to fight on an empty stomach."

Caina nodded. "I'll go change. If anything happens, come get me at once."

Kylon nodded, kissed her once more, and then headed for the northern gate.

Caina watched him go, uneasiness churning within her. Kylon could talk about the Moroaica and Rhames all he liked. Caina could make a fine speech to Sophia about all the enemies she had defeated.

But those enemies were dead and gone. Right here, right now, all that mattered was what Caina could do against Razdan Nagrach and the Hounds of the Iron King.

And Seb was right. She was gambling with her life and the lives of many other people. She knew her plan was sound…but she knew a thousand things could go wrong. Caina had made a lot of mistakes in her life, but believing in her own legend had never been one of them. People could talk all they wanted about the Balarigar and the Liberator of Iramis, but she knew that beneath all those fine words was a frightened woman of flesh and blood, a woman who had made serious mistakes and who wished she was still in Iramis with her husband.

Caina let out a long breath, calming herself, and glanced at the glint of metal on her left wrist. Her pyrikon rested there, having returned to its bracelet form, and she remembered the day she had found it. Or, to be more precise, the day that it had chosen her. That had been a desperate day as well, but she and Kylon had prevailed.

Caina was a woman of flesh and blood, a woman who had made mistakes...but she was also a woman with a pyrikon, a valikon, and a plan.

Her eyes turned back to the sky. Less than an hour until dark, and the huge wall of the approaching snowstorm filled the sky to the south.

It was time to get ready.

Caina returned to the White Boar, making for the room she had shared with Kylon last night.

It took less time to prepare for battle than it had for her meeting with Razdan Nagrach. But this time Caina didn't intend to impress or intimidate the boyar.

She only wanted to kill him. She didn't need to look nearly as nice for that.

Ivan had a leather jacket that fit her, made for a smallish man about her size who had been killed hunting before he could pay for it, though it hung to her knees. That was just as well since the jacket was fitted with thin steel plates to deflect knife blades, and Caina supposed it would at least slow the claws and fangs of the mavrokhi. Beneath the jacket, she wore a padded gambeson, and over the jacket she donned the red coat she had taken from Sigilsoara, buttoning it to her throat. Trousers went on her legs, and heavy boots on her feet, and around her waist went a belt holding the dagger she had taken from Varlov's corpse and a second from the ardivid.

Caina looked at the room's small mirror and winced. The red coat would stand out in the night like a candle flame, and she wished for a Ghost shadow-cloak. That said, the red coat would work for what she planned. She wanted Razdan to be able to see her. She wanted the red coat to taunt him.

Of course, the boyar was capable of answering her taunts with deadly force.

Caina let out a long breath and froze.

She felt the faint prickle of arcane power against her skin. Once more she turned, seeking with the vision of the valikarion, and she saw a faint gray aura, the aura of a powerful warding and concealment spell.

The last time Caina had seen that spell had been in the moments before Rudjak and his men had pursued them to the Sanctuary Stone.

She nodded to herself, crossed to the connecting door to the dining room, and opened it.

And as she expected, the Bronze Witch stood by the window, her withered face in shadow.

She stood with a slight hunch, grasping her bronze staff in both hands as if she needed its support, though Caina noted that the Witch's weight was on her feet in their dusty leather boots. As before, the Witch wore a thick brown dress and a long gray cloak, her face still concealed by the cowl.

"Dear girl," said the Bronze Witch. This time she spoke in High Nighmarian, though her Ulkaari accent remained thick as ever. Between that and her rasping croak of a voice, her words were nearly incomprehensible. "Look at you. An Arvaltyr going into battle against the servants of the Iron King. That is a sight that no one in Ulkaar has seen for a very long time."

Caina stared at the ancient sorceress, considering her next words.

"Thank you for the warning on the road," she said at last, also speaking High Nighmarian. "If Rudjak and the other Hounds caught us there, we would have been finished."

"Such manners!" crooned the Witch. The bronze teeth glinted behind her withered lips. "Rare in the young today. I approve. Well, you are the first valikarion to be seen in Ulkaar since Iramis burned. It would be disappointing if you were slain on the road." Her head tilted, as if looking towards Caina's pocket. "And it would be downright alarming if the ring you carried fell into the hands of Razdan Nagrach."

"And what ring is that?" said Caina, not wanting to give away any information.

"Why, dear girl," said the Witch. "The ring you were forced to take from Sigilsoara. The Ring that once graced the bloody, tyrannical hand of Rasarion Yagar himself. The Ring, incidentally, into which he secured a portion of his powers."

"I see," said Caina. "The Temnoti want it back, I imagine?"

"And the Umbarians wish it for themselves," said the Witch. "As you might expect, neither the Temnoti nor the Umbarians should have it."

"Who should?" said Caina. "You?"

"No one should wield the Ring of Rasarion Yagar," said the Witch. "What do you intend to do with it?"

"I am going to take it with me back to Iramis," said Caina. "The loremasters of Iramis will secure it within the Towers of Lore. It can't hurt anyone there."

"A good place for it," said the Bronze Witch. "There are too many old sorcerous relics loose in the world."

"Believe me, I won't argue."

"The loremasters of old Iramis gathered many such things and kept them safe in the vaults below the Towers of Lore," said the

Witch. "If you take the Ring of the Iron King there, I shall be content."

"Then you are a loremaster?" said Caina. "You seem familiar with the vaults below the Towers."

"Why, dear girl," said the Witch with a raspy chuckle. "Who do you think I am? I am the Bronze Witch of Ulkaar. I have been for centuries."

"Maybe," said Caina. "But I think you might have been a loremaster once upon a time."

The Bronze Witch said nothing.

"Because the spells you use, I can see the Words of Lore in them. I know what a loremaster's spells look like," said Caina. "You're wrapped up in a warding spell like a cloak, probably to keep the Temnoti from locating you through sorcery, but some of the aura leaks out. And that staff you carry. Sometimes I glimpse the aura through your warding spell. I'm not at all sure…but I think that staff might be a pyrikon."

She stepped closer, and the Witch took a sudden step back.

"Ah," said Caina. "That's almost as good as an answer."

"For a young woman," said the Witch, "you are dangerously cunning."

"People keep telling me that," said Caina. "Though I wonder if you are as old as you appear. There are tricks of makeup and posture and clothing that a clever woman can use to make herself look older or younger. I wonder if you know a few of them. Maybe if you stood in the rain long enough, you might look twenty or thirty years younger when the makeup washed away."

The Bronze Witch said nothing.

"Are you a loremaster?" said Caina. "One that has been here for centuries? Or is the staff an office passed from bearer to bearer?"

"Who I am is unimportant," said the Witch. "What is important is what you must do tonight. Because you face a very dangerous foe, do you not? The boyar is coming for you, you specifically, and he brings fifteen of his Hounds with him."

"Then we will face sixteen mavrokhi?" said Caina.

"That is correct, girl," said the Witch. "I have seen your preparations and divined your plan. It is good. But do not underestimate the boyar. He is the equal of one of the great and terrible Hounds who fought alongside the Iron King himself in ancient days. Razdan Nagrach is cruel, but he is wise enough to lay aside his lust for cruelty and torment when his life is in danger…which it shall be so long as you and your husband and your half-brother yet live."

"Did you come here to tell me things I already know?" said Caina. Just as well Kylon was not within earshot. He detested oracles and seers, and listening to the Witch's vague warning might make him lose his temper.

"There is one thing you must understand about the boyar," said the Witch. "One thing you must understand about the mavrokhi. The leader of a pack of Hounds cannot look weak, not for any reason. If he looks weak and fearful, if he is wounded and they smell his weakness, they will turn on him. It is the law of bloody nature. The mavrokhi spirits fill the minds of the Hounds with violence and gives them the instincts of wolves. Wolves follow only the strongest, and he dares not turn back."

Caina frowned. "Are you saying that if I wound Razdan, the other mavrokhi would turn on him?"

"Eventually," said the Witch, "but not in enough time to save you. No, dear girl, reflect on this. Razdan Nagrach knows everything I have told you. He cannot look weak or hesitant in front of his pack brothers. Perhaps you can use that against him."

Caina opened her mouth to answer, and she heard voices from the market below. She glanced towards the window and saw that the sun had set, that men were running and shouting in the market.

Her skin crawled with arcane power, and she turned to see that the Witch had departed once more.

"Useful trick," Caina muttered.

She turned and ran from her room. Sophia sat in the common room, her face tight with fear.

"My lady?" said Sophia. "Is it…"

"Yes, I think it's time," said Caina. "Stay here until one of us comes for you."

Sophia nodded, and Caina ran from the White Boar, down the main street, past the various obstructions, and to the northern gate. The gate stood open, the moonlight glimmering on the dark forest outside the walls. Kylon and Seb stood over the gate with Magur and Valexis, and Caina ran up the stairs to join them.

"What's happening?" said Caina.

Even as she spoke, a chorus of howls rang from the forests outside the wall. They were deep and cold and chilling, far deeper and more terrible than the howls of any normal wolf.

"The boyar," said Magur in a shaking voice. "He has come to take us."

CHAPTER EIGHTEEN

THE BOYAR'S HUNT

Razdan Nagrach raced through the frozen forest on all fours, the cold wind from the south ruffling his fur, the rage of his mavrokh spirit making his blood sing. The mavrokh had already enhanced his senses, and when he took the form of the Hound, the world came alive. He could smell every trace left on the ground, the leaves of the trees, the stink of the town to the south. He could smell his pack brothers as they followed him to Kostiv where the townsmen huddled inside their houses, hoping that the valikarion woman and her foreign husband could save them from Razdan's wrath.

They would not.

Razdan was the lawful boyar of Kostiv, and the lands and the people belonged to him. He would do with them as he pleased, and right now it pleased him to kill the valikarion and her friends and then rebuke the townsmen who had aided her. Razdan had not yet decided how to administer their punishment. Perhaps he would devour Magur's sons in front of him and force him to watch as his pack brothers took the burgomaster's daughters. Maybe he would devour the acolytes of the Temple as Brother Valexis watched…

No. Razdan rebuked himself, forcing the hungry rage in his blood to obey reason. The valikarion first. Caina and her husband and the battle magus had to die. They threatened his rule, and he had to kill them first.

Then, once again, he could do as he pleased with Kostiv.

Razdan moved to the edge of the trees, his sensitive eyes picking out the firelight from within the walls of the town. He heard the rustle as his pack brothers moved around him, though to human ears the Hounds of the Iron King would have been silent. Razdan could hear his pack brothers, he could smell them, but what was more…he could hear them inside of his head.

Their mavrokhi granted them the gift of silent communication.

"There are a few men upon the walls, my boyar," said Rudjak's voice inside of Razdan's skull.

"Yet the gates are open," said Balmin, his rage and hunger flooding the silent communication. "Why? Do they think to trick us?"

"Perhaps the townsfolk have realized the folly of opposing their rightful lord," said Bashkir.

"Perhaps," said Razdan, though he had his doubts. Even in the more tamed parts of Ulkaar, in the south near Risiviri and the villages of the Inner Sea, the gates of a town were always closed at night. Too many undead and malevolent spirits wandered the forests, to say nothing of opportunistic bandits.

Maybe Bashkir was right, and the townsmen sought his mercy.

Or maybe Caina had persuaded them to leave their gates open for some reason.

"Let us rush inside and slay them all!" roared Balmin, his mavrokh's rage thundering inside his voice. Razdan's own mavrokh stirred in response, and Razdan wanted to hear the sweet screams of fleeing prey, to taste their raw flesh, to feel their hot blood pour down his throat as he feasted.

Once again, he forced reason to assert itself.

"Not yet," said Razdan. "Let them know we are here. Let them hear our howls and feel their blood turn to ice. Let them know fear!" The howl of an enraged mavrokh was a terrible thing, and it chilled even the blood of a strong man. If some of the bolder townsmen had decided to aid Caina, perhaps that would dissuade them.

Balmin threw back his head and howled, and the other Hounds followed suit. The music of their hunting cries filled Razdan's blood, and for just a moment he gave himself to the mavrokh's furious instincts and joined in the chorus, his own howl ringing over the empty fields around Kostiv.

Kylon listened to the howls with half of an ear.

They were horrible noises and seemed to reach down his throat and grasp his heart. Varlov's howl at the Sanctuary Stone had been a terrible sound. Hearing sixteen mavrokhi loose their howls at once was a far more intimidating noise.

It wasn't nearly as unpleasant as sensing the presence of their mavrokhi spirits, though. Because Kylon could sense them at the edge of the fields, creeping forward like wolves preparing to spring upon sheep. He sensed their rage and hunger for flesh, their desire to run down prey and gorge themselves upon their victims.

All that fury was directed towards Caina.

Kylon's hand balled into a fist. They would regret that.

"How many?" said Caina in a quiet voice.

"Sixteen total," said Kylon. "Just as we guessed. The boyar and all his so-called pack brothers."

"Good to know we warrant such a response," said Seb. "I would have been insulted otherwise."

"I could have done with a little insulting," said Caina.

One of the mavrokhi moved close enough that Kylon made out the creature in the moonlight. As before, the mavrokh looked like a huge wolf the size of a horse. Varlov had walked on his hind legs, but this time the mavrokh prowled forward on all fours. Despite its bulk, the creature looked sleek and deadly, a perfect machine of flesh designed for killing. The jaws looked as if they could bite through a steel bar without much difficulty, and the claws looked like they could shred plate armor like wet paper.

"I don't know why we bothered to keep the gate open," said Seb. "Those things could go over the walls without much trouble."

"We left the gate open because we want them to come into the town," said Caina. "It's time. Seb, come with me." She looked at Kylon and took a deep breath, seeming to search for words. Instead, she touched his hand, and her emotional sense flooded over him, a mixture of fear and grim determination and love for him and fear for him. More than anything else, she was afraid something would happen to him in the fight.

But the ice-wrapped rage was there, the fury backed by cold calculation that had brought down Rezir Shahan and the Inferno and Cassander Nilas.

"I'll see you when this is all over," said Kylon.

"Yes," said Caina. She gave a sharp nod, and then flashed a smile at him. "Good hunting."

Kylon squeezed her hand once more and stepped back as the mavrokhi howled again. He turned and called the sorcery of water and sorcery of air, filling his limbs with strength and speed.

Then he took three running steps and jumped.

The sorcery of water lent him strength, and Kylon jumped from the wall. He landed on the steep rooftop of one of the houses overlooking the street, and he hurried south, jumping over alley after alley until he passed the makeshift barricade the townsmen had built across the street.

The howls rang out behind him.

A few snowflakes started to blow past, the cold wind from the south tugging at his hair.

###

Caina took one last look at Kylon as he ran across the rooftops, and she turned her attention to the bleak fields outside of the town.

Hopefully, this would not be the last time she saw Kylon.

"Come on," she said, and Seb followed her as she ran down the narrow stairs to the street. The remaining militia on the walls fled, scattering to their positions. Caina did not have Kylon's ability to sense emotions, but she could see their terror.

She hoped their nerve held. By the Divine, after listening to those howls, she could understand their fear.

More howls rang out from outside the walls.

"How frightfully overdramatic," said Seb as they ran for the barricade.

Despite the tension, Caina laughed. "Do you think he'll make a speech first? Talk about his irresistible power and offer us one last chance to submit?"

"I do hope so," said Seb. "There are a variety of rude gestures I would like to employ in answer."

They reached the barricade, and Caina saw the flare of sorcery as Seb worked a spell of psychokinetic force. He jumped, reached the top of the barricade, and vaulted over it, landing on the other side with a clatter of armor. Caina lacked psychokinetic sorcery, so she climbed the barricade the old-fashioned way.

The howls made it easy to hasten.

She stood atop the barricade and looked around as a few snowflakes blew past. Seb waited a few yards behind the barricade, his power held ready. From this angle, Caina couldn't see Kylon, but she saw the silvery-blue aura of his own sorcerous power.

He hadn't called his valikon. Not yet.

In front of the barricade and to her right stretched the alley, now lit by torchlight, militia archers waiting atop the roofs of the nearby houses, bows gripped tightly in their hands.

Behind the barricade waited their other preparations, silent and motionless.

Caina braced herself atop the barricade and faced the northern gate, the wood of an overturned wagon creaking beneath her boots.

Razdan watched the gate as he prowled closer, his pack brothers quivering around him.

There had been a few people standing on the walls, but they had fled from the hunting song of the Hounds of the Iron King. Perhaps Caina had thought to mount a defense there, to hold them at bay, but that would have been futile. The mavrokhi could have climbed the walls with ease thanks to their dagger-like claws, and with enough of a running start, the Hounds could have cleared the walls in a single leap.

But if Caina had thought to hold them at the walls…then why leave the gate open?

Of course. It was obvious.

The main threat to Razdan was not Caina herself but Kylon of House Kardamnos. A valikon would be deadly in the hands of a Kyracian stormdancer, but Kylon was still a mortal man. If one of the mavrokhi got their jaws around his throat or even his leg, the fight was over. At all costs, Caina had to keep the mavrokhi from surrounding her and her husband. That meant she would try to funnel them into a narrow, enclosed space where the mavrokhi would have to come at their enemies one by one.

Contempt flooded through Razdan, and his mavrokh spirit snarled with hunger. Was this the best that the great and mighty Balarigar could do? Pathetic! How he would enjoy tearing her limb from limb! He…

No. Caution. Caution! He could exult in his kill once she was dead.

"Enough," said Razdan into the thoughts of his pack brothers. The howling trailed off. "Enter the town. Remain cautious, and follow my lead. The valikarion is a cunning foe, and she might have tried to prepare traps for us."

He loped forward, his claws grasping at the frozen ground. His pack brothers raced after him, and they flowed towards the gate in a tide of fur and fangs and claws. Razdan scanned the walls for any sign of danger, his ears and nose straining. His mavrokh spirit reached out with its senses, and it felt terrified townsmen huddling within their houses, but no one upon the walls.

The Hounds of the Iron King poured into the main street, and Razdan came to a surprised halt, the mavrokhi growling and snarling around him.

A barricade had been raised across the main street to the market.

Caina stood atop the barricade, her valikon burning in her right hand.

The mavrokhi came through the gate, and Caina's fingers tightened against the hilt of her valikon.

The things were huge, sleek and muscled and terrifying, and their yellow eyes glowed like poisoned flames in the darkness. Their claws rasped against the street with a sound like steel grating against stone, and slime dripped from their muzzles as they advanced. Every one of those yellow eyes glared at Caina, and the weight of their gaze made her skin crawl.

"Razdan Nagrach!" shouted Caina, pointing her valikon at the Hounds. "Have you come to die?"

No answer came from the mavrokhi. Caina knew the creatures could talk in their wolf-forms, but so far, they remained silent. Likely she had puzzled them. Standing atop a barricade and taunting them like this was suicidal. At least, she wanted them to think it was suicidal.

She hoped it did not turn out to be actually suicidal.

Caina made herself laugh, filling the sound with derision. "Are these the great Hounds of the Iron King? Are these the fearsome mavrokhi? I have seen more frightening dogs prowling the alleys of Istarinmul!" A growl came from several mavrokhi. "Perhaps the mavrokhi spirits are not to blame. Maybe they couldn't find any better hosts! Little wonder the Iron King was defeated if he was defended by flea-bitten curs like you!"

This time nearly all the mavrokhi snarled at her. Only one of them, the largest one, remained silent. Likely that was Razdan Nagrach himself. Perhaps the boyar wondered what she was doing.

"Then come!" said Caina. In one smooth motion, she stepped off the front of the barricade, throwing her valikon backward as she did.

She heard the clang as the weapon struck the street behind the barricade.

Caina dropped down the front of the barrier, landed on a wagon wheel jutting from its side, kicked off that, and managed to land with her dignity mostly intact. Her heart hammered against her ribs as she took a few steps towards the mavrokhi with no weapon in hand. They moved closer, and even with the cold wind and the snow whistling past her, she smelled the creatures, the reek of rotting flesh and musky fur filling her nostrils and twisting at her stomach.

Every instinct screamed for her to turn and flee. Instead, she kept walking towards them.

"You want to hunt, dogs?" shouted Caina, flinging her arms wide. "Then come and hunt! Catch me if you can!"

The mavrokhi snarled and surged forward, and Caina whirled and sprinted as fast as she could down the torch-lined alleyway, the archers waiting above her.

###

His pack brothers started to charge, and every fiber of Razdan Nagrach's being screamed for him to join them, to run that arrogant whore down and rip her heart from her chest, to rejoice in her screams as fangs and claws ripped her flesh to bloody strips...

"Stop!" he shouted into the thoughts of his Hounds. "Stop! Stop, you idiots!"

The mavrokhi came to a halt uneasily.

"Lord boyar?" said Balmin, a snarl of challenge filling his thoughts. Balmin's blood was up, and if he did not kill something soon, he was going to turn his wrath against his boyar. Razdan would dispatch him with ease, of course, but fighting amongst the pack while facing a valikarion would be a dangerous mistake.

Perhaps that was what Caina intended all along.

"Look!" said Razdan. "Do you not sense it? She fled into that alley! Can you not see the torchlight? Can you not sense the men on the roofs? She is trying to lure us into a trap!"

Balmin growled again and then fell silent as his brain caught up with his killing fury.

"A trap?" he said at last.

"Have we not done the same?" said Razdan. "Have we not flushed the prey in the direction we wished them to flee? That alley leads to the market, and it is narrow enough that we shall have to go single-file! If we pursue her, likely we shall blunder into the Kyracian and the battle magus. That feeble barricade will not stop us. Instead, let us proceed down the main street to the market. Then we can catch our foes from behind."

The mavrokhi roared their approval, and Razdan and his pack brothers raced for the barricade.

###

Kylon watched the mavrokhi, his heart in his throat.

If they went after Caina, if they chased her down that alley, he was going after them. If they chased her, the plan could be damned. Kylon would race to the alley and interpose himself between the mavrokhi and Caina. The alley was narrow enough that they would have to come at him one at a time, but it would be easy for the mavrokhi to leap over him and come at him from behind.

Plan or no plan, there was absolutely no way in hell he would allow the Hounds to pursue Caina down that alley.

But they didn't.

The Hounds ignored Caina's flight and the torchlit alley and the archers waiting along the rooftops. It was obviously the direction she wanted the mavrokhi to run, and the Hounds ignored it. Instead, the wolf-creatures raced towards the barricade, preparing to leap over it and intercept Caina at the town's market.

Kylon braced himself, preparing to move.

###

The barricade would have been a strong obstacle to mortal men, but to the Hounds of the Iron King, it might have well been a lace curtain. Razdan raced forward, seized the side of an overturned wagon, and leaped, the power of his mavrokh carrying him over the ramshackle barricade and onto the other side. He landed in the center of the street, his paws gripping the cobblestones for balance as he skidded to a stop.

The street was deserted. Razdan had half-expected Caina to have militiamen standing here to fight him, or maybe Kylon and that battle magus, but there was no one. Razdan sensed townsmen huddling behind the windows of the nearby houses, cringing in fear of his wrath.

Then the smell flooded his nostrils.

It was a vile aroma, so strong that it made his stomach twist, and it smelled vaguely like a rotten pine tree. The cobblestones were damp beneath him, and he realized it wasn't from the flurries of snow that were falling from the sky.

Turpentine. She had doused the street in turpentine.

Why the devil had she done that? Did she think to set them on fire? Igniting the turpentine would hurt them, but it wouldn't be enough to kill them, and their mavrokhi spirits would heal the burns in short order.

Especially after they were strengthened by devouring a few victims.

Perhaps Caina had intended the turpentine to blunt the keen noses of the Hounds. And it was working. Razdan couldn't smell anything but the vile reek of the stuff.

But his eyes worked just fine, and he saw the glint of metal.

Then he saw the bear traps, the dozens of bear traps, scattered down either side of the street.

A narrow aisle of clear space, perhaps two yards across, had been left down the center of the street, but to the left and the right of that narrow aisle waited dozens of bear traps. Razdan had been the spearhead of the Hounds' charge, and so he had landed in the aisle and avoided the traps by sheer chance.

But why bear traps? Why...

And in that instant, fury exploded through Razdan Nagrach as he realized that Caina had tricked him.

"Stop!" he screamed into the thoughts of the others. "Stop, stop!"

But it was too late. His pack brothers, fired with fury for the hunt, bounded over the barricade with growls and snarls of challenge, leaping over the rickety barrier in a tide of muscle and fangs and claws.

It would have been a terrifying sight to any mortal watching it.

Except for the bear traps.

The Hounds of the Iron King landed on the other side of the barrier, and dozens of the bear traps snapped shut at once.

The growls and roars turned to screams of agony as iron teeth sank into the flesh of the mavrokhi. The Hounds could heal from almost anything, could recover from anything short of having their heads cut off and their hearts removed, but the iron teeth of the trap plunged into their limbs and stayed there, holding fast with a tenacity that even the jaws of the mavrokhi could not match. The traps closed on paws and limbs, and one Hound even had the bad luck to slip and drive his head into the trap. The jaws swung shut, and the injured Hound could not even scream as the iron teeth pierced his tongue.

The mavrokhi could not heal wounds with the iron teeth still embedded in flesh, and the trapped Hounds went berserk.

With their superhuman strength, they could rip free of the traps, but that would take at least a few moments. And the traps hurt. Razdan felt the agony of his pack brothers flooding through their mental link, and the street erupted with roars of fury and pain. Razdan shouted instructions into their minds, but the mavrokhi were in too much pain to heed him.

He looked around. Maybe four or five of his pack brothers had avoided the traps. He would have to tell them to take human form and help the others out of the iron jaws. Except those caught in the traps had gone mad with pain, snapping and clawing at everything around them. One of the Hounds had ripped away from the trap, leaving his right front paw in the jaws, blood spilling from the ragged stump of his foreleg.

Even the mavrokh spirit would take some time to heal that.

"Idiots!" roared Razdan into their thoughts. "Listen to me! We..."

"Now!"

The shout boomed over the street from above, and Razdan recognized the voice of Kylon of House Kardamnos.

At once every single shutter on the street opened. Razdan roared and whirled, expecting to see archers or maybe Caina herself holding that valikon. Instead, he saw dozens of terrified townsmen and women, all of them holding white lumps of crystal…

Sunstones?

As one, the townsmen activated their sunstones.

The light from a sunstone could not harm a Hound of the Iron King. It kept lesser undead at bay, but the mavrokhi were living creatures. But the sunstones gave off light, brilliant light, especially in the first few moments before their charge of sunlight drained away.

And the mavrokhi had sensitive eyes, and dozens of people held sunstones.

The street erupted with a brilliant blaze of light, and Razdan staggered back, trying to see through the the glare.

"Boyar!" shouted Rudjak into his mind. He had avoided the traps and was trying to free the others from the iron jaws. "From above! From above!"

Razdan lifted his dazzled eyes and saw a blaze of white fire falling from the sky.

###

To Kylon's eyes, it looked as if the main street had suddenly lit up with daylight. The snowflakes glowed golden as they fell past him and landed on the struggling mavrokhi. Eight or nine of the creatures had gotten trapped in the iron jaws. The rest were in the central aisle left clear of the traps, and the mavrokhi appeared confused, unsure how to proceed.

Kylon would not give them time to recover their bearings.

He leaped from the rooftop, drawing all the power of water and air he could manage. The valikon burned in his hands as he lifted it, trailing white fire like a comet. One of the mavrokhi looked up at him, and for an instant, Kylon saw the reflection of the white fire in its yellow eyes.

Then he landed, the sorcery of water strengthening his legs, and he brought the valikon down like a thunderbolt. The power of his blow combined with the momentum of his fall drove the ghostsilver blade forward, and he beheaded the mavrokh. The freezing mist swirling around his blade froze its blood, and body and head dropped to the ground, shrinking back to human form.

The mavrokhi whirled to attack him, and Kylon met their claws and fangs with the ice and white fire of his valikon. One of the mavrokhi lunged at him, jaws snapping, and he thrust the valikon. The creature cringed away from the blade, perhaps fearing what the sword could do to the malevolent spirit within its flesh. Unfortunately for the creature, its right rear leg came down onto an empty trap, and the iron jaws snapped shut. The mavrokh screamed, and Kylon killed it with a blow to the neck.

The other mavrokhi in the central aisle came at him, jaws snapping and claws slashing, and Kylon had no choice but to retreat. The lack of space in the central aisle now worked against him, and he didn't have enough room to dodge properly. A single misstep could bring his foot down on one of those traps, and the iron jaws closed with enough force that he would die of blood loss in short order.

Though the mavrokhi would take off his head first.

Kylon fell back, and only the speed of air sorcery let him stay ahead of his enemies. Once the uninjured mavrokhi got clear of the traps, they would be able to encircle him and take him down.

White fire flashed behind the mavrokhi.

Seb lifted Caina's valikon.

It was a shorter sword than he liked to use, and he had never been fond of curved blades. Yet it was unquestionably a valikon. He felt the thrum of power through the weapon, and the Iramisian sigils upon the blade burned with white fire. Caina had thrown the sword over the barricades before she had run down the alley, and Seb had picked it up, ducking beneath the barricade itself.

He hurried forward, killing a trapped mavrokh as he passed, and threw himself into the fray.

The uninjured mavrokhi were so focused upon Kylon that they did not see Seb coming. He raised the valikon with both hands and brought the curved blade plunging into a mavrokh's back. The ghostsilver sword sank deep into the mavrokh's flesh, and the creature went rigid as the white fire blazed hotter. At once the creature shrank into human form as the sword destroyed the mavrokh spirit, becoming one of the young noblemen that Seb had seen at the Sanctuary Stone.

The man fell dead at Seb's feet.

Another mavrokh started to turn to face him, and Seb raked the valikon across its ribs. The cut didn't draw any blood. Rather, it smoldered and hissed, and the mavrokh threw back its head and screamed in agony as the valikon wounded the malevolent spirit within him. Seb struck again, psychokinetic force driving his arm like a catapult stone, and Caina's valikon found the mavrokh's heart.

As Seb turned to face his next foe, a wild thought occurred to him.

As a child, he had read the tales of ancient Iramis and Ulkaar, and he had dreamed of becoming a valikarion, of wielding a sword of white fire against creatures of twisted sorcery and malevolent spirits from the netherworld. Growing up to learn that all the valikarion had died and all the valikons had been destroyed or lost long ago had been a tremendous disappointment.

He was a battle magus, and a sorcerer could never become a valikarion, but wielding a valikon in battle against the mavrokhi was the next best thing.

Seb had already rejected many of the things that Talmania Scorneus had tried to teach him, and he was pleased to learn that yet another one of her lessons had been wrong.

He ran to attack another mavrokh, the valikon trailing white fire in his black-armored hand.

Panic fluttered at the edges of Razdan Nagrach's mind.

The iron jaws of the bear traps might have caught most of his pack brothers, but the larger jaws of the death trap that Caina Kardamnos had constructed for them were closing tight around him. Recriminations shot through his thoughts in a blur. It was Varlov's fault for provoking a fight with Caina and her companions. It was Sophia's fault for running into the wilderness in the first place rather than accepting her fate. It was his pack brothers' fault for not warning him of the trap.

And maybe it was his fault. Perhaps he should have taken his chances at the White Boar and killed Caina then and there. Or maybe he should have thought up a better plan. Charging into the town like this had been an act of reckless folly. He should have waited until Caina's patience ended and she left Kostiv. Or he should have entered by stealth and murdered the woman while she slept. It would have made him look weak in front of the peasants, true, but getting killed in the street would make him look even weaker.

Now he was trapped between Kylon and Sebastian, both men wielding valikons. Likely Caina had thrown hers over the barricade after her little oration, letting a far more capable warrior use the deadly weapon. Another death scream rang out as Kylon cut down yet another of Razdan's pack brothers, and the panic grew stronger.

It was the Syvashar's fault. The High Priest had thrown Razdan's life away by sending him against such a cunning foe. It was...

Wait. The Syvashar.

A path to victory blazed before Sebastian's mind.

Kylon didn't matter. Sebastian didn't matter. Sophia and the other women chosen for the Hunt and the entire town of Kostiv didn't matter. Even the lives of his pack brothers didn't matter.

The only thing that mattered was killing Caina and taking the Ring from her corpse.

If he could do that, then Razdan could yet salvage this disaster. If he brought the Ring of Rasarion Yagar to the Syvashar, the Temnoti would reward him. Their mighty sorcery would help him reestablish control over Kostiv and punish the rebellious fools who had sided with a foreign valikarion rather than their own lawful lord.

And as for his pack brothers...well, the Temnoti could always help him to create new ones.

"Forward!" he screamed into the minds of the others. "Forward! Get to the market and kill the valikarion! She is the only one that matters. She is the architect of this! Find her and kill her."

Razdan surged forward as fast as he could, lunging at Kylon. The stormdancer stepped back in a blur, the white blaze of the valikarion coming up in guard, but Razdan twisted aside at the last minute. With the direction of his leap changed, he missed Kylon and the blade of the valikon by mere inches, landed beyond the jaws of the iron traps, and kept running. Behind him he heard screams and roars as the other Hounds fought their way free, leaving behind those who were too injured to run or who were still caught in the traps.

He felt their dying screams in his mind as he raced south on the main street. How many were left? He reached through the mental link and recoiled.

Three. Of the fifteen mavrokhi who had accompanied Razdan from the castle, only three others had survived the slaughter at the traps – Rudjak, Bashkir, and Balmin. He felt their rage pouring through the link, rage at Kylon and Sebastian Scorneus – but also at him. Razdan had led them to this disaster. If he was yet victorious, they might unite against him.

No matter. Razdan would deal with that when the time came.

"Get to the market!" he shouted. "Find the valikarion and kill her!"

The market came into sight, the snow falling heavier around them, and Razdan glimpsed the red coat that Caina wore.

CHAPTER NINETEEN

VALIKARION

Caina sprinted through the alley, her boots slapping against the cobblestones. The wind howled from the south, snow blowing over the rooftops and lashing at her face. Already it was starting to accumulate on the streets.

A blizzard was indeed coming.

Caina ran faster, taking care to keep her footing on the increasingly slick ground. On the other side of the houses, she heard the roars of the mavrokhi, roars that were increasingly full of agony rather than rage. It seemed the mavrokhi had blundered right into the trap Caina had prepared for them.

The thought filled her with a vicious elation.

It also filled her with fear. Her husband would be fighting for his life against those monsters. She had left her valikon behind, knowing that Seb could wield the valikon against the mavrokhi far more effectively than she could.

But the mavrokhi might break loose from the trap.

If they did, Caina needed to be ready.

She burst into the market. Already there was a half-inch of white snow covering the ground, glittering and pristine as it reflected the light from the sunstones further up the street. Under other circumstances, she might have thought it beautiful. Right now, she cursed the snow for its uneven footing. Caina ran to the center of the market, the Temple and the burgomaster's house on her left and the White Boar on her right, the mill behind her, and looked up the main street.

The street blazed with light from the sunstones, and she saw a scene of furious chaos. Mavrokhi screamed and collapsed, and dead noblemen lay sprawled upon the cobblestones. Caina spotted the white flames of two valikons, one in the hands of a blur that had to be Kylon, the other in the grasp of a black-armored warrior that was Seb.

But some of the mavrokhi had broken free of the battle and were charging right towards her. Four of them, all told, likely the strongest and most powerful of Razdan's pack. At their head raced a huge mavrokh that looked like a giant wolf out of a nightmare, its venomous yellow eyes fixed on her.

That had to be Razdan himself.

Caina whirled and started running towards the mill.

And then something went wrong.

Caina had grown up on the shores of the Bay of Empire, where it never snowed. Most of her time with the Ghosts had been in the central and western provinces of the Empire, where it rarely snowed, and then two and a half years in Istarinmul, where it never, ever snowed. She had seen snow, of course, and knew that it made the ground slippery, but she had little experience running in it.

Her left foot slid out from beneath her, and Caina lost her balance and fell backward.

The back of her head bounced off the ground, and stars exploded before her eyes.

Sophia Zomanek stared through the shutters of one of the common room's windows, terror flooding her heart.

Caina had told her to stay in the White Boar, and Sophia had, though she suspected that Caina had meant for her to go to her room on the second floor. In truth, that was where she wanted to be, maybe hiding under the bed like she had when she had been a child and nightmares of the fire that had killed her parents haunted her dreams.

But that wouldn't do any good. If the boyar won the battle outside, he would storm into the inn, kick aside the door, and drag her out from under the bed.

If that happened, Sophia was ready.

She had a loaded crossbow on the floor next to her, a charged sunstone in a pouch at her belt, and a sheathed dagger. In truth, she knew that both the crossbow and the sunstone would do little good.

The dagger was for herself.

She would rather cut her own throat than let the boyar take her. Sophia had tried to run, and she had nearly been killed in Sigilsoara and nearly captured at the Sanctuary Stone. There was no place left to run.

Either Caina would kill the boyar, or Sophia would die here.

A flash of red caught her attention, and Sophia peered through the thickening snow.

Caina ran into the center of the market and stopped, staring into the main street. There was no sign of her valikon, of Lord Sebastian or Lord Kylon, or any of the Hounds. For a moment Caina stood there, staring at the street, and then she turned to run.

As she did, she slipped and fell backward into the snow, and Sophia saw her head hit the ground.

Caina lay there, motionless.

Sophia was stunned. Caina always walked with such an economy of movement. How had she lost her balance? Maybe she had never had to run in snow before.

Roars rang from the main street, bloodthirsty and chilling.

The mavrokhi were coming for Caina...and she was stunned in the snow.

Sophia wanted to scream. It wasn't fair! After everything they had done, everything they had escaped, Caina would die because she had slipped in the snow? Caina could have defeated the boyar. Sophia was certain of it. She had seen the golden glow from the street, had heard the mavrokhi scream in fear.

They had been so close!

And then something happened to Sophia that had never happened before.

She was...she was...

She was furious.

Her rage was suddenly stronger than her fear. Bad enough that the boyar had become a demon and brought back the Boyar's Hunt. Bad enough that he would kill her and six other women for the Hunt. But one of the legendary valikarion had returned, someone to make the mavrokhi and the undead and the wicked sorcerers frightened, and Razdan Nagrach was going to kill her.

It was just so...so...

The feeling made her want to scream in outrage. She had always thought that getting this angry made someone feel like they were on fire, but she felt horribly cold, like the blizzard outside had turned her blood to ice.

It wasn't fair!

She snarled, snatched her crossbow, and ran for the door. If the damned wretched boyar wanted to claim her life, then Sophia wanted to die with her hands on his throat and her lips spitting defiance into his stupid ugly face.

In her rage, Sophia Zomanek had found her courage.

All at once, the course of the battle changed.

Razdan pounded up the street to the market, his three remaining pack brothers following him, Kylon and Sebastian cutting their way through the trapped mavrokhi as they started to pursue. The two men might have been sorcerers and warriors of skill, but the

Hounds of the Iron King were faster, and Razdan and his men outpaced them. Caina was standing in the center of the market, no doubt waiting to see how the battle would end, and then she turned to run.

And as she did, she slipped.

Razdan could hardly believe it.

It was sheer dumb luck, the random chance that sometimes ruled the fate of nations and empires. But this time, random chance had favored Razdan Nagrach. Nothing could stop him before he killed her. He would do it as swiftly as possible. No games, no chance to savor her torment, not even a moment to decide what color her strange eyes really were. He would just rip out her throat, take the Ring, and flee.

Then he would see how Kylon and Sebastian and the wretched peasants of Kostiv fared against the Syvashar.

Razdan roared in triumph and surged forward.

Pain went through Caina's head in waves, followed by sheer panic.

She had to get up!

Caina shoved off the ground and jumped to her feet. A wave of dizziness almost took her back down, but she kept her balance.

That was just as well because it let her take a good look at the four mavrokhi charging towards her. They were fast, terrifyingly fast. Caina took an automatic step back and then realized there was no way she could outrun them, no way she could get to the mill before they caught her.

It was almost funny. All those legends and tales about her, and Caina would die because she had slipped in the snow. She glimpsed the white flames as Kylon and Seb ran up the street to intercept the mavrokhi, but she knew they would come too late.

There was only one thing left to do.

Caina held out her right hand and called her valikon. Seb had the weapon, but he didn't need it at the moment, and the shards of silver light assembled themselves into the sword in Caina's hand. She braced herself, eyes fixed on the lead mavrokh. Perhaps she could take Razdan with her in death.

But Kylon would see her die. He had seen his first wife die at the hands of the Red Huntress, and now he would have to see her die in front of him…

Then someone started screaming, a high, shrill shriek of pure rage.

Caina turned her head and saw Sophia running at her, clutching a crossbow. Ever since Caina had met the girl, Sophia's expression had been a wooden mask to conceal her fear, her eyes tense and wary. Now her eyes all but bulged with rage…and her arcane aura lashed and snarled around her. Her untrained sorcerous talent had risen in response to her wrath, and wisps of freezing mist danced around her fingers and trailed from her sleeves.

Razdan glanced at Sophia as she approached, and though his face had become lupine and alien, Caina still saw the flicker of contempt.

Sophia leveled her crossbow and pulled the trigger.

She was a better shot than Caina would have thought. Maybe Ivan had taken her hunting. The crossbow quarrel punched into Razdan's side, rocking the mavrokh, and Razdan growled in irritation, his yellow eyes glaring as his fanged head swung towards Sophia.

Then Razdan started roaring in pain.

An arcane aura flickered around the crossbow quarrel embedded in the boyar's side, the fur around it turning white with frost. Kylon sheathed weapons in freezing mist with his water sorcery, and in her mad rage, Sophia had just done the same, albeit far more crudely. Razdan rocked back again, roaring in enraged agony, and the other three mavrokhi hesitated, looking at the girl in sudden alarm.

Sophia had given Caina one last chance.

"Run!" said Caina, grabbing Sophia's arm and spinning her towards the mill.

Something like lucidity came into Sophia's expression. She dropped the crossbow, and together they sprinted for the mill. Caina slammed into the doors at full speed, and they popped open with a squeal of hinges. Within the mill was a large, barn-like space, with the gears and machinery of the river-powered grindstones on the far wall. There was a loft with a narrow ladder, built so the miller could access the machinery if it happened to jam. A window in the wall above the loft overlooked the river, and a lit lantern and a coiled rope waited next to the window.

Sophia's eyes widened again.

"By the Divine," she said, half-amazed, half-terrified, "what did you do?"

The inhuman cries of rage came through the door behind them.

"Go!" said Caina, pushing Sophia towards the ladder.

###

Razdan ripped the freezing quarrel from his side and threw it to the ground. At least he didn't need to worry about bleeding out. The damned girl's sudden display of sorcery had frozen the wound shut, and already his mavrokh's power was healing the damage.

But he was angry, so angry that he wanted to release his mavrokh's fury and start killing everything in sight. Only by dint of great effort did he keep himself under control.

"My lord?" said Balmin into his thoughts. "Are you well?"

"Kill them!" screamed Razdan. "Follow them into the mill and kill them!"

He ran forward, and the three others followed him. Razdan burst into the mill and looked around. The sight was familiar to him since millers were thieving scoundrels, and he had often inspected the mill to make sure the taxes were being paid. He recognized the grindstones, the machinery attached to the water wheel, the wooden bins for grain, the coal dust that lay scattered over everything like black snow...

Wait. Coal dust?

And cooking oil in puddles here and there.

The air was also heavy with dust from the grindstones. Someone had gone to a lot of trouble to kick it up into the air. Why hadn't Razdan smelled it? Both coal dust and cooking oil had distinctive smells that even a normal nose could detect from a long way off.

The turpentine. The odor of the turpentine had masked everything.

Razdan looked towards the loft and saw Caina standing with one foot in the window, a rope dangling from her right hand.

In her left hand, she held a lit glass lantern.

Razdan stared at the lantern's flame for half a second, puzzled.

And then, in a horrified instant, he understood.

He understood it all.

"Stop her!" he roared. "Stop her before..."

Caina jumped out the window, still holding the rope, and in the same motion, she threw the lantern. It tumbled end over end, the flame dancing within, and fell to the floor.

The glass shattered, and the fire within spread across the floor in a little puddle.

Razdan could not look away from the flame.

It exploded in all directions.

###

Caina's boots hit the frozen river, the ice creaking beneath her. Sophia stood a few feet away from the rope, staring at the window as if she expected Razdan to burst from it.

"Get down!" said Caina, grabbing Sophia and propelling her towards a section of the mill's stone wall without any windows. She crouched low, and Sophia followed suit.

Then the world shook beneath her.

The mill heaved and bucked, and fiery light filled the sky, reflecting off the clouds and the falling snow. A colossal roaring sound boomed into the night, and a gale of hot air screamed past them and onto the river, the ice creaking with the sudden heat.

At last Caina opened her eyes and looked up.

The mill's thick walls stood intact, which had just saved her life and Sophia's life. But the explosion had torn off the roof, and the interior had become an inferno. Caina heard a horrible howling noise and realized that it was a mavrokh screaming as it burned alive.

"How?" croaked Sophia.

Caina blinked and tried to clear her ringing, throbbing head. "How?"

"How did you make the mill explode?" said Sophia.

"Made sure there was a lot of dust in the air," said Caina. "Flour dust. Burns quickly. That and coal dust. Add some cooking oil to the floor after the dust is in the air, and..." She spread her hands to pantomime an explosion. "Did that once in a Master Slaver's palace for a distraction. Morgant the Razor would laugh. I had to burn down another building."

"Morgant the what?" said Sophia.

"Never mind." Caina shook her head, got to her feet, and called her valikon back to her hand. "Come on. This isn't over yet."

Slowly, slowly, Razdan Nagrach swam back to consciousness.

He almost wished he hadn't.

Agony filled him. He was still in wolf-form, but burns covered every inch of his body. His mavrokh was healing them, but slowly, slowly. Razdan had also broken both of his hind legs and about half of his ribs.

Rudjak, Bashkir, and Balmin weren't as lucky. Their final screams faded away inside Razdan's head as the mill fire took them, their mavrokhi spirits released to fade back into the netherworld.

Only sheer chance had saved Razdan's life. He had been standing in front of the door when the mill had exploded, so the blast had thrown him from the mill and into the market. In the process, he had clipped the door frame, shattering his ribs, and the landing had broken both of his rear legs.

But he was healing. He just needed a little time. Once he was whole, he would find Caina, he would rip out her throat and take the Ring and...

Fresh agony exploded through him, and white fire blazed before his eyes.

Razdan screamed...and his mavrokh screamed within him. The spirit seemed to unravel and shred inside of his head, and then it was gone, just gone. Molten agony rolled through Razdan as his body shrank back into its human form, and he lay on his back in the market, the snow falling around him seeming to glow in the light from the flames.

A valikon jutted from his chest, and above the valikon he saw Caina, her hand grasping the hilt.

Razdan stared at her, in too much pain to move or to speak or even to breathe, and suddenly his agonized, delirious mind fixed upon a stray thought.

Those blue eyes. Razdan knew what color they really were.

They were the color of death.

All this time, they had been the color of death.

Specifically, his.

"I did warn you," said Caina.

The shadows swallowed Razdan Nagrach, and he knew nothing more.

CHAPTER TWENTY

LIEGEWOMAN

It snowed the rest of the night, all the next day, and part of the next night.

Caina had never seen so much snow in her life.

Any enchantment she felt at the sight of Ulkaar's snow-cloaked landscape was soon eroded by the sheer damned difficulty of moving about in two and a half feet of snow. Maybe it was just as well that Razdan had attacked when he did. Otherwise, they would have had to fight each other during a blizzard. She could just imagine having to write the boyar another message, asking him to hold off his attack due to poor weather.

But even with the snow, there was still a lot of work to do.

Sophia vomited and then collapsed a few moments after Caina finished off Razdan. At first, Caina had feared the girl had been hurt, but Kylon and Seb had arrived right after that and carried her to the White Boar.

"It's her power," said Seb as he grasped Sophia under the knees, while Kylon's hands went under her arms. "She's exhausted herself. Strong emotion, as you have no doubt seen, can fuel sorcerous power."

"She looked like she wanted to tear apart the boyar with her bare hands," said Caina. By the Divine, she was tired, and her head throbbed where it had bounced off the ground. Even if she hadn't hit her head, she still would have had a headache from the stink of all that turpentine.

She wasn't going to complain, though. The turpentine had worked, masking the smell of the trap until it was too late for Razdan and his surviving Hounds to retreat.

"Everyone has a breaking point," said Kylon. "I think Sophia reached hers and decided that she was going to go down fighting."

"This won't kill her, will it?" said Caina, pushing open the White Boar's door and holding it as Kylon and Seb carried her inside.

"No," said Seb. "It's just sorcerous overexertion. I had it happen a few times during my training. She will sleep for a day or two and then wake up with a nasty headache."

"But she needs to be trained," said Kylon. "She has a strong arcane talent, and if powerful emotion caused her power to erupt once, it is going to start happening with greater frequency. If she doesn't get some training, the next time she's frightened or angry or even happy, she might hurt herself or someone else."

Caina nodded. It was something else to consider.

After that, Magur, Valexis, Ivan and the other leading men of Kostiv came to the White Boar to find out what had happened, and Caina told them the news.

"Then...then the boyar is truly dead?" said Valexis.

"He was set on fire, caught in an explosion, and then stabbed through the heart, Brother," said Seb. "I assure you that he is quite thoroughly dead."

"By the Divine," croaked Magur, his eyes wide. "By the Divine. He...he truly is dead?"

Caina nodded, watching the old burgomaster. "He is. And all his szlachts, too."

Magur started to totter, and she and Valexis stepped forward and guided the burgomaster to one of the benches.

Magur started to weep, but they were tears of relief, not sorrow.

"It's been a nightmare," said Magur. "I knew he was going to kill my girls, but I couldn't do anything to stop him. No one could do anything to stop him. Thank you. Oh, by the Divine, thank you."

Once Magur had mastered himself, the discussion turned to what to do next. Razdan Nagrach had never married, and despite his frequent liaisons, he had never fathered any children. By the ancient law of Ulkaar, Castle Kostiv and the title of boyar would pass to his nearest surviving relative, who turned out to be...

"You?" said Caina, surprised.

Grim old Ivan Zomanek managed to look embarrassed, even chagrined. "Yes, I fear. The Zomanek family used to be House Zomanek, and our ancestors were szlachts in service to the Boyar of Kostiv. We fell on hard times three generations back, and the family turned to blacksmithing to support ourselves. Which we have done quite well, thank you. But we're still noble. Else I would have given Sophia to the Temple to put her out of reach of Razdan."

"Then Castle Nagrach and its lands are now yours," said Magur.

Caina frowned. "Will you have any trouble from the other nobles? The Voivode of Vagraastrad, perhaps? Razdan was one of his supporters."

"Likely not, so long as we are careful," said Ivan. "Kostiv is very remote from the rest of Ulkaar, and the Voivode...well, he might have welcomed Razdan's support, but he didn't like the man."

Seb snorted. "What a shocking surprise."

"If we send the Voivode our taxes on a regular basis, he will be content, I think," said Magur. "I have met the Voivode, and he frankly seems more interested in crushing the Boyar of Risiviri than anything else. We shall send him a message saying that Boyar Razdan was killed while hunting," Caina supposed that was true enough, "and that his nearest relative claimed the castle. If we pay our taxes on time, I doubt he will care."

"That is good to hear," said Caina. From what she had heard of the Voivode of Vagraastrad, he seemed like a man dreaming of becoming a great power in the world. So long as a backwater place like Kostiv did not make trouble for him, he would likely leave the townsmen alone.

Nothing was certain in this world, of course. But Caina did not want to leave Kostiv worse off than she had found it.

The burgomaster and the new boyar took over the conversation, discussing how best to repair the damage from the fighting and how Ivan would take control of Castle Nagrach once the weather cleared. Ivan and Magur had been friends for years, and Caina thought they would work well together.

Later she slipped away to go to sleep, and Kylon joined her.

"I think," he said as he lay down next to her, "we did a good thing today."

"Did we?" said Caina.

"Yes," said Kylon. "Razdan wouldn't have stopped until someone stopped him. Even if he had chosen the wiser course and decided to let us leave with Sophia and the others, he would have chosen new victims for his Hunt as soon as we were gone."

"He would have," said Caina. She frowned.

"Something troubles you," said Kylon.

There was no point in hiding things from him. He knew her too well for that, and since they were touching, he could sense her emotions anyway.

"I wonder why he didn't back down," said Caina.

Kylon shrugged and then yawned. "He couldn't. He was young and stupid and proud, and he couldn't back down without losing too much face."

"That's probably it," said Caina. "But he still should have run once he realized the trap. He could have escaped if he had wanted to, but he didn't."

Kylon shrugged. "Not everyone is as clever as you are, wife."

Caina laughed. "That's very kind, but I wonder...I wonder if someone sent him after us."

Kylon shifted. "To get the Ring back, you mean."

"Yes." Caina stared at the ceiling. "I think someone sent that ardivid after us in the woods as well. We both saw that hooded shadow. Someone had to turn Razdan and his friends into mavrokhi. If the Temnoti are followers of the old ways, then they were the ones who transformed the boyar into a mavrokh...and they might be trying to get the Ring back. And they might have sent Razdan after us to take the Ring."

They lay in silence for a moment.

"Then we take the Ring back to Iramis," said Kylon. "The Temnoti won't be able to get it there."

"No," said Caina.

That was a good plan, but Iramis was a long journey away...and many things could happen in that time.

She turned her head, wondering if Kylon would take her in his arms, yet she saw that he had fallen asleep. A smile went over Caina's face. Her brave husband had killed at eight of the mavrokhi by himself. If he wanted to take her, he could have her...but by the Divine, he had earned his sleep. The aftermath of a brush with death often fired Caina's blood, but she was exhausted, and her head hurt.

Caina kissed him, slumped against the pillows, and went to sleep.

Later she awoke. It was not yet dawn, and the wind howled outside the White Boar. Kylon was still asleep, his breathing slow and steady. Caina's head still throbbed, and she doubted she would get any more sleep, so she rose and dressed in silence. She slipped through the door and onto the balcony overlooking the common room.

The common room was deserted, but Seb leaned against the railing, gazing at the hearth. He had removed his black armor and wore only a rough tunic and trousers and his boots. The lack of armor made him seem more human somehow. He looked up as she approached and offered a shallow bow.

"Couldn't sleep either, I see?" said Seb.

"Not really," said Caina. "I usually sleep after a battle, but my head hurts too much."

"Mmm." Seb leaned back against the railing. "If I may be perfectly candid, what I usually want after a battle is to get drunk and find a woman, but right now that seems unwise."

Caina shrugged. "I'm sure one of the townswomen would be grateful to the man who helped save Kostiv from its cruel boyar."

Seb gave her a surprised look. "Such a thing for a married woman to say."

"I think it's best to see people as they are," said Caina, leaning on the railing next to him, "rather than pretending that they are better or worse than they really are. Both are errors."

"Wise of you," said Seb. Suddenly he grinned. "We did rescue Kostiv, didn't we? Like the valikarion of old."

"We did," said Caina. Something clicked in her mind. "You used to be married, didn't you?"

Seb's smile drained away. "Yes. How did you know? Did Lord Kylon tell you?"

"No. But Kylon didn't need to. You're in mourning," said Caina. "I'm afraid it's obvious, if you've experienced it for yourself, and I have. And you wanted to save Kostiv...probably because you couldn't save your wife."

"I forget how irritating it must be," said Seb, "to meet someone with our deductive abilities."

"It is annoying, isn't it?"

They stood in silence, watching the flames in the hearth.

"Her name was Katrina," said Seb at last. "Aunt Talmania murdered her."

"I'm sorry," said Caina.

Seb let out a long breath. "It is just as well Talmania chose the Umbarian side of the war because I am going to have to kill her someday." He looked down at her. "But only after we get you and the Iron King's relic to Iramis, I think. It would annoy Talmania to no end if the Umbarians failed to acquire the Ring, and the thought of her annoyance pleases me a great deal."

"You were right," said Caina.

"Eh?" said Seb, blinking out of the dark memories of his past.

"We did save Kostiv," said Caina. "And we couldn't have done it without your help. Thank you." She hesitated. "Brother."

Seb paused. "I suspect that may have been a difficult admission for you."

"It was," said Caina. "I hated my mother. I don't like how you remind me of her. I hated my mother, but I came from her, and I don't hate myself...so I suppose it isn't fair to hate you, either."

"If it helps," said Seb, "I'm not at all fond of her either."

"Neither was I," said Caina, "and I knew her personally."

"Well." Seb offered her another bow, deeper this time. "Then I am very pleased to know you, Caina Amalas Tarshahzon Kardamnos. I think I already like you better than my full sister."

"Is she an Umbarian?" said Caina.

"No," said Seb. "I don't think she's loyal to anyone except herself. Will we leave tomorrow?"

"Certainly not," said Caina. "Not until it stops snowing, and not until we can actually travel on the road or maybe on top of the frozen river. I fear we'll be stuck here for at least a week." Hopefully, the snowfall would slow the Temnoti as well.

"We ought to move as soon as possible," said Seb. "I'm afraid that trinket you took from Sigilsoara will draw attention sooner rather than later, and maybe more dangerous attention than the late and unlamented Razdan Nagrach."

Caina nodded. "Figured that out too, did you?"

"I did." Seb shrugged again. "Someone had to turn Razdan and his friends into mavrokhi. The Temnoti are the most likely suspects."

"They are," said Caina. "But I hope it doesn't matter. If we can get out of Ulkaar fast enough, we can take the Ring to Iramis, and then it can't hurt anyone."

"I can't think of a better plan," said Seb. "Have you decided what to do about Sophia?"

"She said she would come with us to Iramis," said Caina. "I suppose she might change her mind, now that she is the heir to the title of boyar."

"At least until Ivan marries some young woman and fathers his own heir upon her," said Seb.

"True." Caina shrugged. "But when she's recovered, I will ask her if she still wants to accompany us. I think she will. She loves her uncle...but I don't think she loves Kostiv."

In all the years since she had killed her mother, Caina had never returned to visit the ruins of her father's house overlooking the Bay of Empire. Perhaps Sophia felt the same way about Kostiv.

"If she is willing and you do not object," said Seb, "I can start training her during the journey."

Caina frowned. "You're a magus of the Magisterium. Her talents are in the sorcery of water, and I hope she will become a loremaster. Would you be able to train her?"

"In the basics, at least," said Seb. "There are many different forms of the arcane sciences, which you know as well as I do, but many of the fundamentals are the same. At the very least I can teach her to keep her power from erupting out of control as it did during the fight. Which saved your life, I know, but any strong emotion might trigger it. If she meets a young man she fancies she might accidentally encase her hands in ice or generate a burst of psychokinetic force."

"I suppose that's one way to keep unwelcome suitors away," said Caina.

"In a fashion, it is not so different than learning a skill with a weapon," said Seb. "The sword, the axe, the spear, the bow, and the javelin are all very different weapons. Yet becoming fit and strong helps master each. What I will teach Sophia is the sorcerous equivalent of becoming fit and strong. When she comes to Iramis and if the loremasters accept her, that kind of training will only serve her."

"Very well," said Caina. "If she is amenable, I see no objection to it."

"If it makes you feel better," said Seb, "you'll be able to see everything I teach her in a way no one else could. After all, no one can lie to an Arvaltyr, or so the legends say."

"People lie to me all the time," said Caina. "They just need to be better at it."

Seb snorted. "That's not the motto of House Scorneus, but it really should be." He pushed away from the railing. "I think I am tired enough to sleep now."

Caina smiled. "Talking to me tired you out, is that it?"

"Another phrase that should be the motto of House Scorneus," said Seb. "Good night, Caina."

"Good night, Seb."

He bowed once more and disappeared into his room.

Caina turned back and leaned against the railing, lost in thought. Her life had indeed taken some odd directions. Once she had hated sorcerers with a passion and would have been happy to see the entire Magisterium destroyed. And now...she was married to a sorcerer, even if he thought of himself as a warrior first, her half-brother was a sorcerer, and she was taking a girl to Iramis to be trained as a loremaster.

Her younger self would have been appalled. Now, though...now she had come to realize that life was more complicated. Some forms of arcane science were innately evil. Others were not. They were like any other form of power. A sword was power, and a man could use a sword to kill children or to defend his family.

She was thinking about arcane power, so it did not surprise her when she saw a flicker of a familiar ward.

Caina turned and saw the Bronze Witch standing a few yards further down the balcony, the bronze staff grasped in both gnarled hands, the glow of the familiar warding spell around her.

For a moment, they stared at each other. Caina caught the glint of the firelight reflecting off the dark eyes beneath the Witch's ragged cowl. The greening bronze teeth also glinted in the light.

"Thank you," said Caina.

"For what, dear girl?" said the Witch.

"Your advice was correct," said Caina. "Razdan refused to back down, even after Kylon killed half of his szlachts."

"Your husband is a powerful warrior," said the Witch, "with a healthy disdain for prophecies."

"Did the Temnoti send the boyar after the Ring?" said Caina.

"Oh, most certainly," said the Witch. "You see, there are ranks in the hierarchy of the Temnoti. The lower rank, the deluded cultists who gather in cellars with the petty necromancers and conjurers, they are dangerous but mortal. But the elder Temnoti, they are virtually immortal and most patient. They were the ones you saw in Sigilsoara, the twisted ones. They were with Rasarion Yagar when he attempted his great spell and the Warmaiden slew him, and the backlash of that spell made them into the creatures that they are now. They are most patient, most patient indeed, patient in a way that you can scarce imagine. If poor stupid Razdan failed, they will simply try again, though they will not show themselves to you. That is not their way. They prefer to operate from the shadows...and they are wise enough not to face a valikarion directly, for no spell will turn aside a valikon's fury."

"A poor choice, then," said Caina. "I also prefer to operate from the shadows."

The Witch cackled. "Indeed! Indeed! Though you're not very good at remaining in the shadows, amirja of Istarinmul and Liberator of Iramis."

"You helped us," said Caina. "Why?"

"Because that is my duty, dear girl," said the Witch. "It has been my duty for a very long time. And I must say you provided some excellent help with that obligation. I confess, I thought Razdan might eat you all. Instead, the mavrokhi are dead, and old Ivan Zomanek shall give the town of Kostiv a better ruler than it has known for quite a long time. If you take the Ring from Ulkaar and secure it within the Towers of Lore, the deaths of many shall be averted."

"Who are you?" said Caina.

"Why, I am the Bronze Witch," said the old woman. "No more and no less. A legend."

"In other words," said Caina, "if the Umbarians and the Temnoti figure out who you really are, they'll try to kill you, so it's safer to hide behind the legend of this Bronze Witch."

The old woman said nothing.

"I know a thing or two about legends, I'm afraid," said Caina.

"That clever tongue of yours," said the Bronze Witch, "is going to get you into trouble, girl."

Caina smiled. "Who says that it hasn't?"

The Bronze Witch snorted once, her lined face twitching into something that might have been a scowl, or maybe a smile. It was hard to tell beneath the shadows of her cowl. Then Caina saw a flare of arcane power, and the Witch vanished without a trace.

She stood in silence for a moment, then shook her head and pinched the bridge of her nose.

Her headache had gotten worse.

"Again?" Caina said. In Istarinmul, Nasser, Prince Kutal Sulaman, and Samnirdamnus had all kept their true purposes hidden from her. Granted, it had worked out for the best, but it was still exasperating.

By the Divine, Caina was tired of games.

Still, it meant that she was tired enough to go back to sleep.

The next morning, she sat in the common room eating a breakfast prepared by a dazed-looking Rachov and his family. The shock of the boyar's defeat still hung over the town, and the townsmen that Caina had seen had a stunned look. Likely it would take a few days before it began to feel real. Kylon sat next to her, eating a piece of bread and discussing the finer points of swordplay with Seb.

Caina looked up as Sophia descended to the common room, tired-looking and bleary-eyed. She stopped at the base of the stairs, seemed to pull herself together, and walked straight towards Caina.

"Good morning," said Caina. "How are you feeling?"

"Very tired," said Sophia. "But alive. Thanks to you, my lady."

"You saved my life," said Caina. "The boyar would have killed me if you hadn't shot him. Thank you."

Sophia shook her head in bewilderment. "I was so angry. I can barely remember it. It was like a dream or something that happened to someone else. I wasn't even scared. I just…I just was so angry with the boyar that I wanted to hurt him no matter what, and the ice exploded out of me."

Seb nodded. "Your power manifested in fury in response to your own rage. If you wish, I can teach you to better control it. Else the next time you are under emotional duress, it might manifest again."

"Yes," said Sophia. "I would like that, my lord. I don't want to feel out of control like that again."

"And if you are willing," said Caina, "we will take you with us to Iramis. You can be trained as a loremaster there."

"I would like that, my lady," said Sophia. "If you would take me with you…yes, I would like to leave Kostiv. And Ulkaar. But I should do something else first."

"What is it?" said Caina.

Sophia took a deep breath and dropped to her knees. Seb raised an eyebrow in surprise. Kylon looked at her, nodded, and went back to his breakfast.

"I wish to swear fealty to you," said Sophia.

Caina blinked. "To me?"

"Yes, my lady," said Sophia. "You saved my life and the lives of those six other women. None of us would have survived if you hadn't come to Ulkaar. I would have died in Sigilsoara, and the Boyar's Hunt would have continued." She stared up at Caina. "You truly are one of the Arvaltyri of old. I...I wish to swear as your liegewoman. Like how a szlacht swears to his boyar." She frowned, thinking. "How do they say it? Yes, that's it. The szlacht says he will be a loyal son as if the boyar was his own father. So I will swear to be a loyal daughter as if you were my own mother."

A tangle of sudden emotions went through Caina at those words.

As if you were my own mother...

It was only a ritual phrase, she knew, and a variant of it was used in every nation in the Empire. Yet it had still struck her in the heart. Caina took a deep breath to calm herself and looked Sophia in the eye.

"You will have to obey me if you do this," said Caina.

Seb snorted. "As if we haven't all been doing what you have told us to do for the last week."

Sophia nodded. "I shall. What greater honor could there be than serving as the liegewoman of a valikarion?"

So they took the oath together, and Sophia swore to serve and obey her, and Caina swore to protect and guide her.

Two weeks later they were ready to depart Kostiv.

Truth be told, Caina had been ready to leave Ulkaar from the moment she had arrived, but the roads were finally ready for travel. The new boyar was most generous with supplies and clothing from his deceased predecessor's castle, and Caina, Kylon, Seb, and Sophia were well-equipped for the journey south.

Caina stood in the market, wrapped in a heavy cloak lined with wolf fur (not taken from a dead mavrokh, thankfully), and watched her breath steam in the air, shivering a little even in her heavy clothes.

"Are you ready to go home?" said Kylon, stepping next to her.

She smiled up at him. "I am home. I told you the day that you asked me to marry you. Home is wherever you are."

Caina took his hand, and he leaned down and kissed her.

"Then are you ready to go someplace warmer?" said Kylon.

Caina laughed. "I have never heard sweeter words from you, husband."

The four of them left Kostiv, following the southwestern road along the river to Vagraastrad.

SORCERERS & PRIESTS

The power of the bronze staff had a limited range, and it took the woman who called herself the Bronze Witch three jumps to travel from Kostiv to the stinking back alleys of Vagraastrad, near the docks overlooking the Kozalin River. Even in winter, the docks reeked, and teemed with laborers going about their business.

No one saw the Witch. A simple spell ensured that.

The Temnoti, though, would have no trouble seeing through the spell. The Witch hastened towards the market below the Voivode's castle, where she would change to her other disguise, the one that the twisted, mutated Temnoti would never suspect.

For they had lost all taste for the simpler pleasures of life.

The Witch needed to be ready. Caina was coming to Vagraastrad...and she was the only valikarion in Ulkaar.

And Caina would need the Witch's help if she was to survive the creatures of darkness that awaited her in Vagraastrad.

The Syvashar glided through the woods, seven of his brothers trailing him in silence, their heads bowed, their limbs concealed within the long sleeves of their ragged brown robes. Any man of

Ulkaar who saw them from a distance would assume that they were a procession of Brothers and Sisters of the Temple.

Any man of Ulkaar who drew close enough to see what they really were would start screaming.

Though briefly. The High Priest of the Temnoti desired no witnesses.

The Syvashar was troubled, but not alarmed. He had intended for the Umbarians to claim the Ring of the Iron King from Sigilsoara and deliver it to their haughty provost.

Unfortunately, Caina Kardamnos had interfered with that.

Then it had seemed simple enough to send Razdan and his mavrokhi against her. Caina might have been a valikarion, but she was only one woman. Razdan would deliver the Ring to the Syvashar, and he could arrange for it to fall into the hands of the provost. The Syvashar would have to make sure that the provost thought that it had come into her grasp by her own efforts, of course, in the same way he had ensured the woman had acquired one of the other five relics of Rasarion Yagar.

A simple plan, so easily executed.

Except Caina had killed all the mavrokhi.

It beggared belief. The Syvashar was over fifteen centuries old, had stood at the right hand of the Iron King as he had ruled Ulkaar, and he had thought he had lost the capacity for surprise.

Clearly, he had been wrong.

Caina represented a deadly danger. She had to be removed and the Ring retrieved at once. The hour for the Iron King's return was almost ripe, soon to be followed by the advent of the Final Night. It seemed unlikely that one valikarion could stop such a momentous event...but it had also seemed unlikely one valikarion could kill that many Hounds of the Iron King.

The Syvashar had made inquiries among the mortal agents of the Temnoti about the woman who had been Caina Amalas. The resultant stories had been contradictory, but most alarming. The

Balarigar and Marsis. New Kyre and the day of the golden dead. Istarinmul and Cassander Nilas.

Iramis returning from the dust of the past.

All these rumors agreed that Caina was a deadly danger.

She had to be killed. No games, no plots. Her death by whatever means necessary.

Fortunately, the Temnoti had many friends in Vagraastrad.

Talmania Scorneus, master magus and one of the five ruling Provosts of the Umbarian Order, rode towards the gates of Vagraastrad.

Annoyance beat within her in time to the hooves of her horse. That damned blizzard had slowed her progress for days, and urgency was needed. The war between the Empire and the Umbarian Order hung balanced upon the point of a knife, and the slightest breeze could tip it in any direction.

Talmania intended to provide far more than a breeze, and the means were here in Ulkaar.

Assuming, of course, she could find the other four relics of Rasarion Yagar.

The Temnoti had helped her to find the Amulet of the Iron King, but the Temnoti were fools. They thought they were manipulating her, but she could see through their transparent plots. She had used the Amulet to summon Sigilsoara, empowering the spell with her own blood, though the soldiers she had sent into the Iron King's castle had all perished.

No matter. She would gather replacements and try again until she succeeded.

And when she succeeded, when she gathered the Amulet, Ring, Sword, Dagger, and Diadem together in one place, then she would teach the Temnoti their place. She would teach the rest of House Scorneus and the other provosts their place.

The Umbarian Order would rule the Empire, and Talmania Scorneus, with the power of the relics, would rule the Order.

She smiled a cold smile at the thought.

Anyone who stood in her way would be crushed.

THE END

Thank you for reading GHOST IN THE RING!

Look for Caina's next adventure, GHOST IN THE GLASS, to be released in the second half of 2017.

If you liked the book, please consider leaving a review at your ebook site of choice. To receive immediate notification of new releases, sign up for my newsletter, or watch for news on my Facebook page.

ABOUT THE AUTHOR

Standing over six feet tall, USA Today bestselling author Jonathan Moeller has the piercing blue eyes of a Conan of Cimmeria, the bronze-colored hair of a Visigothic warrior-king, and the stern visage of a captain of men, none of which are useful in his career as a computer repairman, alas.

He has written the DEMONSOULED series of sword-and-sorcery novels, and continues to write THE GHOSTS sequence about assassin and spy Caina Amalas, the COMPUTER BEGINNER'S GUIDE series of computer books, and numerous other works. His books have sold over a half million copies worldwide.

Visit his website at:

http://www.jonathanmoeller.com

Visit his technology blog at:

http://www.computerbeginnersguides.com

90514596R00186

Made in the USA
San Bernardino, CA
11 October 2018